RAVEN FLIGHT

ALSO BY JULIET MARILLIER

Shadowfell
Wildwood Dancing
Cybele's Secret

RAVEN FLIGHT

A Shadowfell Novel

Juliet Marillier

EMBER

Text copyright © 2013 by Juliet Marillier
Cover art copyright © 2013 by Jonathan Barkat
Map copyright © 2012 by Gaye Godfrey-Nicholls of Inklings Calligraphy Studio

All rights reserved. Published in the United States by Ember, an imprint of Random
House Children's Books, a division of Random House LLC, a Penguin Random House
Company, New York. Originally published in hardcover in the United States by Alfred
A. Knopf, an imprint of Random House Children's Books, New York, in 2013.

Ember and the E colophon are registered trademarks of Random House LLC.

Visit us on the Web! randomhouse.com/teens

Educators and librarians, for a variety of teaching tools,
visit us at RHTeachersLibrarians.com

The Library of Congress has cataloged the hardcover edition of this work as follows:
Marillier, Juliet.
Raven flight : a Shadowfell novel / Juliet Marillier. — 1st ed.
p. cm. — (Shadowfell ; 2)
Summary: "To rescue her homeland from tyranny, Neryn must seek out the
powerful Guardians to complete her training as a Caller." —Provided by publisher
ISBN 978-0-375-86955-6 (trade) — ISBN 978-0-375-96955-3 (lib. bdg.) —
ISBN 978-0-375-98367-2 (ebook)
[1. Fantasy. 2. Magic—Fiction. 3. Voyages and travels—Fiction.
4. Insurgency—Fiction. 5. Orphans—Fiction.] I. Title.
PZ7.M33856Rav 2013 [Fic]—dc23 2012039483

ISBN 978-0-375-87197-9 (pbk.)

Printed in the United States of America
10 9 8 7 6 5 4 3 2 1
First Ember Edition 2014

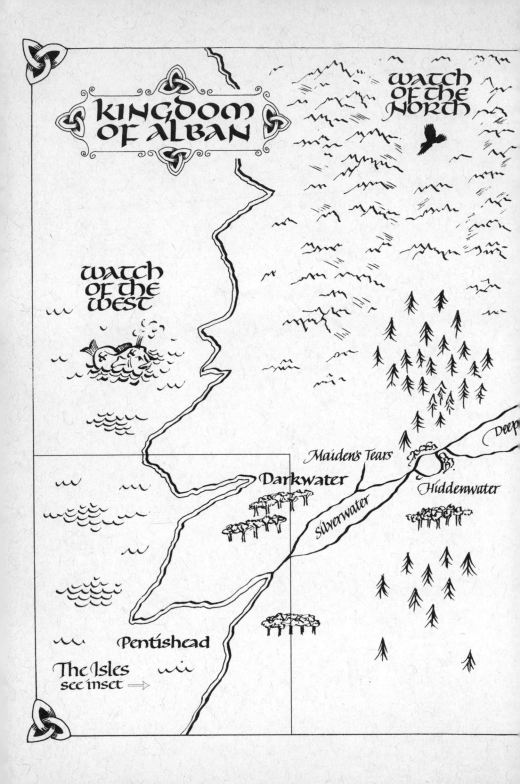

Shadowfell

Giant's Fist

Odd's Hole

Winterfort

Lone Tarn

Howling Rock

Corbie's Wood

Three Hags

Brollachan Brig

Brightwater

WATCH OF THE EAST

Summer-fort

...ater

WATCH OF THE SOUTH

Far Isle

Ronan's Isle

Home Isle

Pentishead

The Cradle

The Isles

N
W   E
S

Chapter One

As the lone traveler approached, the five Enforcers spread out in a line across his path. They waited in silence, a team of dark-cloaked warriors in full combat gear, astride their tall black horses. The fellow was roughly dressed—hooded cloak of gray felt, woolen leggings, battered old boots—and carried only a small pack and a staff. His gait was steady, though his head was bowed. He looked as if he'd been on the road awhile.

"Halt!" called Rohan Death-Blade when the traveler had come within ten paces and showed no sign of stopping. "State your name and your business in these parts!"

The man raised his head. The lower part of his face was covered by a cloth, like a crude imitation of the mask Enforcers wore on duty to conceal their identity. Above this concealment a pair of clear gray eyes gazed calmly at the interrogator. The man straightened his shoulders. "Have I been gone so long that you've forgotten me, Rohan?" Though harsh with exhaustion, the voice was unmistakable. They knew him before he peeled off the makeshift mask.

"Owen! By all that's holy!" Rohan removed his own mask, swung down from his mount, and strode forward to greet their long-absent commander. The others followed, gathering around Owen Swift-Sword. "Where's the rest of Boar Troop? We expected you long ago. When will they be here?"

"Not today." A long pause, as if the speaker must dig deep for the strength to say more. "I must speak to the king. Straightaway. Have you a spare mount?"

"Take Fleet," said Rohan Death-Blade. "I'll go up behind Tallis. You'd best get yourself cleaned up before you see the king; you stink like a midden. Don't tell me you walked all the way from Summerfort."

"I have . . . ill news. Grave news. Keldec must hear it first."

Something in his face and in his voice halted further questioning. They knew that look; they understood the sort of news that rendered a man thus grim and taciturn.

The king's men mounted their horses and turned for Winterfort. Their troop leader rode with them. Nobody spoke a word.

"Up, girls!" The sharp command from the doorway was familiar now. No matter how early we woke, Tali was always up before us. She stood waiting as the four of us struggled into our clothes, tied back our hair, and straightened our bedding. When folk lived at such close quarters over a long winter, keeping everything in order became second nature.

"Hurry up, Neryn." Regan's second-in-command leaned against the doorframe, her tattooed arms folded, observing me as if I were a tardy recruit. "I planned to put you on the Ladder later this morning, but two young fellows have turned up at the door—Black Crow only knows how they got here through the snow—and I'll have to test them today. So you'll be training before breakfast. It's the only time I can fit it in."

My heart sank. When I'd first reached the rebel base at Shadowfell, I'd been weak. Three years on the road, living rough, moving from one place of hiding to the next, had left me undernourished, sick, and slow to trust. When I was on the run, I had not understood why the king's men were pursuing me, only that my canny gift was more curse than blessing. Indeed, I had hardly known what that gift was. It had taken a long journey and many strange meetings before I'd learned that I was a Caller, and that my gift might be key to ending King Keldec's rule.

My first weeks at Shadowfell had been spent resting, eating what was set before me, and having occasional visits from my fey friends Sage and Red Cap, who were lodged somewhere out on the mountain. I had not been invited to join strategic discussions or to study the various maps and charts Regan kept in the chamber where he did his planning. Everyone at Shadowfell had daily work to do, but I had not been asked to do anything except recover my strength. Regan and his rebel band had treated me as they might a very special weapon—they had concentrated on returning me to top condition as swiftly as possible.

Of recent days I had insisted on helping Fingal in the

infirmary, where I could make myself useful preparing salves and tinctures, rolling bandages, and performing additional routine tasks. That freed Shadowfell's healer for other work. Tali's tough winter training regime resulted in a steady stream of sprains, cuts, and bruises for her brother to tend to.

And now, at last, I had been declared well enough to begin that training myself. For my canny gift, so valuable to the rebels, was not enough on its own; Regan would not allow me to work for the rebellion unless I had at least basic skills as a fighter. I would never be a warrior like Tali or Andra or the other women who shared the sleeping quarters. My years on the road had made me tough, but I was too small and slight to be much use in a fight. Still, I needed to be able to defend myself until someone could step in to help me. That was what Regan had said.

"Good luck," muttered Sula, who had tied up her hair with practiced speed and was heading for the door.

"You'll be fine, Neryn," murmured Dervla as she passed me. Finet thrust her feet into her boots and followed the others out while I was still pulling on my skirt. Andra had been on night guard and had not yet come in. Despite our remote location, Shadowfell's entry was constantly patrolled.

"You can't wear that." Tali's dark eyes were not hostile, exactly, but they were not friendly either. Even now, when I had been at Shadowfell long enough to be accepted by everyone else, it was plain she still had reservations about me. "Hasn't Eva found you some trousers? Get them on,

4

hurry up, and wear your boots, not those soft slippers, or you'll end up injuring your ankles."

I made myself breathe calmly as I changed skirt for trousers. Eva, who along with Milla was in charge of domestic matters at Shadowfell, had indeed made me the required garment, since all the female fighters wore male attire for active duty. I should have thought of this. Tackling the Ladder in a skirt would be impossible.

I put on my boots. I plaited my hair. I wondered if Tali would let me go to the privy before we began.

"That was much too slow," she said now. "If we were sleeping in the open and there was an ambush, you'd be dead before you could pick up your weapon at that rate. We can't afford any weak links."

There were things I could have said about the numerous times Father and I had melted away into the woods when Enforcers came near. I could have mentioned that we had managed three years on the run without being caught, until the terrible night when the Cull came to Darkwater and my father perished. But I said nothing. Tali's job was to keep us all fit enough to fight on, to survive, to spread the message of freedom out across Alban. For now, my job was to learn.

"Go to the privy," Tali said, "then meet me at the Ladder. We've got it to ourselves until breakfast is over, and I want to make the most of that. Don't dawdle."

"Ready? Fifty steps this time, and I want it quicker. One, two, three, go!"

I climbed. Tali followed, apparently tireless, staying

5

a few steps behind and keeping a rapid count. My thighs burned with pain. My chest ached. I hardly had the strength to hate her, only to keep on going.

". . . forty-nine, fifty!"

I bent over, hands on knees, chest heaving. Tali stepped up behind me, not in the least out of breath. Now I really did hate her.

"Rest to the count of ten. One, two . . ."

The precipitous stone steps known as the Ladder lay at the end of a long, winding passageway, part of the network of cavelike chambers that was Shadowfell. Who had made the place, nobody knew. It was old and uncanny. From time to time it changed its shape, forming new caverns or hallways, or opening new doors and windows to the outside. There was a clan of Good Folk here, the fey folk of Alban whom the king had decreed human men and women should shun. They lived in the mountain beneath the rebel headquarters, or so my small friend Sage believed. Without the useful gifts they left, the human folk of Shadowfell could not have survived the harsh highland winters. Firewood. Freshly killed livestock. Vegetables that could not grow here on the mountain. The Good Folk teased the rebels with their closeness, but never showed themselves. When I'd first come here, I'd thought it might be easy for me to find and befriend them. My gift as a Caller allowed me to see and speak to uncanny folk of every kind. At least it had in the past. But these particular folk were proving as hard to coax from their bolt-hole as a hazelnut is to prize from its shell.

The Ladder went up the wall of a high, narrow cavern. At the top, the steps opened out to a broad ledge. People said that on a good day the view from up there was breathtaking: a sweeping vista of snowcapped peaks, high fells, and deep valleys. If you were lucky, you might see eagles soaring on the currents of air.

I had never been up before. Clearly the steps had been carved out from the rock by someone with a wicked desire to challenge folk to the breaking point. Either that or their creator had not imagined the use Tali might make of them.

". . . ten. Ready? One, two, three, go!"

I climbed. I might have been almost too tired to move, but I could still obey an order.

"Good," Tali said as I reached the hundredth step and bent double, gasping for air.

"Thanks," I wheezed. From her, this was extreme praise.

"Don't waste your breath talking. Rest for the count of fifteen. Then we're heading for the top."

She counted. I breathed. In the chill of the cavern, I was drenched with sweat.

". . . fourteen, fifteen. Ready? One, two, three, go! Pick up the pace, Neryn! Move those legs!"

There were one hundred and twenty-seven steps in all. By the time we reached the ledge at the top, every part of my aching body wanted to collapse. I held myself upright, leaning back on the rock wall, working to slow my breathing. If there was anything Tali despised, it was lack of self-control. And she had a habit of springing surprises. It didn't pay to lose concentration, even for a moment. She was perfectly capable of making me go all the way back to the bottom and start again.

"You can sit," she said, moving out along the ledge and seating herself with her back against the rock wall and her long legs stretched toward the sheer drop. "You're not a warrior; I do make allowances for that. And the way down is hard on the knees."

Since she had given permission, I sat down beside her. The air was icy. It was a still day, without the whipping northerly that so often came up in the mornings. Low cloud wrapped the mountain closely. No view today beyond a few rocks here, a patch of barren hillside there. Shadowfell sometimes felt like the end of the world.

"What lies north of here?" I asked when I had enough breath to speak. "Are there settlements beyond those mountains?"

"Why do you ask?"

"It looks empty. Trackless." When I had discovered I was a Caller, with the ability to summon the Good Folk to the aid of humankind, I had also learned that I must seek guidance in my craft from the Guardians of Alban. These ancient beings of great power had retreated to places of hiding when Keldec came to the throne. They could not bear to see our peaceful realm turned to a place of fear and cruelty. If I could find them, their teaching would enable me to use my gift to the full, and wisely. I'd met one Guardian already. The Master of Shadows had found me and tested me, then told me in his cryptic way what I must do next. I had three journeys to make and three more Guardians to find: the Lord of the North, the Hag of the Isles, the White Lady. North, West, East. "The Lord of the North must live in those mountains, or beyond them, so when the winter is over, I'll have to go there."

"Without a guide, you could wander about in that area until you died of starvation," Tali said flatly.

"I can forage. I can fish. I know how to make a snare."

"It's not easy terrain. There are few settlements, few good tracks, few bridges. Even in summer, not much grows there."

"At least there will be no Cull and no king's men to contend with, if the north is so empty."

"One thing's certain," Tali said. "You can't do the trip on your own, no matter how much of a warrior we make of you by springtime. Regan seldom sends people out alone anyway, Flint being the obvious exception. He'll insist you take someone with you as pathfinder and bodyguard." She stared out over the cloud-veiled mountains. "If I were you, I'd go west first and seek out this Hag of the Isles," she said. "Save the north for summer. Or do you need to follow a particular order?"

"The Master of Shadows didn't say anything about that. I only know that I need to learn something different from each Guardian."

"Mm-hm." Tali was noncommittal; I could not tell what she was thinking. She lifted an arm ringed with tattoos—spirals, swirls, flying birds to match the ones around her neck—and pushed her dark hair back behind her ear. "It's a long way to travel, Neryn. Perhaps farther than you realize. The north . . . it's an unforgiving place. We've lost a lot of good comrades there."

"I suppose I could go west first." That would mean retracing the path I had taken to come to Shadowfell, a path full of difficult memories. Still, I had to do it sometime. If I went west, there was a possibility—slim but real—that I might see Flint. The thought of him was both joy and sorrow, for when he had left Shadowfell, we had spoken sweet words of forgiveness and hope. We had not spoken of love, not in so many words, for soft feelings were forbidden among Regan's Rebels. But something deep and real had passed between us. Now Flint would be back at Winterfort and living his perilous life as Regan's eyes at the heart of the king's court. Keldec's Enforcer; Keldec's confidant; Keldec's most trusted man. A rebel spy. Treading a very thin line, and in constant danger. I still dared to hope he might return to Shadowfell in time to travel with me in spring. But, knowing he would need to explain away the loss of an entire troop of Enforcers, I doubted the king would let him leave court again so soon.

"Have you thought of asking your uncanny friends to go with you?" Tali asked. "Or one of those folk that are supposed to be living downstairs?"

"The Folk Below, Sage calls them. You sound as if you don't believe in them."

Tali gave me a sideways look. "I'm not stupid, Neryn. I know there's something in these caves apart from us.

Especially now I've seen your unusual friends. We'd never have survived in this place without fey help. But they can't be down that spiral stair. It leads nowhere. You've seen it for yourself. The passageway at the bottom ends in a solid rock wall. Yet Sage insists that's where they live."

I had nothing to say to that. Not even Sage had been able to raise so much as a squeak from the Folk Below.

"So why not ask them to go with you? Sage and the other one? Their magic could help protect you on the way, couldn't it?"

"I don't want to ask them. One of their kind died protecting me, on the way up here. You know iron is a bane to the Good Folk, as deadly as poison. Sage's dear friend died with a chain wrapped around his neck and an Enforcer holding it tight. It was hideous. Cruel. He was just a small being, a creature of the woodland, and he stood up to the king's men so I could escape. Sage has given up a lot for me already. Red Cap has a little baby to look after. If I ask them to come with me and it happens again, I don't think I can . . ."

I felt the weight of Tali's gaze on me. "Believe me," she said, "I know how that feels. It's something you learn to live with, because it's the nature of what we do. This war won't be won without losses. Regan will balance up the value of your gift against the risk of someone getting hurt protecting you, and he'll insist you have a guard. If not one of the Good Folk, then one of us. You'll have to swallow your scruples."

When I said nothing, she went on, "The north isn't

11

entirely empty. There's a regional chieftain there, Lannan, sometimes called Lannan Long-Arm, with a number of district chieftains answering to him. Lannan is kin to the leaders in the northern isles. We've been told his personal fighting force is substantial." She hesitated. "Our negotiations with Lannan are at a delicate stage. Of Alban's eight regional chieftains, this is the most powerful. He hasn't attended the Gathering for several years; his relationship with the king is less than cordial. Distance is his friend. Keldec's unlikely to send a war band rushing up there only to see them lost in the mountains."

There was a pause.

"You understand what I'm telling you, Neryn?"

"That whoever wins Lannan over to their side has a big advantage. Yes?"

"Mm-hm."

"Does that mean Regan is traveling north himself in spring?"

Tali shook her head. "No need. We've a team talking to Lannan already. There's more to Regan's Rebels than this small band at Shadowfell, Neryn. This is the center of the operation, yes; Regan is the beating heart of the rebellion. But we couldn't do it with so few. We're spread out in many parts of Alban, in places where a single dissenting voice has grown into a force for change. We do have to be careful. You know what happens when the king gets the merest whiff of disobedience."

I knew all too well. I had seen villages burned, the innocent put to the sword, leaders who stood up for justice summarily executed. I had lost my entire family to the Cull, the seasonal sweep of Alban's villages that weeded out the rebellious and those with canny gifts. Keldec feared magic above all else. And yet he used it for his own ends. His Enthrallers, of whom Flint was one, were able to work an enchantment to turn someone who had displeased the king into a flawlessly loyal subject. Sometimes, though, the charm went wrong, and the victim became a witless husk of his former self. That too I had seen. It had been the worst night of my life.

"If Regan's teams are spread out all over Alban," I asked, "how do they communicate? How can you put a complete strategy in place when the time comes?"

"We have folk here and there who carry messages. Trusted folk. Believe it or not, there are some of those in Alban still. But, yes, it is a weakness. These things take time."

I thought of the boy who had brought messages to Flint, when he and I had spent the long days and nights of my illness in a little hut halfway up the Rush valley. I had wondered about that boy; wondered if he was like my brother, who had died with a spear through his chest when the Enforcers raided our home village, less than four years ago. Only a fool or a hero would dare carry messages for the rebels. Perhaps such folk were both heroes and fools.

"It's not a quick process," Tali said. "Winning the chieftains over, I mean. Those who are prepared to support a rebellion dare not be open about their intentions. In every stronghold there's someone ready to slip word to the Enforcers for a few pieces of silver. And once they do

13

that, whether their information is true or false, the king's wrath comes down like an ill-aimed hammer, striking innocent and guilty alike. All of us want the rebellion soon, as soon as possible, before people are too worn down to care anymore. But a word to the wrong ears could wreck the whole endeavor." She glanced at me sideways, her dark eyes narrowed. "That means no blundering into unknown parts and saying too much, whether it's a chieftain's hall or a cave housing an uncanny creature of some kind."

"I wasn't intending to do any blundering. And I'll be staying away from chieftains' halls. I'm hoping to avoid human settlements altogether, if I can. But I do need to go, and go as soon as the season allows. If Regan wants my gift as a tool for the rebellion, I must find the Guardians and complete the Caller's training. Though by the time I get back down the Ladder, I may not be able to walk to my bedchamber, let alone all the way to the western isles."

"By springtime," said Tali, standing and reaching out a strong hand to pull me to my feet, "you'll be running up and down these steps without a second thought. You're tougher than you look; must be those years on the road. If you're heading west first, maybe we should be practicing swimming."

"Wonderful," I said, not mentioning that I could not swim at all. "Where would we be doing that, in some ice-bound mountain tarn?"

"Don't put it past me." The merest trace of a smile touched Tali's features. "Now we're heading back down. Don't be too cautious, keep the pace steady, and lean back slightly as you go. I'd prefer not to have to catch you. I won't count, but I want you to imagine there's a big fellow with a big weapon right on your tail. Dawdle, and he'll make sure you get to the bottom uncomfortably fast."

Once I began training with Tali, my daily routine changed. The Ladder was in heavy use during the day, with everyone at Shadowfell but Milla and Eva required to complete a certain number of ascents and descents to maintain their fitness. I took to rising early and going up and down while everything was quiet. The only ones on the Ladder before me were Tali and her brother Fingal, who fitted in the same combat training as everyone else. People said Shadowfell's healer had a rare skill with the knife, and not only for surgery. As for Tali, she worked everyone hard, and herself hardest of all.

When the folk of Shadowfell were not on the Ladder or in the training yard, they were busy with other work: helping Milla and Eva maintain the household, keeping weaponry in top condition, fashioning maps, making plans for the spring's trips out from Shadowfell. I wondered, sometimes, if Regan had established this routine so there would be less time for arguments. Disputes did tend to break out when a small community was cooped up in a confined space, as we were over the long highland winter. It was rare for anyone to venture outside, apart from their activities in the training yard with its sheltering stone walls. The fells were blanketed with snow; ice made the paths treacherous.

I learned new skills. Andra, a strapping red-haired

fighter of one-and-twenty who could match the best of the men in hand-to-hand combat, trained me to use my staff as a weapon. Muscular, hard-faced Gort, who had once been a chieftain's master-at-arms, taught me to wield short and long daggers in self-defense. I was not trained alongside the new recruits, who had been given a trial period over the winter to prove themselves. Regan had ordered that my lessons be conducted in private. Knowing how vital it was for me to be ready when spring came, I worked hard and asked no questions.

Every few days Sage came to the door of the rebel head-quarters, and the guards put away their iron weapons, respecting what she was. They would call me, and I would go to talk to my friend in a little chamber set aside for this purpose. Sometimes Red Cap came with her, but not often. His infant was still very small, and it was cold out in the snow, going to and fro. My fey friends did not like to come farther inside our dwelling, for there was iron everywhere, not only weaponry but Milla's kitchen ladles and tongs, the soup pot, the trivets, and other paraphernalia.

Sage and Red Cap, with the babe, had followed me all the way from the forests by Silverwater in the west, where I had first encountered them. They had helped me, had stood up for me in the face of their clan's doubts, and convinced others of their kind to aid me on my journey. Indeed, I'd discovered that Sage had been keeping an eye on me since I was a child, suspecting that my special ability went something beyond the canny gifts—unusually good sight or hearing, a particular talent at music, an exceptional knack with animals—that a scattering of human folk possessed.

So Sage and Red Cap were here on the mountain, not lodged with the rebels or with the mysterious Folk Below, but in some place unknown to me. Sage had been confident, at first, that the Good Folk of Shadowfell could be persuaded to come out and talk to us, but thus far our efforts to contact them had been fruitless. I had hoped to enlist their help; I had promised Regan I would do my best. Although the Good Folk in general were distrustful of humankind, the Folk Below, with their gifts of food and fuel, had shown goodwill toward the rebels since Regan and his band had first moved into Shadowfell. I had thought I could ask for their help in finding the Guardians—they should know, at least, where to start looking for the Lord of the North. More than that, I'd thought we could win them over to the cause. If the Good Folk could be persuaded to join the rebellion, we had a much better chance of removing Keldec from the throne. The most famous Caller of the past had united fey and human armies to defeat a common enemy.

All very well. Thus far I had not even persuaded these folk to open their door to me. And there lay the problem. My gift was powerful. I had used it to turn the tide of a battle last autumn; I had called out a rock being, a stanie mon, to fall on a party of Enforcers and crush them. That deed weighed heavily on my conscience, and not only because one of the rebels had been caught up in it and had sustained an injury from which he'd later died. Regan's

17

fighters had hailed me as a hero that day. But I did not feel like a hero. Wielding that kind of power horrified me. It made me determined not to use my special talent again until I knew how to do so wisely. I must reach the Folk Below without using my gift; I must not compel them to come out. Sage and her clan had befriended me without my needing to call. Why should not the Folk Below be the same?

My health improved. My strength increased, thanks to good food, enough rest, and rigorous training. I became more used to living at close quarters with many folk. That had been hard at first, for it was years since I had lived in the village of Corbie's Wood, with a family and a community. Father and I had been on our own a long while; and after he died, it had been only me. And then Flint and me. I tried not to think too much of him, for my imagination was all too ready to paint me pictures of Flint at court, Flint in trouble, Flint under suspicion of spying. I dreamed of him sometimes, confusing dreams that I could not interpret. I kept them to myself. He had been my companion in times of trouble, sometimes trusted, sometimes doubted, in the end a friend above all friends. And now he was gone. I must not waste time regretting something that could not be.

I had not kept count of the days, but others had. It was close to midwinter, and even Ban and Kenal, the two lads most recently arrived at Shadowfell, were starting to look like warriors, thanks to Tali's training and their own hard work. We sat in the dining chamber, the only place big enough to accommodate our whole community at once, working on various tasks by lamplight after supper had been cleared away. At one end of the chamber, Milla's cooking fire burned on the broad hearth, filling the place with welcome warmth. Regan and Tali sat together, red head and dark bent over a map spread out on the table before them. They were arguing, though they kept their voices down. Tali had her arms tightly folded. Regan's handsome features wore an uncharacteristic frown.

Eva and I were working our way through a basket of mending. Killen, Shadowfell's most expert archer, had fletching materials laid out on the table before him. Andra was sharpening my knife for me, her eyes narrowed as she worked it against the whetstone. The special sheath I had made, with its protective wards, lay close by. She had not asked me about it, and I had not volunteered any information. I had learned the making of such things from my grandmother, a wise woman. Grandmother's story was too hard to tell, too raw and painful, even now. She had fallen victim to the Cull in the cruelest way, turned into a witless shell by an enthrallment gone wrong. Destroyed before my twelve-year-old eyes as I hid and watched. I had learned to set the memory away where it would not cripple me, and I did not bring it out for sharing.

When Flint had told me he was an Enthraller, one of those who performed the same vile magic those men had worked on my grandmother, I had fled in revulsion. The news had made me physically sick. Mind-mending, Flint had called it, a fine old magic that had been warped and perverted under Keldec. In time I had come to accept the truth of this: that mind-mending had indeed once been a force for healing. Still, I did not speak of my grandmother: neither of the time of her wisdom and love, her strength and goodness, nor of the frail, lost thing she became. Her death had been a mercy.

Big Don was adjusting the binding on a spear. Little Don, a marginally shorter man, was plucking a tune on a three-stringed fiddle and humming under his breath. Others played games—stanies, hop-the-man, or a form of skittles with an elaborate scoring system that seemed to change from night to night. Running totals were marked up on the stone wall with charcoal, and friendly disputes as to their accuracy were common.

The games, I did not care for. No one at Shadowfell knew I'd first met Flint when he beat my father at stanies and won me as his prize. That night was etched on my memory forever. Not long after the game the Cull had swept down on Darkwater and my father had been burned to death. I had trained myself to be calm when folk brought out the board and pieces. I had taught myself not to start in fright every time they made the call: *Spear! Hound! Stag!*

"You should go off to bed," Eva said, giving me a glance. "You look worn out. Been having bad dreams again?"

In a place like this, there was no avoiding scrutiny. "I'm all right. Let me finish darning these leggings, at least."

"Another pair of Tali's," Eva commented. "She wears them out faster than anyone else, and since I'd rather not get my head snapped off, I don't ask her to do her own mending. It's not as if she's ever idle. Does the work of four men, that girl."

Plying my bone needle and hoping Tali would not complain about my uneven stitchery, I allowed my thoughts to wander back to Flint, for it was a dream of him that had disturbed my sleep last night. It was hard to say exactly what we were to each other. Not lovers. Not sweethearts. What lay between us was too deep and too complicated for such words. I feared for him. Despite what he was, despite what he did, I longed for his return. But only if coming back did not place him in still greater danger. I yearned for the time when we could be together in a world without fear. I hoped that time would come before we were too old and tired to care anymore.

"What are you dreaming of, Neryn?"

I managed a smile. "Better times. Opportunities. Good things."

"Ah, well. We all dream of those."

"Even Tali? I wonder what she would do if Alban were at peace."

Tali's dispute with Regan had intensified; she smacked her hand on the table for emphasis.

"I don't see peace coming in a hurry," Eva said. "Even if it does, folk will still need guards, protectors, sentries. There's always work for fighters."

"Tali as a sentry? Give her a day or two and she'd be running the whole army." I realized halfway through this comment that the chamber had fallen quiet and my voice had carried clearly to both Tali and Regan. "I'm sorry," I said quickly, glancing over. "I meant no offense."

"A song!" put in Big Don before Tali could say a word. "What better for a winter night? Who'll oblige us? Brasal, how about you?"

Brasal was Fingal's other infirmary assistant, a young man of brawny build who could lift a patient with ease. His strong hands were useful for bone-setting. He also had a deep, true singing voice.

"Come on!" Little Don plucked the start of a tune on his fiddle, then reached for the bow. "Something cheerful, none of those forlorn ballads of lost loves and misfortunes."

"I'll sing if Regan sings with me. And the rest of you join in the refrain, even you, Tali."

"Me?" Tali's dark brows lifted. "You know I've got a singing voice like a crow's, Brasal. I'll leave it to the rest of you." After a moment she added, "Sing that thing about catching geese, I like that one."

The goose song was lengthy and became sillier as it progressed. Regan added a higher counterpoint to Brasal's melody, and we all joined in the refrain with good will. This made a change from the pattern of hard work that filled our days, and it pleased me to see people smiling. Eva and I sewed as we sang, and Killen's big hands stayed busy with his arrows. When the goose song was done, requests came from all over the room and the singers obliged. Regan's singing voice was lighter than Brasal's, clear and sweet in tone. The fiddle added an anchoring drone and sometimes inserted its own line of melody. The fire crackled; the mead jug was passed around; the mood was mellow.

"Regan." Milla spoke into the silence after a song. "Do you remember that old tune for midwinter, 'Out of Darkness Comes the Light'? I've always loved that." She glanced at me. "My man used to sing it, back in the early days. Back when we needed every scrap of hope we could find."

I nodded understanding. At two-and-thirty, Milla was the oldest person at Shadowfell. She and her husband had been with Regan from the first, along with Flint. Fingal and Tali had joined them not long after. Those six had been the sum of the rebellion then, the tiny flame from which a great fire of hope had flared. Milla's man had died for the cause. Exactly how, I did not know and did not ask. Folk only shared their stories if they chose to; it was an unspoken rule that one did not pry. Likely every person at Shadowfell had a tale of loss and heartbreak in their past, just as I did.

"I remember it," Regan said. "Brasal?"

Brasal shook his head. "I don't know it. You start, I'll try to pick up the tune."

Regan lifted his voice, unaccompanied in the quiet of the chamber. The firelight played on the strong bones of his face; his deep blue eyes shone with feeling. And while his singing voice was pleasant rather than exceptional, suddenly everyone's gaze was on him. Fingers stilled in mid-stitch; playing pieces were set quietly down.

Out of darkness comes the light,
Out of night comes morning,
Out of sorrow rises joy,
In the new day's dawning.
Courage, wanderer! May the sun
Cast its light upon us,
Showing us the path ahead
Into springtime's promise.
Rise up, weary traveler, rise!
Hope's bright beacon lights the skies.

The melody died away; this song had no refrain. For a count of ten nobody made a sound. I could swear not one of us took a breath. Then, into the quiet, there came a din of clashing metal and raised voices. Tali was on her feet in an eyeblink and in front of Regan, shielding him with a skill born of long practice. Andra and Killen were up a moment later, moving in on either side, she with her staff, he with an ax. Tali's knife was at the ready; I had not even seen her draw it from the sheath. Brasal moved into position in front of me and Eva. Five people headed out toward the entry, drawing weapons as they went.

"It's the middle of winter," muttered Eva. "Who'd come knocking but an ice trow or a madman?"

I shivered, waiting. It was all very well to joke about trows. I had met a brollachan last autumn, and although the fearsome creature had proved to be a friend, that was only after he had dangled me by the ankle over an abyss and frightened me half out of my wits.

Shouts from the entry; someone exclaiming in astonishment, "Cian! By all that's holy!"

Regan made toward the door; Tali halted him with a raised hand. She formed a word with her lips, making no sound. *Wait.*

We did not have to wait long. Big Don and Fingal came back into the chamber supporting a man between them. He was wrapped in thick woolen clothing, a cloak, a cloth around his head and shoulders, mittens that looked heavy with damp. A dusting of snow lay on his head and shoulders. Within the shawl-like wrapping that swathed his head, his eyes were strangely bright against a death mask of a face, gaunt and pale with exhaustion. His boots were cracked and worn. The two brought him to the fireside and sat him down on a bench. All around the chamber, weapons were slid back into their sheaths.

"On his own," said Big Don succinctly.

Regan crouched before the traveler, gazed up into the drained face. "By sun and moon, Cian, you look like a ghost! Welcome home. No, don't try to speak. Let's get you warm first. Milla—"

Milla was already ladling broth from a cook pot into a bowl while one of the men poured mead into a cup and set it by Cian. Plainly this was neither madman nor ill-doer, but one of us.

"Not too much," Fingal warned as Cian lifted the cup in shaking hands. "A sip at a time. That's it. Get that cloak off, man. And the boots. Black Crow save us, look at the state you're in. How far have you walked today?"

25

"Save the questions for later." Regan gestured and folk moved back, giving the traveler room. Milla brought the broth; Brasal went out and came back with a blanket, which he wrapped around Cian in place of the cloak and shawl. Under Milla's direction, Little Don carried in a tub of warm water for the traveler's feet. Cian's face regained some color, but bouts of shivering still coursed through his body.

"Who is he?" I whispered to Eva.

"One of ours," she murmured. "From the north. He'll have news. He'd never have attempted the journey in winter otherwise. Just hope it's not bad news."

After some time Cian's trembling lessened, though he still looked shattered and weary. Regan sat close by him, murmuring reassuring words, while Fingal checked the traveler's pulse, looked in his eyes, then sent me to the infirmary to make up a restorative infusion.

"Thank you," Cian said in a thread of a voice when I returned to set the cup before him. "Who . . . ?"

"Neryn," Regan said. "A Caller."

Cian's eyes widened.

"She came last autumn, with Flint. A long story, which can wait for tomorrow. As can yours, my friend—Fingal should take you off to the infirmary and get you to bed." Despite these words, there was a question in Regan's voice.

"No. I must tell you first." Cian made a visible effort to sit straighter, to gather himself. I did not like the look in his eye. All around us, folk were waiting in silence.

"Good news or ill?" Regan was calm—outwardly, at least.

"Both. It cannot wait for tomorrow." Cian glanced at me, then over toward the new lads, Ban and Kenal. "Is it safe to speak?"

"It's safe. Tell us. You come from Lannan Long-Arm. Does this concern the proposed alliance?"

"I have news of that, yes. But . . . there is something else." Cian drew a deep breath; there was a rasping sound in his chest. "Three of us set out to bring word to you. Arden and Gova were with me. They are . . . they are both lost, Regan. We were caught in a storm, heading back over the pass north of the Race. Gova fell; we could not reach her. Arden perished from cold."

A silence, then; heads were bowed all around the firelit chamber.

"What news could be so urgent that it demanded the sacrifice of two of our finest?" Tali's voice was tight with what might have been grief or fury. "What news could not wait until the passes were safe to cross?"

"Tali," said Regan in an undertone. It was a warning; Tali fell silent, though her anger was a presence in the room.

"The news is this." Cian looked straight at his leader. "Lannan Long-Arm will support the rebel cause. He has promised to bring a substantial force to Summerfort and to stand up beside us when we challenge Keldec." Then, as the rest of us were about to break out into a chorus of amazed congratulations, he added, "There's a condition. Lannan believes that if our preparations draw out too long, the king will inevitably get word of what we plan. Should that happen, our cause is lost before we can put the final pieces in play. Our whole strategy depends on keeping the plan from Keldec's knowledge."

Regan was frowning. "I understand Lannan's concerns. We're working toward putting this in place as soon as we can. Did you offer him the incentives I suggested?"

"That was discussed, yes. Should we succeed in removing Keldec, Lannan wants a position as regent, or coregent, until the heir comes of age. If as coregent, he wants the power to approve whoever shares the position. He suggested a couple of names."

"He knows, I assume, that Keldec is likely to bring magic into play in any confrontation with us?"

Cian nodded. "He does; and suggested, almost as a jest, that we attempt to harness the support of the Good Folk in order to counter that. At the very least, he said, if our own folk possess canny gifts, we should make use of those. But . . ." He looked at me.

"But Lannan does not know—cannot know—that we now have a Caller," said Fingal. "A Caller gives us an immense advantage."

I cleared my throat, not sure if I should speak. These people had just learned of the deaths of two of their own; it seemed no time for a strategic discussion. "But not yet," I said to Cian. "I have only recently discovered the nature of my canny gift. I need time to learn its wise use. Two years, maybe three—I won't know how long until I find the people who can teach me. They are all in different parts of Alban."

Cian said nothing.

"Out with it." Regan fixed his gaze on the traveler. "Lannan has set a limit on how long we can rely on his help, yes? Tell us."

"He knows we plan to confront the king at one of the midsummer Gatherings, when the clans are all together in the one place. His ultimatum is this: if we cannot do it by the summer after next, he'll withdraw his support for the rebellion, and instead step away from both Keldec's authority and any alliance with the other chieftains of Alban."

Horror filled me. The summer after next? How could I possibly be ready in time? There were gasps and murmurs all around the chamber; Brasal uttered an oath.

"You're saying that if we can't do this in a year and a half, the north will secede from the kingdom?" Tali's voice was hushed with shock.

"That's bold," said Big Don. "Some might say foolishly so."

"Lannan has kin in the northern isles," Milla said. "And his territories are guarded by the mountains; even Keldec's Enforcers would have trouble sustaining an armed conflict in those parts. Provided his northern kin could supply him, Lannan and his folk could survive without Keldec's support."

"Support!" put in Big Don with a grim smile. "Not the word I'd have used."

Nobody else was smiling.

"The Gathering after next." Regan spoke calmly, but his face told another story. "I would say that was impossible. But here at Shadowfell we don't use that word. Neryn, you understand how much this depends on you. Can you learn the skills you need by the summer after next? Will it be long enough?"

I bit back my first response. Three Guardians to find, all in different corners of Alban; three branches of knowledge to master; and then, the disparate talents of humankind and Good Folk to be brought into an alliance strong enough to stand up against the might of Keldec and his Enforcers . . . all that in a scant year and a half? When I had thus far failed to exchange even one word with the Folk Below? It was . . . I must not say impossible. I was one of Regan's Rebels now, and I must not even think it. "I'll try my best," I said.

Chapter Two

Whether Sage sensed, somehow, that finding the Folk
Below was more urgent than ever, there was no telling, but
the next day she was at the entry to Shadowfell, asking to
see me. Sula had been on guard duty with Gort and came to
fetch me from the infirmary. At the entry Gort was wrapping his weaponry and Sula's in a cloth, and beyond the
opening stood the small figure of my fey friend, her hood
up against the cold, her worn green cloak covering her to
the ankles. She would not come inside until every piece of
iron in her path had been shielded. A chill wind blew the
highland winter in, setting a shiver deep in my bones.

"We're clear," said Gort, tucking the bundle of weaponry away in the alcove near the entry, a place that had
not existed within the intricate plan of Shadowfell until
the need for it had become clear with the arrival of Sage
and Red Cap. It was no wonder the Good Folk referred to
the area around Shadowfell as the Folds. The terrain was
steeped in earth magic. It seemed to change of itself, bare

fell becoming forested hollow, dry stone suddenly shaping itself to hold a mirror-clear mountain tarn, ridge and cliff and cave forming and vanishing in startling defiance of any rules known to humankind. It was a deeply odd place, but one thing about it seemed plain: whoever controlled those changes was not ill-disposed toward Regan and his band. If the land altered, if something appeared where there had been nothing, it always seemed designed to give our band an advantage. The appearance of the storage area near the main entry was one of those useful changes—it allowed not only the temporary concealment of the iron weaponry so feared by the Good Folk, but also ready retrieval of the replacement spears and knives fashioned of other materials, which our guards substituted for their usual armory when Sage and Red Cap came to visit me.

"Come in," I said, ushering Sage through to the small chamber set aside for our meetings. The two guards re-armed themselves with wooden spears and returned to their positions. All the rebels were accustomed to these visits now. "I need your good counsel."

As briefly as I could, I told her of Cian's dramatic arrival and the dilemma that now faced us. I did not know if a year and a half would be sufficient time for Regan's forces to prepare a successful challenge to the king. It didn't sound long; but then, Tali had implied that the northern chieftain, Lannan, had a substantial personal army. The most doubtful part of it was my contribution. Even if I could find the Guardians, even if they agreed to teach me, even if I could learn to harness my gift, what about the Good

Folk? It simply wasn't in their nature to cooperate with humankind—Sage and Red Cap were notable exceptions—and I faced the daunting task of persuading them to help us despite the very real likelihood many of them would lose their lives in the process. And all by the summer after next. Regan had made it plain to me that without their aid, the rebellion was unlikely to succeed. The might of Keldec was formidable; fear would keep most of the chieftains loyal to him.

Sage listened quietly as I set it out for her; indeed, she spoke not a word, but rested her chin on her hands and regarded me with grave eyes.

"I don't really see how I can do it in so short a time," I said. "It's perilous to travel anyway, with the king's men possibly on the lookout for me, or for someone like me. I have no idea where the Guardians are, except west, north, east. I'm hoping I need not seek out the Master of Shadows again; from the way he spoke to me, it sounded as if I might see him from time to time along the way, perhaps when I least expect it, and perhaps that means I don't have to travel south. But the others . . . how do I even know where to start looking? I thought I could ask the Folk Below, but they won't come out. Won't even open their door to us. Yet I have to do it. Regan believes in me. His plan depends on me. I can't let him down."

"There's one answer within your grasp, at least." Sage spoke briskly. "You know it full well."

"You mean I should call them. Use my gift, compel them to open their door to me."

"Why would you not do that, with time running so short? Since they will not open to you when you wait politely, this seems the only way."

There was nothing to say to this. The last time I had used my gift as a Caller, men had died horribly. It hadn't seemed to matter that they were Enforcers, the enemy, and that my action had turned the tide of a battle. Looking at their broken bodies, I had not thought of them as king's men, but as brothers, fathers, sons, and comrades. To wield such power was monstrous. It was only in the face of Regan's eloquent arguments that I had agreed to learn the skillful use of my gift and to aid the rebels in their struggle. The fact was, every rebel faced the same kind of dilemma. Freedom could not be won without immense personal cost. But it felt wrong to use my gift here at Shadowfell. I would hardly endear myself to the Folk Below if I forced them out against their will. And what if something went wrong, and I caused more damage?

"A year and a half," murmured Sage. "Not long. Not long at all."

"There's no need to keep telling me that!"

"No?" She regarded me with brows raised and a crooked smile on her small features.

"I've tried already, Sage, you know that. Every single day I've gone down the spiral stair and waited by that stone wall, thinking they'd come out if I gave them enough time. When I met you and the others in the woods above Silverwater, I didn't have to call. I was by my campfire, and there you were. Later on too—when I needed you, you came."

"Ah," said Sage in a weighty tone. "But we're different."

"You and Red Cap are my friends, as Sorrel was; but not all of your clan believed in me back then. Silver and her cronies were quite hostile. But they came out too, without my making any sort of call."

"We're Westies," Sage said, as if that should explain everything.

"Westies—you're talking about belonging to the Watch of the West? What difference does that make?"

She shrugged, as if the distinction should be obvious. "We're quick, like water. Fluid and adaptable. The Northies—" She lifted her hands in a gesture I took to mean the Northies were almost beyond hope. "They hold fast to their ways. If they choose to, they can make themselves deaf as stone. You'd need something akin to a bolt of lightning to shift them. They'll be aware of your presence; they'll be able to feel it even through that wall they've put up. But they've chosen to ignore you."

"Isn't it more likely they don't know I'm here?"

Sage shook her head of gray-green curls. "You're a Caller. All the Good Folk feel your presence, like a tune they can't get out of their heads, or something buzzing around them that can't be swatted away. It's a matter of how long they can hold out against it. Could be the Folk Below will hold out a year and a half, or longer. Either you head off on your journey in spring without talking to them, or you use your gift to summon them."

"But what if—"

"No *what if*. You need their help. Call them, explain the

wee difficulty Regan's faced with, and ask for their advice."
A pause. "Not that it's for me to tell you what to do, lassie."

A plan began to form in my mind, based on what I
knew of the Good Folk already. Not that I had ever met a
Northie, except perhaps for the owl-like creature that had
saved me from dying of cold on the way along the valley
to Shadowfell. A being of some power, it had summoned
a pack of wolves and turned them small so they could
snuggle around me in my makeshift shelter. So perhaps I
already owed the Northies a favor.

"We need to offer them something. A meaningful
gift, not just the usual offering of food and drink. And it
should be Regan who tells them about the rebellion, not
me. When he talks, everyone listens; everyone is caught up
in his hope and courage. I might only have one chance at
this, Sage."

"If you ask me," Sage said, "a council would be the
thing. A grand council, rebels and Northies, with everything set out for them and a formal request made for their
help. Regan could do it, I suppose. But you'd be the one
would have to get them up here."

"Up here? You think they'd come, even if we shielded
every scrap of iron in the place?"

"Talk to Regan. Talk to that cook of yours. See what
they're prepared to offer. Then we'll go down and you can
call them out and issue an invitation. The sooner, the better, that's my thinking on the matter. You'll have heard
what they say about Northies."

"What?"

"Ask a Northie a question, and you'll wait a year for an answer. Ask two Northies a question and you'll wait two years while they talk it over. Ask three Northies and they'll still be arguing when they're dead and in the grave."

While she waited, I went to find Regan. He was in the dining hall with Tali, Big Don, and Andra, deep in discussion. Milla was stirring something on the fire and contributing a suggestion from time to time.

"1 know Lannan favors Keenan of Wedderburn," Tali was saying. "But Wedderburn's a high risk for us; I don't need to spell out the reasons why. Any approach to Keenan's household would have to be made with the utmost caution. There isn't time for that now, and I don't believe there's need. We have Gormal of Glenfalloch. We have Lannan, and his army is the biggest in Alban, after the king's. Shouldn't that be enough?"

Milla straightened with the ladle still in her hands. "Lannan's hardly going to march his entire army south to Summerfort for the Gathering. That would be like waving a flag to warn Keldec something's amiss. Not to mention the difficulty of moving a large force over those mountains, even in summer."

"Wedderburn is the closest chieftaincy to Summerfort," Andra said. "If we had Keenan's approval to cross his land, we could move men into place without using the king's road."

"The risk is too great." Tali was intent on Regan; I suspected this was an ongoing debate. "I don't know why you insist on pushing this argument. It's quite simple: you can't put your trust in anyone from that family. And besides . . ." She fell silent.

"Go on," Regan said, and the look on his face was one I had never seen before; there was a darkness in it, the shadow of something unspeakable. "Besides what?"

"You know what," Tali said, then looked up and saw me standing in the doorway. "Neryn. What is it?"

"I've been talking to Sage. I think I might . . ." I hesitated, not wanting to confess that I could perhaps have spoken to the Folk Below much earlier, if I'd been prepared to compel them out. "I believe I may be able to speak to the Good Folk today, and I want your permission to invite them to a council. It would be on midwinter eve, and we'd need to offer good hospitality, a feast, maybe music. And a gift; I will arrange that." All eyes were on me, showing varying degrees of surprise; it was known that I had failed so far to speak with the Folk Below, but not exactly why. Nobody said anything, so I cleared my throat and went on. "If they agree to come, we'll have to shield every piece of iron at Shadowfell."

Milla smiled. "Prepare a feast without pots and pans, ladles or knives? That'll be a challenge and a half."

"Regan would talk to them about the rebellion and how they can help us. And I would ask them for help in finding the Guardians, the ones who can teach me. There's another thing."

"Go on," Regan said.

"I've talked about this with Sage and Red Cap, and they

think we should suggest it to the Folk Below. Some of the Good Folk have the forms of birds, or something close. I have met one, Daw, who called himself a bird-friend. Daw is able to send crows to spy and to carry messages. This could be a way of getting word from one of your teams to another very quickly. A crow could fly from Shadowfell to the north, or from the Rush valley to the isles, in far less time than it would take a man to ride." After a moment I added, "I believe that would reduce our losses. It would mean folk wouldn't need to take the kind of risk Cian and his comrades did."

"Birds that talk." Andra's tone was flat with disbelief.

"Let Neryn tell us," Regan said. "You were at the battle last autumn; you saw what she can do. There are wonders here that we can hardly imagine. Talking birds are probably the least of it."

"Daw can certainly speak as we do. And he can make the birds understand." I thought of the owl-like creature that had helped me survive a chill night. "Among the Northies—the northern Good Folk—there's at least one that has a bird form."

"This could make all the difference." Tali's face was alight with enthusiasm now. "It would allow us to coordinate our forces, to ensure everything's in place at the same time. Provided the Good Folk can be trusted, it would allow us to pass on information ten times more quickly. And secretly, since these folk only make themselves visible to humankind if they choose. We must hold this council; we must persuade them to do this."

Her tone troubled me. "It may not be so easy," I told her. "The Good Folk have difficulty agreeing even among themselves. And in times of crisis they mostly go to ground, hide away until the threat is past. Sage and Red Cap are exceptional. It's very possible the others may refuse to help."

"But you're a Caller," said Tali. "Can't you make them help us?"

I hesitated. My instincts told me compelling uncanny folk into action could only lead to disaster. Surely it was best that they stood up for justice because it was what they believed in.

"Seems to me," Milla said, "the first thing we should be doing is thanking them. After all the good they've done us since we came to Shadowfell, it's past time for a bit of recompense. A feast, yes. And a payment of some kind, like the offerings folk used to put out on the doorstep to keep the Good Folk happy."

There was a silence while everyone considered this.

"Can't imagine what such folk would have need of," said Little Don, who was toying with the playing pieces for stanies.

"In the longer term, ridding Alban of its tyrannical ruler is the best gift we can offer," Regan said. "You say the Good Folk would rather hide away. Don't they value the notion of an Alban at peace, a country where they can go unmolested?"

"They may doubt our ability to deliver peace," said Andra. "We are of humankind after all, the same kind as Keldec and his Enforcers."

"Then it's up to Regan to convince them," said Tali. "We need these folk on our side. Once Neryn gets them to this council, he'll have to make the speech of his life."

The spiral stair led down into the heart of the mountain. The first time I had entered the maze of passageways that made up the rebel headquarters, I had almost fallen down here while trying to find my way around. A chill draft blew up from below, turning my flesh to goose bumps. Sage drew her cloak more tightly around her.

"Down we go, then," she said.

I held the lantern; Sage walked ahead. Shadows danced on the stone walls as we descended; the air grew colder.

"Sage," I whispered. "I don't really know how to do this. Call them, I mean." Twice I had summoned stanie men, great, slow beings of stone. I had relied on instinct when I called them, and chanted verses from a childhood rhyme. *Stanie mon, stanie mon, doon ye fa'*. But the Good Folk were of many kinds: brollachans, trows, urisks, selkies, smaller beings like Sage and Red Cap. Perhaps each must be called in its own particular way.

"No need to whisper, lassie. Northies only hear when they choose to. As for how to do it, you'll know. You're a Caller."

We reached the foot of the stair. Before us the stone of the mountain rose up in an unbroken wall. This was the spot where I had waited, day after day, in hope that some-one, some*thing,* would come out to talk to me as Sage and her kind had done in the forest, knowing I was in need.

41

Plainly, in the case of the Folk Below, needing was not sufficient. I set the lantern on the bottom step.

"Think about what they are," Sage suggested when we had stood quiet for a while. "An old, old folk, stubborn and strong. Strong as stone, and as hard to open up. Set in their ways. Not bad folk, but . . ." Her shrug was eloquent.

To win Hollow the brollachan over, I had played a game and sung a song. The same song had awakened a ghostly army on the shores of Hiddenwater. And once, I recalled, all I had done was think *Help!* and a strange mist had come up to hide me from Flint. That morning I had watched him search for me, his face white with anxiety and hurt; I had heard him call my name until his voice was a hoarse whisper. I had so misjudged him.

If these were an old, old, folk, perhaps they still observed rituals, as the human folk of Alban had before Keldec had come to the throne and banned such gatherings for their taint of magic. This had been at the back of my mind when I suggested midwinter for the council. I tried to remember the words Grandmother had used at the turning of the season and at the high festivals. That seemed so long ago. And who was I to give voice to such solemn prayers? My losses had wiped out the last remnant of my faith. Still, I must try, and if the Northies saw through it, then I must try something else.

I moved to stand by the wall, spread my arms wide, and leaned into the stone. I pressed my cheek against its cold, hard surface; my fingers encountered bump and crack and small scuttering thing. I breathed slowly. Behind me, Sage made no sound.

Endure as earth endures, those were the words of wisdom given me on that strangest of days, when the Master of Shadows had tested me. The Northies were not so much like earth as like stone, hard and strong and slow to change. That could seem an obstacle when what was needed was quick decisions and immediate action. But stone was the backbone of Alban, and the strength of all its people—it said so in the song of truth. *Her crags and islands built me strong.* Stone was shelter; it was anchor; it was home.

As I stood there in silence, I felt the strength of stone pass into me; I opened myself to its deep magic. The call woke inside me, rising from my heartbeat and coursing blood, forming words I spoke almost despite myself. "Folk of the North! Folk of deepest earth!" The call was bone and breath, memory and hope, the past and the future. In my mind I held the many faces of stone: the roots of great trees deep in the earth; the cliffs where stanie men stood in their long, silent vigil; pebbles in the riverbed, each different, each a small, lovely miracle. Crags raising their proud heads to the sunrise; mountains under blankets of winter snow. "In the name of stone I call you! Come forth! Show yourselves! I have grave need of you, and it is time!"

Silence, save for the fading echoes.

I stepped back and found I was dizzy; Sage caught my arm, stopping me from falling. "Now what?" I whispered, knowing I hadn't the strength to do it again. The call had only taken a few moments, but I felt as if I had climbed a mountain without stopping for breath.

"We wait. These are not hasty folk." After a moment

43

she added, "If that doesn't do the trick, lassie, I don't know what will."

I sank down onto the bottom step. We waited. It was freezing at the foot of the stair, a stark reminder of how much Regan's Rebels owed to the Northies, for it was not possible for a whole winter's supply of fuel to be brought up the mountain and stored in the caverns every autumn. When stores ran low, the wood baskets were replenished by unseen hands. And even when the fire burned down to coals, the chambers upstairs stayed warm. I clenched my teeth to stop them from chattering; I pulled my shawl more tightly around my shoulders. I wondered if the Master of Shadows had been entirely wrong. Perhaps I did not have what it took to be a Caller after all.

A tiny sound. My skin prickled. A crack was opening in the wall, perhaps a handspan broad and as high as my shoulder. There was lantern light on the other side, illuminating a personage in a gray cloak. The eyes that peered at us through the gap were inimical. The skin of the creature's narrow face and long fingers was as gray as its garment, and around that face hung long, tangled locks of the same stony hue.

"What ye want?" Even its voice sounded gray. Something about it made my flesh crawl; it set a dread in me that went far beyond the cavern and the shadows and the cold. I felt as if we had woken something that was best left sleeping.

I stood silent, unable to find the right words. The thing standing here was not human. It was not even one of the Good Folk; or if it was, it was a kind far different from

Sage and Red Cap and the folk of the forest. As I stared into its hostile eyes, the crack between us began to close.

"No!" I exclaimed, taking a step forward. "Wait! I must speak with you!"

"'Must,'" echoed the creature. "We dinna much care for *must*."

The crack had narrowed no farther. I gathered my wits, wondering why Sage had not stepped in to help me. "Please," I said belatedly, "may we speak with you? I am Neryn, a human woman and a Caller, and this is Sage." I tried to arrange my face into a pleasant expression, though the thing's stony glare unnerved me.

"A Westie." The tone was all scorn.

"Aye," said Sage equably, "a Westie, and not ashamed to say so. I've traveled a long way to be here, across the margin between Watches. Even a Northie can grasp the significance of that. This is not a couple of folk making a nuisance of themselves at your doorway. It's a matter of vital importance. Will you come out and talk with us?"

"I willna. That place up there reeks o' cold iron."

"Then may we come in?" I asked. "I'm bearing no iron, and nor is Sage." It occurred to me that whoever brought up supplies and left them in the kitchen had to come close to Milla's pots, pans, and ladles, so there must be at least one Northie among this clan who could tolerate iron. Now did not seem the time to mention that.

"Come in?" It seemed this was an unthinkable notion. "As if it werena enow that your shoutin' woke every last one o' us frae the lang winter sleep!"

I looked at Sage; she looked back at me, her gooseberry eyes full of disbelief.

"I'm sorry I woke you," I said. "I bring an invitation to your clan. And I need your wise advice on a matter of great importance. But I suppose if Northies go to sleep for the winter, like bears or squirrels, you won't be interested in a midwinter feast, with music and gifts, to thank you for your kindness. And you won't care whether you're part of a council to talk about restoring peace and justice to Alban. All you'll be thinking of is how soon you can go back to bed."

The being's expression became, if anything, still more baleful. "A human lassie," it observed. "And ye're callin' us squirrels and bears."

"That wasn't what—"

"Seems tae me," the creature said, "that if it's good enow for the Big One tae sleep all winter lang, it's good enow for us sma' folk."

The Big One. That was the name the Good Folk used for the Guardians. This was delicate indeed. I must not let this creature slip back into the depths of the mountain; there was knowledge here that could be vital to my journey and to our cause.

"The Lord of the North?" I ventured. "He's part of this winter sleep as well?"

"We dinna speak o' that." The gray-cloaked being set its lantern down on the ground. In the altered light, I saw that its features were those of a wee man, but seamed and cracked like old stone. "'Tis too great a sadness to be put in

46

words. As for the rest o' us, now ye've disturbed our rest wi' all this callin', there'll be nae gettin' back tae sleep till ye've had your say, I reckon. Midwinter, was it?"

"Aye," said Sage. "What better time for a feast and celebration? Mulled ale, good food, fine singing. And did Neryn mention gifts? Invitations like that don't come often these days." She waited for the space of two breaths, then added, "She's a Caller. Did you grasp that? The lassie's asking you nicely, out of the goodness of her heart. She's been down here day after day waiting for you to show your faces, to no avail. Plain discourteous of you, I'd say that was, since I don't for a moment believe the whole clan was asleep for the winter. Or maybe Northies can walk in their sleep, and carry baskets of food and loads of firewood while they're dreaming."

"At dusk, on midwinter eve," I put in quickly. "That's when the feast and council will take place. I give you my solemn promise that every scrap of iron at Shadowfell will be wrapped up and set away behind a closed door. I ask that you attend, please, and let us thank you for your help. And I ask that you listen to our leader, Regan. He has something to put to you, something of immense importance."

"Anythin' more, while ye're askin'?"

"I need help in finding the Guardians," I said. "The Big Ones. Not the Master of Shadows, since he has already come to me, but the three others. If your clan can give me some directions, I will be most grateful."

A weighty silence. "Ye dinna ask much, do ye?" the

being said. "I tellit ye, the Lord o' the North is sleepin'. A lang sleep full o' ill dreams. Wakin' us is ane thing. Wakin' him . . . Ye wouldna wish tae be doin' that, unless ye were oot o' your wits." He stepped back from the opening; the crack began to close.

"Wait, please!"

I could still see one eye, his hand with the lantern, shadows beyond.

The stone halted its movement. "Aye?" came the being's dour voice.

"Please put it to the others. We will prepare the celebration anyway, in hope of your attendance. Please tell them I am here, and what I've said."

"Ach, they know ye're here. Havena ye been creepin' your way into our heads since the moment ye set foot in this place last autumn? How could they not know there was a Caller close at hand? Trouble, that's what ye are, naethin' but trouble. Aye, I'll pass it on." A pause. "For what it's worth." The crack snapped shut; the stone was seamless before us.

"Wretched Northies," muttered Sage. "Don't bother yourself, lassie. They'll be there. They know what you are, and they know they can't refuse. Gifts, you said? I can't imagine what manner of gift would please such a sour-faced creature as that." She gave me a shrewd glance. "You're weary. That was quite a call; went straight to my bones. You'd best get back up there and warm yourself, and I'll be off. Red Cap's only got the wee one for company, and it's not much of a talker."

I reported back to Regan. His eyes showed the same excitement as Tali's had earlier, filling me with anxiety. So much hung on the success of this council, and Regan could not fully understand how hard it might be to persuade the Good Folk to our cause. Although he was pleased with the news, the overall mood was somber. Folk were not doing their usual work but sitting in the dining area, talking in low voices about the loss of Cian's two companions, who could not even be offered appropriate burial. I had a word with Eva and Milla on the subject of feasts and gifts, then found myself so weary I could hardly force my eyes to stay open, though it was still day. Tali ordered me to go to the women's quarters and rest, since I'd be a liability in the training area if I was half-asleep. I did as I was told.

I slept, and dreamed of Flint. Flint standing by a pallet where a solidly built young man lay sleeping; Flint with his hands on either side of the man's face, singing or chanting. Richly dressed folk seated all around, watching him. Their faces intent, their eyes . . . avid. When I woke, my stomach was churning. I only just reached the privy before I was violently sick.

I knew Flint was an Enthraller. I understood that he must sometimes—perhaps often—practice his craft under the king's orders, using it to turn rebellious subjects loyal or to ensure that the canny skills of people like me were used only for Keldec's purposes. It was said many of the Enforcers were enthralled men, rendered by the process into the most reliable fighting force a leader could have. Knowing Flint only complied with the king's orders to keep his true purpose secret did not stop me from being repelled by it to the point of physical sickness.

Milla came by as I was retching into the privy hole and insisted on wiping my face and sitting me down in the dining area to be fed sips of broth. At supper, Fingal inquired after my health and suggested a peppermint tea with honey, which would be efficacious even though there were no fresh leaves, only dried. He would, he said, have suggested I sleep in the infirmary for the night, only Cian was still there recovering from his long journey. Andra, usually more interested in what was going on in the training yard than domestic matters, offered me one of her blankets for the night, since the cold might keep me awake. Big Don made me sit in his usual spot at table, close to the fire. I thanked everyone. I could not explain that my sickness was of the spirit, not the body. As Regan's spy at court, Flint had to act as if he were a loyal subject of the king, even if that meant using his gift to ill purpose. The cause must come before matters of conscience for all of us. Already people had died because of me. If I could not come to terms with this, I would weaken the rebels. I would become a liability.

There were eight women at Shadowfell, including me. We were outnumbered four to one by the men. The women's sleeping quarters accommodated six of us; Milla and Eva shared a tiny chamber off the kitchen. At first I had found it difficult to be so close to the others, though having shelter and a proper bed was a rare luxury for me. As it turned out, the fighters were usually so tired after the long day's work that they fell asleep almost as soon as their heads touched the pillow.

That night I lay on my bed with my blankets up to my chin, forming in my mind a letter I would never write. I told Flint how much I missed him, how I worried about his safety, how I hoped he might return in springtime. How, even though I had a mission to accomplish, my pathway felt lonely without him. How I forgave him the things he must do, and hoped the day would soon come when he need no longer bend to Keldec's will.

Across the chamber Tali was awake too, and restless. She turned from one side to the other, kicked off her blanket then hauled it up again, punched her pillow. I knew better than to ask her what was the matter.

Eventually she said, "Neryn?"

"Mm?"

"Bad dream this afternoon, hmm?"

"I don't want to talk about it."

There was a brief silence. Then, "You dream about him, don't you? Flint?"

She was too sharp.

"Mm."

"You miss him."

"I don't want to talk about it, Tali." Not to anyone, and especially not to her.

"Regan said he thought your dreams might be useful,

especially if they give you a true picture of what Flint is doing. Since the two of you are close, and Flint is a mind-mender with control over other folk's dreams, we wondered if that might be so. You should tell us about them."

I got up on one elbow to look across at her. She was lying flat now, her hair a splash of darkness on the pillow, the rings and twists of her tattoos wreathing her lean body in mystery. I wished I could ask her about those markings, which were extensive, skillfully done, and almost an exact match for her brother's. Those tattoos told a story, and I'd have liked to know what it was. But folk here seldom spoke of the past. There was little talk of families, of home settlements, of loved ones left behind. At Shadowfell it was all the cause and the future.

"It wouldn't be useful," I said. "I only see him in snatches, not long enough to know what is really happening."

"More than a snatch today, surely, if it made you bolt for the privy to be sick."

I said nothing.

"Seems to me the dreams might be more curse than blessing, if they bother you so much."

I hesitated. In the quiet of the chamber, with the other women sleeping around us, it was easier to speak the truth. "Sometimes, yes. But I'd never wish them away. Even if Flint is in trouble or doing something I hate, I'd rather see that than not see him at all. It's a long time until spring. And chances are he won't come even then."

The silence drew out.

"I haven't forgotten what you said about not getting

close," I felt obliged to add. "We are friends, he and I. We journeyed a long way together. Dreaming of him gives me hope."

"Then you're a fool," Tali said. "What do you hope for, true love and happy endings? What if your dreams show you Flint being tortured, Flint spilling out secrets to the king, Flint and his Enforcer comrades sweeping down on another village, hacking and burning as the Cull gets under way?"

"Last night, in my dream, I saw him performing an enthrallment, with folk looking on," I said quietly, though her words had brought angry tears to my eyes. "My grandmother suffered an enthrallment that went wrong. She lost her wits. The dream sickened me. But I still have hope, Tali. I need to believe a happy future is possible for me and Flint; for all of us. If people can't dream of better times, if they can't imagine a future in which they might marry and raise their children, dig their vegetable plot, ply their trade without fear, then the goal of freedom becomes meaningless. Don't you think?"

Tali sat up. "Of course folk want that changed world," she said, turning her dark eyes on me with some intensity. "Of course they want to live without the constant need to be looking over their shoulder or waiting for a knife in the ribs. But it's going to be a long, hard fight, and people are going to die. You should know that, Neryn. You saw what happened to Garven. You saw six of our fighters die in that battle. You heard how Gova and Arden perished bringing news from the north. What's needed here isn't soft dreams of true love. It's anger—the anger that drives a person forward. The fury that keeps them fighting right up to the moment the knife goes in. In our world there's no place for love."

"Be quiet!" came a mumbled complaint from Sula, who had the pallet next to Tali's. "Some of us want to sleep."

"Good night, Tali," I made myself say, though her last words had chilled me.

"'Night." A pause. "You put your case well."

This grudging praise was far more than I expected. "Thanks," I said.

"Be quiet," growled Sula again, putting her pillow over her head.

"Sorry." I closed my eyes.

CHAPTER THREE

MIDWINTER MORNING, AND NOBODY ON THE LADDER. The cavern was shadowy; outside, the sun would be struggling up behind heavy clouds. It was hard to believe that only a year ago my father had still been alive and we had spent the cold season on the road. Midwinter had passed us by as we sheltered in some derelict outhouse or under some shallow overhang in the woods. As I began my climb, trying to keep the pace as brisk as Tali would expect, I told myself I would never forget how fortunate I was to have reached Shadowfell.

I came to the top of the steps, breathing hard. Tali liked us to head straight down again if we could, but today I went out onto the ledge. It was barely light. Rain descended in shifting sheets, moved hither and thither by the wind. I was not first here. By the rock wall stood Regan, gazing northward through the watery veils, his hands outstretched in private prayer.

I would have retreated quietly, not wanting to interrupt

him. But Regan said, "It's a momentous day. Midwinter, and our first meeting with the Folk Below. A milestone on our journey. Will you join me?" So I stood beside him, thinking how remarkable it was that out of the darkness of winter there always came the light of springtime.

"Rise up, brother sun!" Regan's voice was strong and sure. There was no trace of uncertainty in it. "Bear forth your flaming torch! Banish the shadows. March forward in vigor, young and free, and lead us into a new day. Farewell to the dark. Hail to the light!"

"Hail to the light!" I echoed. The stirring words were most apt, not only to the festival day, but to our whole enterprise. Glancing at my companion, I saw that his face was bright with hope. It was a perfect reflection of the light he had invoked. No wonder he inspired such loyalty.

We stood there awhile longer, until the rain became intolerable and we retreated to the steps.

"You must have come up here in the dark," I said.

"I brought a candle. The rain extinguished it for me; as a symbol of new light it was short-lived."

"The prayer was good. I had planned to say one of my own, but I've forgotten the proper words." We began the descent, Regan going first, I following. We went slowly; in my mind I could hear Tali saying, *Pick up the pace! What are you, a pair of old women in your dotage?*

"I doubt if the gods trouble themselves much about the words," Regan said. "What matters is the intention. Only a few of us at Shadowfell observe the old rituals; most have become rather disillusioned over the years."

"But you believe it's worth going on in some small way?"

He did not answer immediately, and when he spoke, he sounded unusually hesitant. "Sometimes I wonder whether all a ritual provides is a comforting familiarity. Such observances lose their significance if few believe in them. For me, it still seems important to acknowledge the turning of the year. To celebrate the times of joyful plenty and to recognize the times of sorrow and hardship. A ritual makes it easier to understand our place in the grand plan of things."

I would have liked to ask about his past, before he became a rebel leader, before Shadowfell began. But that was not the way we did things here. Regan knew far more of my story than I did of his, for before Flint had left for the east, he'd told Regan about our journey along the lakes and up the Rush valley, and how we had been friends, then enemies, then friends again.

"I'm not sure if I believe in gods," I said as my knees started to protest at the long downward climb. "I know the Guardians are thought to be wielders of old magic and immensely powerful. If the gods exist, they must be greater still. And more distant. I think of them when I see a lovely sunrise, or a flock of birds passing over, or the first flowers of spring. When I hear a fine tune played well, or see someone act with generosity or courage." An image of Flint came sharply to my mind, Flint after the battle, kneeling to close the eyes of a dead Enforcer. I would never forget his expression.

My foot slipped on an uneven step and I struggled for balance. Below me, Regan halted; I steadied myself against his shoulder. "Sorry," I gasped. "Tali's told me often enough not to lose concentration."

"You're doing well," Regan said as we continued the downward climb. "When you first got here, you were skin and bone. You wouldn't have managed ten of these steps. Now you're up and down with the best of them."

"Tali's work."

"A person doesn't achieve such a result without determination and hard effort, no matter how well drilled she is."

We reached the bottom of the steps.

"It troubles you, doesn't it?" Regan asked, out of the blue. "The risks. The losses."

I nodded.

"What you have to offer us is priceless," he said quietly. "I wasn't exaggerating when I said your gift was the difference between our winning and losing this struggle. Even with Lannan's support, we can't move a fighting force into Summerfort that will equal the king's. This won't be a conventional battle; much will depend on the element of surprise. And Keldec won't surrender his power easily, even when he sees we're backed by some of his chieftains. We can expect more losses; it will be a bloody confrontation. More than that; I believe the king will make full use of whatever magic he has at his disposal, whether it's the talents of the canny men and women of his court, or something more powerful."

His words turned me cold. "Something more powerful? You mean uncanny folk? How could the king use them? They despise him. They hate the way he's changed Alban. They'd never agree to help him."

Regan hesitated. "If he could find a way to coerce them, he would not hesitate to do so. I know the king's men were interested in you, Neryn; tracking you, hunting you ever since word got out that you might have an unusual talent. That was what Flint told me. Now that you are beyond Keldec's reach, I imagine his agents are looking elsewhere for a Caller. What if there were another to be found?"

Now I felt sick. "Perhaps it's a good thing that we only have a year and a half to do this," I said, trying to keep my voice steady.

"It is just a thought," Regan said, and laid a comforting hand on my shoulder. "Put it aside for now, and let us think of a new day, and the light of the rising sun. Of hope and faith. We meet the Good Folk at dusk, and perhaps set foot on the last and most remarkable part of our journey."

I looked up into his eyes, and saw there the faith he spoke of, bright and true, and behind it the shadow of the deaths, the injuries, the opportunities set aside in the name of the cause. To till the fields or sail the fishing boat in peace; to lie down at night by a loving wife, to father children, to grow older surrounded by a strong community. I wondered, yet again, what dark thing lay in Regan's past, what had driven him to this.

He smiled, and I thought, *Even so, he is a father to his comrades; he is a friend; he is the center of a community. Here at Shadowfell he is all those things. He is a leader.*

By dusk we were ready, or as ready as we could make ourselves. Of all the human inhabitants of Shadowfell, I was the only one who had much experience of the Good Folk,

59

and that had been quite limited, for they were a cautious and reclusive people, not given to mixing even among their own clans. The council would be a challenge—both Northies and human folk would be wary. The Northies might choose not to come up at all. The lure of sleep might be too strong.

All day we had made preparations. The feast had been cooked in clay pots, with the assistance of Sula's canny gift for transferring heat into water. Wooden spoons, copper basins, tin cups, and earthenware platters had been put to use. In a chamber at the very back of Shadowfell, every piece of iron we possessed, to the last belt buckle, was wrapped up and set away behind a fast-closed door.

Eva and I had put the finishing touches on the gift we'd made, and had hung garlands of dried herbs about the dining chamber, which was the only place in Shadow-fell big enough for a council—we hoped the community of Northies was not too numerous. The rebel community had practiced songs and had listened as I explained that Regan would do most of the talking until we discovered how ame-nable the Good Folk were to the proposal we would be putting to them. I warned them that there might be some odd-looking beings, and that they must be courteous even if the visitors spoke somewhat bluntly.

Just before dusk, Sage and Red Cap came to the door and were admitted. Red Cap had his infant in a sling on his back; it was hunkered down against the chill with only the tips of its ears showing. We stood at the top of the spiral stair with Regan and Tali. The rest of the community was waiting in the dining area, where the benches and tables had been stacked at one end, and blankets spread out on the earthen floor in their place.

We heard them before we saw them, and I was filled with both relief and wonder. The sound that drifted up the stair was hard to describe. It was not a chant, nor yet a song; it was something like the sound of breaking waves, and something like crackling flames, and a little like the rustling of leaves in the wind. It made the hairs on my neck prickle.

"Black Crow's curse," breathed Tali.

"Hush," murmured Regan. "Only listen."

The murmuring, rippling sound increased, reaching our ears in a pattern of rise and fall. Light flickered on the stone walls of the spiral stair.

"A procession," I whispered. "A midwinter ritual."

"I'm glad to see the Northies have not forgotten the old ways." Sage made no attempt to lower her voice. She glanced up at Regan. "You can leave this part to me." Her tone was full of authority, and he gave a solemn nod.

The lights became brighter; shapes flickered and danced across the ancient stone as the Northies climbed toward us. Beside me, Regan sucked in his breath.

They were cloaked in uniform gray, but it could be seen that they were of many kinds. Their leader—not the being we had encountered before—carried a glowing lantern fashioned in the shape of a bee. Behind him came many others, some bearing lights, others carrying little baskets or bags. Among them were five tiny beings, each about a handspan tall. They were holding a very small wreath of greenery between them; it was taking some maneuvering to get it, and themselves, from step to step, and the folk behind them in line were showing signs of impatience. I suppressed the urge to offer help, since quite plainly this was something the wee folk either wanted or needed to do by themselves.

There were beings here that seemed hewn from rock, their features, under the gray hoods, made up of cracks, crevices, and holes. They were like smaller versions of a stanie mon, and the sight of them sent me back to that day on the battlefield, the day so many men had perished because of me. One creature was all smoke and flame, and walked without a cloak. Tali muttered another oath and Sage gave her a repressive look. Red Cap had lifted the young one out of its sling and put it on his shoulders, the better to see; it squeaked in excitement, waving its paws.

The Northies' leader was at the top of the stairs. He came toward us, with three others in a row behind him, and pushed back his hood to reveal a face not unlike Sage's—pointed ears, beady eyes, shrewd expression— though in place of her green-gray curls he had filmy hair that resembled cobweb. The others did the same. One was a little woman with dark, penetrating eyes, one a gold-furred, catlike creature, and the third, somewhat taller, a being that fell somewhere between young man and badger, bearing a staff. They halted.

"Greetings," said Sage, taking a step forward. "Out of winter's darkness, you bring us light. Hail the light!"

"Hail the light!" Regan and I echoed, followed, a heartbeat later, by Tali.

"Our solemn greetin' tae ye." It was the little woman who spoke. "Out o' sleep is born wisdom. Out o' winter comes new life. The wise woman passes intae shadow; the warrior awakens. Hail the light!"

"Hail the light!"

As we gave our response, the last of the Northies reached the top of the stair. They gathered in a group, eyeing us suspiciously. There were many of them; the passageway was crowded. The sound that had accompanied the ascent had died down. I still did not know whether they had been singing, or humming, or whether they had created that compelling music by means of a magical charm.

The five tiny folk came forward, bearing their wreath. It was about the size of a woman's wristlet. They stopped in front of Regan and held it up. They were saying something, but their voices were so small and high there was no making out the words. With considerable presence of mind, Regan dropped gracefully to one knee, which brought him somewhat closer to their level.

"A gift to you," translated the cat being. "New growth. New life. New hope is born from winter's darkness. Take it, warrior."

Regan put out his hand, palm up, and the tiny folk laid the wreath on it. "I thank you," he said quietly. "In the time of shadow we rest and are renewed. May the fallow season make us strong. May the light return to us; may its warmth restore us; may its beacon guide us forth." He rose to his feet. "We welcome you to our hearth and to our hall. We welcome you to Shadowfell."

I glanced at Sage, thinking the folk from downstairs would be entirely justified in arguing that Shadowfell was *their* hall, and that Regan's people were only here because the Northies made it possible. Sage's mouth quirked up at the corner, as if she shared my thought. The five tiny folk had gathered around Red Cap, whose resemblance to a pine marten—sleek brown fur and an open, guileless face under his scarlet hat—probably made him seem the least threatening being among us. The infant was uttering little squeals, as if torn between excitement and terror.

"We too have a gift," I said, and from under my cloak I brought out the basket Eva and I had made together. We'd crafted it in the shape of a bird's nest, and it was fashioned from many materials: uncarded wisps of wool; spun and dyed thread; twigs and dried leaves gleaned from Milla's stock of herbs; five white stones knotted into a leather cord; patches of cloth from various worn-out garments, cut in the shapes of moons and stars; little plaits of hair, black, russet, gold; feathers, cobwebs, and dry seedpods. I supported it on my two palms and knelt down so they could see. Nestled within were tokens sewn of felt and stuffed with dried peas. We had made flowers and fish and leaves, rabbits and owls and mice, a thistle and an acorn. I hoped it would please our visitors.

"My name is Neryn, and I am responsible for disturbing you during your winter sleep, as you may know," I said. "This is Sage and Red Cap, from the Watch of the West.

64

This is Regan, Shadowfell's leader, and this is Tali, his second-in-command. We offer you the work of our hands."

The cobweb-haired man and the little woman stepped forward and took the basket between them. "Aye," the wee man said, touching the fabric with a careful finger, "there's old knowin' in the makin' o' this, 'tis plain in every corner." He glanced up at me. "Who was it learnit ye hearth magic, Caller?"

"My grandmother was a wise woman; what she taught me went into the making of this. Eva, who is expert at sewing, helped me. And every person who lives at Shadowfell—every human—contributed something. A strand of hair. A thread from a favorite garment."

"We offer it as a token of thanks and respect," Regan put in. "I hope our meeting will be one of amity and goodwill. Please come into our hall. The human folk of Shadowfell are gathered for our council. Afterward, we invite you to share our midwinter feast." He did not ask them for their names. I had warned him that the Good Folk were slow to reveal such details, especially to humankind.

"I tellit ye," the whisper from somewhere among the Northies was all too audible, "nae guid can come o' this. Soon as we're in this ha' the fellow mentioned, they'll be shuttin' the doors, and it'll be a wee knife in the back for every last one o' us."

"You will be safe here," Regan said. "We have no reason to wish you ill. If not for your support and generosity, we could not have made our base at Shadowfell. Now we seek your wisdom; hence the council. Will you come?"

The Northies entered warily. Our own folk, who had moved back to stand around the walls so our smaller guests could sit in the center on the blankets, did their best to look calm, but even though I had warned them, the sight of the more unusual beings made brows lift and eyes widen. Whispering went around the chamber.

Our visitors seated themselves in a circle. At Regan's nod, our own people formed an outer circle. Sage and Red Cap sat on either side of me, with Fingal and Regan next. The five tiny folk were in front of us.

I made a quick count and found that there were exactly as many Northies in the chamber as rebels. We had two on door guard; but perhaps they did too. I did not see the being that had challenged Sage and me on the day I called the Folk Below.

There was a silence. Perhaps Regan was waiting for me to speak; I had thought he would address the visitors first. Then the little woman of the Northies, who had given the ritual greeting, rose to her feet. "We're no' here altogether o' our ain free will," she said, looking at Regan, then at me. "Ye ken that, I expect. 'Tis not our way tae mingle wi' humankind, nor tie ourselves up in your disputes and difficulties. There's twa things have drawn us tae your council. First, the Caller; we canna ignore her voice. Second, we had a visitor. No' the Caller or the Westie. Another visitor, frae the north. Trouble's brewin'. The Master o' Shadows is up and walkin', and him that should be keepin' the Master in check canna be woken frae sleep. Seems the time for bidin' awa' and waitin' for the shadow tae pass ower is gone."

After a pause, she said, "Because o' that, I'll dae what we seldom dae, and gie ye some names tae make this simpler. I'm Woodrush. This is Hawkbit"—she gestured toward the wee man with cobweb hair—"and that is Pearl-Wort." She pointed to the catlike being. "And now," Woodrush said, "ye can tell us why that fighter o' yours, the one wi' the pretty patterns on her skin, isna sittin' doon like the rest o' ye, but standin' there wi' her staff in her hand, ready tae sweep around and fell the lot o' us."

Tali was standing in the shadows behind Regan. The other female fighters had changed their clothing for the winter feast—even Andra was in a gown—but Tali still wore her trousers, tunic, and boots.

"I'm doing the same thing that fellow of yours is," she said crisply, using the staff to indicate the tall Northie, the one who somewhat resembled a badger. He stood on the opposite side, in a position that exactly mirrored hers. She was guarding Regan; he was stationed behind Woodrush, Hawkbit, and Pearl-Wort. "Protecting what's most precious."

"Oh, aye?" Woodrush's gaze was searching. "Wouldna that be your spears and knives?"

"I'm a warrior." Tali's voice was perfectly calm. "I value my weapons, don't doubt that. Both the iron ones and the others. But swords and knives can be replaced. Some things are irreplaceable."

"A man dies," observed Hawkbit. "Another steps up tae tak' his place. Isna that the way of it for your folk?"

"It's not so simple," said Tali. "For now, I will lay down

my staff if your guard does the same, and if you give me an undertaking that both Regan and Neryn will be safe from any harm for the duration of this council."

"Tali—" Regan made to say something, perhaps to tell her no such promise was required. But the Northie guard was already setting his staff on the floor. He met Tali's gaze across the double circle, and there was respect in his eyes. After a moment she too put down her weapon. Neither of them moved to sit in the circle. Trust, it seemed, went only so far.

The Northies were quiet for a little. Then a being pushed back its hood, revealing that it was another catlike creature, black as night, its eyes an icy blue.

"We ken ye hae big plans," it said, looking at Regan. "And we ken ye seek tae involve our kind, force us tae help ye if we willna agree tae what ye propose." A glance at me. "Set it out for us now; let us hear it."

"Wait a bit." The warm voice was Milla's; she had come out of the kitchen corner with a tray of little cups, and behind her was Brasal with a jug. "Councils make thirsty work. You'll take a wee drop of my honey mead? And we have some morsels here to nibble on while you talk." Eva was there too, kneeling down to proffer an earthenware platter laden with cakes delicate enough for the tiniest fingers. "The food is safe," Milla added. "You must be aware that I get a good many of my ingredients thanks to your generosity, and I'm happy to be able to return the favor in a small way. Please enjoy it."

The Good Folk helped themselves; there were murmurs

of appreciation all around the circle. The basket Eva and I had fashioned was passed from hand to hand and admired. When both Northies and rebels had been served with food and drink, Regan stood up and the chamber fell into an anticipatory hush. What Woodrush had meant about the Master of Shadows and someone needing to be woken from sleep, I did not know. But it seemed the Good Folk had their own reasons for agreeing to talk to us at last.

"I won't draw this out too long," Regan said with quiet assurance. "Thank you again for agreeing to come out and show yourselves, and to sit with us in this hall and listen. I understand why your kind chooses to remain largely invisible to ours, and I salute you for taking this risk."

"We wouldna hae done it, but for the Caller," someone muttered from the Northic circle.

"Hush your mouth, Vetch," said the wee man, Hawkbit. "Dinna interrupt the laddie, he's just gettin' goin'."

"I am Regan, as perhaps you know, and I formed this band with a group of like-minded people some years ago. Our mission is to remove Keldec from the throne of Alban, to end his reign, and to ensure fair rule until such time as the heir is of age. In fifteen years as king, Keldec has transformed our peaceable realm into a place of fear and oppression, where nobody is truly free. The chieftains are cowed into obedience; they know that to speak out against the king's might is to risk the destruction of everything they hold dear. There's not a soul in all Alban untouched by this. Each autumn the human inhabitants cower under the scourge of the Cull, and in the seasons between nobody can trust his neighbor." He paused to draw breath. In the packed dining hall, there was not a sound. "The old rituals are all but forgotten; folk no longer trust in gods. Your kind have been driven into hiding by Keldec's fear of the uncanny. He has little understanding of the Good Folk, but he distrusts your influence, hence his laws forbidding our kind and yours to meet and speak together. Above all, he fears human folk with canny skills—people like Neryn here, and certain others among our band." His gaze rested briefly on Tali; on Sula; on one or two other rebels who had skills unusual enough to be considered canny. "But Neryn in particular, since she is a Caller."

Woodrush asked, "Why is this king afraid o' magic? In older times, human folk used hearth magic, such as went into the makin' o' that wee basket, and thought little of it. Did the king's mother and father no' teach him right ways as a bairn?"

"Folk talk of a foretelling," Regan said. "An old woman spoke over his cradle, saying he was destined to die by a canny hand. Keldec grew up in fear of that. It is possible all the ills that have befallen Alban under his leadership have stemmed from that fear. The folk of his inner circle support and encourage him in his actions against the people of Alban. He and Queen Varda will do whatever they can to prevent the prophecy from being fulfilled, at least until their son is old enough to assume the throne."

"Their son?" This question came in many fey voices.

"An infant," Regan said. "And yes, I know a son does not take the throne on the death of his father; at least, not here in Alban. It is a wise law that gives the right to contest the kingship to all the sons of women in the royal line. But Keldec does not care for that law; he sees no reason why it should be followed. And he will deal harshly with anyone who dares challenge him on the matter."

"Who is the true heir?" asked the fey guard, whose eyes were bright with interest.

"He's a child still," said Regan. "There could be other claimants, but he is closest in blood: the grandson of the king's maternal aunt."

"The laddie would be needin' verra careful keepin'," the Northie guard commented.

There was a brief silence, then Regan said, "He is in a place of safety."

It was a measure of his audience's understanding that nobody asked where.

"With so much held secret and the price of speaking out so high," said Pearl-Wort, "how can you know so much of the king's thoughts, his hopes and fears?"

Another silence. "We have eyes at court," Regan said. "Eyes close to the king."

"If the heir is so young," a wizened Northie in a sheepskin coat spoke up, "why do ye trouble tae seek our aid now? Put a wee laddie on the throne and Alban will be a' brawlin' chieftains, and worse than ever."

"We cannot wait until the heir is grown," Regan said. "The support of our most influential ally depends on our moving against Keldec quite soon. To hold back longer from action would spell the death of the rebellion. We need this ally; and we need your help. To answer your question about the heir, I believe a joint regency made up of certain chieftains would be adequate until the boy is a man."

"Oh, aye," said Hawkbit. "Ye need our help, ye say. Doin' what, exactly?"

"Until the final stand, we must continue to build support all across Alban. A movement such as ours is not like a conventional army. While we must prepare ourselves as a fighting force, our main role has from the first been to draw together like-minded folk and to win the support of those who love justice and peace. To persuade them that it's worth taking the risk. An evil is eating at the heart of Alban. We cannot let it consume us. We must make an end to the Cull; we must make an end to the fear and distrust that have marred our once-great realm. We must reestablish the authority of the chieftains and the practices that allowed power to be shared among them. Keldec has a mighty army. We must make one mightier still."

His voice rang through the chamber, setting goose bumps on my skin.

"Alban is wide," said Pearl-Wort. "From the green glens of the south to the crags of the cold north; from the western isles to this king's court in the east. Many chieftains; many clans. And that's just the human folk. Our own kind are everywhere. Enough for an army, certainly. But widespread, and not of one mind. How could you draw them together?" The creature's gaze took in Regan himself, then moved to Tali, to me, to the rebels seated in their circle. "A handful, that's all you have."

"Shadowfell started with a handful," Regan said, smiling. "But there are more now. Those of us you see before you make up the heart of the operation; here at Shadowfell our planning is done and our decisions are made. But we have teams elsewhere in Alban, and other loyal folk who shelter us when we cross country, and who bear our messages at great risk to themselves. Of the eight chieftains still remaining in Alban, two have agreed to stand with us when we challenge the king; one of those two, in particular, can provide a substantial fighting force."

"So ye'd still be fightin' the king's Enforcers," said Hawkbit. "We dinna doubt your bravery. Your sanity, now that's another thing."

"You should not doubt Regan." Tali spoke up for the first time. "This is a different kind of war. At the end there will be an armed confrontation, yes, and you are right—the king's Enforcers are formidable in combat. But don't discount our ability in battle; we accounted for an entire troop in the autumn, thanks in part to Neryn's use of her gift."

The wee man in the sheepskin coat spoke up. "'Twasna your ability won that battle; 'twas the aid o' a stanie mon, one o' our folk. Without that, the king's men would hae made an end o' ye all."

"That's unfair," rapped out Tali. "Besides, how can you know that?"

"Ye hae eyes at court," the wee man said. "We hae eyes everywhere. We dinna miss much. As for *unfair*, what's unfair is this king who's set all at sixes and sevens, so a body canna sae much as draw breath wi'oot Callers rappin' on the door and stirrin' us all up."

"Enough!" It was Woodrush who spoke, getting to her feet and turning a ferocious glare on the speaker. "'Twas the Caller drew us up tae talk wi' human folk, aye, and that was against our natural inclination. But we're here now, and I dinna plan tae waste the time bickerin'. The rest o' ye, if all ye can do is complain, then drink your mead, eat your cake, and hold your tongues." She motioned toward Regan. "This man's a guid man. Ye ken he keeps the auld observances; ye've seen him performin' the rituals in his ain way, season by season, faithful tae the traditions o' Alban. Why else would we hae bothered tae keep his band o' rebels supplied ower the lang winters in the Folds? Now he needs help, and he's runnin' short o' time. We know change is comin' and there's nae stoppin' it. 'Tis hard for me to say this, for 'tis no' the way o' our folk tae join wi' humankind in their wars and disputes. But this is different. The fate o' Alban's at stake and the time for hidin' awa' is ower. If there must be change, let's mak' sure it's change for the better."

"Short of time," echoed Pearl-Wort. "How short?"

"You understand, I am sure, that all our plans must be kept secret," Regan said. This was something we had discussed endlessly in preparation for the council, for if word got out among the human populace of Alban, the rebellion would be over before it really began. "We've taken great pains over the years to keep it so. If Keldec got the slightest indication that an organized rebellion is taking shape, the Enforcers would hunt down every last one of us. As it is, the attacks and skirmishes that occur from time to time as we go out to spread the word are fraught with risk. You know, perhaps, the practices the king's men use to extract information from captives." He glanced at Andra.

"You can tell them," she said.

Regan gave her a nod. "Andra and her brother Manus were in my team from quite early days," he said. "They were captured by the Enforcers while on a mission, and subject to beatings and worse while the king's men sought to break their will and extract their secrets. After two nights they managed to escape and headed off into the woods. But Manus was severely injured and could not move quickly. A day later, while Andra was fetching water from a nearby stream, the Enforcers found their makeshift shelter and recaptured her brother. He was by then too weak to talk; no use to them. It was Andra they wanted. So they strung Manus up and began to kill him very slowly.

"Our folk are supplied with certain substances that can be taken in such an extreme to end their own lives. But the king's men had removed the bags Andra and Manus had when they were first captured, and with them the two lethal doses.

"The cause comes first for all of us, no matter what. That is the rebel code. Andra could not save her brother. If she had tried to rescue him, she herself would have been recaptured. The Enforcers would have worked on her further, perhaps subjected her to enthrallment. Manus, now weakened to the point of death, would have been considered of no further use to them, and killed. So, from a place of hiding, Andra watched her brother die. Then she slipped away into the deeper concealment of the forest, and at length brought the tale back to Shadowfell."

Utter silence. Andra was so still she might have been a warrior of stone, her strong features set grim. I thought of my brother, Farral, who had died in my arms after the raid on Corbie's Wood. At least I had held him; at least I'd been able to say goodbye.

"Aye," said Hawkbit eventually. "Aye. Ye want an undertaking we'll keep this secret? Ye have it."

A subdued chorus of *aye*s from the circle.

"If we want the support of the most influential chieftain, we must confront the king at the next Gathering but one," Regan said. "The midsummer after next. We'll have to achieve a near miracle. But then, it is most rare for our kind and your kind to work together in cooperation. If we can do that, I believe the mission will succeed."

At this point, Milla brought the platter back around with a fresh supply of sweetmeats. Red Cap helped himself to a small confection, then divided it neatly into five, passing a piece to each of the tiny folk, who seemed to have taken a fancy to him. When the infant squalled in protest, Woodrush bid it rather sharply to hush, then handed it the honeyed violet from atop her own sweetmeat.

"So far, so good," murmured Sage.

"You'd best tell us the plan," said Hawkbit. "The Gatherin'—'tis held at the king's stronghold by Deepwater, aye? In the Watch o' the West?"

"That's right, at Summerfort," I told him. "The chieftains attend with many of their household retainers. Ordinary folk come too. In the past it was an opportunity for the clans to mingle, celebrate, play games, and do business. Under Keldec it has become something very different. All of his court will be there, and every troop of Enforcers."

The Northies' guard moved, coming over to seat himself beside Regan. He did indeed have the look of a badger, though his features were those of a young, sturdy man and he wore a shirt and trousers of old, soft leather over his black-and-white pelt. "Name's Bearberry," he said by way of introduction. "What you'd want is a sort of ambush, aye? Your own folk planted in the crowd, disguised as farmers and washerwomen and travelers. And you'd be wanting these chieftains to have their fighters all ready to back you up. If not, the king's men would make mincemeat of you before you could say a word."

"Enforcers would cut ye doon like barley stalks in autumn," said Vetch.

"If they tried it now, aye," Bearberry said. "But there's time. Remember what Whitlow told us—the Caller has to travel to the Big Ones; without that, she won't be able to lead when the time comes. While she's away learning, we might be making ourselves useful. There's plenty of ways to do that, and they don't all involve fighting."

Whitlow. That must be the gray-cloaked door warden. I found I was holding my breath in anticipation, for this was starting to look like the change of heart we so badly needed.

"Quite right," Regan said carefully, "and I would very

77

much welcome your advice on that. Neryn plans to set off on her journey to find the Guardians as soon as the spring thaw arrives. Others will travel also. We have hopes of winning over one more chieftain, at least, before next winter; possibly two. And we need to get word to our other teams, make sure everyone knows exactly what is planned. Our folk are spread widely across Alban, and reaching them takes time. We are only human, and there is only so much ground we can cover. And there are many dangers. Distrust has clawed its roots deep into the soil of Alban."

Milla came around with the mead jug to top up folk's cups. The chamber seemed to grow warmer. I did not see anyone leave the double circle, but in a corner, a wee man was strumming on an old crooked harp.

"There are two things we're hoping you can offer," Regan said. "First, strategic advice. Ideally, since we are all here at Shadowfell and shut in by the winter, we can meet again and exchange ideas. You understand, I suppose, what Neryn's presence means. When it comes to the final confrontation, we will need your kind on our side in order to prevail. There are workers of magic in the king's household. We must be able to withstand what they can do."

Suddenly every eye was on him. Cups halted halfway to open mouths; crumbs of cake fell to the floor unheeded.

"So," said Vetch, "we come tae the point at last. What you want is for us tae stand up against an army o' folk wi' iron weapons. You want tae destroy every last one o' us."

"No!" I said. "We would not ask that of you. I know some of the Good Folk can withstand cold iron. The stanie men, for instance. Others too." I remembered Sage standing strong against a pair of armed Enforcers, using her little staff to shoot out fire. She had won me time to escape them. "If I can reach the Guardians and persuade them to teach me, surely I can learn to call only those of you who are strong enough to stand up in that battle."

"Reach them, persuade them, learn a particularly tricky kind o' magic, and be ready tae call humankind and Good Folk into a grand battle in a year and a half?" Woodrush's brows went up. " 'Tis nae small thing."

"Neryn is no ordinary woman," said Regan. "If you will help her, she can do it."

"The Lord o' the North is sleepin'," said Woodrush. "They say he canna be woken, not even by his ain folk. The White Lady—we know little o' her. The Hag . . . she'd be the one tae try first, seein' as you are a woman o' the west yourself. Could be that old creature's prepared tae be found, if word's come tae her ears about the Master o' Shadows. If he's out and about, anythin' can happen."

"Is it possible . . . can you tell me where I might find the Hag of the Isles?" I ventured. "In the west, of course, but there are many islands there; I could spend all spring and summer looking, and I must travel north as well before next winter."

" 'Tis secret knowledge you're seekin'," Hawkbit said.

Sage had been unusually restrained. Now she rose to her feet and faced the little man. "Regan has shared his secret knowledge with you," she pointed out. "He's passed on information that could see his whole venture wrecked and each of his folk at the mercy of the Enforcers, should you betray him. Don't tell me our folk cannot match that."

A kind of shiver went around the circle of Northies; then Woodrush spoke. "So be it, then. Set your wee cups down; show the lassie her way."

The Northies rose to their feet and joined hands, all but the tiny folk. A ripple went through the air, and I felt my skin prickle with the awareness of magic working all around us. Then someone whistled a few notes, like the start of a sea chantey, and to a collective gasp from the rebels, there appeared in the space within the circle a seascape in miniature: most of it churning ocean, with a hummock of land rising here and there, the larger ones grassed, the smaller mere rocky outcrops against which the waves dashed themselves, sending a fine salt spray into the air. I could feel the droplets on my face; I could hear the wash of the waves.

"Get on out there, Twayblade," ordered Hawkbit. By the edge of the map, the tiny folk were emptying out the basket Eva and I had crafted as their gift. One of them climbed in, and the basket, now a boat, headed out across the wavy map.

"Ye must set out frae a place called Pentishead, down the coast frae Darkwater," Hawkbit said, setting a shiver in me. I never wanted to go back to Darkwater as long as I lived. "There are high cliffs to the north and hidden skerries to the south. Fix the peak o' Ronan's Isle to the north o' your prow, or ye will founder before ye reach the sheltered moorin'." The wee boat passed the inner isles, heading westward. "A lang way. A lang, hard row. Beach your craft in the cove on Ronan's Isle, then tak' the narrow pathway tae the west, ower Lanely Muir. At the end o' that path, ye'll get a sign."

The tiny being demonstrated every stage of the journey as Hawkbit spoke: the long row between the isles, the boat drawn up on shore, a steep climb from the anchorage and a walk to the west. It crossed the moorland to the far end of Ronan's Isle, where sheer cliffs dropped away to the sea. There it sat down, gazing out in the direction of the setting sun. Warm light illuminated its wee features.

"Done," said Hawkbit. The Northies released their grip on one another's hands and the image of sea and islands vanished. The chamber was once more our familiar dining hall, now under the ordinary light of lanterns. Savory smells drifted over from the cooking area. The Northies sat down in their circle, the tiny folk among them. Woodrush retrieved the basket and began repacking the contents.

"'Twere a grand wee boat," someone said in a tone of regret.

"That was . . . impressive." Regan sat down cross-legged a little behind Hawkbit. "Sit down, all of you." This was addressed to our own people, who seemed incapable of moving after the startling display.

"Aye," said Hawkbit, grimacing. "Dinna *loom*."

"Thank you," I said. "That was the best map I could ever imagine. Am I right in thinking Ronan's Isle is not the farthest island to the west? I thought I saw one or two beyond it."

"Aye, ane or twa," said Woodrush. "But dinna gae beyond the spot Twayblade showit ye."

"We are deeply grateful," Regan said.

"I willna say we're happy tae help ye." Hawkbit's dour expression left no doubt of that. "The lassie seekin' out the Big Ones, that's ane thing. Us gettin' wrapped up in fightin', that's different."

"It's not all fighting." The Northie guard, Bearberry, spoke directly to Regan. "We ken your people head out in spring on their various missions. What's to stop one or two of ours traveling with every team of yours? While you conduct your business, we could pay a wee visit to our own kind, for they can be found everywhere in Alban. We could pass on the word that things have changed, that we're all working together now. You won't find any traitors among our people, though there may be some closed ears and closed doors. There's ways of knocking on those doors, even those that are barred fast, and being heard."

An outraged muttering arose from the Northies at this speech, which was indeed remarkable in its boldness. Bearberry, I thought, had the courage of a true warrior.

"Us travel wi' the likes o' them?"

"Ye've lost your wits, laddie!"

And then, from Hawkbit, "Ye're suggestin' we travel ower the border? Oot o' the Watch?"

"Have you thought," offered Sage, "that there might be no need to go in company with the human folk? We've our own ways of crossing the land, and they carry us far quicker than a pair of human feet or the hooves of a riding

82

horse. All you need do is find others of our kind within the Watch of the North and carry Regan's message to them. Tell them that a rebellion is afoot, and that there's a Caller in training, and that when the time comes, we need to be sure of their support. That's what this is all about, isn't it?"

Every eye turned to me.

"I believe so," I said. "However many of the chieftains we have on our side, at the end Keldec won't go down easily. Not only does he have the most powerful army in Alban, he has magic. We must fight magic with magic, or we cannot win. Once I'm properly trained, I can bring uncanny folk together to fight against the king's forces. Bearberry's suggestion sounds very good to me. You could get the word out to your own kind all across the north."

"You say we can carry the word in our own Watch," Woodrush said to Sage. "But what about the other Watches? You'll have told your own folk in the west. But that's only two from four."

"Aye." Sage sounded dour. "And I can't say I've spoken to every clan in the west, nor convinced every single body that this is a good idea. There are some stubborn folk among us, but I don't suppose that's a surprise to you. As for south and east, I know little of them."

"But ye dinna care about borders," put in Vetch. "Ye can hop ower there and tell 'em yersel'."

"Ach, hold your tongue, you silly wee man," snapped Woodrush, startling me. "Is Sage a sorceress, that she can be in a' parts o' Alban at the same time?" She stood up and looked around the circle, and folk fell quiet. "We need tae take a risk," the little woman said. "Ye know it as well as I do. We must go out, not only through the north, but ower the border as well. If Sage and Red Cap can do it, so can we. We ken what's afoot. We ken it's a time o' great change for all o' us. I say we divide up. Some gae north, some south, some east. If more work's needed in the west, Sage and Red Cap attend tae it. Each time we find a clan that's willin' tae help, their ain folk can move out and spread the word farther. Start small, grow bigger. That's the way it'll be."

"Aye, if we're no' squashed under the boots o' king's men before the summer's ower," muttered Vetch.

With impeccable timing, Milla came back at that moment bearing a deep bowl from which fragrant steam arose. My mouth watered. "I couldn't help overhearing some of what you were saying," Milla said, setting the bowl down in the circle and fishing a wooden ladle from her apron pocket. She had an eye on Vetch, whose wrinkled face wore an intractable look. "Of course, you'll have noticed that not all of us go away over the summer. There's always work here preparing for the next cold season. Drying and salting fish, not to speak of catching them; trips out onto the fells to find and gather herbs; picking and preserving the berries that can be found in the valley. Sewing, mending, cleaning, storing things away. And, of course, there must be someone here to keep the place ready when our people pass through and to relay messages. Usually that's Eva and me. I imagine it's the same for you folk; always something to be done back home. So you can't all go."

"Oh, aye," said Vetch. He looked somewhat relieved.

"Now, who will try my hot pot?" Milla asked as Eva brought a stack of little bowls. "There's plenty for all. I used the plump hens someone very kindly left at the door this morning, and I've stuffed them with mutton-fat porridge. It's a tasty old dish my grandmother taught me to cook. Brasal, will you fetch the mead, please, and pour everyone another cup?"

I think perhaps we wore down their last resistance with our good hospitality. All of us ate, the rebels from larger bowls, and it was indeed a hearty midwinter feast, the sort of meal I remembered from my early childhood. The fire crackled on the hearth. One of the Northies had brought out a miniature set of pipes, whose sound blended surprisingly well with that of the wee harp. Little Don found his fiddle, others added whistle and drum, and Brasal was persuaded to sing. He started with a sad ballad and followed it with the goose ditty, which the Northies greeted with riotous applause.

At a certain point Regan and Bearberry went out into the hallway, where they stood in earnest conversation for some time. A little later, Tali went to join them, and then Woodrush. I stayed where I was, between Sage and Red Cap, enjoying the music and good fellowship. If Regan needed me, he would call me.

Red Cap's infant had fallen asleep, cradled in its father's arms.

"Does the child have a name yet?" I asked.

Red Cap shook his head. "That's given at one year old. If they live so long, they've a chance of growing up."

I was silenced. I had never asked him if the child had a mother or where she was. I had assumed the babe was strong, or Red Cap would not have brought him halfway across the highlands, following me.

"Bairnies are rare among our kind, and so doubly precious. The wee one looks robust, I know, but he's fragile like all of our infants. He's done well to thrive so long."

My mind filled with things I could not say. Folk had to make their own choices. If his words had made me sad, it would be wrong to say so. "You're a brave spirit, Red Cap," I told him instead, "and a fine father. The wee one is lucky in you."

Red Cap gave a nod but said nothing.

"You know, don't you," Sage said, "that we won't be traveling with you in springtime, even if we all head west. That fellow, Bearberry, was right—it's time for us to go back home and make sure Silver and her cronies haven't undone the good work we started."

"I'll miss you."

"You won't be on your own," Sage said. "That fellow of yours might be back from court by then, and if he isn't, no doubt Regan will give you one of the others as a guard." She glanced around the chamber, where human folk and fey folk were engaged in a number of animated discussions. Big Don was trying out the harp, which looked like a toy on his knee. Finet sat cross-legged, drawing with a piece of charcoal on a scrap of bark from the woodbox; the five tiny folk were clustered around her, watching and chattering in their high voices.

"I understand." The thought of bidding Sage and Red Cap farewell made my chest hurt. They had been staunch friends to me, loyal, brave, and true. But even if we were all heading west, I knew it would not be safe for us to travel together.

"Don't look so downcast, lassie," said Sage. "We'll meet again, I know it. Maybe by then I'll have persuaded Silver to set her doubts aside."

"Do that, and you can do anything," said Red Cap.

The fire died down; the midwinter feast was consumed; the mead cups were filled and drained, filled and drained again. The musicians played fast reels and slow laments and a few tunes that were without question of fey origin. Brasal sang a lullaby; he and Bearberry together rendered an old song of farewell. Last, we sang the ancient anthem forbidden by Keldec: the song of truth. Not all of us had singing voices as pleasing to the ear as Brasal's or Regan's, and many of us were weary, but when our voices rose as one, fey and human together, I felt the stones of Shadowfell come alive with the power of it. My skin prickled. Tears started in my eyes. The last line seemed to echo on in the chamber long after we fell silent. *My spirit is forever free.*

Then, without another word, the Folk Below collected their belongings and formed a procession as before, Hawkbit leading with the lantern, the others following in turn. Pearl-Wort carried the basket that was our gift to them. Milla had packed up some leftover cakes and other morsels, and these were borne away in the small baskets and bags the Good Folk had brought with them.

Woodrush lingered beside Sage. "Blessings o' the season on ye, wise woman," she said, and took Sage's hands in hers.

"May the White Lady light your footsteps, wise woman," said Sage, and for an uncanny moment, as they looked into each other's eyes, they seemed as alike as twins. The moment passed; Woodrush turned toward me.

"Travel safe, Caller," she said. "There's a long road ahead o' ye."

I bowed my head respectfully. "I hope you too will be safe. Your presence here tonight honors us."

"Ye comin'?" Vetch looked back over his shoulder at Woodrush. The others had all filed out of the chamber, on their way to the stair.

"Aye, I'm comin', foolish wee man." Her tone was affectionate as she moved away.

I got up and followed her out. Regan was standing at the top of the stair. As the Northies passed down, he bade each a grave farewell. For Bearberry he had more words, and the young Northie lingered to talk to him. I thought each had recognized in the other something of himself. Fingal stood by Regan, watching. When our guests were halfway down the stair, they began to sing. This time there were words in it, but they were in a tongue I could not understand. I guessed the song was of renewal, a ritual chant to honor the night of turning, when the wise crone sinks into her long sleep and the bright warrior awakens. Tonight the year began its slow ascent to light. The human folk of Alban had allowed such lore and wisdom to fade

away. Yet here, in this unlikely place, the hand of friendship had been extended between folk long distrustful
of each other. We had not only reached a truce, but also
found a shared pathway forward.

The last of our visitors vanished below; the light from
their lanterns faded and was gone. We stood there in silence for a few moments. Then Fingal, who had hardly
said a word all evening, spoke in a tone of awe. "They told
me they have healers. Imagine what we could learn from
them, given time."

"Such cooperation did not take place even in the years
before Keldec," Regan mused. "This evening's work has
been truly astonishing. The enchanted map . . . This is beyond anything I hoped for, Neryn. Bearberry confirmed
that some of his kind have the power of flight, and that
some can communicate with creatures, including birds.
I hardly need tell you what an immense difference that
could make to us."

"Anything they share with us we must use with caution," I said. "The power of such gifts is balanced by peril."

"Of course," Regan said, but there was a light in his
eyes that told me his thoughts were far ahead, seeing the
day when Alban would be free again.

Tali came strolling through from the dining area, a half
smile on her lips. "So," she said, coming to lean on the wall
beside me. "You did it."

"*I* did it? Hardly."

"You think they'd have come up here for the first time
ever, and eaten our food, and offered us all kinds of help

if we hadn't had a Caller among us? Come on, Neryn, you're no fool. It's your presence that draws them out. It's your canny ability that's finally turned them to our way of thinking."

This thought made me deeply uncomfortable. "All of us did this together—Milla with the food, Eva with the gift, Regan with his stirring speeches, you and your warriors with your readiness to clear the place of iron and do without your weapons for a day. Besides, they spoke of changing times and the Master of Shadows—only a small part of this is my doing."

All three of my companions were smiling as if I were saying something mildly amusing.

"A Caller," said Fingal. "Maybe we're starting to realize what that is. And maybe it's more than any of us expected."

CHAPTER FOUR

IT WAS HARD TO LEAVE SHADOWFELL. FOR SO long I had been without a proper home, without the certainty of enough food and a roof over my head at night. For years my only purpose had been keeping my father out of trouble and surviving one more day. Now I had a purpose so grand it hardly bore thinking about, and it was time to move on with the journey.

The plan was to seek out the Hag of the Isles, then head northward to find the Lord of the North in time to get home to Shadowfell before autumn storms made the mountain tracks impassable. An ambitious plan, with little allowance for the vagaries of the weather or the possibility either Guardian might choose not to cooperate. But it was the only one we had.

Sage and Red Cap, with the child, were already gone, heading west toward their home forests and their own people. They would carry the message out among the Good Folk in their Watch. As for the Folk Below, once they had made up their minds to help us, they had startled us with the efficiency of their preparations. They had organized their clan into groups that would set out soon to spread the word across the Watch of the North. Bearberry had been up the stairs many times, often with Hawkbit or Woodrush, to discuss strategy with Regan. The rebels had various missions to undertake before midsummer, when folk would return to Shadowfell to report their progress. Regan and Fingal were heading south to meet with a rebel group in Corriedale.

Regan and Fingal. That had been a shock to everyone, and most of all to Tali. She always traveled with Regan as his personal guard, standing at his right hand, keeping him safe. Always. Her presence by his side meant Shadowfell's leader survived to inspire and invigorate us. There was no doubt his stirring speeches, his bright-eyed enthusiasm, his unswerving dedication to the goal were what kept us all strong.

But when the time had come for Regan to allocate tasks to his team, he had announced that in view of the vital nature of my mission, Tali would be going with me as my guard and protector. Tali hadn't said a word. It was not her way to lose control in public. But I'd seen her face turn sheet-white. I'd seen her clench her jaw and curl her hands into tight fists. I doubted she'd heard what Regan said next, about how my safety was his first priority, so he was giving me Shadowfell's most able and versatile warrior as my companion on the road. Had there been any chance Flint would reach Shadowfell in time, he would have been the one to travel with me; but he had not come yet, and we all knew it was unlikely he would be here at all. Regan did not include him in the plans.

There followed some challenging days. Regan and Tali argued behind closed doors. Tali stalked about with a face so shuttered and grim that nobody but Fingal dared speak to her, and when he did, she snarled at him. Our bedchamber was a place of tight silences and averted eyes. Tali was like a storm confined in a small space, near bursting with wounded fury, but too proud to talk about it save in her private protests to Regan. It was not that she objected to the job of guarding me, Fingal told me, but that she believed Regan would not be safe without her. Since Fingal himself was to be Regan's guard now, that suggested Tali had a lack of faith in her brother, and I could see that Fingal was somewhat put out by this.

"At least, if Regan is hurt, he'll have you there to patch him up," I told him, attempting a joke. Shadowfell was too small to hold Tali's rage, and everyone was edgy. The only good thing that could come of this was that Shadowfell's warriors would head out on their expeditions in top fighting condition, thanks to the extreme rigors of their current training. An angry Tali made a fearsome taskmaster.

At a certain point she accepted the inevitable and the arguments ceased. She gave me curt instructions about what to pack and told me, without consultation, which path we'd be taking. She avoided talking to Regan.

He seemed much as usual. He sat down with Bearberry, Hawkbit, and me, and we went over what the Folk Below had shown us at midwinter. Tali and I both knew the way to Darkwater, a settlement on a western sea loch. But we would not pass through the place where my father had died. Instead, we would make for Pentishead, some miles to the south, and embark on the voyage Twayblade had demonstrated in the nest-boat: out between the inner islands, then to Ronan's Isle, steering clear of the skerries.

"What about a boat?" I asked.

"Leave that to Tali," said Regan. "Once you're out of the mountains, you'll travel as a pair of women seeking work. It's the best choice for avoiding notice. Once you reach the coast, you'll likely find someone to ferry you over for a few coppers. Flint has been expert thus far at keeping the king's attention away from the outer isles, using the argument—true enough—that they're hard to reach and not many folk live there. That can only be to your advantage."

"There are sure to be Enforcers on the road now spring's come, especially around Summerfort. The idea of traveling openly does scare me."

"Between Tali's good judgment and your instincts, I'm confident you'll reach the isles safely." A pause here, as he turned his searching blue eyes on me. "Believe me," he said, "it never gets any easier to send the folk of Shadowfell out across Alban, not knowing how many will come back in one piece. We've lost a few over the years and never found out what befell them. But we have work to do, a message to spread abroad. With Tali to protect you, you've a better chance than many of making the journey without coming to harm."

I said nothing, only nodded. A look passed between Bearberry and Hawkbit. It told me they, like me, were thinking this perceptive human leader had missed the important fact that the Good Folk had played a significant part in keeping me safe on my journey to Shadowfell, and perhaps in those difficult years before. Sage had been watching over me from a distance for some considerable time. Never mind that; Sage was gone. I did need a strong human companion, and there was no doubt Tali was strong, though whether she could be a good companion was yet to be seen.

The rebels left Shadowfell a few at a time, taking advantage of breaks in the weather, going their separate ways. The night before Regan and Fingal departed, I dreamed of Flint riding out from Winterfort with his Enforcer troop, though I could not tell where they were headed. When I woke, Tali was sitting on her bed, polishing an already gleaming knife by the dim light of the lantern that hung out in the hallway. I caught her eye, but the look on her face told me to hold my tongue. I lay awake for some time, as was usual when Flint had appeared in my dreams, and she said not a word. Later, when I had dozed fitfully and woken again, she was folding garments into a pile with meticulous precision—she, who tended to throw clothing in a heap on the floor, unless it was her combat gear, which was cleaned and oiled and stored with as much care as her weapons. I thought of things to say and discarded each of them in turn. Eventually I slept again. When I woke, soon after dawn, she was up and gone. Perhaps she talked to

Regan before he left, perhaps not. When the time came, I bade him and Fingal farewell with the best smile and the bravest words I could find. But it seemed to me that when Regan went down the mountain, Shadowfell lost its heart.

Tali and I were next to go. As we made our way down to the river and across the shaky rope bridge, I tried not to wish it were Flint walking beside me. The longing for him was a physical ache in my chest, all the stronger because we had walked this path together, coming the other way.

We passed the place of last autumn's ambush, where the bodies of Flint's Enforcer comrades had been piled up and burned. No sign was left of that carnage. If there had been remains, the rebels had made sure they did not lie there long. We went by quickly, not talking.

We did not take the path along the valley past Corbie's Wood, the burned village that had been my childhood home, for we wanted to avoid the busier tracks as long as possible. Instead, we went by Lone Tarn, along the ridge that looked westward over the valley. It was a journey of several days from Shadowfell to Three Hags Pass. By night we sheltered in caves, or under overhangs, or—once—in a tumbledown hut: not the place where Flint had tended to me when I was sick, but a ruin that was home only to spiders and beetles. Tali and I barely spoke to each other, except for her curt instructions about taking the left fork or the right, or keeping quiet, or waiting while she scanned the territory ahead. When we camped for the night, she set snares; a rabbit or two supplemented the supplies we carried.

I had wondered if Silver's clan, the Good Folk who had

helped me when I came the other way, would appear again. Once past Lone Tarn we were back in the Watch of the West, their home territory. But then, Tali was armed; Silver's people had steered clear of me while I was with Flint because of his iron weaponry. My own knife traveled in its protective sheath. Tali would not shield her blades. "I understand the difficulty," she'd said. "But there are many dangers between here and the coast, including troops of Enforcers, and I can't protect you without iron. I need my own weapons and I need them ready to use."

Traveling with Tali was quicker than it had been with Flint. I was fitter, of course, after a winter of warmth and good feeding, not to speak of all that running up and down the Ladder. But there was more to it. I began to realize how careful Flint had been for my welfare on that earlier journey, making sure I rested and ate well, pacing the walks to suit my shorter legs, often refusing to let me help with the tasks of making and striking camp. Tali treated me as an equal or, on occasion, a not especially useful underling. She made few concessions. When night came, I slept the sleep of sheer exhaustion.

Once we were over Three Hags Pass, Tali changed into her female clothing. From here on we would encounter more and more other travelers, and the less of a warrior she appeared, the less likely she'd be to attract attention. There was no need for her to say she hated wearing a skirt; the way she walked in it made it perfectly clear.

With the pass behind us we were in the Rush valley, where the river tumbled and roared and swept its way down to lose itself in Deepwater, close by the king's stronghold of Summerfort. So early in the season it was unlikely Keldec would be in residence, but there would be Enforcers guarding the place, and folk coming in and out with supplies—while the king only lived at Summerfort in the warmer months, he maintained permanent households both there and at Winterfort in the east. There was only one road down the valley, and that was the king's road, which crossed the Rush by the king's bridge, where there were always guards. We wouldn't be using that bridge.

"Hollow will let us over," I told Tali as we descended the upper valley in our working women's clothing. Tali had a swathing kerchief around head and neck, concealing her unusually short hair and her tattoos. "He'll provide a night's shelter too. I just need to speak to him nicely, make sure he remembers me."

"A brollachan."

"A brollachan, yes. No stranger than some of the others you've encountered in recent times."

"Aren't brollachans fiercely territorial? That's what I recall from the old stories. The idea of sheltering in one's house doesn't sit well with that."

"Hollow can be fierce; when I first met him, he almost knocked me off his bridge. But we soon became friends. It's just a matter of saying things in the right way."

Tali glanced at me sideways. "Or being a Caller."

I shrugged. "It probably helped, though I never called Hollow. His job is to leap out when anyone sets foot on his bridge and stop them from crossing. But we're approaching the other way this time."

"Wonderful. What happens when a brollachan thinks he's being attacked from the rear, by stealth?"

"It will be all right, Tali, I promise. Just one thing."

"What?"

"You'll have to wrap up your weapons. Not so much to protect him—I'm sure he has the strength to withstand iron, or he wouldn't have been able to hold the bridge for so long—but as a sign that we mean no harm."

She said nothing, simply looked ahead down the track, where now we could see a scattering of farmsteads on either side with strips of grazing land behind, and farther down the hill the narrowing of the valley that signaled the entry to the defile. In that place, for the length of two miles there was only room for the track and the river; sheer rock walls rose on either side. When Enforcers had caught up with me there, only my gift had saved me.

"No need to put your knives away until we're nearly at Brollachan Bridge," I told her. "It took me half a day to walk between there and the defile last time. Of course, I was sick then. We'll be a bit quicker."

"You're not looking so well now." Tali glanced across at me.

"There's a farm farther down where I sheltered and woke to find myself cornered by folk with pitchforks," I said. "Just about everyplace on this path has bad memories. Even Hollow's lair. A friend of mine died by the bridge. That was the only time I've seen iron used as a weapon against the Good Folk, and it was hideous. If you'd been there, you'd understand why I insist on knives being guarded."

After a moment she said, "I do understand, Neryn. I

99

just don't like it much. I'd rather fight with a good blade than use my hands or a nearby lump of rock. Let's hope this Hag of the Isles has some insights into the problem of iron. It looms as serious if we're expecting these folk to stand up beside us when the time comes."

We passed the farm where Flint and I had been sheltered overnight. We passed two more dwellings. There was nobody around, though smoke from hearth fires threaded up into the cold morning air. Then without warning Tali grabbed my arm and pulled me down into the concealment of a drystone wall.

"What?" I whispered, my heart juddering.

Tali put a finger to her lips. We waited, motionless. After what felt like a long time, there came the sound of bleating, movement on the path down the hill, a sharp whistle, the bark of a dog. Memories crowded me. I clenched my teeth and tried to concentrate on the here and now. Let these folk pass; let us get down to the defile unnoticed. Let me not meet someone who remembered me from last time I was here.

"Now," murmured Tali, who had put her head up to scan the track. "Quick."

No running; I knew that without being told. Instead, it was a creep from stone wall to outhouse, from outhouse to trees, from trees to rocks, each time waiting under cover until Tali gave the sign that it was safe to go on. I could hear the sheep still, up behind a run-down barn. The barking had ceased; maybe the dog was too busy to scent strangers close by. Only when we were clear of the scattered settlement and within a few hundred paces of the defile did I risk speaking, and I kept my voice down.

"Thanks. I didn't see them coming."

"Doing my job, that's all. Now wait here while I go and look through the defile. We're not going in until the road's clear ahead."

The canny gifts possessed by some human folk, thanks to a fey ancestor, were of numerous kinds. Tali's gift was unusually sharp eyesight. I stayed crouched in the concealment of some low bushes while she went forward. The way she moved made a mockery of her disguise; every part of her body was finely tuned, on guard, ready for whatever might come. Before we left Shadowfell, she'd set out for me what I should do if we were attacked: keep out of things and let her do the fighting. Escape by any means I had at my disposal—my staff, my knife, my canny gift. I had reminded her that if I called the Good Folk to help us and others saw the encounter, word would soon get back to the king's men. *If you must use it to save yourself, use it,* she'd said. *Regan needs you. And, Neryn? Never forget the rebel code—the cause comes first, no matter what. If you can escape by leaving me behind, that's what you do.* Each of us had a little packet of hemlock seeds concealed in her clothing. Since the death of Andra's brother, the rebels had carried these close to their bodies, within quick reach. When Fingal had given me mine, I had asked him whether anyone had ever used the seeds. His face had gone very still. And he'd said, "Best that we don't speak of that."

Tali was back, crouching down beside me. "Folk

approaching the defile from the other side. Not Enforcers; people on foot, with children. After them it's clear. We wait. Up there." She jerked her head toward the oaks on the hillside behind us.

The trees were leafless still, providing scant cover, but we found a hollow sheltered by rocks. There we waited, taking the opportunity to drink from our waterskins and eat a little of Milla's waybread. There was no talking. After some time a family of five came out from the defile: a man and a woman, each carrying a sack of grain, three weary-looking children with bundles, and a little dog. As they passed the point nearest to our hiding place, the dog pricked up its ears and turned its head toward us. But one of the lads had it on a rope lead, and when it pulled in our direction, he cursed it and hauled it after him.

They moved on up the valley and out of sight. Tali checked the defile again, and now someone else was coming. We waited until a boy had passed through with a bow over his shoulder and a pair of rabbits dangling, limp, from his hand. Someone would eat well today. Tali checked a third time and gestured for me to come down; the defile was clear.

"Right," Tali muttered. "Straight through, and if I'm wrong and someone comes, we don't speak unless we have to. And if we do have to, we stick to the story."

"It would help if you could walk a bit less like a warrior," I murmured. "Couldn't you slump a little?"

"Not every woman of Alban is a downtrodden drudge, Neryn. I don't see you doing any slumping."

"No, but . . . never mind."

It was shadowy in the defile. The river coursed along beside us, swollen by the melting snow. Its voice clamored in our ears. The rock walls threw back the sound, making one river into many. Tali set a quick pace; I made sure I kept up. As I passed, I murmured a belated thank-you to the stanie mon somewhere in the cliff above us, the one who had hidden me when the Enforcers came. Not his fault that the farm folk had found me and apprehended me soon afterward. He had answered my call straightaway; he had saved me from torture, enthrallment, maybe death.

We were nearly through when Tali halted suddenly, and I just avoided crashing into her. She put a hand up, signaling silence. I felt the thump of my heart; I made myself breathe slowly. Then she turned and mouthed one word. *Enforcers.*

No going back. We sprinted forward to the place where the defile broadened and the Rush valley opened out again. I still couldn't see anyone on the road ahead, but Tali led me at a run onto the open ground that lay between track and river. Here, the remnants of old drystone walls ran across barren terrain dotted by coarse grasses and the odd scrubby bush. A few goats grazed on the sparse pickings. The only farmhouse was at some distance, on the eastern side of the track.

"Quick!" Tali glanced back over her shoulder, toward the road. Ahead was a stretch of wall less broken than the rest. "Come on, Neryn!"

We reached the wall; dived down behind it, lying flat on the hard ground with our packs beside us.

"Don't move," Tali muttered. "Don't make a sound."

The wait felt endless. My throat was dry; dust went up my nose and I had to force down a sneeze. My body ached with cramps. But Tali had trained me well, in both endurance and strength. I held still. I kept quiet. And eventually, over the sound of the river, I heard hoofbeats on the road from Summerfort. I stayed flat, listening as they passed us and moved on into the defile. At least three riders, maybe more.

"Now," breathed Tali. I rose to my feet, wincing as a cramp stabbed through my legs. Tali shouldered one bag; I grabbed the other. Dust was still rising from the riders' passage as the two of us headed toward the river, keeping low. The ground was uneven. My foot went into a sudden hole and I almost twisted my ankle. My breath was coming hard; my chest hurt. "Here," Tali muttered, reaching for my hand. "Up ahead, those trees. Keep your head down."

We reached the trees. Only then did I see that the natural contour of the land in this spot provided a hiding place. The riverbank was higher here, and between the alders was a sheltered hollow that would be invisible from the road. We threw the bags down and clambered after them. My heart was racing. If not for Tali's canny eyesight, we'd still have been in the open when the king's men came by.

"My guess is they'll ride back down before long," Tali said. "They were traveling too light to be headed over the pass. Must have some business at those farms. Just as well we weren't caught higher up."

"So we wait here until they go by again?" I tried to match her calm tone.

"Mm-hm." She settled in a spot where she could see

over the riverbank to the road, which lay some two hundred strides away.

"What if they don't? What if you're wrong and they are headed over the pass?"

"Unlikely, in my judgment. Now tell me—this brollachan cave we're headed for, can we get there straight along the riverbank? Pity we don't have a boat." She took her gaze off the road for a moment to look down at the river, a churning mass of gray water from one bank to the other.

"You're joking."

"It would certainly get us downstream fast. The problem might be stopping before we washed up at the river mouth in full view of the Summerfort sentries."

As a joke, it was distinctly unamusing. "We can get most of the way along the bank," I told her. "Right at the end, there's a sort of stony hill on this side, and we have to climb that to reach Hollow's cave and the bridge."

"I think I remember the spot, though I never saw any bridge in this valley except the king's bridge."

"Brollachan Bridge is hidden by the hill. It's only a log." *Only* was hardly the right term for the monumental tree trunk that spanned the gap between rocky rise and cliff face. "I hope Hollow's in a good mood today."

"What'll he do if he isn't?"

"He likes games. The kind of games that could end up with someone falling a long way."

Tali gave a slow smile. "We'll see about that."

"He's a friend, Tali."

"As I said."

It was late afternoon before the three Enforcers rode back through the defile—long enough for my imagination to provide a picture of what might be happening in one or another of those lonely farmsteads. At a certain point in the afternoon, a column of smoke arose from the approximate direction of the farms. Neither Tali nor I made comment. We heard no screams, no sounds of weapons being drawn, no dogs barking. But maybe we were too far away for that. The smoke was thinning by the time the king's men came riding by, the silver on their bridles glinting in the sunlight, their horses uniformly tall and black. The men's faces were concealed by their Enforcer masks, dark cloths wrapped over nose, mouth, and chin. None of them was Flint. I would have known him instantly, mask or no mask.

As soon as they were out of sight, we moved on. We followed the east bank of the Rush, staying in whatever cover we could find, but there was nobody on the road now, and nothing stirred in the valley save birds passing high above us and a goat or two in the fields. I had no sense of Good Folk anywhere nearby. Perhaps Tali's weapons were keeping them away.

We reached Hollow's hill not long before dusk. Tali was edgy. I had asked her to wrap and stow her weapons when the hill came into view and she had complied without a word. Now her hand kept moving to her belt, reaching for a knife that was not there. The hill loomed dark under a sky now thick with clouds; it would rain tonight. Hollow's hearth fire would be welcome.

"He might jump out and yell," I warned Tali. "Keep your weapons wrapped up. He knows I'm a friend. It will be all right once he sees me."

"As long as he recognizes you before he rips our heads off, fine with me."

"I'll go first." I climbed the narrow path between the rocks, using my staff to help me balance. The light was fading fast. At every step I anticipated a great shout from above, for when I had dared set foot on his bridge the first time, Hollow had hurled a fearsome challenge. I found I was holding my breath, waiting for the moment when his booming voice would ring from the rocky hillock.

We climbed and climbed, and there was nothing. Only the moon low over the horizon, and a high-pitched sound as something flew overhead. Now we must be almost level with the cliff path on the far side of the river, where Sorrel had died and Sage had held off two Enforcers to allow my escape. And still the place was quiet. Could it be that Hollow only guarded the front door, not the back?

We reached the end of the path. A shadowy passageway led straight into the hill. No sign of the brollachan. I could see no light from within Hollow's lair, neither the warm glow of a lantern nor the flicker of a hearth fire.

"Call him," Tali whispered.

No need for a canny call here, only the kind a traveler might make at a friend's doorway. "Hollow, are you there? It's Neryn."

Nothing. I tried again. "Hollow! It's Neryn, Sage's friend. You helped me last autumn when I was in trouble. I'm here with another woman. May we come in?"

Silence. I looked at Tali; Tali looked at me. Soon it would be too dark to move around safely on these rocks. Besides, there was nowhere else to shelter.

"Don't tell me," she said, taking off her pack and setting it on the ground so she could rummage inside. "Make fire without using a knife, light a candle, then walk into some creature's lair with only my bare fists to defend both of us. Yes?"

"Use your knife. But wrap it up again as soon as the candle's burning. He can't be gone. Guarding the bridge is his mission, his solemn trust. He'd have come with me and protected me on the journey if not for that."

"Really?" Tali was working efficiently with flint and knife; she had a supply of compressed tinder in her bag, and a beeswax candle in a holder. "So where is he?"

"Maybe asleep. Or on the bridge. I don't know."

She said nothing more until the candle was alight and her materials were stowed in the pack again. "Neryn, this could be a trap." She was keeping her voice to a murmur. "There could be anyone in there. The two of us, with no proper weapons at hand, wandering along a narrow tunnel with a nice little light to warn folk we're coming—that's asking for trouble. If your friend were here, surely he would have come out by now."

"We must go in. Maybe he's sick or hurt."

"We'd be better off finding a place to shelter among these rocks, and having another look in the morning."

"If it's some kind of ambush, whoever it is will have heard us by now. So your suggestion doesn't make much

108

sense. We need to go in. If Hollow isn't there, we can at least make a proper fire and sleep under cover."

As if in answer, rain began to fall in pattering drops. Tali put up her hand to shield the candle. "Black Crow's curse! All right, but you carry the candle. I want my staff ready."

There was no ambush. We made our way cautiously through a network of dark tunnels, guessing at the right direction. Our candle was the only light. It felt a long way. It felt much farther than I had walked last time I was here, when Hollow had bid me farewell at the back door.

"Hope you're right about this," Tali murmured. As she spoke, I felt a movement of the air suggested the narrow tunnel was opening out. We stepped forward and into Hollow's cave.

"This is it," I breathed.

The fire on the broad hearth was a pile of whispering ashes. Above it the roof arched high; shadows moved oddly in the candlelight.

"There are bones everywhere." Tali's voice was hushed. "Hundreds of bones."

"He collects them." I set down my bag and staff. "We may as well make a fire; there's a woodpile over there. We should save the candle." Where was Hollow? Surely he wouldn't leave the bridge. Had the Enforcers been here? Had I been wrong about the brollachan's ability to withstand cold iron?

Tali set her belongings down and fetched an armful of firewood. I stirred the ash heap with a long stick.

"Tali!"

She was by my side in a moment.

"There are glowing embers here. He hasn't been gone long."

She made no comment, simply went about getting the fire burning again with the efficiency she turned to every task. I took out some provisions and set them on one of the flat stones that furnished Hollow's lair.

Tali started suddenly. "What was that?"

I listened, and for a while heard nothing. Then it came, a thready whimpering from somewhere in the dark recesses of the cavern.

"Give me the candle." I moved cautiously in the direction of the sound, taking care not to trip on the bones, which were not in a tidy arrangement as Hollow liked them, but scattered here and there on the ground.

Over by the wall was a pile of old sacks, and from deep within, a pair of frightened eyes peered out. I released my breath and knelt down, not too close, for I knew from experience how hard the pookie could bite. "It's his friend," I told Tali, feeling suddenly cold. "Something bad must have happened. Hollow wouldn't go off and leave the pookie on its own."

As if it understood, the catlike creature began a mournful wailing, but when I tried to coax it out, it hissed and retreated farther into the sacks.

"Food," I said. "Cheese, in particular. And it likes to be warm, so let's build up the fire."

Tali was doing so even as I spoke. "What in the name of the gods is a pookie?" she asked.

"I'd never heard of one until I came here. It's Hollow's only companion."

It took me a while to get the little creature out, even with morsels of cheese as a lure. Eventually it crept toward the fire and settled itself on my folded cloak, shivering. The embers suggested Hollow had been gone less than a day; the pookie was not starving, though once it was out, it ate as if it hadn't seen a meal since my last visit in autumn.

Tali settled herself out of biting range, watching the creature as we ate our own meager supper. There had been no hunting or trapping today, and we needed to make our provisions last. "Can we get over this bridge without the brollachan?" she asked after a while. There was no need for her to spell it out: with Enforcers active in the valley, it was doubly important for us to avoid the king's bridge. And Brollachan Bridge was the only other way.

"We could." I glanced at the pookie, which had sidled closer and was curled up against my leg. "It's a matter of keeping your balance and not looking down. Once we're over, there's a small settlement to pass through, then a track that leads to the woods above Deepwater. Last autumn the king had sentries along the hill on this side, and the local people were in the habit of telling them when strangers passed through."

"Hmm. Well, this place is good shelter. I never knew about this bridge, and I've been up and down the valley more times than I can count."

"People don't talk about it. If you ask them, they either tell you there is no bridge, or they say whoever attempts to cross ends up being washed down the river, stone dead. That would be Hollow's doing."

"But he let you across."

"After testing me, yes. Hollow is old and strong. I can't think what has happened to him."

"There's nothing we can do about it," Tali said, "so let's get some sleep. We'll move on in the morning. And, before you ask, we're not taking that creature with us. If I wanted another traveling companion, it wouldn't be one with a shrill voice and a bottomless stomach."

Morning came, and still Hollow had not returned. We packed up in silence while the pookie perched on the rocks, staring at us. It was an odd-looking creature, a little like a cat, but with a hairless tail and enormous ears. Perhaps I was imagining the look of reproach in those gleaming eyes.

"What about the fire?"

"I'll bank it up; it'll keep the cave warm for today, at least. Maybe he'll be back soon." I hoped the pookie could find food in these underground ways or on the hillside beyond. It felt entirely wrong to leave it on its own. What if Hollow never came back?

"Don't even think of it," Tali said over her shoulder. How she knew what was in my mind was a mystery. "The creature is a burden we can't afford. We must go swiftly and quietly. We've lost half a day already. I want to be in the safety of those woods before there's too much movement on the road. Where's this bridge?"

I dealt with the fire, then led her out through the

passageway to the west. The bridge was a single log of immense length, set high above the Rush. At the far end it rested on a ledge partway down the cliff face. A precarious path led from there to the high track toward Deepwater. It was barely dawn; I hoped it was too early for sentries.

It had rained during the night and the bridge was wet. I reminded myself that when I'd done this before, I had been weak and ill, and Hollow had leapt up onto the log to challenge me. He had made me play a game of catch, using the pookie as a ball. And I had fallen, as so many had before me, but Hollow had caught me. After that, we'd been friends. "The thing is not to look down," I said, my stomach churning.

"Check that your pack's secure." Tali was assessing the bridge and the hillside beyond, perfectly calm. "Hold your staff crosswise and use it for balance. Scuff your boots in the soil here, you'll get a better grip. Best if you go first; you've done this before."

That was ridiculous, since this was the kind of feat she excelled at; most likely she wanted me to go first so she'd have some chance of grabbing me if I slipped. I hitched up my bag, tucked the hem of my skirt into my belt, and gripped my staff with palms suddenly slick with sweat. I stepped onto the bridge. Fixed my gaze on a point at the other side where there was a rock a bit like a dragon's head. Said Flint's name to myself a few times, silently, as if it might be a lucky talisman.

"If you're ready, go on. I'll be right behind you." Tali sounded completely confident, as if she hadn't the least doubt that I could walk across quite steadily. It helped. I headed out onto the log, one foot before the other, not trying for speed but maintaining a rhythm, because if I hesitated, I would have too much time to think. One foot. The other foot. Adjust the staff. Keep looking at the dragon's head. Keep breathing, in, out, in, out. A long way. In the middle a fresh breeze caught us, coming down the river from the snowy mountains to the north. In, out, in, out.

"You're doing well," came Tali's voice, a murmur now. "More than halfway there."

One foot. The other foot. The staff a little up, a little down. *Don't drop it, Neryn.*

"Stop!" Tali's voice was tight with alarm, but quiet enough not to startle me into falling.

I froze in place, my heart hammering. "What?" I squeaked.

"There's something over there. On the path. Back up, Neryn."

Back up? It was hard enough going forward. I couldn't see anything on the ledge at the end of the bridge. I turned my head carefully, making myself look up the path toward the cliff top. And there, coming down from above, was a nebulous dark shape, a thing of mist and shadow. Within that strange veil could be discerned legs like tree trunks, fists the size of platters, dark penetrating eyes above a grinning mouth full of formidable teeth.

"Back up!" repeated Tali in an urgent whisper.

The dark form was moving fast; he was at the bridge before I could take another step, walking out toward us, reaching out a huge hand. "Hold on tae me, Neryn. We canna hae ye fallin'." He led me forward, and in no time I was safely on the ledge, and Tali was coming down after me, her eyes wide with shock. "Sorry I wasna hame tae greet the twa o' ye," Hollow said, giving Tali a good look up and down.

"You're safe; that's all that matters. I was worried about you. Hollow, this is my friend and guard, Tali. We sheltered in your cave last night; we fed the pookie and made up your fire."

"And now we'll be getting on," said Tali.

"Oh, aye," said Hollow. "I was comin' tae that. Will ye no' cross back ower, and I'll mak' ye a bittie breakfast tae see ye on your way? I ken ye're in a rush, but this ledge isna the coziest spot for a chat."

Tali glared at me, as if this delay were my doing. "We've no time for this," she said.

"Ye're headin' off on a mission, and ye've nae time tae heed a warnin'?" The strange mist was dispersing from around Hollow's massive form, revealing more clearly his blockish frame and his rough-hewn features. "Ye'd be plannin' on headin' up that way, aye?"

"We're going west," I said. "To the isles, to find the Hag. This is the safer path down to Deepwater. We wanted to avoid the king's bridge."

"Weel," said Hollow, scratching his chin, "ye wouldna be wantin' tae tak' this path. But ye shouldna be followin' the king's road neither. The wee wumman, Sage, was by here no' sae lang since, and tellit me what's planned. I took it on masel' tae check the coast was clear for ye, knowin' ye'd be by here soon. There's king's men on guard by the track up yonder." He gestured up the path we had planned to take. "Gae that way and ye'll walk right intae them."

Tali stared at him. "You checked the coast was clear, you say. That took all night?" It was a challenge.

"Tali," I said, "Hollow is a friend. I told you."

She narrowed her eyes at me. I reminded myself that it was her job to keep me safe; I might need to get used to this kind of thing.

"We'll come back over with you," I said, making the decision. "You're right, this is not the place to discuss things." Chances were I was standing on the very spot where Sorrel had died in agony; chances were Tali was in the place where Sage had fought a desperate battle to keep the king's men at bay while I fled across the bridge. "Especially if there are Enforcers just around the corner."

"O' course," Hollow said, "I could hae got rid o' them for ye. But that didna seem wise. I dinna want them comin' up in numbers, stormin' the brig wi' fire and iron. Yon cave's a handy shelter; chances are your folk may need it again."

We walked back over the bridge. Hollow insisted on going sideways and leading me by the hand while Tali came behind, her silence heavy with doubt. When we were halfway across, the pookie emerged from the entry on the other side to stand by the bridge, quivering and giving out little shrieks.

"Silly wee gomerel," said Hollow fondly. "Doesna care

for bein' on his ainsome; jumps at shadows. Didna bite ye, did he?"

"I didn't give him the opportunity."

"Gets up tae mischief when I'm awa'. Scatters ma banes, chews on the beddin', lets me know he's no' best pleased."

Back in the cavern, we set down our belongings again— Tali kept her staff close—while Hollow went off down another passage and returned with a substantial joint of meat, most likely from one of the local sheep. This he laid on the coals to cook. Then he set about rearranging the disordered bones until the hearth was encircled by an orderly pattern, with skulls at precisely placed intervals. The largest of these looked like an ox's, complete with great horns; the smallest was tiny and delicate, a shrew's or vole's. When all was to his satisfaction, the brollachan gave a contented sigh, sank down on a large stone, and turned his gaze on us, solemn now. The pookie leapt into his arms and clung, chirruping.

"Mightna be the way ye wanted tae spend the mornin', but I'm glad I caught the twa o' ye before ye met up wi' the king's men. And at least ye'll get a good feed wi' me."

"I'm so happy to see you, Hollow. I thought you might be gone right away. Or hurt."

He eyed me. "'Twould tak' mair than a few poxy En- forcers tae hurt me, Neryn. But the twa o' ye—Sage tellit me your companion there is a braw fighter, but nae lassie's braw enough tae fend off a troop o' king's men hung about wi' iron weaponry. Dinna ye try tae tell me otherwise," he added quickly when Tali made to speak. "If ye're as guid as they say ye are, ye willna lead Neryn intae peril, and that's a fact. Listen now. I ken ye dinna want tae be waitin' here wi' me any langer than ye must. It didna need Sage tae tell me the sand's runnin' through the glass quicker than ye thought. 'Tis all ower the place now; wee folk passin' the word, birds and creepin' things tellin' how we should be gettin' ready for a big fight."

"Already," breathed Tali. "Sage left Shadowfell only a matter of days before we did. How could she have spread the word so quickly? I thought the Good Folk were slow to trust."

"Ye suggestin' a brollachan's fibbin' tae ye, lassie?" Hollow stretched his mouth in a grimace.

"Getting accurate information could mean life or death on this journey. I'd be stupid not to check it. And my name's Tali."

"The lassie has a tongue on her," Hollow said, the grimace turning to a grin. "Our folk hae ways o' passin' messages, and ways o' crossin' country, that your folk canna understand, lassie. Tali. That's a guid strong name."

She gave him a tight nod.

"I told ye the word was bein' passed abroad; I didna say those that are passin' it are happy wi' it. But change is afoot. The Master o' Shadows is walkin' the land, and a Caller's stepped up. Sage tellit me ye passed your test, Neryn. That the Master came tae ye o' his ain will. So there's nae doot ye can mak' the difference."

"I hope so, Hollow. But I do need to get to the isles, to find the Hag and do the first part of my training. And now that time's so short, I'll have to go to the north as well before next winter."

"The Lord o' the North? They say he's sleepin' and canna be woken."

"The Northies said that. They implied that he was the one who should be keeping the Master of Shadows in check."

"That's the old balance: earth and fire. Water and air. Mebbe ye can call him out, Neryn. Seems naebody else can."

The task ahead was becoming so daunting it made me feel sick. I said nothing.

"Hollow." Tali was trying for a more courteous tone, though I could see the wish to be gone in her restless fingers and the little frown that never left her dark brows. "You say we can't use this cliff path because of Enforcers. The only alternative is the king's bridge, but you say we shouldn't use that either, and I agree entirely. It would be a foolish risk. What choice is left to us, go home or wait here indefinitely? You know we have very little time to accomplish this. The isles, the north, home before the autumn storms."

A lengthy silence, then, as Hollow turned the meat on the coals. A rich, savory smell filled the cavern. "There is a wee path," the brollachan said eventually. "I dinna ken if ye'd be wantin' tae go that way. A secret path, 'tis. Human folk canna find it on their ain. But Neryn's no' the common kind o' human folk. If ye care tae use it, I'll show ye how."

"A path," Tali echoed. "Where?"

"Straight up the cliff frae the brig, ower the hill, west as the raven flies. A bittie later the way curves tae the south. It comes out by Hiddenwater. Ye'd want tae be guid at climbin'."

"Due west," mused Tali.

"So we could bypass Summerfort altogether," I said. Even better, we could get as far as Hiddenwater without setting foot near the well-traveled path that ran beside Deepwater.

"Wait a moment," said Tali. My heart sank. "If the path goes the way you describe, it would have to cross Wedderburn land, for part of the way, at least."

"Ach," said Hollow, throwing his hands wide, "I dinna understand your clans and holdings and chieftains. The four Watches, they're auld and easy to grasp. But those others, they're the lines drawn by human folk for their ain purposes, and make nae sense tae me. What's wrong wi' walkin' on Wedderburn land? Is there an auld curse, or a sheep disease, or is the chieftain o' those parts another such as that king o' yours, the fellow that's set Alban all at sixes and sevens wi' his thirst for power?"

"We don't know," Tali said, her mouth grim. "There's old history between that chieftain and our leader. I won't go into details, but we've no cause to expect a welcome if we're caught crossing his land. Still, given the choice between that or the keen eyes of the Summerfort sentries, your wee path seems the safer option."

"Do you know the path well, Hollow?" I asked. "How good is the cover? How long would it take us to reach Hiddenwater?"

"'Twould be quicker than gaein' down the valley and

along the lochs. There'd be risks, aye; but ye wouldna be needin' tae pass close by this fellow's stronghold. Keep tae the north o' that, cross a wee river ower a ford, pass a hill wi' a crown o' standin' stanes, and after that bear southwest. Ye'll find oaks, pines, rocks. Guid cover, aye. And if ye dinna gae south afore ye pass that hill, no' sae many settlements. For a woodcrafty lassie such as yoursel', 'tis a guid way."

I looked at Tali.

"We have no real choice," she said. "Time's short. I'm not taking you over the king's bridge, it's just too risky. And the original plan is no longer viable. So we'll try this path. Agreed?"

"Agreed," I said, thinking her method of consultation left something to be desired. "But we have breakfast first. I don't imagine we'll be making campfires on Wedderburn land, unless we're pretty sure nobody can see us. So this might be our last hot meal for a while."

CHAPTER FIVE

WE MOVED WESTWARD, FOLLOWING HOLLOW'S wee path. After the first challenging climb up the cliff, it traversed a landscape whose hollows still held patches of stubborn snow, printed by the feet of creatures out foraging for what lean pickings they could find. Tiny mountain flowers popped up tentative heads, spots of white or yellow among the rocks. The path was often hard to find. Hollow had told us to look for certain signs: a little pile of white stones, blades of long grass twisted into a loose knot, a row of last autumn's leaves threaded onto a stick, telling us to go left or right, uphill or down. Here, I felt the constant presence of magic. There were Good Folk everywhere, though they did not show themselves directly.

The weather warmed a little, and the bare hills began to put on a tentative cloak of green. Occasional stands of pine softened the landscape, and in these we heard the songs of birds. At night, as we sat by our meager campfire, there came the hunting cries of wolves. We kept our fires small, mindful of the need to go unseen, at least until we were off Wedderburn land.

We reached the river on the third morning. It was broader than Hollow's description had suggested, and if there was a ford, clearly it was not in this spot. The water-way wound through a valley whose slopes were thick with alder, birch, and willow. Stony outcrops broke the tree cover here and there. Even so early in the season, with spring's new growth barely begun, it was hard to see far in any direction.

We halted on the pebbly shore. Tali slipped off her pack; I did the same. Each of us kept watch while the other knelt to drink; we refilled our waterskins.

"Your friend said *cross a wee river*," Tali said. "I suppose this is it. You rest, I'll look for the ford. Keep under cover."

I settled myself, with the two bags, half under a row of straggly bushes, and she headed off upstream. Within the space of a few breaths she was out of sight.

I was glad of the opportunity to rest my legs. Pride meant I did not ask Tali for breaks unless I was incapable of going on, and she did not often suggest them. I sat qui-etly, listening to the conversation of birds in the woods and the gurgling of the water. At times like this it was al-most possible to forget what a sad and sorry place Alban was. There were Good Folk somewhere close by, up in the trees or in the great stones that lay along the river valley like pieces tossed aside from a game for giants. I wondered if they might show themselves while Tali was not with me. It was at just such moments, on my other journeys, that a little voice had piped up with *Neryn, oh, Neryn,* or a small being had raised its head out of the bracken to gaze at me. Perhaps I should leave out an offering for them. We still had a supply of Milla's waybread, a hard-baked, long-lasting substance that sat heavily in the belly but was welcome at the end of a long day's walking. I would break off a morsel and put it on a piece of flat bark for them to eat when we were gone.

I was fishing in my bag for the food packet when I heard Tali's signal—not a shout, but a hooting cry like an owl's. A warning. I froze. Then came men's voices and the sudden tramping of booted feet on the stones, closing in fast.

We'd practiced. I had my knife in my hand within the space of a breath. I kicked the bags under the bracken, then crouched still, weapon at the ready.

"That way!" A man ran across the shore, passing without seeing me. Another emerged from the trees, following. They headed in the direction Tali had taken, soon vanishing from view around a massive rock. Had she managed to run and hide after sending that warning call, or was she trapped?

Shouting broke out from beyond the rock, the skid of boots on stones, a thud, a curse. At least three men, perhaps more. I knew what I was supposed to do: keep out of the way, leave the fighting to Tali. She'd drummed it into me often enough. If I could hide or flee, that was what I should do. My knife was only for self-defense. I might have better combat skills than I'd possessed last autumn, but I was a beginner by her standards, and my help would likely prove more of a hindrance.

Metal clashed; a man let out a chilling scream of pain. Then came Tali's voice, cursing. There was a note in it that told me she was hurt. Cold sweat broke out on my skin. The knife shook in my hand. I couldn't do it. I couldn't bolt into the woods, saving myself and leaving her behind. She might be Shadowfell's best fighter, but the numbers were against her. What if I created a diversion, gave her an opportunity . . .

Over the years I had learned to walk as a hunting creature walks, my feet making little sound. I moved with care now, avoiding the pebbles beside the water, going instead on the rough grass higher up, edging around the big rock. Tali yelled again, a fearsome challenge. I inched forward, right hand gripping the knife, left hand brushing the rock.

She was surrounded. Her staff lay on the stones, beyond her reach. With a knife in each hand she was keeping them at bay, ducking, turning, constantly in motion, never quite where they expected. There were four of them, and three had hunting knives. One man was bleeding from a cut to the cheek; another seemed to have hurt his leg, but still they circled Tali, taunting her.

"Slice my friend with your blade, would you? Just let me get close enough, girlie, and I'll show you what a knife's for!"

"What's that on your skin, canny magic? Shall we cut you open and see if you bleed like a real woman?"

"Go on, fight me! Let's see what you're made of, witch!"

I hesitated, not sure if Tali had seen me. I was at least six strides from them. My heart drummed. If I ran straight forward shrieking, could I win Tali enough time to seize the advantage? I might at least get a chance to do some damage before they grabbed me. I sucked in a breath and stepped out from cover, and someone seized me from behind, knocking the knife from my grasp.

"What have we here?"

All eyes turned in my direction. For a moment Tali's attackers froze, staring at me and my captor, and in that moment she struck once, twice, and two men went down. Then, with a roar of outrage, the biggest of the men delivered a blow to her head, sending her staggering toward the other one still on his feet.

"Leave off," my captor growled. "That one might be a stinger, but this one's a soft kitten. We could all sleep sweet tonight, fellows. I say tie them up and bring them with us. Why not enjoy them before we finish them?"

Tali kicked out, aiming for a man's privates, but the strike to the head had left her unsteady and the two of them grabbed her, one bending her arms up hard behind her back. She went white, teeth sunk in her lip.

My captor marched me forward. He was strong; there would be no point in struggling. Knife in hand, he addressed me. "Stand still, kitten, or your friend gets gutted like a codfish. You!" This was to Tali. "Try anything and I cut the little one, nice and slow." He released his hold on me and squatted down to examine the two injured men. One was groaning as he regained consciousness. The other lay sprawled unmoving on the stones.

"He's dead," said one of Tali's captors, a young fellow who looked almost as pale as she. His tone was flat, unbelieving. "Coran's dead."

The man who had held me rose slowly to his feet. Between the others, Tali was trying to stand tall, but she looked close to fainting. Blood was running down her neck from the head wound, staining her shirt crimson.

"You killed him," the man said. "You killed my friend."

The look in his eyes told me I had only a few moments to act. No choice, then. I met Tali's gaze, trying to warn her. The river. The water, flowing deep and strong through the valley. Alban's lifeblood, from the smallest stream to the shining loch to the great ocean. I opened myself to the power of it, and silently I called, *Help us! Quickly, help!*

The river roiled and rose up. It was over our feet, our ankles, our knees in an instant. It washed over the fallen men, carrying them swiftly away. The three shouted in alarm, and one of Tali's captors released his hold. Quick as a flash she wrenched free of the second, no longer near fainting but apparently her old self again.

The water rose to my waist. A figure rose with it, taller than a tall man, a being all ripples and eddies and swirls, its features discernible as darker patches in the watery substance of its face. Flotsam adhered to its head, forming what might be hair or a hat, and within its body twigs and leaves washed about as if carried on the natural flow of the river. In its liquid face a mouth opened, a great dark cavity, and one of the men let out a terrified oath. Another shouted in a foolish display of defiance. The man who had been holding me waded as fast as he could toward dry land. In an eyeblink the creature reached out a great watery hand and gripped him around the waist. It tossed him up—a shower of droplets arched through the air, catching the light—and out into the river. He vanished beneath the surface.

"Don't hurt us! I can't swim!" shrieked the younger man, while the other gave a wordless wail of horror. The creature wrapped a hand around each, lifting them so their feet were clear of the water. Tali and I retreated to the shallows, drenched and shivering.

The river being spoke, its voice a thundering torrent of sound in which I sensed rather than heard words. "Wash, dip, splash, drown?"

Tali glanced at the eldritch creature, then quickly away. "Tell it not yet," she said. "Not till they've answered some questions."

"Wait, please," I said, my teeth chattering. Somewhere under the cold and the shock was the dawning knowledge that once again I had used my gift to deliver not only rescue, but also death. That man, the one not killed by Tali, would not survive being swept downstream unconscious.

"You!" snapped Tali, addressing the two men. "What are you doing here? Why did you attack us?"

The river being gave the men a shake, as if this might jog their memory.

"Speak up!" Tali said. "Or do you prefer to join your companions in the river? Who sent you?"

"W-we were h-hunting," one fellow stammered, whey-faced. "D-deer. Boar. R-rabbits. No harm in that."

"*Who sent you?*" Tali was formidable at the best of times; when angry, she was truly fearsome.

"Don't let it hurt me!" spluttered the other man, his feet hanging just above the water's surface. In his terror he had lost control of his bowels. "Hunting, that's all!"

"What sort of hunters are you," I said, "that you feel entitled to attack women by the wayside whenever it pleases you? Which household did you come from? Tell us the truth, or my friend there holds you underwater, and how long he keeps you there is anyone's guess." I felt within me the being's fluid presence, its links to the rivers and lochs and tarns of the highlands, its long story stretching back and back in time, perhaps to the days of other Callers. I did my best to meet the murky patches that were its eyes.

"Dunk, wring, soak, drench?"

"Let them answer first," I said. And to the two men, *"Where did you come from?"*

"Last chance," put in Tali. "Speak or drown."

"W-W—"

"Wedderburn," the second man gasped. "Keenan of Wedderburn is our lord. Not sent to kill— only—"

"Only what?" Tali snarled. The river being's hands dipped lower. The men went in up to their necks.

"Look out for—for folk out of place. Folk wandering. No more than that."

"Look out for them and kill them." Tali's voice was flat. "Or no, take your pleasure with them first, then kill them, wasn't that the plan? Is that what your *lord* told you to do?" There was a look on her face that truly frightened me.

"G-g-g—"

"Enough," Tali said, and turned her back.

The river being held still, keeping the two suspended. So far as I could tell, it was looking at me. "Plunge, toss, drown, change?" it inquired.

The men turned agonized faces toward me. Neither spoke.

"We can't let them go free," I said, my heart thumping. "Not now." The moment we released them, they'd be straight back to Keenan with their story, and if he didn't believe the part about watery monsters, he'd surely be interested in two young women on the road, well armed and combative. He'd be interested in any sign of canny gifts, and if these men could put two and two together, they'd have realized the significance of the way this creature spoke to me. But I would not order the being to drown them. I grasped at the meaning of its last word. "Change?"

A smile appeared on its fluid features. It lifted the two and threw them high into the air. As they tumbled, screaming, back down toward the river, the thrashing of limbs and the billow of clothing became the shimmer of scales and the whip of narrow bodies, and two gleaming fish dived into the moving flow of the water. They would live to see another day. But not as men.

"Black Crow save us!" muttered Tali. Her face had turned greenish white, as if she might be sick.

The water retreated, sinking to knee level and lower. The being began slowly to slip back into the body of the river.

"Thank you!" I managed. "You saved us. We are in your debt."

"Go," murmured the river being. "Learn. Lead." Then, with a sound like a sigh, it rippled and vanished into the flow.

We stood in silence a few moments, then Tali said, "We can't linger here, someone may come looking for those so-called hunters. And we still have to cross the river."

"I doubt if that will pose any problem now," I said, with a glance toward the water. "Let me look at your head, at least. You took quite a blow. And I have something else to do, something important."

We retrieved our bags. Tali's staff and knives were gone, as was my own knife. I cleaned and bandaged Tali's wound, saying little. My mind was full of what I had done; full of the death I had delivered. I had called out that being to perform acts of violence. Cause or no cause, it felt wrong.

While Tali packed up, I set out an offering of waybread on a flat stone and spoke words of respect and greeting to the unseen inhabitants of this place. I added a prayer for the men who had died or been forever changed here. They had performed their own act of violence. But, like the Enforcers who had fallen in last autumn's battle, they had been sons, fathers, brothers, husbands. Someone would mourn their loss; someone had loved them.

I was bone-weary; the use of my gift seemed to weaken me. But there was no time to rest. We made our way upstream and found the ford, a broad, shallow crossing over small stones, the water babbling cheerfully along, only a finger-length deep. Washed up on the bank was a long, cloth-wrapped bundle.

We approached with caution. The thing was too small for a body.

"That's a cloak," Tali said. "One of those fellows was wearing it."

She was right. The sodden cloak still bore a clasp shaped like a battle-ax, perhaps their chieftain's household emblem. Tali unrolled the garment to reveal our missing weaponry, wet but otherwise unharmed. "By all that's holy," Tali muttered. "You have some powerful friends."

A bout of shivering ran through me.

"You're tired," she said, turning a shrewd gaze on me. "I'm sorry, we must keep moving. I don't want to be on Keenan's land a moment longer than necessary. Let's hope the standing stones your friend mentioned are in sight from the top of the hill there. Once we find a safe bolt-hole, we'll camp for the night, make a fire, change our clothes, and get these wretched things dry. As for what happened just now, I don't even want to think about it. Not yet anyway."

I made no argument, though it would have been more comfortable to walk in dry clothing. This was no place to strip off and change. Where one party of hunters had traveled, others might follow.

Tali led off at her usual brisk pace. We splashed across the ford and headed up the hill, where the same subtle signs as before marked the fey path.

"Tell me one thing," I said.

"What?"

"Were you faking weakness back there, hoping to catch those men off guard? You looked on the point of collapse. You have a lump on your head as big as a man's fist. It was streaming blood. I'd have expected you to slow down just a bit."

For a little she did not answer. Then she said, "The pain

132

was real enough. I've taught myself to keep going unless an opponent actually knocks me out cold. That has happened once or twice, but only in practice."

"Really? Who did it?" I could not imagine any of the Shadowfell warriors achieving such a feat.

"Regan," she said. "My brother. Once each. A while back; they couldn't do it now. Andra came close once. It wasn't all pretense, Neryn. Those men caught me off guard, and I wasn't quick enough in my defense. I saw the look you gave me, warning me that you were going to try something, and I did exaggerate a little in the hope that I'd get a chance to break free. That thing in the river . . . Whatever I expected, it surely wasn't that. You called it, didn't you?"

"It was the only thing I could do to save us." We scrambled up a tricky section of path, and for a while all my breath was needed for the climb. When we reached a patch of level ground, I added, "When I told Regan I didn't want to use my gift yet, it was the truth. I'm not used to killing. I probably never will get used to it, even though I know we're fighting a war and it has to happen. And there's another thing. Every time I use my gift, every time I harness the support of the Good Folk, there's a risk that someone will see and take the story back to the Enforcers and to the king. I might draw them straight to us."

"I did tell you to stay out of it if we got into a fight."

I held back the obvious comment.

"But if you had," Tali said it for me, "we'd both be dead. So I owe you."

"The way I see it, we're on the road together and we help each other."

"Mm," she grunted, and continued to climb, long legs steady and sure on the track. I hitched up my wet skirt and followed.

That night we roasted a skinny rabbit in the coals and ate better than we had for a while. We sat in a silence that, if not quite amicable, felt less strained than before. Our damp garments dripped and steamed on the bushes around the fire.

"You think we're over Keenan's border now we've passed the standing stones?" I asked her, more to fill the silence than anything else.

Tali spat a small bone into the fire. "As far as I can tell. Tomorrow we'll be heading south, toward the lochs. More folk around; more need for caution. But you must know that already—you must have come over from Darkwater by the same track, or one very close."

"Mm."

She turned her perceptive gaze on me. In the firelight, her eyes were touched with points of gold light. "Still weighed down by conscience? Even though what you did saved both our lives? Neryn, the rebellion depends on your gift. Without you, there's no chance we can do it in the time we have. You need to put these scruples behind you; if you can't, they'll become a burden too heavy for you to carry."

"It would be bad enough if I were the one sticking the

knife in or drowning people. It's even worse if I make one of the Good Folk do it for me. I know you're a fighter and accustomed to killing. But wouldn't you feel bad if you made an innocent person kill someone else?"

"Neryn, that thing at the river, that water creature—it certainly didn't strike me as in any way reluctant to help you. Nor did your alarming friend Hollow. And didn't you hear what the river creature said at the end?"

"Go. Learn. Lead."

"Exactly. It knew who you were. It knew what your mission was. It wished you good luck with it. There was a moment earlier on when I wondered if we'd end up drowned too, purely by accident. Still, we could have swum to the bank and climbed out."

I did not reply.

"Don't tell me you can't swim."

"Not much." After a moment I said, "Not at all, really. I'll try not to fall out of the boat when we cross over to the isles."

"Wonderful." She wiped her greasy fingers on her skirt. "I'll have to hope the sea beasties of the west are as favorably disposed toward you as the river creatures seem to be."

Soon afterward we rolled into our blankets and lay down beside the dying fire. We were camped in woods, under the shelter of a stone outcrop. It was a still, clear night, winter-cold. Above us stars pricked out a brilliant pattern on the dark sky. The moon waxed pearly white.

I was still pondering the extraordinary events of the day. "What was it made you want to stay clear of Wedderburn?"

I asked. "When Hollow asked about it, you said something about old history."

"It's complicated." Tali's face was somber in the firelight. "There are several reasons for steering clear, even though Wedderburn is strategically placed. Regan made the right choice when he went south instead."

"What reasons?"

"Nothing that need concern you." She rolled over, her back to me. "Go to sleep. Long walk tomorrow."

We moved on. Closer to the lochs, the hillsides were more densely forested. With every passing day, oak, beech, and ash put on fresh leaves, welcoming the new season. Here the snow was only a memory. Flowers lifted bright heads above a rich carpet of last autumn's fallen leaves. Birds chirped, busying themselves with nest building.

Spring rain fell often, swelling the streams and slowing our progress, though we pressed on in all weathers. The waybread was finished. But with the season advancing, mushrooms, wild greens, and roots could be found in the woods. We caught fish in the lochans and set snares for rabbits.

There came a morning when we climbed to a vantage point and saw the shining expanse of a broad loch to the southeast, nestled among forested hills. Hollow's wee path had allowed us to bypass Deepwater altogether.

"We'll be close to the road by nightfall," Tali said. "And walking on it in the morning. It'll be busy. Keldec will have substantial forces back at Summerfort by now. They'll be moving to and fro, and so will ordinary folk. For us, ordinary folk are almost worse than Enforcers."

"They can hardly be worse." When a settlement or household incurred the king's wrath, the Enforcers acted without mercy. They had no regard for human life or human dignity. I had seen what they could do.

"They're harder to read. An Enforcer makes no secret of his loyalty. He acts as you'd expect a king's man to act. A farmer or fisherman might be anything. Friend or enemy. Helpful or treacherous. Terrified or prepared to take a risk. We'd best practice our story before we go down there."

"Don't forget to wear your kerchief, and keep your sleeves rolled down. Those men at the river noticed your tattoos."

Tali ran her hands through her dark locks, which were cropped to finger-length, making her stand out from a crowd even without the body markings and proud carriage. "And hide my weapons again, yes? Just as well a fighting staff can double as a walking stick or I'd have to disobey Regan's orders."

This remark made me curious. "So you usually obey them?" I asked. "You seem so strong in your own opinions, I thought . . ."

"I'm a fighter. Regan's a leader." She turned and headed down the hill. I scrambled after her. "In a war, you obey your leader," she said, still striding ahead. "If you don't, everything falls apart."

There was a reservation in her voice. I took a risk. "But?"

"It can be hard to set aside the past. You must know that as well as any of us. I've done it. Fingal's done it. Flint's done it. Regan . . . He struggles with it sometimes. If he has any weak spot, it's that."

"I know something happened to Regan. Or to his family. Flint told me once that it gave him good reason for what he's doing now."

Tali looked over her shoulder. Her expression was somber. "More than enough reason, Neryn. But that story's his to tell."

"I understand."

"Another man might have taken vengeance in blood and fire, or made an end of himself. Regan is stronger than that. There's a light shining in him, moving him forward: the light of freedom. That's what draws all of us to follow, to take risks, to keep on fighting when we see our comrades fall beside us. But there's no light without shadow."

Our path came out at the edge of the woods; we looked down on the road linking Deepwater to Hiddenwater, the smallest in the chain of lochs. For a while we stayed in the shelter of the trees, assessing what movement there was: carts, riders, people on foot herding stock. A group of Enforcers swept along the way. Folk scattered before the drumming of their horses' hooves. The Cull was not until autumn, but that would not stop the king's men from breaking down doors and putting the disloyal or the canny to the sword. Out of sheer terror, ordinary folk would lie about their neighbors. To protect his own skin or that of a wife or child, brother would denounce brother. I wondered if Keldec had kept Flint close by him this spring, perhaps ordering him to stay at Winterfort until the court moved west in time for the midsummer Gathering. For more nights than I could count, I had not dreamed of him. Wherever he was, I hoped he was safe.

We camped one last night in the woods, without a fire. When morning came, we packed up, rehearsing our story in whispers. Tali was Luda, I was Calla, the name I had used before when on the run. Not sisters; with one of us tall, dark, and athletic and the other slight and fair, that seemed likely to give rise to questions. We were friends and neighbors from a settlement called Stonyrigg, in the western isles, and we were returning home after a visit to Luda's sister, who had wed a man from the north. The distances involved were farther than most ordinary people would dream of traveling for such a purpose, but the story should be good enough to get us to Pentishead and, with luck, over to the isles. That was if folk did not notice how ill Tali's upright carriage, authoritative manner, and snapping dark eyes sat with her drab working-woman's clothing.

For me, it was easier to go unnoticed, provided I did not betray my canny gift. I was neither exceptionally tall nor unusually short. As far as I knew, I was neither strikingly beautiful nor startlingly ugly. In my ordinary attire, with my walking staff and small pack, I could be any traveler. I had a knife, yes, but so did most folk. A person had to be able to make fire. She had to have some means of defending herself on the road. As for my footwear, my old shoes with their delicate stitchery had been left at Shadowfell. Now I wore a pair of sturdy walking boots. My hair, which when newly washed was honey-colored, was tightly plaited and pinned up under a kerchief similar to Tali's. A bracing dip in a stream was the closest we'd come to bathing since we left Shadowfell; if folk noticed anything, it would probably be the way I smelled.

"What are you smiling at?"

"Not at you, I promise. I was thinking about how filthy I am and wondering how long it'll be before I next have a hot bath. I doubt the Hag of the Isles lives in a place with such luxuries."

"There's always the sea," Tali said. "A nice cold bath. You could play with the seals. That's if I succeed in teaching you to swim."

"Let's cross that bridge when we get to it. Shall we move on?"

There was a series of difficult firsts: the first day's walking down on the road; the first time we exchanged wary nods with other travelers; the first night spent at a wayside inn, where a few coppers bought us a bowl of watery porridge and a flea-ridden pallet. We'd wanted to avoid such places, which were collecting points for gossip and rumor, but sudden heavy rain cut our day's walk short and gave us no other option for shelter. We spoke as little as possible and headed for bed soon after our meager supper. Over the meal we heard talk of new arrivals at Summerfort, a troop of Enforcers, maybe two troops. There was speculation as to when they would ride out and which direction they would take. Last autumn's Cull had been thorough; only the western isles had been entirely spared. That did not make folk safe from unexpected visits, from fists pounding on doors and masked men asking hard questions. If the king's men didn't like the answers they got, people were apt to find themselves strung up or worse.

We left the inn soon after dawn, heading west toward Hiddenwater.

Early-morning light touched the guard tower at Summerfort, where Owen Swift-Sword stood alone. To the south lay the expanse of Deepwater, lustrous as a dark pearl. Close at hand the Rush branched as it flowed into the loch. Behind him, to the north, lay the mist-shrouded peaks of the Three Hags. Beyond was the way to Shadowfell.

The creak of footsteps on the ladder. "Owen? You up there?"

He reached out, grasped his comrade's hand, hauled him up to the platform. The two stood side by side awhile, looking out, not talking. To the west, wooded hills, the lakeshore winding away, the road to the isles. To the east, below the tower, the practice area, where already twelve men of Stag Troop were engaged in an early-morning drill. Beyond, the way to Winterfort and Keldec's court.

Rohan Death-Blade cleared his throat. Glanced toward the ladder. Down in the practice area, the men had set up targets for archery. "They're ready," he said. "We can be on the road as soon as you give the word."

"Mm." His troop leader's gaze did not move from the practice area.

"Some advantage in moving before Bull Troop gets here. You saw how the fellows clashed at Winterfort."

Owen nodded, but made no comment.

"About the target in the isles," Rohan said, dropping his voice to a murmur. He moved to the ladder, took a look down, returned to the parapet once more. "You know that job's best covered by a man on his own. Two at most. Sail over with more than that and the quarry will have gone to ground before anyone sets foot on shore."

Things unspoken lay heavy between them.

"Islanders are stubborn folk," said Rohan. "Could be a lengthy process getting information out of them. Lengthy and untidy. One man, covert operation, quick strike—in my opinion, it's the only way to do the job."

"You volunteering?"

"You must be joking." Rohan grimaced. "Have you ever seen me get on a boat if I can avoid it? We could split the troop, send Tallis north with one team while I take the other south. Regroup when the targets are all accounted for."

Down below, Tallis's arrow flew straight to the distant mark. A small chorus of congratulation broke out.

They stood watching a while longer. If there was an obvious omission in Rohan's strategy, neither spoke of it.

"It's a sound plan," said Owen Swift-Sword levelly. "Call the men together after breakfast and we'll tell them."

Before dawn we headed down to the road. It was too early for folk herding stock or driving carts to market. With luck it would be too early for Enforcers. We walked in silence, each keeping her thoughts to herself. I had dreamed of Flint, and that was enough to keep me quiet. He'd been at Summerfort, watching his men as they trained in the yard. Talking to another Enforcer. His blunt features, so dear to me, had borne an abstracted expression; his gray eyes had been troubled. What the two had spoken of there was no telling. Whether it meant Flint was at Summerfort now, or whether the dream was created by my longing for him to be close, I could not say. But something of my feelings must have shown on my face, for I caught Tali looking at me from time to time, eyes shrewdly assessing.

As the road approached Hiddenwater, it wound between barren, stony slopes. The small loch lay in a deep bowl, sheer rock walls almost encircling it. The water was pearly gray under a sky of vaporous clouds. Here and there a hint of the dawn to come brightened the stark stones. The wind was from the west, an eerie whistling along the lonely track.

"Hear the ghosts," I murmured.

Tali looked at me as if I were touched in the wits. "The story of this place is well known, of course: an ancient battle with many fallen. But what folk hear as they pass through is only the wind."

"You're wrong. Warrior-ghosts haunt this place; the sound is their voices, crying out."

"Nonsense, Neryn. How can you know that?"

"I know because when I came the other way, I saw them." It had been a momentous encounter. A turning point in my life.

Tali made no comment, but something had changed in her expression.

"Walk quietly," I said. "If anyone can catch sight of them, surely it's you."

"I'm carrying iron."

"These are warrior-spirits, the ghosts of the dead, not Good Folk. If they want to come out, iron won't stop them."

We were halfway around the narrow path that skirted the loch when we heard the marching of their feet behind us, soft but regular, then a voice whispering *Halt*. Tali whirled, staff up in defensive mode. I turned more slowly.

They stood in a neat double line, eyes bright in their skull-like faces. Their warrior garments were rent and stained, their boots cracked and broken. Some wore helms of leather, some were bare-headed, their hair ragged, their beards wild. Here and there an ugly wound split a skull or left a limb hanging crooked and useless. One young fighter had a great hollow in his chest, as if an ax had cloven his body nearly in half. From somewhere down the line came a faint skirl of pipes and the *rat-tat* of a ghostly drum.

Tali stood frozen by my side, her staff gripped in both hands.

"We greet you, warriors of Hiddenwater," I said, doing my best to look like the fighter they had once asked me to become. "How do you fare?"

Well enough, Caller. The answer came from everywhere and nowhere. *What news?*

"You bade me fight. I am preparing for that fight. Others too. My companion here is one of them."

Their eyes went to Tali. To her credit, she met that hungry gaze with confidence.

144

"Brothers, I salute you," she said, and to my astonishment I heard a tremor in her voice. Not fear; she was afraid of nothing. "What mighty battle brought you to this sad extreme?"

They gathered closer, breaking their formation to encircle us on the path. A chorus of whispers told the tale: *We were camped yonder, under the trees that once grew in this vale. Conal's men came down on us by night, as we slept. Broke the ancient truce. Blood on the stones. We fought hard. We fought long. We fell.*

"What was the ancient truce?" Now it was Tali who seemed hungry; her hands were white-knuckled on the staff.

A sigh ran through the spectral troop. *Yonder lies Corriedale,* the whispers told us, and several hands pointed roughly north. *And yonder Ravensburn, our own place.* They pointed south. *The truce let men of each holding use this track from seeding to harvest; from lambing to the autumn culling of stock. Our chieftains were long at war, but folk must have a livelihood. Conal broke the truce. His men set a stain on their honor that night. They left us dying in our blood, and they bore away our chieftain.*

"Ultan of Ravensburn," breathed Tali. "They cut off his head and set it up on the parapet of Conal's stronghold at Corriedale for folk to throw stones at. The tale goes that for many nights the moon in those parts showed blood-red, and Ultan's head could be heard crying out, 'Shame! Shame!'"

The spectral host had fallen utterly silent. I too had nothing to say. Tali's response had astonished me.

145

Roll up your sleeves. One voice, every voice.

Tali passed me her staff, then obeyed the request, revealing the elaborate tattoos that circled her arms from wrist to shoulder, chains and swirls and flying birds. She took off her kerchief and pulled down the collar of her shirt to show the row of birds around her neck.

A wordless whispering of excitement broke out among the warriors, a restless vibration that made my heart thump. A tall, lean fellow walked forward through the crowd; the others fell back to let him pass. In life, he might have been handsome. He carried himself straight. His hair was long and dark; his tattered clothing had once been that of a leader. As he approached, he rolled up his ragged sleeves, and on the pallid flesh of his arm were inked chains and swirls and flying birds. *You are one of us,* the ghost said, and *One of us,* echoed the others. *Ultan's heir,* breathed the ghost. *A warrior.*

"I am a warrior," Tali said, "but I am not Ultan's heir, and neither is my brother. Ravensburn fell to our enemy long ago; it is lost to us. But we are of Ultan's blood, and we are still fighting. Not for a single territory or a single stronghold. We pursue a far greater cause. We seek freedom for all Alban. Freedom from tyranny, freedom from terror, freedom to build our land anew. No doubt men of Corriedale died here that night, along with the heroes of Ravensburn; there must have been bitter losses on both sides, for I see you fought long and hard. Corriedale's fallen were treated more kindly after death, I imagine. But they were no less dead for that. In our war, old enemies will fight, not against each other, but side by side." She paused. The tattooed man had reached out tentative fingers toward her neck, where the dark birds of Ravensburn followed their straight, unswerving path. "You are my kinsman," Tali said, and I saw to my astonishment that tears were running down her cheeks. "My ancestor."

Ultan was my father. In the harsh, faint ghost voice I heard a fierce pride. *My name was . . .* The warrior hesitated, as if reaching for something almost fled. *My name was Fingal.*

"I am descended from your daughter," Tali said. "My brother is named for you. So we keep your memory alive and honor your courage. Our land may be lost, but the blood of Ravensburn flows strong and true. Know that, my kinsman." She reached up a hand to dash the tears from her cheeks, and I saw in that gesture the same pride I had seen in the ghostly warrior.

"It's almost day," I said. When I had encountered these spirits before, they had vanished with the first rays of the sun. "We must say our farewells and move on."

Keep her safe, Fingal said. *Keep the Caller safe. That is your mission. She carries the flame. Guard her with your life. Farewell, daughter of my daughter.*

"Father of my father, farewell." Tali was fighting to keep her voice steady.

"Farewell, warriors of the west," I said. "I have not forgotten what you taught me. Weapons sharp; backs straight; hearts high."

Weapons sharp; backs straight; hearts high. Farewell. . . . And they were gone.

Beyond Hiddenwater lay a broad area of farmland, a place I had crossed by night coming the other way, ducking from one sheltered spot to the next with my heart in my mouth. Tali had decided we would go straight on, since the alternative—hiding up on the hillside until dusk—would lose us a whole day's walking. Once past the farmland we would be on the wooded shores of the next loch, Silver-water, and could go on under reasonable cover.

I asked no questions, and she held her silence. What had struck me most strongly was the way the spectral warriors had shared their story with her, as if she were one of them. And it seemed she was: theirs by blood and theirs by calling, a warrior of Ravensburn. When I had first encountered the ghostly comrades, last autumn, I had thought the past all but forgotten for them. Perhaps, when they had bidden me sing the song of truth, that ancient anthem had woken their memory. Or perhaps the spark had been Tali herself, a vibrant, passionate warrior as they had once been, a fighter who wore the clan patterns by which they had lived and died. *Guard the Caller,* they had said. They knew what I was. They knew what I could be.

There were folk about on the farms, letting chickens out to forage, hanging clothing on a line, forking a dung heap. A tired-looking horse pulled a cart laden with lumpy sacks. A girl with a dog herded sheep from one walled field to another. We kept our heads down and walked on by. Not far to the shelter of that wooded hillside. I imagined Sage and Red Cap up there somewhere, looking out and exchanging wry comments as they watched our progress. Judging by what Hollow had said, word of the mission was spreading fast among their kind.

"You! On the road!"

I snapped out of my reverie. Tali's hand moved to her concealed knife, but she did not complete the movement. We halted, and Tali leaned on her staff.

A man had come to the edge of the nearby field and was examining us over the drystone wall. He was a burly individual with a pitchfork over his shoulder. At the far side of the field a younger man stood watching, a similar implement propped against the wall beside him. The field smelled of pigs, though no pigs were in sight, only a ramshackle sty.

"Fine day," Tali observed in neutral tones.

"Where are you headed?"

My skin prickled. Nobody asked this kind of question anymore. Nobody shared information with folk they did not know.

"West," Tali said.

The man grinned, showing blackened teeth. "Any fool can see that. How far west?"

"Home. The isles. Long way; we'd best get on. Good day to you." Tali lifted her staff.

The man's gaze sharpened; his companion strolled over to stand beside him.

"The isles, is it?" the first man said, and something in his tone warned me that our prepared story might not be good enough here. "Which part are you from, then?"

I spoke before Tali could mention Stonyrigg. "You

wouldn't know the place; it's small. I'm hoping to see my brother before we cross over. We heard he might be riding out from Summerfort soon, heading this way." I paused for effect, then added in what I hoped was a convincing tone of pride, "He's with Stag Troop."

"Best be moving on, Calla," Tali said. "The morning's passing and it's a long walk."

Neither man said another word. Indeed, they might have been frozen where they stood.

"Good day to you," I said politely, and we walked on, doing our best to keep a steady, relaxed pace.

It was only when we had crossed the last of the farms and were making our way up the hillside into the sheltering woods on the far side that Tali spoke. "Black Crow save us! What happened to Stonyrigg?"

"He sounded as if he knew the isles. I thought he might say *No such place*. With two of them, and two pitchforks, I didn't fancy the odds, not to speak of the tales people might tell afterward even if we did get away."

"A couple of farmers with pitchforks are no match for me, Neryn. But I see the point." She paused to help me up a steep stretch of hillside. "Your brother, an Enforcer. Great story for shutting people up, true. But what happens if Stag Troop rides by and the fellow happens to mention that Calla was asking after her brother?"

"What farmer in his right mind would go up to an Enforcer and talk to him about his sister?"

"True." We stood atop the rise to catch our breath. From here we had a fine view back over the patchwork of walled fields to the rocky hills around Hiddenwater. I could not pick out which field was the one where the men had been working, but Tali shaded her eyes against the sun, and said, "The two of them are still there, forking soiled straw out of the pigsty. Good sign; nobody went running to share the news that two disreputable-looking women were on the road." She set down her pack and reached for her waterskin, glancing at me. "Sit down awhile, Neryn."

"I'm fine." The response was automatic; I worked hard every day to keep up with her. But it was not true.

"Sit down. That's an order." She passed me the waterskin and watched my hands shake as I took it. Under her assessing gaze, I subsided onto the rocks.

"I'll be fine soon. Sorry."

"You're white as chalk. Are you hurt?"

I shook my head. "I'm all right. Those men, talking to them, it brought back some bad memories, that's all. Last time someone asked questions like that I ended up tied to a post, wrapped in iron chains, waiting for an Enforcer to come and take me away. I thought I'd gone past that, but clearly not. I'm sorry."

"No rush to move on. We're in good cover here." Tali fished out her packet of food and passed me a wedge of dry bread. A few coppers had obtained us supplies from the inn.

"I'm fine, Tali, I can go on."

"Eat. It'll help. And stop saying you're sorry. You showed presence of mind down there. Gave me a bit of a fright, but you were probably right to change the story.

The farther west we go, the more likely it is that people will know the isles." She took a chunk of bread for herself. "This stuff is as hard as stone. We'll soon be able to dispatch enemies with our teeth." She dribbled water from the skin onto the dried-out crust. "Maybe I can go fishing while this Hag of yours gives you lessons in spellcraft. Our diet could surely do with improvement."

CHAPTER SIX

WE CAMPED IN THE WOODS ABOVE SILVERWATER, close to the waterfall known as Maiden's Tears. The fall gushed like a lovely veil down the hillside, bordered by lush ferns and mossy rocks. The pool at the top was full of fish, and we caught enough for two days' meals. We had made excellent time, reaching the place well before dusk.

While Tali scaled and gutted the catch, I went off to gather firewood. Last autumn's storms had brought down plenty of useful sticks and branches. I was making my way back to the camping spot with a load when I heard a noise that sent my heart leaping into my mouth. Hooves drummed on the road down the hill, signaling the approach of a large number of riders. I froze in place, waiting for them to pass.

Someone shouted and the hoofbeats ceased. They had stopped at the foot of the hill. Many horses. Many men.

What now? Creep back to Tali, then head farther up into the woods, or keep still and hope they would move on soon? Perhaps they had only stopped to adjust a load or water their horses, for the stream must flow across the track somewhere down there, perhaps as a shallow ford. But Tali might not have heard them. She might come looking for me. What if she made a noise, called out?

I laid down my load of wood as carefully as I might a clutch of new-laid eggs. Just above me was a rocky outcrop. I went straight up, placing my feet with unusual care. *Climb like a marten,* I told myself. *Not a sound.*

At the top I went down on my belly and wriggled forward. No sense in finding a vantage point if all it achieved was to reveal my presence to someone below. I looked down over the wooded hillside. Much of the road was obscured by foliage, but through a gap I glimpsed a flat area beside the track, a number of big black horses, riders in dark cloaks dismounting. Enforcers. How many I could not count, for they moved in and out of view. Many. Perhaps a whole troop. Packs were lifted down, bedrolls unstrapped, horses led out of sight. It looked as if they were camping for the night.

Tali met me halfway back to the pool. Her expression told me she too had heard them. We held a rapid conversation in glances and gestures. *Packs, staves, waterskins, knives. The fish? In my bag. The rubbish? Buried. Keep quiet. Up the hill, fast as you can. You all right? Yes, you? Mm-hm. Go.*

We climbed far above the pool, to an area dense with bramble-netted rocks, a place a traveler would enter only if she were stupid or desperate. From up here, we heard no sound of horses or men. The lakeshore below us was hidden by the trees; there was no way of knowing if the troop was seated comfortably at the bottom by a campfire or spread out on the hillside tracking us. The light was fading fast.

"A bit higher," Tali whispered. "Up there near the ridge, see? Pick up the pace, I want to be under cover of those rocks before dark."

I gritted my teeth and moved on after her. The brambles had etched their own bloody tattoos on the skin of my arms. There was a jagged rent in my cloak. My feet hurt. What upset me most of all, foolishly, was that there would be no fire and therefore no fish tonight. Not for us, anyway.

By the time we reached the outcrop, I was stumbling, unable to see my way. Tali did not have the same difficulty.

"Over here, Neryn." Even so far above the loch shore, she kept her voice to a murmur.

There was a slight overhang and beneath it a hollow, comfortable enough provided the weather stayed dry. We settled there.

"I was looking forward to that fish," Tali said, getting out the remains of her dried-out bread. "But not enough to eat it raw."

"Do you think they were after us? Because of what I said to that man on the farm?"

"I doubt it. If they'd been tracking us, they'd have had men up in the woods, not riding on the road. Besides, you may be of interest to the king, but he's hardly going to send a whole troop of Enforcers thundering after you."

I said nothing. From the moment I'd spotted the troop,

I'd been imagining Flint among them, at the bottom of this very hill. So close. My longing to see him was an ache in my chest. Foolish. There was no good reason to think this was Stag Troop, save for that dream of him at Summerfort.

"At least we know where they are and that they're heading west," Tali said. "Be glad it's not culling time. Be glad they got there before we made a fire, not after, or they'd have been up the hill in a flash to see who was out wandering so late in the day." She sat in silence awhile, then added, "They'll be on the road ahead of us. Well ahead, since we're on foot."

I said nothing.

"They could be going to Pentishead. If they take that road, we may need to change the plan. Go up the coast to Darkwater and find a boat there."

Go to the place where I had watched the Enforcers sweep in for the Cull. Where I had seen my father burned to death. "The Northies did give us precise directions. That included heading out from Pentishead."

"Maybe so, but I know where Ronan's Isle is; I can find it from anywhere on that stretch of coast. The Northies would hardly expect us to walk into Pentishead if it was full of Enforcers."

Darkwater. The prospect made my insides shrivel up. It drained away all my courage.

"Neryn? Do you understand?"

In a war, you obey your leader. "I understand."

Lying awake in the encampment, Owen Swift-Sword thought of Shadow. Many times he had regretted leaving her behind, though she was in good enough hands. It wasn't easy to

156

conceal such a horse, all sleek, high-bred lines and muscular strength. You couldn't put a beast like that out to graze with mountain ponies, unless you lived so far from the tracks of men that there'd likely be no grazing beyond lichens and mosses. She was far away; there seemed no chance she would be his again, unless the whole of Alban changed.

Now he had Lightning, one of the horses that had found their way back to Summerfort after the cataclysmic rockfall in which the men of Boar Troop had perished, high in the mountains, while pursuing erroneous rumors of rebel activity. An accident. A disastrous accident. Only one survivor: himself. At least, that was the story he had told, the one Keldec had chosen to believe. He wondered, sometimes, if the king was lonely. Perhaps Keldec had accepted his unlikely account rather than lose a man he regarded as a friend. He had so few friends.

Boar Troop had left their horses by the stream, hobbled, before they'd entered the rocky area where Regan's forces had ambushed them. Coming back down, alone, he'd set the animals free. There had been no other choice. One or two of them had kept pace with him as he walked along the valley, until he'd gone up to the high track to lose them. Riding an Enforcer mount back to Summerfort had not been part of his plan.

Not all the horses had found their way home. Some had probably perished in the highland winter; some might have been taken in by farmers, though most folk would see the peril in this. Among farm horses, an Enforcer's mount would stand out like a fine-bred hunting hound among scruffy terriers. And nobody wanted to face the penalty for stealing what was, essentially, the king's property.

Lightning, easily recognized by a small white blaze on his otherwise night-black coat, had belonged to Gusan. Now, as Owen lay among his sleeping comrades, the image in his mind was not of the dark sky above, spangled with stars, nor of the slumbering forms of the others, their bellies comfortably full after a supper of freshly caught fish. It was of Gusan lying dead on the battlefield, his leather breast-piece split open by the mighty blow of Tali's ax. His eyes blank. His face like pale parchment. The wreckage of his body, and the crimson pool beneath, fast-spreading.

There was no escaping it. He had led them there. He had led them to their deaths; he had swung his sword in support of Regan's Rebels in the battle. And now here he was, heading west on the king's mission with another troop of comrades around him, men who trusted him, men who believed in him. And if there was need, he would do it all again. What kind of man did that make him?

From the woods above their camping place came a high shriek of pain, abruptly cut off. Something hunting. Something dying. *A man unworthy of friendship,* he thought. *A man unworthy of love.* He closed his eyes, willing himself not to think of Neryn.

As we went farther west, the terrain became steep and rocky, the forested glens giving way to a far starker landscape, in which great seams and crevices split the stone like the marks of a giant's ax, and the air smelled of the sea.

The plan was to come as close to Pentishead settlement

as we could while staying off the main track. If the king's men were there, we would retreat and head north. If there was no sign of them, we'd risk going down to the bay and asking for a lift over to the isles. There would be fishing boats going in and out every day, if the weather stayed fair. With luck, someone would be prepared to take us.

It was a long walk, and a difficult one. Traveling alone, I'd have been much slower. But Tali found paths where it seemed no paths existed. Her tireless determination pushed me farther than I had believed I could go. Only once, as we lay beside yet another meager fire in yet another windswept corrie, she said, "Aren't you tempted to ask the Good Folk for help when you get cold and hungry or when it just seems too far to walk? That thing at the ford did exactly what you needed it to do. And I imagine there might be similar creatures everywhere we go. I've noticed how you put offerings out for them each morning before we move on. You could make things much easier, couldn't you? You could call out some flying creature to transport us over to the isles right now with no need to worry about Enforcers. You could ask your uncanny friends to provide better shelter, a hot meal, all sorts of things. But you don't."

"Until I find the Hag, I'm like a blind person feeling a way forward. The gift is so powerful. It's frightening. It would be wrong to use it for convenience—if we're hungry, for instance, or if we want to get somewhere more quickly. It should be saved for the times when it's the only solution. When it makes the difference between life and death. If I hadn't called the river being, we'd both have been killed."

"That creature had to be there to be called," Tali said.

"Did you know it was in the water? What if there hadn't been any uncanny folk in that place?"

"I felt them. I knew they were close. As they are here, all around us." I glanced across the windswept hillside, a place of tumbled rocks, gorse, thistles. Lichens, yellow, white, purple, crept with gentle insistence over the stone, softening the gray. "In the rocks. In the earth. Everywhere."

"But they don't come out as you say they did when you were traveling alone," Tali observed. "They don't visit our campfire and stay for a wee chat."

"If you wrapped up your knives, they might."

"Ha! Out here in the open, with just the two of us, it'd be foolish to take such a risk. With Enforcers in the district, doubly so. Neryn?"

"Mm?"

"Why are some of the Good Folk afraid of iron, when others aren't troubled by it? When that thing came up out of the river, there were weapons everywhere, not only mine but those men's as well. And afterward, someone took the trouble to wrap up our knives and deposit them where we'd find them."

"That's a question for the Guardians," I said. "I hope the Hag of the Isles will have some answers."

"You may be seeing her quite soon," Tali said. "We should reach Pentishead tomorrow."

"Then let's hope there's no sign of Enforcers, and we find a nice little boat and a cooperative boatman to sail us across," I said, attempting to be cheerful.

"More likely we'll have to trust to some leaky craft too unseaworthy to be of value to the local fishermen. And row it ourselves."

I hoped very much that she was joking.

The sun was in the west as we climbed the last rise next day, and the air above us was alive with wheeling gulls. I could hear the great, restless wash of the waves. We came to the top, and there before us was the sea, deep blue-gray and dotted with whitecaps. The isles lay in that vast expanse like a pod of strange sea creatures, some near at hand, some losing themselves in mysterious veils of mist. A larger island, closest to the coastline, had a settlement of low stone-and-thatch dwellings. On the sloping pasture-land behind it grazed hardy sheep. I could see a jetty and a row of boats pulled up on the shore beside it.

Immediately below us lay Pentishead settlement, a straggle of cottages and small jetties fringing the bay, with the main track coming in around the shore. It wouldn't be easy to get down there; we'd be descending what amounted to a cliff path, and the rock looked broken and crumbling. To attempt it under cover of darkness would be inviting a long, damaging fall.

"I'm going along there to get a clearer view," Tali said, indicating a place where the hilltop rose to a cluster of high rocks. "Stay here and keep still."

I moved back and sat down in a place I judged to be reasonably well concealed. I made myself recall the Northies' strange map of the isles and the path they'd bidden us follow. The wee boat had passed south of that bigger island, the one closest to shore. It had threaded a course between many other isles, until the tiny Twayblade had made landfall on Ronan's Isle, far to the west. The Northies' map had shown at least one islet beyond it; I recalled it as high and flat-topped with towering cliffs all around, a place likely inhabited only by gannets.

When Twayblade had enacted the voyage in the safety of Shadowfell's dining area, it had looked peaceful. The ocean out there, stirred by a bracing westerly, was a different matter. Tali couldn't really be expecting me to row, could she? I was much stronger than I had been, but that looked . . . *Don't say it. Don't say it's impossible.*

The wind gusted; out of nowhere, something flew straight at me. I flinched, throwing my arms up to protect my face.

"Kaaa." The visitor made a neat landing by my feet. I breathed again. Only a gull. It did not seem alarmed by my presence, but stood with its head cocked to one side, examining me with its curiously ringed eye. "Message for ye," it said.

Not a gull, then. I looked more closely. If this was one of the Good Folk, its disguise was utterly convincing. The beak, the feathers, the spindly bird legs— Oh. Like the white owl I had encountered in the north, this creature wore little boots on its feet. And now that I looked at its head again, I could see an awareness in its expression that was not at all birdlike.

I scrambled to collect myself. "A message? What message?"

"Tomorrow. Before sunup. North cove, by the auld jetty."

My skin prickled. "Who gave you this message?"

The bird turned its head the other way. "Kaaa!" it remarked, then lifted its wings and was gone.

I worked on slowing my racing heart. What did this mean, that Tali's suggestion had proved prophetic, and that the Good Folk would take us over to the isles? Had Sage and Red Cap spread the word about the rebellion so effectively that it had reached the far west before us? Surely that was impossible.

Could this be a trap? To the best of my knowledge, the Good Folk would not turn against a Caller. I suspected they could not. They might doubt me, but I did not think they would lie to me. Perhaps they had been watching us all the way, tracking our progress but keeping their distance.

Tali was back, crouching down beside me. "No sign of them," she said. "I can't see a camp, or any horses, or a building large enough to house them." Her gaze sharpened. "What?"

"I got a message. From the Good Folk." I told her the details.

"Tomorrow! So soon." Her dark brows drew into a frown. "It makes more sense to keep our distance from the settlement for a few days, at least, so we can be sure the Enforcers are well away. We could get a nasty surprise the moment we step out of cover."

"This may be our best, perhaps our only, chance to get across to the isles," I said. "The Northies showed us the map. They gave us detailed instructions. They seemed to know where the Hag might be found, even though I'd been told that she was in retreat, gone away deep. If we don't go down there at the appointed time, it might be viewed as an insult."

She gazed westward, arms folded, saying nothing.

"The light's fading. We must make a decision. If we're to be at this north cove before dawn, shouldn't we find a place to camp a bit lower down?"

"A pox on it," she muttered. "I don't like this. All right, get your things and let's move down the hill. Not that there'll be much camping. A swig of water, a bite of dried meat, and a night under a bush will be about the sum of it. I don't suppose you noticed a north cove on the wee folk's map, did you?"

"No. But the bay's small enough. If we make our way to the north end, it should be easy to find."

In the gray before dawn we crept down to the settlement. The place was sleeping and the only sound was the murmur of the sea. Yesterday's gusting westerly had died down. A gentle breeze blew in its place. It was a good morning for fishing. Early as it was, folk would soon be about.

Behind one cottage a dog barked, running to and fro at the end of its rope as we passed. I tried to be silent as a ghost, subtle as a shadow. The paths were of crushed shells; we walked on the earth beside them. My heart was beating fast. My staff felt slippery in my hand. When a bird flew over, squawking, I nearly jumped out of my skin.

It was not a big settlement. We reached a track that skirted the waterfront, by the jetties with their moorings for larger boats and the pebbly beach on which the one- or two-man craft were pulled up. The sea looked calmer today, but not so calm that I could easily ignore my churning stomach. Out by the skerries the water rose in white surges; the wind would get up soon enough. Those boats were so small.

Neither of us spoke a word. As we walked by the last cottage, Tali jerked her head toward the north end of the bay. She moved on along the shore path; I followed her. The sky was growing brighter, but I could not see any sign of a second cove. The beach seemed to stretch all the way to the high northern headland.

Tali kept walking. I hoped she could see something I couldn't, for it was almost day, and now that we were out in the open, as soon as someone saw us, we'd have to revert to the old plan and ask if we could pay someone to ferry us over to Ronan's Isle. That would mean explanations, and explanations made things even riskier than they already were.

Before sunup, the messenger had said. We didn't have long. From behind us in the settlement came sounds of activity now, someone opening shutters, the trundle of something on wheels, perhaps a handcart, the dog barking again. A rooster crowing a morning greeting. Another responding in enthusiastic competition.

Tali came to a sudden halt. I stopped behind her, waiting as she scanned the terrain ahead.

She turned to me and nodded. Although I did not know what she had seen, my heart lifted. We moved on more quickly, and after a while I saw a jumble of rocks on the shore where perhaps a stream ran down into the sea, and beyond it a little cove, tucked almost under the looming headland. Still we did not speak, though Tali's walk became a stride.

Along the path, past the rocks, and now I could see it: on the pebbles of the north cove was a boat, small but sturdy, the kind of craft that could go under oars or sail. And someone beside it, a man who was already pushing the boat down to the water, readying it to put to sea. I had exercised perfect control during the walk; I had maintained my silence, following Tali's lead. Now I put my hand over my mouth to stop a cry from bursting out. Never mind the masklike cloth that covered most of his face, the clothing that might have belonged to any fisherman, the lack of a warrior's accoutrements. It was Flint. One look and I knew.

"Shh," warned Tali under her breath as we made our way down to the boat, though the crunch of our boots on the pebbles made nonsense of this. But, then, she did not mean, *Be silent*. She meant, *Keep control of yourself*. This was a mission; my first for Regan's Rebels. I must act like a warrior. I must think the way Tali herself thought. So I spoke no greeting; I held back, not rushing to embrace him as I longed to. His gray eyes met mine over the makeshift mask, wide with astonishment—this was as much of a shock to him as it was to us. I held Tali's staff while she helped him push the boat into the shallows. I waited until he was ready to help me in. I sat quietly in the stern as the two of them loaded the bags, climbed aboard, and took up the oars. The rising joy in my heart, nobody could see.

                    *   *   *

With powerful strokes Tali and Flint rowed the little craft
out from the shore, only shipping their oars when we were
well clear of the breaking waves. Then, with barely a word
exchanged, they hoisted the triangular sail, moving with
perfect balance to tighten and secure the ropes. Flint came
to sit beside me, unfastening a cord that had held the tiller
in a fixed position. The wind carried us on a bobbing, scudding course to the southwest.

   "All right, Neryn?" Tali was as much at ease here as she
was in combat or running up steps; plainly, both she and
Flint were experienced sailors.

   "Mm." The waters were heaving, and I was already feeling queasy. But I kept my eyes on Flint. He had stripped
off his mask as soon as we were well clear of the shore. Had
I forgotten how lined his face was? He looked much older
than his two-and-twenty years. Since I last saw him, something had set a new shadow around his eyes. This was not
a handsome face like Regan's; it was not a face that folk
would remember as striking or unusual. It was the face of
a fighter, the nose crooked, the skin slashed by the lines of
old scars. A plain, strong face. But pleasing to me. His eyes
were of a lovely gray, clear and honest.

   Flint was not a man who smiled often, and he did not
smile now, but the way he looked at me said everything I
needed to know. It was like an embrace. To gaze into his
eyes was to feel my body wake to his. What was between
us had not grown colder with time apart.

                           167

"How in the name of the gods did that happen?" he asked.

"We might ask you the same," said Tali over her shoulder. She'd taken up a position in the bow. "We're headed for Ronan's Isle, following directions the Good Folk gave us. One of them told Neryn to be down in the cove there before dawn today. We were expecting a boat, maybe even a boatman, but most certainly not you. And it seems you didn't expect us. Are you traveling alone? A troop passed us on the shores of Silverwater some days ago. Was that . . . ?"

"You were so close? No wonder my dreams were disturbed that night." Flint frowned. "I came to Pentishead with the troop, but I'm on my own for now. I take it you're seeking out a Guardian, part of Neryn's training."

"The Hag of the Isles, no less."

"I'd thought Regan would send Andra. Who went with him?"

"He decided Tali would be best able to protect me," I said hastily, seeing her expression. "Fingal went with him." We had not spoken of this since we left Shadowfell, but I guessed her mind was often on Regan and whether he would be safe without her.

"And you?" Tali asked Flint. "Are you still on the king's business? Surely Keldec didn't sanction another solitary mission after the losses of last autumn. Though he must have accepted your explanation, or you wouldn't be here at all."

"He accepted the story." There was a heaviness in Flint's voice. "Others were less ready to do so, and have made that known to me indirectly. I'm on thin ice now. As for why

I'm here, Stag Troop has a mission. We split into three; one team went north, another south. The third part of the exercise is me. I meet up with the others when the job is done. I won't give you further details. But . . . it seems possible that I have unexpected support; otherwise, I would not be alone here."

"The Good Folk?" I asked, not sure what he meant.

"No, Neryn. Support from within my troop. I cannot be more specific than that. I could be wrong. I may find myself trapped and betrayed, but it seems one, at least, may have an inkling that I am not what I seem, and may be providing both warnings and assistance."

I thought immediately of the man he had been with in my dream, a fair-haired warrior with an open face. I remembered how that man had glanced over his shoulder as they conducted their intense conversation on the watchtower.

"You'd want to be careful," Tali said, then the boat hit a patch of rough water and the two of them were busy keeping a steady course while I tried hard not to be sick.

When things were back under control, Flint asked me, "Did I hear right earlier? One of the Good Folk told you where and when you'd find me? How could that be?"

"A lot has changed since last autumn," I said. "They are helping us now, spreading the word about the rebellion to their own kind everywhere. The being that brought me the message looked almost exactly like a gull. Perhaps another creature observed your preparations, especially if you got the boat ready yesterday."

"How could they know who I was? That troubles me."

"Sage knows you. Maybe that was enough; I don't know. They promised secrecy."

"Even so."

The nearest island was close now. On the shore, folk were busy, loading nets and supplies, pushing boats into the shallows.

"Flint, how long can you stay with us?" My attempt to sound calm failed miserably. He reached out and put his hand over mine. The warmth of his touch went deep within me, making my breath catch.

"I'll see you safe to Ronan's Isle. But I can only be with you a day or two." He glanced at Tali. "I'll leave the boat with you. She's easy enough to sail single-handed in calm weather. I know folk over there; someone will ferry me back."

As we rounded the southern tip of the island and headed into more open water, the vessel gained speed, scudding over the choppy swell. I clutched the rail, my stomach protesting. Under the deep discomfort of seasickness, a confusion of feelings welled in me. Flint was here, right beside me. His presence was a blessing, a most wondrous surprise. He would soon be gone. But we would have time together on the island. We might steal a precious night together. As for the Hag of the Isles, I could hardly believe I might meet her this very day.

"Look ahead, Neryn," Tali said. "If you keep your eyes on the horizon, you won't feel so sick."

I lifted my head and looked westward. There were so many isles. I had seen them sprinkled on the Northies' magical map, but I had not thought they were so numerous or so varied. Tall, cliff-bounded towers; low-lying rocky skerries; here and there more substantial islands, on which the light of the rising sun showed me settlements and walled fields, stock grazing, threads of smoke rising from hearth fires. There were few trees; the westerly had bent those hardy enough to survive into prostrate surrender. On the sea, numerous vessels were heading out to their favored fishing grounds. Many were similar to our craft; we might perhaps complete our voyage without attracting undue attention. It seemed the community of the isles might be far bigger than I had thought.

The farther west we sailed, the more creatures I saw. Seals basking on the rocks. Something large and sleek just under the water, keeping pace with our boat. Gulls; many gulls, flying above us, beside us, skimming over our wake, alighting atop the mast or on the rim rail to turn their heads and examine us. Their eyes were not as fey as those of yesterday's messenger, but there was something in their gaze that went beyond mere hope of scraps from a fisherman's catch.

"Unusual number of birds," Tali said.

"Mm." I found I was checking their feet. None wore shoes.

"Neryn," Flint said quietly. "Look ahead, there." He pointed westward, indicating a gap between two larger islands. Beyond, I saw only open sea stretching to the end of the world.

"I don't see anything."

"Ronan's Isle. Slightly to the north of our prow."

Black Crow save us! How far out was it? Would we be lurching about on these waters all day?

"In shape it's something like a whale," Tali said. "And there's a flock of birds—see, just over there, flying in an arrowhead shape and heading straight toward it."

Now I saw it, a speck in the ocean, so small I could not really tell if it resembled a whale or a haystack or a pudding bowl. "Oh. It's a long way."

"We'll be there when the sun reaches its peak," Flint said. "It's too far to go under oars, certainly, unless you have the strength of a bear. A place seldom visited."

"You've been there before?" It was, perhaps, another of those questions that should not be asked. He had grown up in the isles; somewhere in this widely scattered realm was the place where he had learned his craft from a wise old tutor. Somewhere too was Regan's childhood home, where he and Flint had become friends. Where something had occurred that had made Regan the leader he was, and set in him a burning will to restore Alban to justice. I had dreamed of Flint here as a small boy. Even then he had looked lonely.

"Not for a while."

"You can make yourself useful, Neryn," Tali said. "Pass us the waterskin, get out some provisions. Not that there's much left. I look forward to some fresh fish."

"I have supplies," Flint said. "In the bag, there."

I did as I was told. Flint's food supply included fresh bread, a luxury Tali and I had not seen for some time. I handed each of them what seemed a reasonable share.

"You should eat, Neryn," Flint said as I packed the rest away.

172

"I'm not hungry." I had thus far managed not to retch out the contents of my belly over the side. I was feeling useless enough without that.

"Best eat." Tali's tone was neutral. "Even if you're sick afterward. A couple of mouthfuls, at least. And make sure you drink some water."

"Is that an order?" I attempted a smile.

"It is. When we reach Ronan's Isle, it's your turn to be leader. Dealing with uncanny beings, especially ancient and powerful ones, is not my strength."

"Here," said Flint, passing me the waterskin. "Drink. Eat. Then keep your gaze forward, to the destination. By midday we'll be on solid ground."

More birds came: not only gulls but terns, gannets, and puffins, a soaring, wheeling banner around our little craft. So much for going unnoticed in these waters. I hoped people would assume we'd taken an especially good catch.

As we traveled on westward, the other craft were left behind. Out here, the islands were farther apart, the skerries more treacherous. The sea grew turbulent, and I soon lost my meager meal over the side. My companions were stern-faced and silent, fully occupied in keeping the boat on a steady course. I tried to fix my eyes on the destination. To take my mind off how wretched I felt, I hummed under my breath the song of truth, the old forbidden anthem I had once sung for the warrior-shades of Hiddenwater, and later for a lonely brollachan. There was a verse in it about the Guardians, its words mysterious but strangely comforting:

White Lady, shield me with your fire;
Lord of the North, my heart inspire;
Hag of the Isles, my secrets keep;
Master of Shadows, guard my sleep.

I had met the Master of Shadows, and he had not been a restful sort of being. If he watched over a person's sleep, it would likely be full of nightmares and sudden, startled wakings. If the same principle held true for the entire verse, perhaps I could expect the Hag to be a gossip and unreliable. Who was there to hear secrets in a lonely place like that isle ahead of us? The Master had a curious little dog. Maybe the Hag liked birds.

Time passed. Ronan's Isle changed from a dot to a blob, and from a blob to a discernible mass of land that was indeed whalelike in shape, high without being unduly steep, and big enough to house a community of sorts. A cluster of huts fringed the near shore, and there were boats drawn up on the shingle, as at Pentishead. Nets hung from poles, drying in the midday sun. A pair of old men sat side by side on a bench gazing out to sea. As Tali and Flint brought our craft in to the shore under oars, they watched us without getting up.

Relief to be on dry land at last did not overwhelm my caution. "What about . . . ?" I murmured, indicating the men with a jerk of the head.

"It's safe here," Flint said.

I could not believe this. Nowhere in all Alban was safe,

save Shadowfell. Where the king did not have eyes and ears, there were always ordinary folk ready to betray their neighbors. "But—"

"It's safe, Neryn." Flint helped me out of the boat and onto the pebbles. I waited while he and Tali hauled the craft up and secured the rope around a stone slab. As we'd reached shore, the birds had risen in a cloud, then winged away across the island. A solitary gull watched us from the rocks nearby. "These folk know me."

We slung on our packs, grasped our staves, walked up the beach. My knees were wobbly; I could not balance. If anything, I felt sicker than I had on the boat. And now here was one of the old men, rising without haste, walking over to take my elbow and guide me to the bench.

"Sit ye doon awhile, lassie, ye're the hue o' fresh cheese. No' a sailor, are ye?"

And while I muttered a thank-you, the other old man said to Flint, "I hardly knew ye, laddie. The winters sit hard on ye." He examined Flint, his blue eyes bright and farseeing in a face seamed by age and weather. "How lang will ye be bidin' in these pairts?"

"A day or two, old friend, no more. I've come only to see Neryn and her guard here safely across." Flint nodded toward Tali, who was standing somewhat apart, scanning the terrain around us as if Enforcers might appear at any moment despite Flint's promises of safety. "I'll be needing a lift back to Pentishead."

"Oh, aye." The tone was measured. I thought it would take a lot to disturb the natural calm of these two islanders.

They seemed like men who had seen many storms come and go, and who had the measure of most folk. But not Flint, I thought. Plainly they knew him. They knew him well. They spoke to him as if he belonged here; he addressed them with the respect due to familiar elders. But if he had once been one of them, surely he was no longer. A king's man. An Enforcer. Worse than that, an Enthraller. Could it be these folk knew nothing of his other life?

"One o' the lads will ferry ye tae the mainland, when 'tis time," the old man said.

"Twa days," commented the other ancient. "'Tisna lang. There's folk will be wantin' to see ye. Three winters, that's a guid while tae be awa'."

Flint made no response to this, but came to crouch down beside me. He took my hands in his. "Where do we go now, Neryn?"

"Take the narrow pathway to the west, over Lanely Muir," I said, quoting Hawkbit. "When we get to the end, we wait."

"The lassie doesna seem fit for a lang walk," observed one of the old men. "'Tis quite a way."

"I'm perfectly fit." I rose to my feet. The ground tilted; I fixed my eyes on a point straight ahead and managed not to fall. "If the boat will be safe here, we should move on." As I spoke, the solitary gull took flight, following the narrow pathway that led from the sheltered bay up the hill before us. This was a place of stone and rough grass; nothing grew higher than my knees.

"Your wee boatie will meet wi' nae harm."

The old men watched us go. Halfway up the hill I

looked over my shoulder. The two of them were back on their bench, gazing out across the water, where a single fishing vessel moved on the swell, a mere speck in the immensity of the sea. Looking back eastward, I saw the humps of the bigger isles, part veiled in sea mist, but I could not see the mainland. It was a strange feeling to be thus cut off from the rest of Alban. Something inside me longed to stay here, to ride out the storm in safe harbor as so many of the Good Folk had chosen to do when Keldec's rule plunged our peaceful realm into darkness. To leave cruelty and hardship, wars and struggles, for other people to deal with.

"All right, Neryn?" Tali was climbing the track with her usual ease, seemingly not in the least tired by the trip.

"Fine."

The gull flew above us, moving in slow circles to keep pace. An ordinary bird in every respect, complete with webbed feet. But nothing was ordinary here. For now, as my legs reacquainted themselves with solid ground and the queasy feeling subsided, I began to sense the strength of Ronan's Isle, an old, old strength. Magic breathed from every stone. The air was alive with it. The sea that circled the isle whispered tales of wonder. There were Good Folk here, no doubt at all of that.

"You should wrap up your weapons now," I told my companions. "I feel uncanny presences here. The Hag may be close."

In fact, Flint was carrying no visible weaponry, though I doubted he would go anywhere completely unarmed.

Tali took out the cloak she had put in her bag, slipped her knives from their sheaths, wrapped them in the garment, and stowed them without a word.

We climbed the hill, and found ourselves on the edge of a broad, treeless area that must surely be the Lanely Muir the Northies had mentioned. There was indeed not a soul to be seen here, only some tough-looking sheep with wool in long, twisted locks, grazing with new lambs by their sides. To the south, at a distance, a cluster of low stone dwellings huddled behind protective walls, and between them and us stood stacks of peat drying in the wind. I could see the dark gouges in the earth where folk had been digging, and here and there a patch of water shining amid the brown. Above the moorland the spring sky was alive with birds.

The gull led us, now winging ahead, now alighting on a stone or a stretch of tumbledown wall to wait while we caught up. We made our way across the island to the west, where the rising land of the moor gave way, with shocking abruptness, to sheer cliffs. There had been cliffs on the Northies' map, but nothing could have prepared me for this. The height was immense—surely we had not climbed so far? The cliff edge was split with crevices, its uneven surface treacherous. Here and there sections had broken away to stand alone, craggy giants with the ocean washing white around their feet far, far below us. Each solitary stack was crowned with a colony of nesting gannets, and in the nooks and crannies of the precipice more birds roosted. The noise of their voices filled the air, a constant screaming. Birds dived to the sea below and rose with fish in their beaks. Others circled above, perhaps seeking their own young among a myriad of squawking, jostling creatures.

"What now?" Tali had eased off her pack and was looking along the cliffs, one way, then the other.

"We wait. Perhaps not right here." I recalled the tiny Twayblade seated on the very edge of the cliff, dangling his feet over the mind-numbing drop. "We might sit over there by the wall."

The drystone wall had probably been erected to keep the livestock from coming to grief. It seemed whoever had built it had run out of energy quite soon, as the wall stretched only a short distance along the cliff top. We sat, our backs to the stones, our faces to the endless sea. The gull flew off with a squawk.

"Couldn't we explore along the cliff top?" asked Tali. "Maybe look for some sign of her? I don't know where a Hag would live, but you mentioned a cave. She's hardly going to come strolling along looking for us."

"We wait because that's what we were told to do. We don't go exploring. We might blunder in somewhere we're not welcome and cause offense. I'm here seeking a big favor. I need to approach it in the right spirit." It occurred to me that when I'd met the Master of Shadows, he had indeed come strolling along looking for me, if in a somewhat roundabout way. I had not sought him out; he had approached me.

Silence, then. Flint was beside me, his legs stretched out, his hand right beside mine. I found myself wishing, unreasonably, that Tali were somewhere else.

"Tell me more about this change in the Good Folk,"

Flint said eventually. "I thought your friend Sage was unusual in her support for the cause. But it seems the tide has turned far sooner than anyone expected."

We broke the news to him that Lannan Long-Arm had set a time limit on his support. We explained the council at Shadowfell, and the Good Folk's belief that a season of change was upon all of us.

"Sage and Red Cap left Shadowfell to spread word of the rebellion to their own kind in the west," I said. "The Good Folk of the north, those who live under Shadowfell, were going on a similar mission. And there was talk of using birds, or fey folk who can fly, to carry the message. I was wondering if word had traveled ahead of us. Now that we've found you, I'm sure of it."

"Birds. Extraordinary. But, then, you have a habit of making the extraordinary happen."

Tali told him about Regan and the others: where they had gone, what they hoped to achieve before next winter closed the paths. Flint listened in silence. Of his own business he told us nothing. The sun moved into the west; the shadows began to lengthen. Flint took off his cloak and put it around my shoulders. Tali was restless, getting up, walking a few paces, sitting down again.

"Gifts," I said, realizing I had forgotten this important aspect of dealing with the Good Folk. "We should make an offering to show goodwill."

"You think the Hag's going to come out for a scrap of bread or a strip of dried meat?" Tali sounded unconvinced. "That's about all we have to offer."

"Could we make a fire? Perhaps find some herbs and cook some kind of soup?" A hag, I thought, might have few teeth left; I imagined her dipping the bread in the warm soup to soften it. It would be a comforting meal in the chill of the sea wind.

My warrior companions tackled the task with the same calm efficiency they'd applied to sailing the boat. Tali went off and helped herself to a supply of peat, which she carried back in her cloak. I hoped there might be some way we could repay the islanders; in a place that had so little, everything would be precious. A second trip yielded the withered remains of a bush that had succumbed to the winter weather, and Tali soon had a campfire burning on the landward side of the low wall. Meanwhile, I went out onto the moorland in search of herbs, returning with a better harvest than I had expected, for sage and thyme both grew here, sending their roots deep between the rocks, and by a lochan where long-legged birds waded, I found a supply of early cresses.

By the time I got back, Flint had water boiling in the small cook pot he carried everywhere, and various ingredients ready to add: a handful of oats, the dried meat shaved into slivers, some wizened mushrooms that had seen better days, shreds of vegetable matter that might have been carrot or turnip.

"I thought it best to wait for your approval," he said, looking up with one of his rare smiles.

"That looks good to me. You carry vegetables in your pack these days?"

"I brought a few things from Pentishead."

A sharp memory came: Flint feeding me as I lay grievously sick. Flint so patient and kind, at a time when I'd believed him my enemy. How much had changed since then. And how little time we had. Only two days. Let there be time alone. Let there be time for me to talk to him properly, to touch, to tell him . . . So much to be said, and none of it possible with Tali present, Tali who was always quick to remind me that soft feelings were chinks in a warrior's armor. I felt, already, that she was watching us.

"At the very least, the three of us will get a good supper," I said.

Tali came to crouch by the fire and warm her hands. "I hope the plan isn't to sleep out here on the cliff top if nobody comes."

I said nothing. If nobody came, there was no plan. We would spend some time on the island, I supposed, and I would try to find some Good Folk here and ask if they knew where the Hag was to be found. I could call them to help me if I must. But I would not call a Guardian. That would truly be overreaching myself.

"Someone will come," I said with more confidence than I felt. "If it's not until tomorrow, we can sleep in the shelter of this wall."

Tali's expression told me what she thought of that suggestion. The wind was blowing hard now, stirring up the ocean all around the island. Out to the west I could see a small, cliff-bound isle I remembered from the Northies' map. Today it wore a collar of white. I imagined wild breakers lashing the rocks. Not even seals would go in there.

"Does that island have a name?" I asked Flint.

"Far Isle. Populated mostly by seals."

"It looks too steep even for them."

Flint seemed about to speak, then apparently thought better of it. Instead, he took up a stick and gave the broth a stir. I leaned across and dropped in the herbs I had been shredding. The mixture smelled good.

"I'd have liked some fish," Tali said. "Tomorrow, maybe." She glanced at Flint. "Won't you be needing the boat?"

Flint made no reply. It occurred to me that Tali's delicate question had nothing to do with his getting back to the mainland. She was talking about his mission in the isles, whatever it was. A mission for the king. He would hardly be going about that with the assistance of the local fishermen. He had friends on Ronan's Isle, or so it seemed. What if he had been sent here to kill someone?

Flint sat silent, gazing at the glowing peat, the flickering flames, the mixture simmering in the pot. It was plain he had no intention of offering us any information.

Time passed. The broth smelled ready to eat, and I realized I was hungry. The sun was low, setting a gold light on Tali's strong features. Flint remained wrapped in his thoughts.

Suddenly Tali's gaze sharpened. She rose slowly to her feet, putting up a hand to shade her eyes. "What in the name of the gods is that?" she said.

It was a cloud—a swift-moving cloud approaching over

the sea, from the lonely cliffs of Far Isle. Birds. A great throng of birds, a flight to dwarf the flock that had heralded our arrival on this shore. And below them in the water, sleek and elegant as a swan, came a boat.

"I thought you said that place was only inhabited by seals," I murmured as the hairs on the back of my neck prickled with awareness of the uncanny.

But Flint said not a word.

CHAPTER SEVEN

WE STOOD NEAR THE CLIFF TOP WATCHING AS the craft approached. It came in a gliding motion, passing over the turbulent waters as if on a tranquil loch: a long, low vessel with a high prow, its sail of a shimmering pale fabric that surely should have been torn to shreds by the sharp westerly wind. The great cloud of birds cast a shadow on the sea, and yet where the boat cleaved the water, there was no shadow, but pale light.

"A woman," Tali said, narrowing her eyes against the sun. "Dressed in a hooded cape. A big man with her. Or is it a creature?"

"Is she old? Young?"

"I can't tell," said Tali. "Her hair is long. Could be white, could be fair. She's sitting very straight. Broad shoulders. Looks tall." After a moment she added, "The boat seems to be sailing itself."

The air around us throbbed with magic, a dangerous magic the likes of which I had not sensed since the Master of Shadows revealed himself to me in Odd's Hole.

"It's the Hag," I said. "I can feel her power." I was both elated and sick with terror.

Flint stood close beside me. He still hadn't spoken. Now, as the uncanny boat came nearer, he put his arm around my shoulders, heedless of what Tali might think. I closed my eyes. My fear eased; my heart quieted. I felt the warmth of his touch in my whole body. *Store this up,* I told myself. *Keep this feeling for when he's gone.* I rested my head against Flint's shoulder; he whispered something I did not catch.

"Turn, turn," muttered Tali urgently. I opened my eyes and realized I had been in a kind of dream. The boat was very close to land now and showed no sign of slowing. "Black Crow's curse, what is she doing?"

The cloud of birds was almost upon us; the boat went out of sight, somewhere down at the base of the cliffs.

"She'll be smashed to pieces," Tali said in flat disbelief. "There can't be a landing place down there."

The birds passed over us, not squawking and crying, but silent. They circled, then landed, a sea of white along the cliff top and all around us. On the wall close by I spotted a gull wearing little boots.

"We must do something—fetch help—" Tali moved perilously close to the cliff's edge, craning her neck.

I looked at the uncanny bird. It turned its head to one side and stared back.

"We should wait," I said. "That was no ordinary boat and no ordinary sailor." When I'd seen the Guardians in that vision, in Odd's Hole, the Hag had said, *Be fluid as water.* "If it's the Hag, her strength is water magic. Maybe she doesn't need a landing place."

"How can we just wait? What if . . ." Tali fell silent as Flint and I moved back to the fire and sat down, side by side. After a little she came over and stood beside us, arms folded. "I hope you're right," she said. "If we could have saved someone and did nothing . . ."

"If an ordinary fishing boat went in under there, the crew would be dead before you could fetch help," said Flint. "Or are you suggesting we descend the cliff on a very long rope?"

"That's just it," said Tali. "Even if they do land, how will they get up?"

"Smells good," someone said. All three of us started in surprise; the person had come from nowhere. She was standing behind Tali now, long silver hair flowing down over her shoulders, rivulets of water running from her robe to pool on the rocks around us. We rose to our feet.

The woman was certainly tall. She could look down on both Tali and Flint. Her stance was proud. Hers was a strong face, the nose jutting, the cheekbones prominent, the jaw firm. Her eyes . . . They were odd indeed, elongated in shape, and of many colors: deep green, seal gray, the blue of a summer sky, and the blue of the sea under winter clouds, all at once. Her mouth was wide and thin-lipped, her expression calm. A hag? I would not have called her that. Perhaps she was old, but she seemed more . . . ageless. Her skin was not the wrinkled parchment my grandmother's had been at the end, but pale and unblemished.

"Welcome to our fire," I said when I had found my voice. "Will you share our supper?"

Tali made a little sound, and I saw someone else come up behind the woman. If she was human in shape, save for those eyes, her companion most certainly was not. He stood as tall as she, but his form was rounded, massive, sleek under a cloak of shining weed. His face was something between a man's and a seal's, and though his bulk was formidable, he wore an expression that could only be described as kindly. My grandmother had told me stories of selkie folk, beings that were part seal, part man or woman, creatures that changed their shape between land and sea. But here we were on dry land, and the being was neither man nor seal, but . . . himself.

"You are both welcome," I said shakily, regretting that we had not taken the time to catch some fish while we could. "Please, sit with us awhile."

The Hag, for I was sure this was she, sat down gracefully by the fire, her hair a pale shawl over her shoulders and down her back. Her robe was of shifting green and had many layers. Its fabric seemed rough, the edges tattered and torn, but the effect was pleasing. It was as if the garment had not been made, but had grown around her as naturally as foliage on a plant. Her companion lowered himself to the ground beside her. I tried not to stare. The creature had limbs like a man's, he sat like a man, but no man ever had such a strange, compelling face. After a moment, Flint seated himself beside me. Tali remained standing, her staff in hand.

"There is no need to stand guard," the Hag said. "Unless,

of course, you have a particular fear of birds. Sit where I can see you."

Tali opened her mouth to argue, then thought better of it. She took a place on my other side. There was nothing relaxed about her pose as she met the Hag's penetrating gaze.

With Flint's assistance I ladled the brew into bowls. We only had three among us. Seeing this, the Hag turned her head to meet the strange eyes of her companion, and from somewhere within his swathing weedlike draperies he produced a pair of half shells.

Nobody said another word until we had finished our meal, Flint and I sipping the brew from the shells, the others using bowls.

"So," the Hag said, setting down her empty bowl. "A long journey for you, and barely begun. Word came to us that you'd had a bit of help along the way." When I looked at her blankly, she added, "One of the river creatures."

"Oh. Yes, I . . . We were attacked, and I had no other choice. If the river being had not come to our aid, we would have been killed." I hesitated, not sure how much to reveal so early. "I try not to use my gift unless I must. I know how perilous power can be when not properly controlled."

"Aye? Then you know something, at least." She examined me, her changeable eyes drawing me in. "Neryn, is that your name?"

"Yes. My guard here is Tali, and . . . this is my friend." Flint used various names, and he might not wish to be introduced to a stranger by any of them.

"Oh, aye, we ken who the laddie is."

That was the second time I'd heard my formidable man called a laddie. So she knew him; or knew of him, at least. Perhaps she knew every creature that walked these isles, animal and human, canny and uncanny. I cleared my throat, not sure whether to get straight to the point or spend more time in preliminary niceties.

"You'll be wanting to come over to the island, then."

Clearly the Hag preferred a direct approach. "I was hoping you might be prepared to teach me. To begin my training in the wise use of my gift. I see you have been told some of my story already. Did the . . . messenger . . . explain why it is I need to learn this?" *Come over to the island.* So the Hag did live on that lonely, cliff-bounded rock out there, the gannets' roost. A formidable place. Isolated. Uncanny. Safe. A place where Flint and I might be left alone for a day, a night, another day, to walk together, talk together, perhaps to sleep side by side as we had done before, but not quite the same, because each of us knew now how precious those times were. . . .

"Aye," said the Hag, startling me out of my daydream. "When one of your kind steps up like this, there's only one reason for it, and that's a change in the pattern of things. As for teaching you, I'll be wanting to find out how much you know and how much you need to know. That will take time."

"How much time?" Tali asked the question I had decided to hold back.

The curious eyes turned to meet the dark ones of my guard. "Long enough," said the Hag mildly. "Longer if we

190

sit about here exchanging the time of day. We should be on our way."

"So we do have to sail over to that little island?"

"Afraid of the sea, are you?" The Hag's eyes were the gray of ocean under storm as she gazed at me.

This question was a test. If I pretended to a courage I did not possess, she would see through it instantly. I thought quickly and gave her an honest answer. "I would be foolish not to be afraid, since the sea is many times more powerful than any human woman."

"Neryn can't swim," put in Tali. "It's not unreasonable for her to be scared of boats."

"Gather your possessions," said the Hag, getting gracefully to her feet. Her strange companion also rose. "My vessel stands ready."

A crazy thought came to me, that she might bid us jump from the cliff top. The Master of Shadows had once commanded me to leap into deep water after all. And how else were we to make our way to whatever anchorage lay at the cliff's foot? How had she and her companion reached us so quickly, save by magic? No path could safely traverse such a sheer drop.

She turned to walk away along the cliff top. After a few strides she halted, and the rest of us halted behind her. The Hag turned.

"One companion only," she said, looking at me. Her glance moved to Tali, then to Flint.

"No," I breathed, and my heart clenched into something tight and painful. "No, that's not—"

"You may bring only one. Choose quickly."

Flint had become suddenly still. I looked up at him. His face was a stony mask. "There's no choice about it," he said. "Tali is your guard and companion. She must stay with you."

Hot tears flooded my eyes. To wait so long, and then not even have time to talk to him properly, not even to have a moment alone, not . . . I wanted to say it wasn't fair, but that would be a child's complaint, and this was not a child's business. I forced myself to turn toward the Hag and give her a respectful nod. "I understand." Try as I might, I could not keep my voice steady. "Please, may we have a few moments to say goodbye?"

The Hag folded her arms. I could almost feel her counting.

Tali reached out to take my staff from me. She jerked her head toward the stone wall, indicating that we should go a little distance away. This unexpected kindness made the tears spill from my eyes. We moved away from the others, Flint and I, until we were standing up by the wall. Tali turned her back and stared out to sea. The Hag and her companion simply stood there waiting. Whatever I might want to say to Flint must be said within their hearing. *Don't show her your anger,* I told myself, *or she might refuse to teach you, and then where would you be? Don't let your feelings get in the way of the cause.* That had never been so hard as it was now.

"I'm sorry," I whispered, taking Flint's hands in mine and wishing he would let that mask slip, just for a little. "I wanted this more than anything . . . time together, even

192

a day, after so long. . . . I had hoped you might be there in spring. At Shadowfell." Old habits were hard to break; I found myself glancing over my shoulder before I spoke this name. "Thank you for bringing us safely across." I couldn't say anything of what I felt, I couldn't speak a tender word, I couldn't tell him how I missed him and feared for him every day, how I longed for him to be close, how my dreams of him confused and troubled me even as I clung to the glimpses they brought me. "This is hopeless," I murmured, freeing a hand to scrub my cheeks.

"Be safe," Flint said. "Tali will guard you well. This is a rare opportunity, Neryn; seize it with all your strength." There was, perhaps, a very slight unsteadiness in his voice. But maybe I only imagined that.

Silence for a few heartbeats, no longer. We stood with hands clasped, looking into each other's eyes. Then the Hag said, "Time to go."

"I wish—" That was all my tears allowed me to say.

"I too, dear heart," said Flint, and now I heard in his voice what his exemplary self-control had kept from his face. He felt as I did, as if his heart were being wrenched out of his chest. "Perhaps this is best. We are each other's weakness."

"We are each other's hope," I said, and although every instinct urged me to throw my arms around him, to press my body against his, to hold him close, I withdrew my hands from his and took a step back. To be a warrior of Shadowfell was to put the cause before all else. "Be safe. Dream of good things."

He said nothing, but I felt the weight of his gaze as I

turned and walked away, down to where the Hag stood tall and quiet, waiting for me. Tali had been transferring items from Flint's bag to her own, fastening the straps. Now she put my staff in my hand.

"I'm ready," I said. I did not turn back; if I looked at Flint now, I would fall to pieces.

"Farewell, comrade!" Tali called to him. "Safe journey."

"Farewell," he said quietly, and it was the saddest thing I ever heard.

"Come," said the Hag. "Follow me." She spread out her arms, raising them high, and there was a whirling sensation, as if sky and sea, cliff top and flock of birds, were turned and tumbled in a great wind, and we were turning and tumbling too, helpless before its power. I clutched the staff, wondering if we might be blown all the way across to Far Isle. But no; the wind stopped and the whirling motion ceased, and here we were in the boat, putting out from the foot of the cliff with the gulls wheeling and dipping around us, their shrill voices raised now in an echoing chorus. The waves crashed against the rocks behind us; wherever the boat had been moored, it surely could not have been there. But there was nowhere else. Tali was pale with shock; I imagined I looked even worse, red-eyed, sniffing, startled, and sad, not to speak of the way my stomach was protesting about the movement of the boat. The Hag sat serenely beside me, amidships; her selkie companion was in the stern, half-reclining on a padded bench. Gulls perched all along the rails, their heads turned uniformly westward.

When we were some distance out from shore, I looked

back, craning my neck to find the spot where we'd been on the cliff top. Was it there, near that deep fissure that sliced the rock face like a mortal wound? Or there, where I thought I could make out a short length of drystone wall? I could not see him. Not anywhere.

"Look forward, not back," the Hag said. "All is change. Do not regret. Instead, learn."

What was I supposed to learn from this? That losing someone you love hurts? I had learned that lesson long before I met Flint, learned it over and over. As for *All is change,* that part I understood. Water was the Hag's element. Water was all change, from the icicles that frosted the eaves to the boiling pot on the fire, from the bog that sucked down the unwary traveler to the tear on a baby's cheek. From this heaving ocean swell to the mysterious, still pond above Maiden's Tears, where pale fish glided by moonlight, rising to their sacrifice on the fisherman's hook.

But some things did not change, I thought, watching Tali as she sat in the bow with the wind blowing her dark hair around her stern features. Courage, for instance. Dedication to a cause. Comradeship. When they were strong and pure, when they came from deep in the bone, those qualities could hold fast against all odds. Surely they could. If that was not true, then how could Regan's Rebels succeed in their mission? And what about love? If love changed as easily as the turning of the tide, did that mean Flint and I might become enemies again, and lose the precious thing that had grown between us?

I was still turning this over in my mind when we

reached Far Isle and sailed straight on past it. The look on the Hag's face forbade questions such as *Where are we going?* I saw, as we passed, that Far Isle was not the uninhabited rock we had assumed it to be, but had on its western side a settlement above a sheltered anchorage where a number of fishing boats were drawn up. Higher up was a swath of grazing land dotted with long-haired island sheep like those we had seen on Ronan's Isle. I saw walled gardens, washing on a line, and, farther around the bay, seals basking on the flat rocks above the water. There were women on the rocks too, gathering something—seaweed, shellfish—but not one of them looked up as we passed. Either they knew the Hag and her unusual companion already, or they could not see us. The vessel headed on into the west; this island too fell away behind us.

"How much farther?" Tali asked the question for me.

"Humankind lacks patience."

"By your standards, perhaps," Tali countered. "Under the circumstances, it seems a reasonable enough question. It will be night soon, and I see no land ahead."

"You are the guard. It is not for you to ask."

Tali's dark eyes narrowed. "My job is to keep Neryn safe," she said, and there was a note in her voice I had heard before, one that tended to make folk obey her without further argument. "She hates boats. She feels sick. You made her leave her friend behind. We expected to land on Far Isle; didn't you say that was where we were going? My job is to protect a person from danger. Danger comes in many different forms. It doesn't always consist of a big man with a weapon."

The selkie's mouth stretched into a smile.

"You think the Hag of the Isles dwells among human folk?" The Hag did not sound annoyed by Tali's challenge, merely surprised. "That would be reckless indeed. We have long shunned their company, though the folk of Far Isle know us. They are true islanders: a different breed from the rest of you." Her changeable gaze went from one of us to the other. "The Caller has much to learn. But the learning itself—that is quite simple. Your own job, simpler still. Guard the Caller with your life."

I saw Tali bite back an angry response. I hated the thought of anyone dying for me, even though I knew any of the rebels was prepared to do just that—Regan's orders put my safety ahead of anyone else's. I was Shadowfell's secret weapon.

The boat sailed on westward. Seeing that neat settlement with the smoke rising from its hearth fires and the setting sun shining on its grassy field, I had allowed myself to think about a comfortable bed, a good meal, and a little time on my own to grieve the loss of Flint before I must begin my training. This was plainly not to be. The vessel continued on its path, and the cloud of gulls kept pace. Now they were joined by sea creatures, seals and other, stranger beings, diving and swimming and dancing around the vessel.

There was, eventually, another island. Hardly an island; more of a rock. As we approached it, our vessel maintaining its stately passage through increasingly choppy waters, my heart sank still lower. *This* was where the Hag lived? *This* was where Tali and I must stay while she taught me?

There was nothing here but sharp edges, tangled weed, and a few clinging shellfish. I looked at Tali. She looked at me. The boat came up close to the skerry, and Tali gathered her possessions, including the well-wrapped iron weaponry. I saw in her eyes the decision to be fluid; to let what would happen, happen. With a warrior's control she relaxed her body and made her face calm.

The boat edged in beside a rock shelf, needing no rope or oars to hold it in place.

"Get out," said the Hag. "You are her guard and companion; keep her safe."

Tali got out onto the rocks, then reached to help me step over from the boat. The selkie moved along the craft, and somehow my bundle and my staff were there on the rocks beside me, and now the boat was moving away with both the Hag and the selkie still aboard.

"Wait!" I called in panic. "You're leaving us here? Why? I'm here to learn, I mean no harm. . . ."

"I should have known," muttered Tali as the boat set sail once more, apparently straight back to Far Isle. "Of course they don't live out here, who would? My guess is the two of them are off home to a nice wee cottage, a warm supper, and a snug bed."

A sharp gust caught us, driving salt spray into our faces. I teetered a moment. The rocks were slick under our feet. It would be so easy to fall. I imagined thrashing about in that churning water, and how impossible it would be to climb back up, even supposing I could swim to the rocks. This skerry was about twice the size of the dining area at Shadowfell. In a storm, the waves might wash right over it.

"Right," said Tali. "Shelter. Food. Fresh water. Who knows how long we've been dumped out here for? Follow me, and watch your footing. I'd rather not have to dive in and fish you out."

The situation was dire. There was no shelter beyond a shallow cave a little higher up, and even that was wet. I wondered when it would be high tide and how far up the rocks the sea would come. Tali examined every corner of the islet, her mouth tight. There was no fresh water. We got out our cooking pot and wedged it in a crevice. Rain might fill it; a wave might as easily wash over and ruin any drinking water we gathered. Beyond a few shellfish clinging to the rocks there was no food to be had.

"We'll ration our supplies, including our water," Tali said with commendable steadiness. "And we can throw in a fishing line. We'll be eating our fish raw. There's no making fire without fuel. As for those barnacles, a person could ruin a good knife getting them off the rocks, and there'd be barely a mouthful in each, but we will need a few for bait." She gave me a penetrating look. "Not much of a welcome, is it? Are we certain she actually wants to help?"

"She did come to meet us." I gathered my cloak more tightly around me; all my clothing was damp. "This must be some part of the learning."

"Black Crow's curse! Well, whatever it is, I hope it's over quickly. I would say this isn't the worst place I've ever spent the night in, hoping to take that stricken look off your face, but I'd be lying."

"Your job isn't to make me feel better."

"No?" There was a trace of a smile on her face as she

eyed me. "Come on, let's do what we can to make this shelter habitable. And pray for calm weather."

The shallow cave was a meager refuge. Neither of us slept more than a snatch at a time. The wind screamed in our ears. The harsh voice of the waves was all around us. Under a clear sky, it was bitter cold. Tali made me lie against the rock wall with her in front of me, which meant she bore the brunt of the gale. We'd put on every garment we had and spread the two blankets over us, but the cold was unrelenting. I felt it in my chest, in my temples, in my ears. I wrapped my shawl around my head and considered why the Hag would have done this. Hadn't I already shown, over and over, that I could endure hardship? Hadn't the Master of Shadows acknowledged that I had the Caller's gift? She'd come to fetch us. Shared our meal. Ferried us in her boat. She seemed to know quite a bit of my story. And now this. It made no sense at all.

Huddling against Tali's back as my hands and feet grew numb, I wondered if the two of us would die of cold before morning. What had I done wrong? What had I said to bring this down upon us?

"Get up," Tali said suddenly, stumbling to her feet, awkward in the cold and dark. The moment she moved, I felt the true force of the wind.

"What—"

"Get up." Now she was hauling me to my feet. "Stamp your feet, clap your hands. Not over there—" She grabbed my arm, steadying me as I wobbled on uneven rocks. "Stay on this flat part or you might fall. Keep moving about. We can sleep by daylight, when it's warmer."

"You're crazy," I muttered, making a clumsy effort to obey. My limbs had lost their feeling and lack of sleep had made my head muzzy. "If we had the Ladder here, no doubt you'd be making me run up and down it in the dark."

"If that was the only way to keep you alive, yes." She was swinging her arms, stamping, stretching. The moon showed me her white face, her dark eyes, the cloud of her breath in the freezing night air. "Pick up the pace, Neryn. This is the kind of thing I trained you for. Don't let me down now I ask you to put it into practice, or my initial assessment of you will be proved right."

A small flame of anger awoke somewhere inside me. "Oh, and what assessment was that?" I bent and stretched, stamped and clapped, hating her as we'd all done from time to time when pushed too hard.

"That you were a wee girl wandering where she didn't belong, trying to do a job that was far too big for her. A girl who hadn't the first idea what kind of life she'd need to live if she became one of Regan's Rebels. Like a snowdrop poking its hopeful head up in a field of thistles."

"Not very flattering," I muttered between squats. "But, then, my assessment of you was harsh in its turn."

For a while she did not rise to the bait. She held her silence as she got down on the rocks to stretch out in the exercise known among the recruits of Shadowfell as the Plank. If she was still limber enough to do that, she had far better resistance to the cold than I did.

"Well, then?" she asked eventually, still balanced on toes and fingertips, her body stretched in a strong, straight line.

"Well, what?"

"I'm sure you want to tell me what you thought of me, that first day."

"When you apprehended me and marched me to Regan for questioning?" We both fell silent then, for that had been a day of blood and death. The rebels had won their battle; it had been a victory. But their losses lay heavily on the folk of Shadowfell.

"I was surprised. Impressed that a woman not much older than me could be a leader of warriors. I thought you were formidable. Angry. Rude. I decided we were destined to dislike each other. It was plain you thought me nothing but a nuisance." I paused, finding it too hard to talk and perform Tali's exercises at the same time. There was no doubt I felt somewhat warmer, but the moment I stopped moving, the bitter cold would envelop me once more. "Tali, we don't have to do this all night, do we?"

"Depends on whether you want to wake up in the morning." A pause. "Are there Good Folk out here? Couldn't you ask them for help?"

"There's something here, or nearby. . . . But that could be part of the test. Not calling if we can survive without it."

"Mm-hm. I'd say this situation is pretty close to desperate. It certainly will be within a few days."

"If it comes to that point, I will call them, I promise."

A silence. Then she said, "Don't worry about me. You're the one who matters. Make sure you don't let this go on so long that you risk your health. After all, I'm only the guard."

Clearly, the Hag's remarks had disturbed her. "We're comrades, Tali," I said quietly. "Partners. We look after each other. That's what happened at the river, the last time I used my gift."

She said nothing for a while. The two of us began the sequence of exercises again, side by side.

"I'm sorry." I heard that the apology cost her something to make.

"For what?"

"I misjudged you at the start. And for a long time afterward."

"You did, yes. And I misjudged you."

"Which bit, angry, rude, or formidable?"

I felt myself smiling. "You know you can be all three. But there's more to you than that. Kindness. Courage. Sound judgment. It took me a while to see those things."

"Your mind was on Flint, no doubt."

That was enough to make me halt the sequence of bend, stretch, run on the spot to the count of ten. "Tali."

"Mm? Keep moving, Neryn."

"Why do you think Flint's here? In the islands?"

"When a whole troop rides somewhere outside culling time, it's usually to visit a chieftain's stronghold. There can be all sorts of reasons for that, from investigating rumors of disloyalty to drumming up support for some venture to come. But there's no chieftain in the isles now. If the troop split up, perhaps they've been ordered to account for a number of individual targets—local leaders who've dared speak out against the king, folk who've been reported as exhibiting canny skills. Keldec's still looking for a Caller—you know that, don't you?"

"I know." The thought chilled my heart.

"Since Flint's come over here on his own, his most likely purpose is assassination. Who the target might be, I can't imagine. The king's left the western isles out of the Cull for the last two autumns."

My attempt at running on the spot had become a sad shuffle. My legs were refusing to accept that it was not bedtime. I did not want to think about the implications of her words.

"Take a rest, Neryn. We'd best not exhaust ourselves, since we have limited food and water. But don't stand completely still or you'll get cold again. Walk on the spot and rub your arms. Sure you don't want my cloak?"

I shook my head. "You need it. I'll be all right." I did as she suggested, for the chill was quick to return as soon as I stood still. "All I wanted was one day." This came out of me without warning, as if what was pent up inside had only been waiting for a moment of kindness to be set free. "Just one. One day, one night. After so long. She didn't have to do that, there was plenty of room in the boat. . . ." I made myself stop. I'd never have shown my weakness in front of Tali if I hadn't been so desperate for sleep.

"I hate to be blunt, Neryn, but for you and Flint it's probably better this way. He has a job to do. A job that's going to be hard for him, either way. Put him out of your mind and concentrate on surviving."

With the coming of dawn the air slowly warmed, but the wind was a constant presence, whipping at our clothing, clawing at our skin. I offered to fish; Tali pointed out that she'd have to watch me anyway, in case I fell in, so she might as well be the one to throw in a line. In the event, I sat beside her, helping bait the hooks with morsels of shell-fish. I gazed over toward Far Isle, wondering what the Hag was expecting me to do.

"I've been in tighter corners," Tali said.

"Really?"

"Not much tighter, to tell you the truth. I wonder if the plan is that I teach you to swim and then the two of us splash back over there."

"I hope you're joking."

She managed a lopsided grin. "I wouldn't attempt such a feat even on my own, and I'm a strong swimmer. Have you considered that she might be testing your common sense? If there are Good Folk somewhere close, what harm in calling them now?"

"Not yet. We can last one more day, at least." It surely couldn't be as simple as that.

"Once our waterskins are empty, we'll be in trouble without steady rain. And we can't store much. As for the lack of shelter, that's going to take a toll over the next few days. We'll be cold and tired, and we're likely to get impatient with each other. And we'll become careless. I don't need to spell out what that could lead to."

There was a tug on her line, and all her concentration was on pulling in the catch. I watched as she landed a sizable codfish, which she killed with one quick blow.

"Good," she said. "We eat today, at least, and save our rations for tomorrow. How are you at gutting and scaling?"

In response I put out my hand for the fish. "Why don't

you sleep while I do this? This may be as warm as the day's going to get." She made to protest, but I forestalled her. "I'll sit up next to the shelter and I won't go anywhere near the water. Promise."

"Don't leave fish guts all over the place. We're going to get filthy enough as it is."

A sequence of difficult days passed; we kept count with scratches on the rock. Just before our water supply ran out, we had a night of thunderous rain. If we'd had the means to collect it, we could have filled fifty waterskins. As it was, we gathered enough in the cooking pot to replenish the ones we had. The next morning we found a rock with a natural hollow at the top, brim-full of rainwater.

"Funny we didn't notice that before," Tali remarked, running her hands through her salt-stiffened hair.

"We're tired. Missing something isn't surprising. It's when we start seeing things that aren't there that you need to start worrying." I was trying to force a comb through my own hair, which was all knots. Much more of this and I'd be hacking it off as short as Tali's. "Sometimes I look back eastward and think I can see Ronan's Isle, and a moment later it's nothing but mist and shadows. And to the south, once or twice I've caught a glimpse of a bigger island."

"The Cradle, it's called."

It surprised me that she knew this. "Is that where Regan once lived?"

Tali hesitated. Clearly this came into the category of information I did not need. On the other hand, the long days of isolation, cold, and damp made the two of us desperate for any distraction. "Mm-hm. One of the largest islands. Several settlements. Or there were, back then. Regan's father was chieftain."

"And Flint?"

"Wherever it was he trained, it was kept secret. Close enough for him to visit the Cradle by boat. He always came on his own. A capable sailor from early days."

I hesitated, wanting to ask her how she and Fingal had first met the others, but knowing such questions went against the accepted codes of Shadowfell. "So Regan was a chieftain's son," I mused. "That doesn't surprise me. Then he could have been ruler of the isles. Or were there brothers?"

"It's his story, not mine. Yes, there were brothers. And sisters. And now there's nobody. He had a choice: claim the chieftaincy and be cut down, or flee and live to fight a bigger battle. And that's all I'm telling you." Her features were tight, remembering. "In that time there were two island leaders, one in the north, one in the south. Keldec got rid of both, and now I imagine he thinks the isles a safe place, sparsely inhabited, with any figures of power snuffed out. Though Flint's current mission suggests that might have changed."

"There's the Hag. She's most certainly a figure of power."

Tali grimaced. "If the king knew she and the other Guardians were still about, there's no telling what he might do. It would certainly be a lot more than sending one Enforcer to deal with the problem. Keldec greatly fears what he sees as the uncontrolled use of magic, whether by Good Folk or humankind."

"Uncontrolled. Meaning, not controlled by *him,* yes? That explains a lot. I'd thought it strange that he has En-thrallers at his court, and other canny folk too, people like you and me, when he's so afraid of magic."

Tali shrugged. "If folk are loyal to him, he can be confident they'll use their talents for his purposes, I suppose. Possibly Flint and the other Enthrallers have turned the minds of every canny person at court, so all of them slavishly obey the king's will. I've never asked Flint about it and I don't imagine you have either."

I made to answer, but a fit of coughing overtook me. It left me with an all-too-familiar feeling: that there was an iron band around my chest. I felt the scrutiny of Tali's dark eyes.

"I'm fine. It's nothing. Why don't you lie down and try to sleep awhile? No need to fish today, there's enough left over." After days on the islet, we no longer thought in terms of food being cold or raw or less than fresh. What we caught, we ate.

The cough was persistent. I did my best to muffle it as I sat hunched in my cloak, obeying Tali's rule about not straying on my own. Not that there was far to go anyway. Beyond the small, flattish area by the shallow cave, the rocks were pitted with cracks and holes, a nightmare of sharp edges and sudden drops. The sea washed constantly against the islet as if keen to swallow it whole. Sometimes it tossed up seaweed, little fronded pieces and long, tough ribbons of kelp. We'd tried eating the smaller bits, but they had made us sick.

Today the sky was filled with long clouds like banners. I gazed toward Far Isle and allowed myself to picture the Hag's boat sailing over to fetch us back. She hadn't sent so much as a single bird to check if we were alive or dead. Not a gull. Not a crab. Not a tiny worm. Behind me in the shelter Tali lay still, a blanket over her, her dark lashes tranquil on her pale cheeks. Against the odds, fast asleep. I wished her good dreams.

I was in a half dream myself, born of weariness and hunger, when I noticed something out of the corner of my eye. What was that down at the water's edge, tumbling and turning in the wash of the waves?

"Tali!" I said sharply. "Wood! Quick!"

She had been sleeping heavily and was slow to rouse. Too slow—the precious timbers would float away before we could secure them. I scrambled down the rocks, slipping and sliding, until I thought maybe I could reach them without falling in. Wavelets slapped up over my feet, drenching already wet shoes. I set one hand on the rocks for balance, used the other to tuck the hem of my skirt into my belt, then stretched down.

"Neryn, wait!"

Her voice startled me. I teetered, then righted myself, heart pounding. In that turmoil of dark, shifting water, I would not last to a count of five. I'd go under before I could snatch a breath, and Tali would likely be drowned trying to save me. I waited, and the wood began to drift away.

"Here." She was beside me, passing me her staff. "I'll hold on to you; you lean out and hook it in closer. Ready?" She braced her legs and held me around the waist. I leaned out over the churning waves.

"Good," Tali said as the staff caught the floating wood and drew it in toward the rocks. "Steady; just hold it and let the water do the rest. That's it. . . ."

We managed to get six pieces of wood in; the rest drifted beyond our reach. Six solid lengths of timber, dark and heavy with seawater. They had perhaps been part of a ship, some vessel that had foundered on a skerry like this one. We dragged our bounty up to the shelter.

"Too wet to burn," Tali said, hands on hips as she examined the wood. Each piece was a handspan broad and about one good stride in length. "And it won't dry out in this place. Besides, there's nothing to get a fire started with, unless you feel like chopping off your hair."

"My hair's as wet as everything else," I pointed out.

"So, no fire. But we can make these into a barrier to keep the worst of the wind out of our shelter. Two sets of three, tied in place—I have rope in my pack. We can anchor it around the rocks."

"With maybe seaweed for caulking," I suggested. "We could hammer it into a pulp and squash it into the gaps."

"Mm-hm." She was already getting out the coil of rope. "I'm not keen to cut this; we may need the full length some other time."

"For cliff-scaling."

"That's a joke, I take it."

"The best I can manage under the circumstances."

After a moment she said, "You're doing well, Neryn."

"Thank you." Her praise was rarely given, and all the more precious for that. "I couldn't have done it without you."

"We haven't done it yet," she said, hands busy with rope and boards. "Whatever it is. But yes, it's easier when you're not on your own."

By the time the barrier was finished, I was yawning, worn out from the usual sleepless night. Tali went off to fish and I lay down in the shelter to rest. As I drifted off to sleep, it came to me that the Good Folk might not have abandoned us after all. The rock with a water-storing hollow had appeared after we made the best of the islet's meager offerings. Those floating timbers might have been guided in our direction when we had shown we were prepared to hunker down and get on with surviving. Maybe the next thing would be a boat, and rescue. I fell asleep heartened, despite the cold.

I could not have been more wrong, for when I woke before dusk, it was to find myself alone. Our bags, our staves, our waterskins lay on the rocks beside me. But Tali was gone.

CHAPTER EIGHT

MORNING. THE WASH OF THE SEA, THE SCREAM of gulls. Three days now, and each waking the same. The quick glance around, expecting to see her long, lean form; the tattoos dark against her pale skin; her shrewd, mocking eyes. The return of memory like a leaden weight. The sick, hollow recognition that I was all alone.

I sat in my blankets, sheltered by the odd arrangement of boards and rope, the last thing she had done that day before she went off to fish and vanished. At first, when I'd found her gone, I'd panicked. I'd searched frantically, shouting her name until I had no voice left, clambering desperately to every corner of the skerry in case I'd missed some clue. And then I'd forced myself to think clearly. How likely was it that Tali, capable, strong Tali, had fallen into the sea and drowned without so much as a shout? This was part of the test. She'd been removed. While I was sleeping, the Hag had come and taken her away.

When that day had turned to night, I had done the

exercises she taught me, keeping my body warm in the long, lonely time of darkness. Bend, stretch, run on the spot. Squat, kick, rise. Attempt the Plank. Start over again. With gritted teeth and eyes streaming tears, I had kept on going. At last, worn out by exhaustion and sorrow, I had slept, and woken to an empty dawn.

And now here I was, three days later, still alone, still waiting. *Keep to the routine,* Tali would have said. *It gives you something to hold on to.* I made myself chew on a lump of raw fish, swallow a careful mouthful of water. My chest hurt, and it was hard to get the food and drink down.

Last night I had dreamed of Flint: Flint running, running as if death were snapping at his heels. His face ashen white, his eyes wild. An angry sky above, wind whipping his cloak. Someone with him, another man in dark clothing, trying to halt him, shouting, gesturing. Flint snarling a response and pushing on past.

There was no way to know if what I had seen was past, present, or future, or only a product of my own exhaustion. But I could not shake it from my mind. He was in trouble. Something had gone wrong.

No point in this; there were no answers. I got up, folded blankets and cloak, tidied the area as best I could. The air was full of salt spray, the rocks slippery underfoot. Heavy clouds massed overhead; rain was close.

There were raw, angry patches on my skin, and I itched everywhere. My clothing hung in filthy tatters. *Hope,* I muttered to myself. *Got to have hope.* I realized I had sat down again, in a daze, too weary to remember what I was doing from one moment to the next. There was a longing in me to roll back into the damp bedding and shut my eyes to the world; to sleep until I woke no more. Something, some thread of awareness, kept me where I was, sitting with my arms around my knees, looking east toward Far Isle. Flint. Flint in trouble. How could I give up if he was out there somewhere, running from disaster?

Call for help, Neryn, before it's too late. If you wait until you're incapable, you're a fool. That voice was Tali's. But surely it wasn't as simple as that. There must be something I was missing, something I was supposed to learn from this. Must I show I could hold back until the very last extreme before using my gift? Or prove my common sense by using it before I was too weak to summon the will? Both were too simple. The Hag had sent me out here for a purpose. When I'd failed to do whatever it was she wanted me to do, she'd made things harder by taking Tali away. What wasn't I seeing? What wasn't I understanding?

The rain came, at first in scattered droplets, then in a steady drizzle, and finally in a great, thunderous down-pour. There was no point at all in trying to shelter. The rain drowned everything. It was like a great fist hammering the rocks, a huge voice roaring its song of power. Nothing to do but sit helpless under its bruising strength. The ocean had never seemed so vast, my friends never so far away. My tears flowed warm against the icy chill of my skin. . . .

And that was it. *Be fluid as water.* The power of the call was not my power. It was the power of deep earth, of mu-table fire and pure air. Here in the west, it was the mighty power of water. The sea, the rain, the tears, the cold sweat on our bodies. Everywhere.

As if it only had been waiting for me to see the truth at last, the storm passed over and was gone. The air cleared. Pools lay in every hollow of the skerry; the clouds parted to let a ray of pale sunlight through, and the miniature lakes shone like mirrors of gold and bronze and silver. It wasn't a call that was needed, it was a ritual. Or at the very least a prayer: an acknowledgment that my gift depended on the power of Alban, its lakes and mountains and forests, its caves and hilltops and secret places. A Caller's magic lay, not in herself, but in the natural world; she must learn to let that magic flow through her.

I had seen my grandmother perform the seasonal rituals when I was young, though even then their practice had been outlawed. I could not remember the words she had used, but I did recall the basic pattern of it. I rose to my feet, dripping, and picked up my staff. I scraped my wet hair back from my face. Around me, moisture rose from the rocks in small clouds under the meager heat of the sun. My head felt strange; I hoped I would not faint before I reached the end.

Make a circle; pace it out; use the staff to point the way. At each quarter, stop and acknowledge the Guardian. "Hail, Lord of the North, Guardian of Earth. . . . Hail, White Lady, Guardian of Air. . . . Hail, Master of Shadows, Guardian of Fire. . . . Hail, Hag of the Isles, Guardian of Water."

I must find words to show I had begun to understand

why the Hag had left me out here on my own. "I greet the spirits of this place, spirits of water and of stone. Hail to the ocean with its secret depths and its powerful surges; hail to the creatures who swim there, wrapped in its embrace, nourished by its life. Hail to the storm. Hail to the rain that falls on field and forest, bringing forth new life; that quenches the thirst of wanderer and bard, warrior and cottager, creature of field and woodland and high mountain." The words were coming to me more freely now, half-remembered, half-invented. A pity it hurt so much to breathe. "Hail to the power of water. Hail to the patience that sees it shape stone; hail to the tenderness of a child's tears, and to the delicate perfection of an icicle. The thunderous torrent; the still tarn on whose shining surface long-legged insects dance. May I be fluid in my understanding. May I shape myself to the task before me. May I learn the language of water."

What was next? There should be a ritual fire; aromatic herbs, perhaps the sprinkling of mead or fresh water. All I could do was pour a little rainwater onto the stones by my feet. "For my ancestors," I murmured. "For my family. For those lost on the journey. For my comrades. For everyone who fights for a better world. May I be guided. May I learn the wisdom of water." There should be far more to it, but my legs would not hold me up any longer. I could hear the rasp of my breathing; it had sounded just like this when I had fallen so sick last autumn, coming up the Rush valley. "Let me be a vessel for the wisdom of water," I whispered, then curled up under my sodden cloak and closed my eyes.

When I woke from a feverish half sleep, it was to find a tiny weed-wrapped bundle beside me. Opening it with shaking fingers, I found inside a little bannock, as warm and fresh as if it had just come off the fire. The smell was sunshine and kindness and well-wishing. It was hearth and home and comfort.

I resisted the urge to cram the food into my mouth, making myself savor each wondrous, buttery mouthful. I ate half. A quarter I rewrapped and stored away. The rest I broke into three small pieces, which I laid on the rocks above the shelter. "Thank you," I whispered. "Thank you for your help." I could not find the strength to look about and see if whoever had left this gift was still on the skerry. I closed my eyes again.

Next time I woke there was a pillow under my head, and a small personage squatting close by, watching me with beady eyes. This was no gull, but a man-shaped being somewhat similar to Hawkbit. He was a being of the sea and the isles, with a long hooded coat of gray feathers, and hair like that of an island sheep, all twists and knots, woven through with strands of weed and little shells. I sat up and was overcome with coughing.

"Drink up, lassie," the wee fellow said, and held out a tiny cup. "'Twill not harm ye. Herself would have ye strong and bright for the learnin'. The draft will soothe the throat and give ye heart."

I drank. Whatever was in the cup, it flowed down my dry and aching throat with a honeyed ease, then spread a blessed warmth through my tight chest. Under the wee man's scrutiny I finished it all. "Thank you," I said. I did indeed feel remarkably stronger.

"Aye," my visitor said. "Ye'll do. Eat up the bannock ye set by, she'll be here soon."

"She?" I rummaged for the leftover bannock, so carefully saved.

"Herself."

No doubt, then, that the Hag was coming. So I had got it right at last; my makeshift ritual had worked. Unless she planned to ferry me halfway back to Far Isle, then drop me over the side. This had been a cruel test. And perhaps not entirely necessary, for when I had called the river being, what had been in my mind was the way that stream connected with its tributaries and springs and flowed down to join the great water of the loch. I had used the knowledge of water in my call. And with the Folk Below, my mind had been on the deep mysteries of earth. When I had used my gift, I had always been respectful.

I ate the last piece of bannock. I began to pack up my sodden, weather-stained belongings. I fought down rising anger.

"Ye'd be wantin' tae mak yerself a bittie calmer," the wee man advised, watching me. "Nae lassie argues wi' Herself."

Right, of course. The Hag was a Guardian; I needed her. Beside her, I was small and insignificant, a speck in the long history of Alban. If she'd done this, she must have had good reason for it. I was alive and unharmed; as far as I knew, Tali was safe. Provided the Hag was prepared to teach me now, I had no grounds for anger.

"I'm sorry," I made myself say.

"Nae apology needed for me, lassie. Here, let me carry that for ye."

"Can you tell me . . . is my friend safe, the one who was on the skerry with me? Where is she now?"

"The lassie wi' the fightin' eyes and the pretty patterns on her skin? She's ower yon, wi' Herself." The wee man glanced toward Far Isle. "Or no' wi' her, precisely. She's among the human folk, keepin' herself busy wi' this and that. She'll be right glad tae see ye again. Dry your eyes, lassie, and hold your head high. I see the boatie comin'."

I mopped my eyes with the rag he offered, but the tears kept flowing. Somehow the little man and I got the bags and the staves, the bundle of weaponry, and the sodden bedding down to the water's edge, and there, approaching with stately balance, was the Hag's elegant vessel, and in it her pale-haired figure sitting proud and straight. The selkie loomed behind her, weed-swathed. The wind was from the west, and yet the silken sails bellied out, carrying the boat toward us. She could conjure the weather, then. Waves, winds, tides, storms. How easy for her to pluck a woman from a rock in the sea while another slept.

I schooled my features, trying to breathe deeply. My chest was still tight, though the potion had helped. I waited without a word while the vessel drew in next to the rocks. In a blur of movement the selkie was out and beside me, and my belongings were in the boat. The wee man put up a hand to help me balance; I stepped aboard and seated myself in the bow. The small one seemed in no hurry to hop over himself.

"Are you not coming with us?" I asked.

"Ach, no, I've ma ain wee boatie." He pointed, and now I saw a tiny coracle of wattle and skins bobbing on the waves a little farther along, apparently held there by the same magic that allowed this larger vessel to maintain its position without rope or anchor.

The selkie slid into the sea, graceful despite his bulk. I did not see the moment of changing. With a twist and a roll, he plunged deep and was gone. The little man scrambled into his frail slip of a boat, picked up a paddle, and bobbed out to sea. The waves slapped and rushed at the skerry; farther out, the swell was monstrous.

"Grand wee boatman," observed the Hag. As the tiny craft was lost to view in the heaving waters, the westerly caught our sails and we headed back toward Far Isle. "Now, let's have a look at you." Her gaze was very direct. Perhaps she saw right inside my mind to the tangle of relief and resentment there. I met her stare, holding my head high. I had not endured all those lonely days for nothing. Weary as I was, I did not plan to crumple in exhausted defeat.

"You're not happy," she said.

"For a while, when you took Tali away, I thought she had drowned. I know you must have had your reasons for subjecting us to this test. But . . . what you did . . . it did not seem altogether right."

The Hag spread her hands, palms up. "You came to find me. You sought learning. Have you learned nothing from this experience?"

Breathe, Neryn. Count to five before you answer. "I learned that a Caller does not possess any magic of her own. She is a . . . a channel, a conduit for the power that exists in nature." I could not help adding, "But deep down I knew that already. I feel it every time I use my gift."

The Hag made no comment, only kept her gaze on me, deep and penetrating. Perhaps she expected some other answer.

"I'm not sure why it was necessary to do this," I said. "It seemed somewhat . . . cruel."

The Hag smiled. "You thought, perhaps, that a hag might be tiny and bent, toothless and frail, happy to drop gems of kindly wisdom in your lap as you fed her sippets of bread dipped in watered mead? Was that it?"

I recalled making the soup up on the cliff top and thinking it might be soothing to an old woman's stomach. "I am not such a fool as to underestimate any of the Guardians," I said. "I fear and respect you. I understand what power you can wield if you choose. I will be deeply grateful if you agree to teach me." Since she seemed to be listening attentively, I went on. "I believe you already know something of my story. A messenger told Tali and me where to find our friend with his boat, ready to cross to the isles; the same messenger was on the cliff top when you came up to meet us. It does seem that word of our mission has come west and that you are prepared to help. You may know, then, that I have lost many of those dear to me. That the rebels are my family now. That I have friends among the Good Folk, trusted and true friends. You know, perhaps, that I have spent years fending for myself and evading the notice of the king's men." I paused.

"Go on."

"Tests of strength, tests of courage, tests of knowledge and wisdom, all of those I accept as preparation for the path that lies before me. When I met the Master of Shadows, I showed him that I met the requirements for training as a Caller. He accepted that I had demonstrated the seven virtues. This time on the skerry . . ."

A silence, then, "Go on. Cruel, I think you said."

A sudden wave of weariness came over me. "I have a question," I said.

"Aye?" She was leaning forward now, as if this mattered where the rest of it had been of little significance.

"Were you displeased with me?" I asked. "Angry that I had used my canny gift several times already, without any proper training? If you were only waiting for me to recognize the power of water, and my own powerlessness, why did you need to spirit Tali away?"

"Angry? No. You have used your gift more sparingly than you might have done. Learning to hold back is important. Birds brought me the tale of your encounter by a ford, when you summoned one of my river folk. On that occasion you acted with due respect. A clumsy call, perhaps, but made in the right spirit."

"You haven't answered the question: why?"

The Hag lifted her hand, and the boat came to a sudden halt. We rocked on the waves, halfway between the skerry and Far Isle.

"What do you think I will do next?" asked the Hag, her shimmering pale locks blowing around her strong face. "Tell me. Say exactly what is in your mind."

"Drop me overboard for daring to challenge you?"

She stared at me a few moments, her eyes a swirl of blue and green and every shade between, night and day, sea and sky, pelt of seal and shining fish scales. Then she threw her head back and roared with laughter. "No wonder the Master of Shadows was so taken with you," she spluttered. "You may look like a gust of wind would snap you, but you've remarkable strength of mind, and you have endurance. You'll be needing both if you're to take the path of a Caller. As for tossing you over the side, if I did that, Himself would only lift you back in again. See, he keeps pace with us." She pointed, and I saw beneath the waves the selkie circling the boat, a graceful, mysterious shadow. "Then he would chide me for treating you too harshly. Besides, I'd have folk to answer to if I happened to lose you on the way; they've been pestering me for your return as it is."

They? Who was there, apart from Tali?

"Neryn," the Hag said, and her voice was different now, more solemn, but also warmer. "You arc safe. You will soon be well again. Perhaps the test seemed unduly hard. But a Caller is a rare thing; we must be sure you are strong enough to do this. Strong enough to learn; brave enough to endure the losses this path will mean. I saw how hard it was for you to bid your man farewell. At the end, you may indeed be all alone. If that is unbearable, if you cannot do without your friends, if you cannot go on without love and support and comradeship, then best you give this up now, before you travel farther down the path. Weigh it up, lassie. It's indeed a hard road."

Fresh tears stung my eyes. I blinked them back. I would not let the first note of kindness reduce me to a weeping child again. "I know it's hard. All of us understand that." I drew a steadying breath and squared my shoulders under my filthy, wet clothing. "I want to learn. I hope you will teach me, and when I am ready, send me on to the Lord of the North. Even if it means losses and heartbreak, this is something I have to do. For Alban. For those already lost and ruined and broken. For all of us."

"Mm-hm. You make a good wee speech. What if I told you we would start learning now, right away? What if learning meant going back out to that skerry and sitting there another five days, ten days, twenty days, with only a knife and a fishing line for company?"

I will not cry. I will not be angry. "If that will teach me to be a better Caller, then I will do it," I made myself say. My tone was perhaps less than placatory, but it was the best I could manage under the circumstances.

She laughed again, a full-throated sound of sheer pleasure. I could have hit her.

"I can be kind when I choose," she said, grinning. Her teeth were white and sharp, the teeth of a young, strong woman. "You may rest for a few days before we begin."

"Thank you." I tried not to imagine a warm bath, clean clothing, a soft bed. She had promised none of these. "Will I see Tali again?"

"Aye, you will. That lassie does not trust me an inch. She'll be waiting on the jetty, like as not."

We sailed on around the southwestern corner of Far Isle, and I saw ahead of us another little cove, and a precipitous path zigzagging up what seemed a sheer cliff. In the cove was a jetty, and beside it a tiny shelter. There were people on the jetty, but I could not make them out clearly.

"I like your anger," the Hag said mildly. "I like your resistance. It makes you less than courteous, but altogether more interesting. Let us sail for shelter. There are storms in the west, and they will pass this way at dusk. Your skerry will be underwater."

The vessel made its graceful way into the cove, and as we drew closer, I saw that there were indeed several folk on the jetty waiting for us. A man in heavy woolen gear, perhaps a fisherman, holding a boat hook. Beside him, unmistakable, the lean, tattooed figure of Tali. She raised both hands in a salute of welcome.

And . . . a third person. A tall, blunt-featured man in a worn gray cloak, his scarred face wearing quite openly its love and anxiety. The sight of him snatched away my breath. Against all common sense, against every decision that would have kept him and his perilous secret safe, Flint had come back to the isles.

No time for talk, then. The vessel came in, the fisherman held it against the jetty with his boat hook—hardly necessary, but the Hag made no comment—and Tali held out a hand to help me ashore. I stepped onto the jetty and threw my arms around her, and then around Flint, blinded by the tears I had held back all the way from shore to shore. Then I stepped away, wiping a hand across my cheeks. I had seen the looks on both my comrades' faces, and I knew I must speak before either of them did.

The Hag had not moved from her boat. Beside it in the shallows, the selkie's head broke the surface. He bobbed there, regarding us with mellow eyes. I wondered what he was to her. Lover, husband, friend, guardian, conscience? *He would chide me for treating you too harshly.*

"Thank you for bringing me safely here," I said to the Hag, and when Tali would have spoken, I silenced her with a quick gesture. The strength I had gained from the wee man's draft was ebbing fast. I had spoken with some discourtesy on the boat; I had been angry. It was plain the others felt the same. I was not ashamed that I had challenged the Hag, but we must put this behind us now. She would teach me; that was enough.

"I will return for you in due time." She fixed me with her gaze. "Rest, recover, consider those matters of which we spoke. The folk of this island will shelter you. They will ask no questions. They will reveal no secrets." Now she turned that look on Flint. "Step down to the boat. Collect your friends' belongings." Then, in a different tone, "You'd want to be leaving this shore as soon as you can, laddie."

I saw Flint gather himself, swallow furious words. "With your permission," he said carefully, "I will stay until tomorrow."

The Hag looked at me.

"Please," I said.

She did not say yes or no, merely watched as Flint got into the boat and passed the staves, the bags, the bedding, the bundled weapons across to Tali. If Tali was relieved to get her knives back, she gave no sign of it, merely took each

226

item and stacked it tidily on the jetty. Her features were well governed now, though the set of her body told me a different story. When I tried to help, she murmured, "I'll do it, Neryn." Flint stepped back onto the jetty.

I waited for the Hag to say Flint must leave immediately. Such a decision would be typical of her, I thought. But she said nothing, simply exchanged a glance with the selkie, whose sleek head still showed above the water by the boat. It was only an instant, and then he dived down and was lost to our eyes. The Hag looked at the fisherman, and he withdrew the boat hook. The vessel turned and headed out to sea. The selkie swam alongside, a dark form keeping steady pace. The Hag did not look back.

Silence for a few moments. Then the fisherman put the roll of bedding over his shoulder and picked up the two bags, and Tali hefted the weaponry and the staves. I looked up at the zigzag path to the top of the cliff. I wanted to be strong. I wanted to make Tali proud of me. I wanted to show Flint that I was a worthy member of Regan's Rebels. But my chest hurt, and my legs felt like jelly, and my eyes were blurry. "Just give me a moment to get my breath," I said, or perhaps I did not say it aloud, for rocks and sea and white faces began to swirl around me, and I was falling down, down, so far down.

Then up again, in Flint's arms, to find myself over his shoulder with my head dangling.

"I'm sorry, Neryn," he said. "But it's steep. I need one hand free to get you up safely."

We climbed. After a while I shut my eyes. I didn't

much care for cliff paths even when I had my own feet and hands to rely on. I clenched my teeth and ordered myself not to faint or otherwise disgrace myself.

"It's all right," Flint said. "I have you safe. We'll soon be in shelter."

"I can't believe she did that to you," came Tali's voice from somewhere behind us. "What if you'd died out there?"

"Thought . . . you . . . ," I managed.

"Shh," said Flint.

We reached the cliff top and he lowered me gently to my feet. My knees buckled; I could not stand. He picked me up again, this time in his arms as if I were a child, and we walked on. It was a small isle. We soon reached a southern settlement, nestled in a hollow a mile or so inland. Its size surprised me. There were at least twenty cottages, each with its drystone wall and its well-protected vegetable patch. Trees were very few, but I spotted one or two survivors, near-prone from a lifetime of westerly gales. Smoke arose from hearth fires; chickens pecked on the pathways. From not far off came the peaceful voices of grazing sheep. This place, I thought, was surely like the Alban of old, the Alban before Keldec.

By the time we went in the gate of one of the little houses, I was struggling to stay awake. The fisherman dropped the bags on the doorstep, exchanged a few words with Tali, and went off. Tali pushed the door open. Flint carried me inside and deposited me on a bed. I was too tired to do anything but lie back on the pillows.

"Get off the bed, you're wet through." Tali put an

armful of folded clothing on the storage chest. "Flint, turn your back."

He went to busy himself making up the hearth fire, while Tali helped me strip, then dress in what must be borrowed garments—a shift, a woolen dress, a warm shawl. "They're generous folk here," she said, making an attempt to comb out my hair with her fingers, then giving up. "We have the use of this house, they've lent us clothing, and we'll be provided with food and fuel as long as we're here." She gave a crooked smile. "Not like Alban at all, is it? And yet, more like Alban than anywhere."

She collected my sodden garments and took them off out the back. Flint covered me with a blanket, then stroked my filthy hair back from my face, gazing down at me. The only thing I could think of was that I might sleep too long and wake to find that he was already gone. This was the precious time I had wished for the day we met the Hag. I could not bear to lose it all over again.

"Wake me up," I murmured. "Please. Not too long . . . Flint . . . why . . . you here?"

"A dream. I saw you out on the skerry, all alone in the storm. Coughing as you did last autumn, when you nearly died. How could I not come back?"

Perhaps I should have realized this as soon as I saw him in my own dream, but I had not thought he would act so rashly. "Saw you . . . ," I whispered. "Looking like death . . . running . . . too risky . . . the others . . . the king . . ."

"Don't trouble yourself with that," Flint said.

"But . . . but what about . . ."

"Sleep now." It was an order. "We'll wake you before dusk, I promise. Here you can have a warm bath, a good meal, time to recover."

"Don't . . ."

Tali appeared beside him, wearing her most ferocious frown. "Stop talking, Neryn. You're safe, you can rest. We'll still be here when you wake up; nobody's planning to leave you on your own. Shut your eyes now, and not another word out of you."

Well practiced at obeying her commands, I closed my eyes and surrendered to sleep.

By nightfall I was well rested. I had bathed, then consumed a bowl of vegetable broth, a hunk of grainy bread, and a small cup of watered mead. The food had been brought by a woman of the island. She hadn't come in, but I'd seen her at the door, where she'd spoken with Tali and handed over the basket. Something else too—Tali had produced a tiny bottle with a curious stopper made from a seed, and added a drop of the contents to my mead.

"I was given instructions. By the Hag, after she brought me back here. Both for this, to restore your health, and for afterward. Where to go for your learning; who's to take you there and bring you back. All thought out, perhaps from the first. I was surprised she didn't give me my own set of orders, for while I'm waiting."

"What will you do?"

Tali shrugged. "In a place like this there's always work to be done. Mending things, digging the vegetable patch, helping with stock. Might go some way to repaying these folk's generosity."

We had the cottage to ourselves: one sizable room with several shelf beds, a privy out the back, and a lean-to where animals could be housed in winter. There was no livestock about the place now except for a large gray cat with a tattered ear, which had come in while I slept and settled itself heavily on my feet. Now we sat over our mead, the three of us on benches before a little hearth fire. I had been woken, not by Tali and Flint, but by a violent storm sweeping across the island, rattling at the shutters and pounding on the door with such force that I knew the Hag had been right—if she had left me out there one more day, I would have drowned. Now the island had fallen quiet. The distant sound of the sea was like the peaceful breathing of a creature worn out by a tumultuous day. The cat had shifted to my lap. It had one eye slitted open, as if not entirely sure it could trust us.

Flint was beside me on the bench, his arm around my shoulders. I felt the warmth of his thigh against mine, the occasional brushing of his fingers against my hair. Tali said not a word about this. Her opinion was all in her eyes. *Oh, you fools. To risk so much.*

"I don't understand why this Hag subjected you to such a grueling test," Flint said.

"Neryn coped well," said Tali unexpectedly. "But I concur with you that the test was extreme, and it's hard to understand the reasoning behind it. Can we trust that the Hag won't do something like this again, Neryn?"

"I had hoped," Flint said, "for one certainty at least: that for the period of your training you would be safe."

I rested my head against his shoulder. I must speak truthfully, though a lie would ease his mind. I hated to think of him back among the Enforcers, or worse still at court, where he must tread so carefully every moment of every day, being distracted by thoughts about my safety. "There's no certainty, Flint. But we must go on. We need the Good Folk. We need their support when we challenge Keldec. I have to learn, I have to become expert, I have to be able to call them to battle without fearing the result will be some kind of catastrophe. If the training puts me in peril, that's the way it must be."

"I'll be praying that doesn't happen," said Tali with a grimace. "Not much scares me, but that surely did. Not only being snatched up and conveyed over here on the back of a selkie, but before that, watching you get thinner and paler, and hearing you coughing, and knowing you weren't going to call her even if you were down to your last breath."

"I would have called some smaller being. Not Herself."

"But she sailed across to meet us; came up the cliffs to share our supper. What brought her if not your gift?"

"She came because she knew it was time. Just as she arranged for us to be on the shore when Flint was there with the boat. It's the messengers—birds and other creatures. What we started at Shadowfell, with our council, has moved with startling speed."

I had wondered if they would talk of Regan and the others, and how they might be faring, but perhaps they had done that while I was sleeping, for neither of them spoke of it. After a while our conversation dwindled and died to a murmur here, a few words there. We sat quiet, wrapped in our own thoughts, while the fire crackled and the cat purred on my knee. In my mind was Flint's mission to the isles, the one he had carried out for the king. And his return here now, solely because a dream had shown him I was in trouble. I wanted to ask him if he would fall under suspicion when he returned; if the rest of his troop was back in Pentishead already; if he would be able to invent a plausible excuse for racing off without proper explanations.

But I didn't ask. He wouldn't tell me anyway; he'd say it was something I need not know. All I could do was hope he could talk his way out of trouble yet again. I feared for him. His double life could not go undetected forever.

I must set those things aside for now. Tonight was a gift. I must not darken it with my fears for tomorrow.

Gods, I was tired. Even after that sleep, my eyes were closing now despite my best intentions. I put up my hand to shield a yawn.

A glance passed between Flint and Tali.

"I'll be off, then," she said, getting up. "Sleep well, the two of you, and don't forget entirely who you are and what it is we're here for. I'll be back at dawn. You'll be wanting to get away early."

"Good night," Flint said, perfectly calm, and after she had slung on her cloak and gone out the front door, he moved to bolt it after her.

I was fully awake now. "*Tali* agreed to go and sleep somewhere else?"

Flint was standing just inside the door, in the shadows.

His expression was difficult to read. "Only after I promised we would be mindful of all the reasons why this was not a good idea," he said. "If you prefer, I can call her back."

"No!" I protested, then felt myself blushing. This was not at all what I had expected. A somewhat awkward night with the three of us in the same sleeping quarters, yes. That would likely have meant Tali and me sharing the big bed while Flint took one of the others. The best I had hoped for was to snatch some private conversation with him while she slept. "No, of course not."

Flint came over to crouch in front of me, taking both my hands in his. "I hoped this was what you wanted," he said a little unsteadily. "It was one reason I came back. The look on your face when she said you could only take one of us . . . But, dear one . . . I don't intend that we . . . I believe some things must wait. You and me . . . what is between us . . . Our lives are perilous. Every moment of every day, we're in danger of discovery. The closer we become, the more likely that one of us may be used against the other. That is the way Keldec's forces work. Neryn, we cannot risk lying together as lovers. What if I got you with child?"

My mind leapt treacherously to the image of a child Flint and I might make together, a boy with strong, blunt features and beautiful gray eyes. I imagined myself singing him to sleep; I let myself picture Flint carrying him on his shoulders, a wide-eyed toddler gazing out over the sea. Then I banished those images from my mind. What Flint had said was right. To have a child who might fall into Keldec's hands was unthinkable. "Tell me what you do want," I said.

A sweet smile appeared on his face. "What I truly want must wait for another time," he said. There was a long pause; I knew he was thinking of the time of peace, the time when Keldec was gone, and wondering, as I did, whether that time would come too late for us. "For now, I will be content, more than content, if we lie side by side as we once did by our campfire."

"Really?" I asked, smiling in my turn, though in truth my heart was beating fast now, and my breath coming unevenly. "As I remember it, as soon as we woke up, we moved apart. And then pretended we had not been lying quite so close that night."

"Believe me," Flint said, "I have relived that morning many times. Are you happy to share this bed with me tonight, so we can sleep in each other's arms?" Unspoken was the understanding that at dawn he would be gone; that it might be years before we had another opportunity to spend a night alone together. That, for us, this might be the one and only time.

"That was what I hoped for, when we first came here," I said, getting up. "Only . . ."

"I promise I will not—"

"I'm not concerned about that. Only that I may fall asleep quite quickly, and that you may find that a little . . . insulting."

Flint laughed. I realized I had never heard him do so before. *Let there be a time in the future,* I prayed, *when he laughs with his children, and plays on the shore with them, and spends all his nights in loving arms. Let us have that.* To whom I was praying I did not know. The future was in our own

235

hands. If we wanted a world where such things were possible, it was for us to make it.

"Sleep all you will, dear one," Flint said, pulling down the covers on the bed. "I will be content to hold you. Come, lie down by me."

It was a sweet night, a night that would return many times later, in memories and dreams, to sustain me through loneliness, fear, and confusion. By warm firelight we lay down together and explored each other's bodies with gentle hands and courteous mouths; we brushed and touched and stroked with tenderness and passion. We were home and comfort and friend, lover and partner and wondrous new world to each other. We were careful and slow, and at the time when our bodies became too urgent in their need, we moved apart and lay side by side, hands clasped, whispering the tender words we had never spoken before, save in our dreams. The fire died down to glowing embers; the timbers of the cottage roof creaked in the wind. In the distance, the waves sighed against the shore. The cat jumped onto the bed, then crept across to wedge itself solidly between us. And I drifted into a deep, healing sleep.

When night was over, we opened the shutters on a sky washed by the storm to a pale, clear blue. All that we needed to say was already said. Before the settlement was fully awake, Flint was gone.

A few days later, when I was restored to health, I began to learn the wisdom of water.

CHAPTER NINE

TALI KEPT COUNT WITH SCRATCHES ON A STONE outside our cottage door, groups of five, one line with four across it, like little trees. Perhaps she had thought ten days might be sufficient, or twenty, or thirty. The trees became a grove, a wood, a forest. The days grew longer and warmer, and the island sheep got fatter. And still I was learning.

Tali and I sat on a wall above Hidden Cove, looking out to the south under a sky filled with strange clouds, here a tall tower, here a three-headed monster, here a cruel figure with a flail. Below us, the sea was churned to angry white-caps. There was not a fishing boat to be seen.

"Surely she must be able to tell you how much longer," Tali said. "Ask her, at least. You know how vital it is that we move on soon."

"I can't ask." It was impossible to explain how wrong that would be. All day, every day I had spent with the Hag, practicing, endlessly practicing. It was not for me to question her on anything. Her power was immense; I wondered, now, that I had ever thought to challenge her.

Most days we worked in her cavern, which was spacious and earthen-floored with a fine view out to the west. Thus far I had done very little calling. Instead, I had spent a great deal of time standing utterly still with my eyes shut, feeling in my inner self the working of waves and tide, or the subtle movements of fish out there in the ocean. Breathing as they breathed; learning the great rhythms of the sea. Feeling the same patterns in my blood and in my breath, and becoming one with them. This kind of learning could not be rushed. It must happen in its own natural time. I could not explain this to Tali. The Hag's wisdom was secret; I knew this without being told.

"We have to be patient. When I'm ready, she'll let me go."

A weighty silence followed. We had both hoped to be back at Shadowfell by midsummer, or at the very least, to be well up the Rush valley before the roads became crowded with folk heading for the Gathering. For even though that celebration had become a testament to Keldec's cruelty, people still flocked there in the hundreds to watch the games. If any major household did not send representatives, its lord and lady might be seen as suspect at the least, and at the worst openly defiant. The consequences of that could be dire. Folk would begin to move well before midsummer day in order to be sure they did not draw attention by arriving in the Summerfort area late. And even if we took the same route we'd used coming west, we could not avoid the main tracks entirely.

"I don't understand why you can't just ask her. Explain to her that you have to visit the north too before winter."

"She knows that. Tali, I can't press her. What if she rushed things and let me leave before I was ready, and then, when I needed to use my gift for the cause, something went wrong because I'd missed a vital part of the training? I know how urgent it is to move on. But we do have to be patient about this."

"It's not just the risk of being on the tracks when they're busy. If we're back at Shadowfell for midsummer, at least some of our folk will be there, and we can talk about progress and make new plans. This enterprise is picking up speed; it's vital that we keep in touch."

I said nothing. I knew she was worried about Regan. I suspected she was only waiting until we returned to Shadowfell to pass the job of guarding me on to someone else and go back to her old job as our leader's shadow.

Tali sighed. "It feels wrong to be here so long. This place—it lulls a person into a false sense of peace. And that's dangerous. Keldec and his forces are still out there maiming and killing, making new laws to torment the people of Alban, grinding the chieftains' faces into the dirt. People still live every day in fear. And over here, folk go about their lives as if none of that existed. They act as if all that matters is shearing the sheep or hauling in a catch." She glanced over her shoulder, in the general direction of the settlement. "Not that I grudge them contentment. That's what we all want. But I need to be out there *doing* something about it, not wasting my time kicking a ball around with a bunch of children while I wait for you."

"Then go," I said.

A silence.

"I mean it, go. Between the Hag, the Good Folk, and the islanders I'm perfectly safe here. The place is remote. The Cull doesn't come to the isles, or hasn't in two years. If it's so important to get back to Shadowfell, leave me and go back on your own."

She got up and began to pace, every part of her restless. "Don't be stupid, Neryn, of course I can't go without you. The mission Regan gave me was to guard you. To keep you safe on your journey. That includes the trip back. The suggestion is ridiculous."

"Either you do that, or you exercise patience. I'm sorry you're unhappy, but we have to wait until she says it's time."

Tali came back to seat herself on the wall beside me. "Sorry," she muttered. "It's just . . . as long as he doesn't . . ."

"As long as he doesn't what? You mean Regan?"

"If you knew the story, you'd understand better."

"Is that the story you keep saying is not yours to tell? I've grasped enough to know that a catastrophe befell his family, that there was nobody else left, that he gave up his claim to the chieftaincy of the isles in order to go to ground and start the movement to dethrone Keldec. Isn't that all I need to know?"

"It wasn't Keldec's Enforcers who swept down on Regan's household and kept killing until everyone but him was gone." There was a look on her face that chilled me. I could only describe it as savage. "It was one of the chieftains of Alban. The king required a demonstration of loyalty; the man had a choice: perform this deed or see something similar happen to his own family and retainers. Keldec delights in such games. So he got his demonstration, and the isles lost a fine chieftain, along with his heirs."

"I saw a district chieftain hanged last autumn," I told her. "Dunchan of Silverwater. The Enforcers put him to death in front of his family. His wife challenged them and they killed her too. That household was lucky to lose no more."

"How was it you were there?"

"I was passing by, in the woods above Dunchan's stronghold. I watched and moved on. There was nothing I could do."

"But there's something you can do now."

"Yes. Too late for Dunchan and his wife. But not too late for all the others Keldec and his forces could destroy if nobody acts to stop it. Tali, where was Regan when his family was killed?"

She grimaced. "With Flint, on another island. They came back to find . . . well, you can imagine. The attackers were still on the Cradle, watching things burn. Regan wanted to rush in and exact bloody vengeance, the two of them against hundreds; he was possessed by fury. If Flint had not been with him, he would certainly have got himself killed that day. Instead, the two of them turned their boat around and slipped away into the dusk." After a little, she added, "The man who carried out that raid believed his forces had accounted for the whole family. That was what he reported to the king. Regan had another name then, you understand, another identity. Nobody knows he's still alive. Except us. Except the rebels. And not even all of them know who he was before."

This was enough to silence me completely. She had just entrusted me with the most powerful and dangerous of secrets. If revealed to the wrong person, this knowledge could be Regan's death sentence.

"And now you're wondering why I would tell you such a thing," said Tali. "You know as well as I do that this is the kind of information we don't share unless it's absolutely necessary for strategic reasons. In its way, this is that kind of reason. The chieftain whom Keldec ordered to carry out that raid was Boran of Wedderburn."

"Wedderburn . . . The territory where we were attacked on the way here? Didn't they say their lord's name was Keenan?"

"Keenan is the son; Boran died a few years ago. Keenan's an unknown quantity. He's one of the chieftains we haven't yet approached. The treatment you and I received at the hands of those so-called hunters hardly inspires confidence. When put to the ultimate test, Boran was faultlessly obedient to Keldec. Though, to be fair to the man, that must have cost him dear. It would take great strength of character to refuse such an order."

"You believe Boran should have said no and seen his own household put to the sword instead?" An unwelcome thought was in my mind, that it was precisely this kind of manipulation that Tali feared could be carried out on Flint and me, since we had been foolish enough to develop tender feelings for each other. "Didn't the king ask Boran to carry out the raid because he doubted his loyalty? His son may not be a king's man through and through."

"We don't know why Keldec asked that of Boran. But yes, when he imposes this kind of task on someone, it's usually because their loyalty is suspect."

"It's a terrible choice. A man might take his own life rather than obey. Or flee with his family, turn his back on home forever, if he could."

"That's what this is all about: impossible choices, and being brave enough to make them. Yes, even if it means a man's nearest and dearest are sacrificed for the greater good."

"You would stand by and see your own children die in order to prove that point?"

Tali's eyes were turned away from me, out toward the sea and the southern isles. Her jaw was set tight. "I have no children. I never will. I have no husband, no lover, no family. Only fellow rebels, others like me. All of them understand how it has to be. Hard. Cruel. Brutal. Full of choices like the one Andra had to face. That makes it all the more vital to keep what we do under strict control. You and Flint—that's out of control now, or he'd never have come back here when he dreamed you were in trouble. It was unplanned, it was foolish, it was too risky. He knew I was here. He knew I was looking after you. Flint is dedicated to the rebel cause. It's his life. But he didn't come back because of that. He came back because he loves you. It's a weakness. I see in his eyes that if he had Andra's choice, and if it was you who stood to be sacrificed, he couldn't do it."

At this point I saw Himself on the path, approaching us. His form, on land, was that of a robustly built man; he walked on feet like any other man, and within the layers of his weedy attire he had arms and hands that he used as a man did. He was, all the same, profoundly Other, a creature of deep water and tides, his flattened features and dark bright eyes telling of wonders we human folk could never dream of. Every day, when the Hag was ready for me, he would come up to fetch me. He never spoke. I had never learned his real name, if indeed he had one a human ear could comprehend. But I was always happy to see him. There was no doubt he was kindly disposed to both Tali and me, and I suspected his influence made the Hag somewhat easier on us than she might have been.

"He's here," Tali said. "I'll be waiting in the usual spot before dusk."

"Thank you."

"It's yourself, then." This was the Hag's daily greeting, delivered without emphasis while she examined me closely, as if since yesterday I might have turned into someone else.

"It is, and I bid you good morning." I had my staff with me, as well as a waterskin and the remains of last night's supper in a covered dish. She and I would share this offering at some point during the day's work. "A fair day." She'd never told me how I should address her, so I avoided using terms like *my lady,* which so obviously didn't fit. I simply made sure I sounded respectful.

"Aye, it is. And just as well, since we'll be out on the cliffs. Ready?"

"As ready as I can be." We made our way from the cave mouth along a ledge. Far below us, great waves pounded in to smash themselves on the rocks. Above and around us screamed an army of agitated birds.

"Breathe," said the Hag. Sure-footed as an island lad collecting eggs, she stepped along the narrow pathway, her back straight, one hand lightly touching the rock wall beside her. I breathed and followed.

The ledge rose gradually, rounded a headland, became broad enough for two to sit side by side without immediate risk of falling.

"You can sit down," she said.

We sat, gazing out to the west.

"You've made progress."

I bowed my head. Her praise warmed me, but I could not assume anything from it.

"What is your greatest need?" she asked me. "As a Caller, what is it you must be able to do?"

Before she had begun to teach me, I'd have taken my answer from ancient tales. A Caller's purpose was to unite Good Folk and humankind in a battle against evil. But now I saw it rather differently.

"I must be a . . . a conduit. I must bring the understanding of water, earth, fire, and air to everything I do. I must use that wisdom for healing. Learning. Restoring peace. Mending what is broken."

"Words, words," said the Hag. "Peace. Healing. Mending. But first war, struggle, death. What of your part in that? Your rebels will not win their time of peace without more losses."

"I'm expecting it to be difficult," I said. "Here in the isles we are surrounded by wonder, by beauty, by natural power. In a place like this I can feel the flow, I can feel it working through me. I know it won't be the same at the end, when we confront the king."

"Indeed not. But you have used your gift on a field of battle."

"Used it imperfectly."

"Folk will die, Neryn, even if you become the most expert Caller Alban has ever seen. Folk will be cut down. Your folk. My folk. You cannot command the course of a battle without seeing losses."

There was a question I had kept back, hoping the answer might come up as part of my training. Now seemed the time to ask it. "Is there a way to protect your folk against cold iron? I have seen its effects and . . . you speak of losses, and I understand that they are part of any battle. But I can't expect Good Folk to fight alongside us when the enemy is armed with iron swords and spears. Many of the smaller folk would have no defense against that."

She looked at me awhile, her strong features somber. "It is a weighty matter," she said. "The answer does not lie with me."

My heart sank. I said nothing.

"Some can resist iron," the Hag went on. "Some it weakens; some it destroys. I can teach you to call one from many; to shape your call to a particular being. But on a field of battle, where all is disturbance and confusion, that may not be enough. I know of no charm that can be thrown

246

over a whole army to shield them. If there were such a spell, only the most potent mage could wield it."

Then it lay beyond my reach. I felt something akin to despair.

"You might ask the Lord of the North, if you can wake him from his sleep. Iron comes from earth. Perhaps he has his own answers." She narrowed her eyes at me. "Fix your mind on the true purpose of your quest," she said. "What lies beyond the sorrow, beyond the losses, beyond the battle?"

"Peace. Justice. Freedom."

"Aye. Good things, fine things. You must not let these doubts obscure them."

I nodded, knowing I must accept her wisdom. We sat on awhile in silence, then she said, "Close your eyes. Go through your cycles of breathing."

I did so; the breathing was a discipline she had taught me early, to calm the mind and body and make myself open to the power that must flow through me, power I would use in my call. It took time. Time I would surely not have on the field of battle.

"Somewhere out in the bay, a hungry seal hunts for fish," the Hag said. "And somewhere, a school of fish hides from her, wise enough to find the concealment of an underwater reef and wait until she passes. Call the seal toward that hiding place. Then bring one fish out to her. Only one."

"But . . ." Seals? Fish? My gift was not to call creatures, only Good Folk.

"No ordinary seal. And among a school of ordinary

fish, one that is not quite a fish. You have learned much, Neryn. Find them. Call them."

"But then—"

"There will be death? Do you imagine these gulls feed their young in the nest without the deaths of fish? Do the seals swim from isle to far isle without taking a meal on the way? Do those folk up in the village keep their sheep and chickens for their suppertime conversation?"

This had nothing to do with seals eating fish or human folk eating chickens. She'd implied those were Good Folk down there, Good Folk in the shape of creatures. I hated this. But if I were eventually to send Good Folk into battle, I must summon the will to do it.

With eyes closed, I breathed with the ocean. In my mind, I drifted with the gulls on the swell. The waves cradled me, until I dived beneath into a realm of light and shadow, a mysterious place of drifting weed and sudden darting fish. I was one with the water. Its power ran in my veins; my heart beat with its ebb and flow.

I sought the hungry seal and found her not far from the rocks at the cliff's base, swimming slowly, sensing the fish nearby but unable to find them. Held her in my mind, her sleek body, her need for sustenance, her knowledge of her young one, waiting for her return. And the fish; there they were, under a rock shelf, in darkness. Safe. *Call one fish out to her. One that does not belong.*

They were all the same. Narrow pale bodies, round eyes, delicate fins. Quiet together. I wrapped my mind around them, fluid as water, and felt it: one here was not the fish it appeared to be. Into my open thoughts came a cross little voice, saying *Ca' me oot tae me death, would ye, and for naethin' but a bittie learnin'?*

I nearly stood up and said I wanted none of it then. But I did not. I stayed strong, and called the wee one out from under the reef. The seal took it in one bite.

"Ah," said the Hag, drawing a breath like a sigh, as if she had witnessed it all at first hand. "It gets no easier, lassie. But you'll have the strength for it. When the time comes, you surely will."

I learned to summon the small strange creatures of rock shelf and skerry. I learned to call the beings of shore and cliff face. A sizable clan of uncanny folk lived there, concealed in chinks and crannies, existing alongside the roosts of seabirds. Gulls would rise, startled, as a stony visage or mossy head poked up out of the rocks to look about.

Sometimes Herself would take me out in the boat and make me call beings of the deep, fey ocean creatures with long fronded tentacles that would swim alongside us awhile, moving with their own stately grace. I learned to control my seasickness. I learned to keep my breathing steady, though the boat still scared me. I learned to concentrate on the call and block out everything else. Sometimes creatures died because of what I did, though only in the natural way of those that live in the ocean or on the shore. I was not sure she understood what this cost me. But sometimes I thought perhaps she knew all too well, since I had done the same when I bid the stanie mon fall, and when the river being drowned one man and turned two into fish at my request. I learned that in the end, only I was responsible for my actions.

Herself was good at springing surprises—the sudden appearance of the selkie on the boat, come from nowhere at all; an abrupt change from calm to storm, so I nearly fell overboard; a flock of gulls swooping down to circle me, squawking, as I attempted a particularly difficult call.

"You must be prepared for anything," she told me. "The expected, the unexpected. The sudden shock; the betrayal that creeps up on you with gradual pace, so it's at your back door before you recognize it." She reached out to take my hands in hers. "Be as fluid as water, and as strong. Nothing stops water. Water is eternal."

When Tali's rock was covered in a forest of scratches, there came a day when my teacher made me stand at the cave mouth with my eyes shut from early morning until the sun was in the west, its rays warm on my face. A long vigil: I knew I was being tested.

Her instruction, when it came, was familiar. "Find a shoal of fish, swimming northward now beyond the head-land there. All are fey. Among them, find one with a red dot below its left eye."

Far quicker now from daily practice, I had it soon enough. The glittering shoal, and the tiny minds quite alien to my own. One among the many had a slightly greater space around it, as if its fellows shrank a little from it. The small red mark.

"Follow this creature as the others leave it."

They swam off, sunlight through the water catching their movement and turning it to a shining streak before they vanished. One fish left alone, a tiny speck in the immensity of the sea.

"Follow him."

This was harder; the creature was so tiny, and he swam in short, panicky darts, now here, now almost out of sight. I bent all my will on tracking him as he moved through the water. I was the water. I was his terror, his need for survival.

He swam up to the surface, the sun lending him a sudden brightness. Above, the dark shadow of a gull, hovering.

"My creatures are efficient hunters," came the Hag's voice from beside me. "Keep your wee one safe. Keep him alive."

It was the hardest call I had yet attempted. The small one was in a panic, every sense attuned to flight, deafened by fear. He darted one way, then the other, deeper, shallower, in and out of the light. The gull was in no hurry; it kept pace, beating its wings a few times, then gliding above the prey, waiting for the right moment to snatch. My call had no words in it. I was the sea current washing the small one toward the concealment of the reef; I was a wavelet moving a tiny raft of floating debris over to hide him. I was a watery embrace, cradling him, bearing him to safety. *Not much farther. Come, come on.*

"Your wee one is flagging. Do not let him die."

He was exhausted. His mind was blank with terror, adrift and helpless. The gull hovered, ready for the strike.

I was not aware of making a choice. I called *Come up!*

and in my mind was Himself, a powerful and ancient island presence, grave and good and kindly. *Come up and save this wee one from death.* All that I had learned, all that the Hag had taught me, and all that I knew before, I put into the call. The words in my mind were simple, but my intention included far more: *Do no harm as you come, to yourself or to any creature. I hope you will see this as an amusement, not as an imposition.* I tried to hold both selkie and fishling in my mind: great and small, strong and weak.

I did not see what happened, exactly. Even if my eyes had been open, we were too far away, too high up. But I felt it. The water moving, the selkie cleaving a powerful path through the waves, the little fish finding itself washed sideways under a projecting shelf of rock, where it sheltered in a minuscule cavern. The selkie passing by to surge up from the water and plunge down again in play, and the gull in its neat boots flying high, swooping low, until it became quite obvious the whole thing was a game. I opened my eyes to find that both selkie and gull were indeed visible, down below us in the sun-touched waves, dancing about as if mightily pleased with themselves.

I swayed, suddenly dizzy.

"Sit down." The Hag took hold of my arm, moved me back from the cave mouth, and helped me sit. "Eat, drink, rest awhile." She fetched the food herself, making sure I drank from the waterskin, dividing the supplies into two portions. I could hardly summon the strength to pick up a piece of bread, let alone take a bite of it.

"Eat," she said again. "You surprised me. Took a harder

path. You could have called the bird. What if Himself had decided not to cooperate?"

"Then I would have made an error in thinking I had learned enough to summon him."

Herself smiled, revealing her sharp white teeth. "None of those tricky answers, lassie. It's not the Master of Shadows you're dealing with. Say plainly why you made that choice, and don't mince your words."

"I thought you were testing me. It seemed a good time to try . . . another step."

"Testing yourself, aye?"

I could not tell if she was pleased or offended by what I had done. "I meant no disrespect. Even though Himself does not talk to me, not in words, I sense he is very wise. And I think he enjoys a joke. If I had not known that, I would not have called such a powerful being when this was only an . . . exercise." I hesitated. "No, that's not quite right. There was a life in the balance, and every life matters. It burdens me that some were lost along the path of my learning. Every life is precious, from the smallest to the most powerful. From a wee fish to . . . yourself." The only thing I did not add, would not, was that I thought maybe she and the selkie were a team in more than one way; that perhaps he moderated her magic and her choices, even to the extent of being her equal in power and influence. This was a deep kind of knowledge, one that lay beyond words.

"Aye," was all the Hag said. "Oh, aye."

We shared the food in silence, then she made me rest awhile, lying on the cave floor breathing in slow patterns until I had recovered my strength. It was a long time before she spoke again.

"Do not be concerned about overreaching yourself. You understand the natural order of things; you're in no danger of forgetting it. If you were, I would not be teaching you. It's a balance you must always keep, Neryn, for a Caller must on the one hand be sure and confident in the use of the gift, and on the other hand have no desire for personal power, no ambition to rule or to dominate. You know the perils that could lead to."

"I do."

"You understand, don't you, that if you should fall into the hands of the king, he'd likely not want to destroy you, but to use your gift for his own ends?"

"Yes. We've known that from the first."

"Then take the greatest care on your journey, for although your gift is not yet fully developed, it is strong. The risks are high. You carry within you the power to save Alban from this king's tyranny. You carry also the potential for great harm, should others seek to turn you to their will."

"I understand."

"Well, then," she said. "You'll be off to the north, and good luck to you."

It took me a moment to understand. "You mean . . . I am finished here?" And on my lips was the word *Already?* though that was quite the opposite of what Tali would have said. It did not seem possible that I had learned all the Hag had to teach me.

"For now. I think we will see you in the isles again someday. But you've a long journey ahead of you before that time comes. The Lord of the North . . . they say his folk cannot wake him from sleep, for he's sunk deep in sorrow. They may welcome you, if they believe you can rouse him. The White Lady has long kept her light veiled; she will be hard to find. As for the Master of Shadows, he is a wayward creature. There's no knowing what to expect from him."

I was still recovering from the startling fact that I was released from training and free to go. I knew these were good tidings. If we moved quickly, we could be at Shadowfell in time to see the others; with luck, I might complete my training with the Lord of the North before winter. But . . .

"You look less than delighted," the Hag observed dryly.

"I am . . . pleased. Surprised. And sad that I will be leaving the isles. You've given me a rare gift. The learning has been hard at times. Testing. Different. But I will miss it, and I will miss you."

She grinned. "Now, that does surprise me. Should I have been harder on you, I wonder? Crueler? Or is it not me you'll be missing, but Himself, with his quiet way of getting into folk's hearts?"

"I will miss both of you, and I will miss the isles and the fine people who live here. This place is like the Alban of old, Alban as it should be. I never lived in that Alban; Keldec became king in the year of my birth. If we win our war, if we restore peace and justice and ordinary lives for everyone, I would like to settle here. With . . . with my man. But I shouldn't say that. I shouldn't even think it. That's perilous. It's forbidden."

Her grin had faded. "You need your dreams," she said. "You need hope. Go on now, tell your friend the good news, for it is good, and say your farewells to the folk who have helped you."

"We'll have to arrange a boat—"

"One of the lads will ferry you over. We'd best send a bird to eye out the situation at Pentishead, make sure it's safe for you. Tell your guard not to rush into anything. Wait for my word."

"Of course. And thank you. Thank you from the bottom of my heart."

"Ach, away with you! Be brave, be strong, be wise. That will be the best thanks for me."

On the shore at Pentishead, a boat was burning. I saw the smoke as we headed northward on a fishing vessel crewed by a pair of taciturn islanders, and Tali with her sharp eyes told us what it was. There were Enforcers in Pentishead, so our boatmen would be dropping us at Darkwater instead. I sat in the stern, keeping out of the way, my mind full of the night my father died. In a boat moored at the Darkwater jetty. A boat all aflame. As my belly churned with sick memory, I told myself, *Be brave, be strong, be wise.*

Tali had not offered to help sail the boat, but sat beside me wrapped in her own thoughts. I could guess what was troubling her. From Darkwater our path would be longer.

Every delay made it less likely we could reach Shadowfell by midsummer. I imagined she was revising her strategy, calculating what paths we might take, perhaps whether we would risk crossing Keenan's land again to win ourselves a few days.

Far Isle slipped away behind us; the plume of smoke became a ribbon, then a thread picked apart by the wind. Grim-faced, the fishermen kept their gaze northward. Particles of ash floated in the air around us.

The boat moved on through sea mist and smoky shadows, bearing us to Darkwater. We left the isles behind.

Chapter Ten

Our boatmen put us ashore near the mouth of Dark-water Loch, some distance from the settlement. As soon as they had unloaded us and our belongings, they turned the boat and headed back out to sea in the gathering dark.

We made camp in the remains of a ruined croft. We had supplies, thanks to the kindness of the islanders, and if we could avoid people's notice on the way, so much the better. As it was, when I rose next morning, it was to find Tali gazing eastward along the loch and muttering to herself.

"What?" I asked, trying not to snarl. My back was aching; I had become used to the comfortable bed on Far Isle.

"Enforcers. Rode into the settlement at first light. At least three of them; I can see horses that don't belong to any local farmer. We won't be going that way either. Pack up quickly, let's be gone before anyone decides this would be a nice spot for a morning walk." Her tone softened a little as she looked at me. "It should be safe to go down to the water and wash your face, wake yourself up a bit. I'm sorry if you wanted to go up there and say your goodbyes. It's not to be."

It was less than a year since the night my father died. It felt as if an age had passed. "I've said my goodbyes," I told her. "He's with me wherever I go. Tali, there is no other path. Only the main track, and the little one that goes up the hill right behind the settlement, the one Flint took me on last time."

"I'll find a track. Get moving, wash, and pack your things. We'll eat later, when we're safely away from here."

She did not say it, but it was in my thoughts as I splashed my face in the salt water of the shallows, threw on the rest of my clothes, and stuffed my belongings in my bag. There were Enforcers in Pentishead; there were Enforcers at Darkwater. Might they not have a presence all the way from here to Summerfort?

There was no going by the main track. The king's men were everywhere. Tali took me north, then inland, planning to come back southward to the track Flint and I had once used. But the way was all steep rocky climbs and sudden treacherous drops, a landscape full of perils even for the most seasoned wayfarer, and painfully slow to traverse.

Days passed, precious days, with little ground gained. Our supplies ran low again. What woodlands existed here were small and sparse, not like the forested hills farther east, where a skillful person could trap rabbits or forage for herbs and roots. Any creatures who survived in this place were fast runners and expert hiders. We rationed what we had, refilled our waterskins whenever we could, and kept on going.

Tali did not like admitting she had made a mistake. She was seldom wrong, and to err on such an important matter was galling to her. But the path she chose, at some points the only possible path, led us farther and farther north and became harder and harder. One morning, after a night spent sleeping among barren hills, we climbed to a vantage point and looked out over a landscape of daunting wildness: high mountains to the north, a deep valley to the east with more mountains beyond, lower hills to the west, and beyond them the gray expanse of the sea. As the raven flew, we had not come far at all. And there was no way ahead.

"All right," Tali said, as if the thing had been settled between us already, though I had held my tongue and let her lead me, believing that if she said she could find a path to the Rush valley, she could do just that. "We're going back. If I thought there were a way to get straight to your Lord of the North from here, I'd suggest we change the plan and do that. But there's no way we can cross those mountains."

"Going back. You mean back to Darkwater."

"What do you think I mean?" It was a snarl. I knew her well enough to realize her anger was not directed at me.

"The Enforcers might be gone by now, I suppose." I offered this tentatively, wondering if silence might be a wiser option.

"I've no intention of taking you right through the settlement, Neryn. I'm not stupid. I'll find another path." A silence. Perhaps she was waiting for me to say, *I've heard that before.*

"We'd better be moving, then." This was a disaster either way. Make good time, and we would arrive on the road to Summerfort when everyone was heading for the Gathering. Be slow, and we would meet them coming back. Go to ground somewhere until they had passed, and we had no chance of reaching the Lord of the North before winter.

It was much later, when we had been walking all day and were starting to look for a place to settle for the night, that she said, "I'm sorry, Neryn. I was sure I could do this." When I did not reply, she went on, "Thank you for not saying what you might have said. I'll get you to the Lord of the North in time. I promise."

"Don't promise," I said. "You can't control the Enforcers. Or the weather. I know you'll do your best, and that's enough. Now let's find somewhere to camp before my legs give up and you have to carry me."

By the time we reached the Darkwater area again, we had stopped talking about getting to Shadowfell by midsummer. Quite clearly that was now impossible. Looking down on Darkwater settlement from the concealment of the forested hill behind, we saw Enforcers patrolling there, masked figures on long-legged dark horses. Signs of last autumn's raid still marked the place: the jetty was half-burned, and there were houses with patched-up doors and shutters. I whispered a prayer for my father, whose bones lay down there in the bay somewhere, washed by the endless tide. We hastened away, turning our steps eastward.

For the next two days we made good progress, following a snaking path through the hills. At night we camped without fire, for although we were off the main way, this region had more farms and settlements than the north, and we did not want to attract attention any sooner than we must. On the third day, as we drew closer to Silverwater, it became impossible to go unnoticed even in the forest. Folk were on the move and headed in one direction only: toward Summerfort. They went mostly in small groups, carrying bundles on their backs. Here and there we saw a child in arms or a dog running alongside. The travelers' faces were not bright with the anticipation of feasting and entertainment, but wary, as if we were not the only ones wishing to avoid attention.

There were some exceptions. A group of young men, joking and laughing, stopped to greet us at a fork in the track, asking if we wanted company on our way. It seemed they had been drinking ale, and perhaps that explained their boldness. Tali managed a laugh in response and said no thank you, her husband would not be happy with the idea. To my great relief the lads did not press the point, but went on their way. We waited until they were out of sight, then took the other fork.

Our story had changed to suit the circumstances. Calla and Luda were from a tiny settlement north of Darkwater, and had been allowed time off from their farmwork to attend the Gathering. It was the most plausible reason for heading east: a reason nobody could question, since half of Alban seemed to be doing the same thing. Once close to Summerfort, we would seize the first opportunity to head up into the woods again and bypass the Gathering altogether. What better time to get up the Rush valley unnoticed than when the eyes of Keldec's court were on the midsummer spectacle? The Enforcers would all be there; the settlements of Alban would be spared their ominous presence, at least for a while.

Eventually Silverwater came into view, a long, shining expanse of freshwater amid tracts of pine and oak forest. The trees were in full summer garb, lush and green; it should be easy to find concealed paths through that woodland, which was the place where I had first met Sage and Red Cap last autumn. Would they be anywhere near? With so many men and women on the road, it seemed unlikely the Good Folk would come out. Most people carried knives for their own protection, and few, if any, would trouble to shield them with charms, even if they knew how. To uncanny folk, the very air must reek of iron.

We sat awhile on a flat rock, high on a hillside, looking out over loch and forest. The day was fair, the sky a sweet blue with scudding clouds like tufts of swansdown.

"Neryn."

"Mm?"

"I've been thinking. From this point on we might be safer on the main road, in the crowd. On these side tracks we'll be noticed every time we encounter other travelers. If we walk with a bigger group, or at least near one, we've a better chance of blending in."

"There will be king's men down there, keeping an eye out for anything unusual."

"We're not unusual. We're just two more women on the road. Keep to the story, say no more than we absolutely must, and we can get through safely. We should be on the shore of Silverwater by tonight. Easier to join the crowd now than suddenly appear just before Hiddenwater, where we've no choice but to use the only track."

"All right. If that's what you think is best."

"You don't sound convinced."

I did not tell her the thought of sharing the road with Enforcers made me feel sick. It was all very well for her; she had not seen her brother impaled on an enemy spear and choking on his lifeblood. She had not seen her grandmother turned into a witless shell at the hands of an Enthraller. She had not been captured and believed herself about to undergo the same fate. But no, that was unfair. I did not know Tali's story. Alban being the place it was, very likely her past had its own share of horrors. "I know we have to do it sometime soon," I said. "But I'm afraid. I can't help it. If something goes wrong, I won't be able to call, not down there."

"Indeed, so make sure you're not tempted. Whatever happens. I mean that, Neryn. Whatever happens. Do you understand? The king's men mustn't get the slightest sniff of the fact that you're a Caller. Not the least hint."

The look on her face terrified me. "I know that," I muttered.

"I can keep you safe in most situations, though if I'm

supposed to be a farmworker, it's clearly best if I don't have to fight."

Her weapons traveled rolled up in the bedding, apart from one knife concealed on her person. She had her staff, of course, which I had cause to know she could employ with great skill in both attack and defense. In a fight against a single Enforcer she might well win, even so lightly armed. To do so would be almost as perilous as my using my gift, for such acts never went unpunished, and the king's punishments were delivered with both speed and savage efficiency.

We camped in the woods one more night. The next morning we joined the crowd on the road. Here the foot traffic was supplemented by ox-drawn carts, by small groups of highborn folk on horseback, and by the occasional flock of sheep or herd of goats that still had to be moved along, Gathering or no Gathering. Even here the mood was subdued, for wariness and distrust had worked their way deep into the fabric of Alban's people during the years of Keldec's reign. In the main, folk gave us sideways looks, then ignored us. The most we got from anyone was a nod, a word or two on the weather or the crowded road. We returned these cursory greetings in kind. Making friends was not part of the plan.

Tali's theory proved to be correct: despite the press of folk, progress was quicker on this more direct path. I hated it. I could see from the tight set of Tali's body that she was uncomfortable too. Every word and every gesture had to be guarded. We walked all day, and when the fading light made going on impossible, we did what everyone else did: found a suitable spot by the road to make a rudimentary camp. The distrust between folk was not so great as to prevent each encampment from sharing a fire: everyone helped gather wood, and everyone enjoyed the warmth. Our supplies being scant, we went down to the loch and fished, competing with many others. We were lucky; or maybe we were more practiced. We shared our catch with a family that had been keeping pace with us on the road, a farmer and his wife with two shy daughters. The girls were close to the age I had been when the Enforcers came to Corbie's Wood and tore my world apart. I wondered why their parents would choose to take them to the Gathering.

In time we came to Hiddenwater, where the warrior-ghosts had recognized in Tali the proof that their chieftain's noble line lived on. She walked by that lonely loch with her raven markings hidden, and folk stretched out before and behind, eyes uneasy, tongues silent. Everyone knew the place was haunted. Perhaps only Tali and I were aware of how close those presences were, though we saw nothing of them, only heard, in the chill wind that whistled through the bowl-shaped valley, the echo of pipe and drum.

"We greet you," I whispered into a fold of my shawl. "We honor you. Today we must pass on by." Beside me, Tali strode forward, her eyes shining with the memory, her jaw set like a fighter's. I jabbed her in the ribs, scowling. "You're walking too fast for me, Luda."

She rounded her shoulders, slowed her pace, became more of a girl and less of a warrior before my eyes.

"I hate this," she whispered. "Every wretched step of it."

"Me too. I hope it's not too much farther."

She blinked at me, then fell silent. Calla and Luda, after all, were going to the Gathering for the very first time. The closer we got to Summerfort, the more important it became to play our parts every moment of every day.

By Deepwater we encountered the group of noisy young men again. They camped near us and kept everyone awake with their oaths and ribald stories. The couple with the two daughters settled as far from the youths as they could, and Tali and I spread out our bedding alongside them, well away from the fire. We ate cold fish left over from the previous night, then settled to sleep. But the voices went on, loud, combative, slurred by too much ale.

"A pox on you, good-for-nothing maggot, I can beat you anytime!"

"Just try it, you sick whelp! You'll get what's coming to you."

"Call me names, would you? I'm more man than you are!"

"Get up and show us, then! Let's see the size of you!"

"*Calla.*" The sharp whisper was Tali's. A fight had broken out among the youths and was drawing in other men from the encampment. Someone ran across the area and fell over one of the two young girls, who screamed in fright; her father rose to his feet, fists bunched. "Get up, back away quietly." Into the shadows, she meant, out of sight and out of trouble. I scrambled to my feet.

The farmer had stepped in front of his daughters and was confronting the fellow who had woken them. "Keep your distance, lout. And hush your noise; there's folk here need their sleep."

"*Calla, move.*"

I backed away, beyond the circle of firelight.

"Who are you calling a lout, old man? Hit me, go on, hit me!"

"Calm down," the farmer said, not giving an inch. Behind him his wife had put an arm around either daughter, like a hen spreading her wings to protect her chickens. "You've had too much ale, lad, that's about the size of it. Take a breath, back off, leave the rest of us alone. There are children here." It was an impressive display of self-control.

"You mean those girls hiding behind you? Children? Those are fine big lassies, ripe for the taking. One for me, one for my friend here—"

The farmer's blow landed on his jaw and he went down like a felled tree. That should have been the end of it, but with roars of outrage the other youths surged forward, and suddenly what had been a foolish scrap became something far more dangerous. The farmer was strong and sober, but angry; the youths were slowed by drunkenness, but there were six or seven of them to the one of him. The other travelers retreated into the shadows, as we had, not wanting to get involved. The woman and her two girls stood paralyzed with fear as the farmer took one blow after another. Now he was reeling, staggering, his punches wide of the target, his face red with effort. Two men held him back. Two more moved in on the mother and daughters.

I couldn't use my gift, not here among so many folk.

But how could I stand by while an innocent man was hurt and two little girls were assaulted? A man was grappling with the farmer's wife, trying to prize one of the girls from her arms. One of the youths seized the other girl and threw her, shrieking, over his shoulder.

"This one's mine!" he shouted.

The farmer was down, with two men kicking his prone form. I quivered with anger and frustration, desperate to run out there and do something.

"Leave that man alone!" Tali strode forward, staff in hand. "Step back and be quick about it." Her voice cut through the din with calm authority. With the firelight making a flickering pattern of gold and gray on her strong features, she might have been a vengeful goddess from ancient times. Almost before I could draw a shocked breath, she executed a precise sequence of movements with booted feet and staff, and the two attackers were lying on the ground beside the farmer. "You! Put that girl down right now or you'll be joining them. Back off, the lot of you. Your behavior is a disgrace."

The youth set the girl on her feet and she ran to her mother, who was on her knees beside her husband now, checking his injuries. The other girl, showing considerable presence of mind, was fetching a waterskin and a cloth from their belongings.

"What sort of woman are you?" The young man's voice was shaking with bewildered fury. He advanced on Tali. Behind him, one or two of the others—perhaps less drunk or with better judgment—hovered as if uncertain whether to support him. "I'd say there's something wrong with you, that's what I'd say." He cast a glance around the firelit encampment, as if to draw in the silent onlookers. "Something not right. No woman fights like that. No ordinary woman. Give her a knife, someone. Let's see how she does in a real fight."

Tali had not moved. She stood relaxed—I knew from experience how deceptive this pose was—with her staff upright by her side, held loosely with one hand. One of the youths passed the combative one a knife; another held out a similar weapon to Tali.

"I have my own knife," she said levelly. "But I shouldn't think I'd be needing it." She laid the staff down carefully, then walked forward. "Are you quite sure you want to do this?" she asked politely. "Might it not be wiser to pack up and leave this place, so the rest of us can get some sleep before tomorrow's walk?"

The young man surged toward her, shouting abuse and slashing with his knife. Tali scarcely seemed to move, but a moment later the weapon was flying through the air and the assailant was sprawled on the ground at her feet, wheezing. The knife landed among his companions; they shrank back to avoid injury. Tali made play of dusting off her hands.

"Pack your things and go," she said quietly. "I don't care if it's the middle of the night. These good people don't want your company. You sully the ground you walk on. You pollute the air you breathe. Is this the best you can do, drinking and quarreling and taking your anger out on ordinary folk who've done you no harm? You should be ashamed of yourselves. Go. Now. And think on my words. You're young, you're strong, you're healthy. Make something better of your lives."

In the hush that followed, I heard the older girl sobbing quietly and the groans of the farmer as he came back to consciousness. And I heard, as the young men gathered their things and walked out of the encampment, someone muttering, "What ordinary woman fights like that? Something wrong there."

Later, while the encampment slept, Tali and I lay close together and conducted a conversation in whispers. I did not chide her for breaking our self-imposed rules. She did not apologize for drawing attention.

"Maybe we should head up into the hills."

"Now, in the dark?"

"Tomorrow, early. Those men might talk."

"There are people everywhere, Neryn. You saw them. Running off now is more likely to create suspicion. It would look like an admission of guilt. We should stick to the plan, stay with other people, blend into the crowd."

To this, I had nothing to say. If that was her idea of blending, we were in serious trouble. But I understood entirely why she had done it.

"Another few days and we'll be close by Summerfort. That's the time to break away, when people's attention is on something else."

"If we went now . . . they could hide us, maybe. Sage's clan. I could ask them."

"No!" The protest was sharp, and there was a sleepy

mumble from someone nearby, reminding us of the peril of unguarded words. "You can't bring them out, Neryn, not with so many people around. It's too risky. Now we'd better be quiet. Try to get some rest."

We headed on eastward. Today the farmer and his family were giving us a wider berth. They did not speak to us, nor did they offer to share their food, but turned their faces away rather than meet our eyes. Even among themselves they weren't talking much. The others who had camped alongside us had dispersed into the greater crowd, and on the next night we slept beside strangers, apart from the farmer's family, who established themselves on the opposite side of the encampment. No doubt they knew Tali had taken a risk to defend them, though just how much of a risk only the two of us understood. No doubt they were grateful. But folk feared trouble, and with Summerfort so close and Enforcers out on the road in increasing numbers, they dared not be seen speaking to us in case the young men had been right, and Tali's outstanding combat skill was a canny gift. If we had not been so on edge, we might almost have laughed at that.

On the second morning after the attack on the farmer, the throng on the road was so big that it became hard to make any progress at all. A cart got its wheels stuck in the ditch ahead of us and overturned, spilling a cargo of flour sacks, some of which burst as they landed. We were trapped in a crush of people behind this obstacle, waiting for a group of frazzled men to clear the way. I had never felt so tempted to bolt up into the woods and hide. I longed to be by a campfire with my fey friends, listening to Sage's wise advice and watching as Red Cap tended to his precious infant. The wee one must be almost a year old by now; I hoped it was thriving back in its home forest, if indeed they were here and not out spreading the word across the west. I missed them. I missed the Hag and Himself. I wondered where Flint was now. It was a long time since I had dreamed of him.

"Hold still there!" A man's shout, deep and commanding, snapped me out of my reverie. The crowd fell silent. A rider threaded his way through, coming from behind us: a masked rider on a tall black horse, the harness jingling with fine silver. Behind him came two more. Suddenly, everyone was standing very still indeed. And although, before, there had hardly been room to move, somehow room was made for the Enforcers.

They rode up to the fallen cart and halted. Two got down and began issuing crisp orders; the third stayed on his horse, his gaze moving over the crowd. After a moment he bent down to speak to someone standing beside him.

"*Calla.*" Tali's voice was an urgent undertone.

"What?"

"Take this. Take my knife. Vanish into the crowd. Now."

No time for questions. I managed to snatch the bag as she slung it off her shoulder. I grabbed the knife and stuck it in my belt. As I shrank back into the press of bodies, thankful that folk's attention was all on the king's men, I heard the sound of hoofbeats behind me, and the Enforcer's voice, closer now.

"Is that the woman you saw?"

"That's her."

I knew that second voice; it was one of the boorish youths from our encampment. Nausea rose in my throat. I clenched my teeth on a cry of protest.

"You! Halt!"

Not me; Tali. This was what she'd anticipated. She'd spotted the young man close to the Enforcers and known what was coming. And since there'd be no getting herself out of this particular tight corner, she'd stepped away from me so that I would not be taken too. For Tali was not Regan's secret weapon: I was.

I could not move farther away without pushing people aside and drawing attention to myself. I must hope nobody chose to identify me as her traveling companion. I watched, my belly churning, as the Enforcer swung down from his horse and seized her by the arm. This time she chose not to fight. She stood silent, passive, as the king's man delivered a brutal blow to her jaw, sending her reeling; as he pinned her arms behind her back and bound her wrists together; as he flung her up over his horse, on her belly, and remounted behind her. She hung there limp and silent. I cursed the promise that would not let me use my gift to save her.

The cart and its spilled contents were cleared from the track. The Enforcers rode off eastward, and Tali was gone. Taken for the king. Taken for the Gathering. *Why didn't you fight back?* I asked her silently, but I knew the answer. Not because one woman against three Enforcers would be ridiculous odds—that wouldn't have stopped her. She'd reasoned that the less of a scene there was, the more likely I could slip quietly away.

The crowd followed the riders; I was drawn along with everyone else, heading toward Summerfort. All day I walked, until my back was on fire with pain and my legs were shaking with weariness. There were moments when I might perhaps have made a run for it, headed up a side track without attracting too much attention. But it was never truly safe. Carrying the two bags, I would not be able to climb quickly to the cover of thicker woodland, and if I stopped to repack, folk would notice. There might be someone here who had seen me and Tali walking together earlier. One of those young oafs might think to amuse himself by turning me in as well.

So I plodded on, stopping briefly to drink and to force down a mouthful or two from our meager rations. When the glittering water of the loch began to darken and a wash of violet-gray spread across the sky, I drifted after a group of folk who were looking for a place to camp, and settled myself on the northern edge of the spot they chose, a narrow strip of level ground between the road and the steep wooded hillside. It was not the most comfortable place, but that was good; with luck, no more would come to join them.

As the dusk deepened, I unpacked Tali's bag and transferred the contents to mine. Her knives I rolled in a shawl and stuffed into the bottom; it seemed unlikely I would be using them. *I'll keep them safe for you*, I told her. *I'll keep them oiled and polished and ready*. I folded her clothing as flat as

I could; when she escaped, she would want her trousers, her boy's tunic, her gauntlets, her wrist braces. In an inside pocket of her bag something small was tucked away. I drew it out, and in the pale light of the rising moon I saw that it was a tiny bird carved from oak wood, a raven, wrapped in a square of soft woolen cloth. *You will fly again,* I told her, and now I could not hold back my tears; they flowed hot down my cheeks. *You'll fly swift and straight as the raven. Nobody can bring you down.* They would take her straight to Summerfort. A fine, strong fighter. If she'd been a man, she'd have made a perfect Enforcer, once they rendered her loyal. But women did not become Enforcers. What would they do to her?

What comes next, Tali? I asked her. *What is the plan now?* I knew what she would tell me. *On your own, you'll be safer in the forest. Get off the road and head straight back to Shadowfell.*

"Sorry," I whispered, tucking the little raven into my own bag. "You're not just a comrade, you're my friend. And I'm not leaving you behind."

Chapter Eleven

My father had told me about the midsummer Gathering. Before Keldec's reign it had been a celebration of all things good in Alban, an opportunity for the chieftains to speak with the king and his councillors, a chance for ordinary folk to show their mettle in games and tests of skill and strength. There had been music, dancing, feasting. The gates to Summerfort's practice area had been flung open so people could go freely in and out from the great encampment that sprang up on the banks of the Rush, close to the place where it flowed into Deepwater. The Gathering had been held over three days and nights. It had drawn folk from all over Alban, and when it was finished, they had headed home with new heart.

Some things remained as before: the opening of the gates, the folk camped by the river, the three-day festivities. There were still games. But the nature of those games had changed. For Keldec had seen in this fine old celebration an opportunity to display his power to the chieftains and to anyone else he thought needed a reminder of what loyalty meant. He saw in it a chance to offer entertainment and mete out punishment at the same time. There was strength and skill enough on show. What had vanished was the heart and soul of the old Gathering, where prowess and courage went hand in hand with friendship and honor. Keldec's Gathering was a travesty.

Still, I was here, camped along with many other folk in one of the tentlike shelters that had been erected for the purpose on the open ground outside the walls of Summerfort. The fine old willows that had graced the river mouth when I'd passed this way with my father had been felled, leaving only sad stumps.

What else had Father told me? That all the clans would be represented at the Gathering, each wearing a color or symbol by which their allegiance could be recognized. That if a chieftain was not present in person, he needed a very convincing excuse or he would soon be the target of Keldec's wrath. Sending a senior member of the household, such as the chieftain's wife, eldest son, or senior councillor, might suffice if that representative said the right things to Keldec or to Queen Varda. It might just as easily swing the other way, with the person taken hostage against the chieftain's ongoing loyalty.

The Gathering also gave king and queen the chance to test the allegiance of their own household, including their fighting forces. For that reason, every troop of Enforcers would be at Summerfort right now, along with many of the men-at-arms of the attending chieftains. The encampment was vast; alongside the shelters for ordinary travelers, there were grander, private pavilions and well-organized horse lines. Smoke curled up from cooking fires. Grooms led animals down to the river to drink; serving folk passed by with bags of feed on their shoulders. With so many folk sharing the shelter, it was not too difficult to avoid undue attention, provided I kept my head down and my mouth shut. Only once, when I was pondering how I would feed myself until the Gathering was over and I could bolt up into the woods and forage, I was startled out of my reverie by a polite little cough. Looking up, I saw the younger of the farmer's daughters, the one whose sister had been assaulted, standing there, holding out a bread roll. Over her arm she had a basket, in which more rolls nestled in a cloth.

"Take it," the girl murmured, glancing one way then the other. Before I could stammer out a surprised thank-you, she thrust the roll into my hand and was gone.

There were places where foodstuffs could be bought for a copper or two: rolls, bannocks, griddle cakes, fried onions, sometimes fish. I did have a small store of coin, but going up to the food stall seemed too great a risk. That girl's act of kindness had reminded me how dangerous this was for me. Her family knew I'd been Tali's companion on the road. It was only one step from that to someone telling the Enforcers.

I broke the roll into three, ate one piece, and tucked the others away. My own supplies were down to almost nothing. I could not afford to let hunger make me weak and confused. Whatever happened here, I needed my wits about me. If Tali was still alive, I was sure she'd make an attempt to escape. I must be ready to help.

She would be furious if she knew I'd come here instead of heading straight for Shadowfell. I'd never be able to explain to her why I'd taken such a risk. *It was beyond foolish, Neryn. You put the cause in peril.* I prayed that I would get the opportunity to hear her lecture me once more. I tried not to dwell on the strong probability that there might be nothing I could do to save her.

It was the eve of the Gathering. In the morning I'd have to go through those gates and mingle with the crowd inside; there would be Enforcers everywhere. Already they patrolled the perimeter of the encampment, eyes watchful over the half masks that concealed their identity. None of these men was Flint. I knew I would recognize him immediately, even masked and hooded.

But he would be here somewhere. He might even be in his old place at the king's right hand. Had he seen Tali brought in? Was there any way he could help her? Tali had told me every rebel would put the cause before a comrade's life. Flint had proved that wrong when he raced back to the isles after his dream of me alone on the skerry. Our night together had been precious indeed; I could never wish it had not happened. But his action could have led to disaster—he would at the very least have had more difficult explanations to make on his return. Tali had been right. The only way to win this fight was by shutting off our feelings, by making ourselves into weapons for the cause. Feelings weakened us. They created complications and traps.

Why, then, was I not on the way to Shadowfell, seizing the chance to get safely up the Rush valley while the eyes of the king's men were on Summerfort? Why was I still here?

"A demonstration of loyalty," the king said. "That is what I require."

"Yes, my lord king." Owen Swift-Sword kept his voice quiet, his breathing steady. What would it be? A fight to the death? An order that he inflict punishment on the innocent before a cheering audience? *I am become a travesty of a man,* he thought. *I sicken myself.*

"Owen," the king said. His tone was softer now; he spoke not as ruler to subject, but as friend to trusted friend. "You understand the need to go through with these performances, so authority is maintained among the people. There are those who have questioned some of your recent actions. Raised doubts. Doubt breeds unrest. You comprehend how vital it is that everyone close to me is seen as entirely loyal."

"Yes, my lord king."

"Owen. Look at me."

He lifted his head, looking up from where he knelt on the hard stone floor at Keldec's feet. They were alone in the small council chamber, while beyond bolted door and shuttered window the household worked late into the night, preparing for tomorrow. The king did not care for surprises. Every element of the Gathering would be under tight control.

Keldec's expression was benign. His narrow features

were softened by a half smile; there was a conspiratorial twinkle in his eye. "You know I would prefer not to go through with this," he said. "You know I want to trust you. Even now. Even after this."

"Yes, my lord king."

"Owen. We are friends, are we not?"

"We are, my lord king."

"You were not the only Enforcer to stray beyond the boundaries of acceptable behavior this year. You must be seen to face appropriate punishment, as the others will. I could require you to do battle with another of your kind. That would provide fine entertainment; my people enjoy a display of strength and skill, and nothing surpasses a fight to the death between peerless warriors." A pause, carefully judged. "Or I could require you to excel in a feat of endurance or a test of will." A longer pause. "But I have devised something special for you: something that will remind my people what power this court can wield. I want that message to be clear to my chieftains. You understand the importance of that."

"I will be ready, my lord king."

I had seen Keldec's forces at work before. I had seen my village burned, my brother killed, my grandmother destroyed. I had watched as the Cull swept down on Darkwater; I had seen a boat go up in flames with my father aboard, along with other innocent men. I had been on the hillside above Silverwater looking on, the day a good chieftain and his wife were slain before their entire household. I should have been prepared. But nothing could prepare me for this.

Within the stone wall that encircled Summerfort's practice area, a second barrier had been erected, a waist-high fence of woven wattles to keep the crowd from the area where games and contests would be held. Folk poured into the section behind the wattle fence and I went with them, carrying my belongings. Not what Tali would want me to do; surely not where Flint would want me to be. But I knew in my bones that Tali would be part of today's so-called games. If she had a chance to make a break for it, somehow to slip from her captors' clutches, I must be here to help her. Foolish; ridiculous; unlikely: yes, it was all those and more. But she was my friend, and I could not abandon her.

With such a press of folk, it was impossible for a short person like me to see much other than the backs of those in front. People kept saying *Move over!* and *Sit down!* but nobody was listening.

I stood there with my bag and staff, wondering if I would spend all day trying to guess what was happening out in the open area. Then a burly young man standing near me leaned over with a smile.

"Little thing, aren't you? You should be up in the front. Move, you fellows, let the lassie through!" He elbowed forward, clearing a path for me all the way to the wattle barrier, and there I was, like it or not, with the best view anyone could hope for, and him right behind me. I'd be visible to anyone who might remember I was Tali's companion on the road; visible to Flint, if he made an appearance. Still, it was a big crowd and the distance across the practice area was two hundred paces, at least. There would be plenty to hold people's attention.

A blare of trumpets, and the crowd fell silent. Then the trumpets sounded again, and now through the open gates of the fortress came a long procession of folk. Blocks of color—a group dressed in red, another in blue and white, a third in brown and yellow—suggested these were the households of Alban's eight chieftains, though I counted only six groups. I guessed Lannan Long-Arm was not here; another too had chosen to risk the king's ire by staying away.

Behind the richly clad chieftains, their families and councillors, came men-at-arms wearing the same hues. The noble folk moved to the raised seating and their warriors stationed themselves around it. My mind went to next midsummer and the challenge. This was a formidable array of fighting men. There were Enforcers all around the open area too, standing guard, watching the crowd, ready for anything. And now from the fortress came the rest of them in their uniform black, but with one difference: today they wore tunics bearing their troop emblems in silver on the breast: Bull, Hound, Eagle, Horse, Wolf, Seal. And there was Flint, marching at the head of Stag Troop. Masked, like the others, but unmistakable. I made myself look away. I felt his presence so strongly that it seemed I must draw his eyes to me; I realized the full enormity of my being here, at Summerfort, on my own within the walls. If Tali was brought out, if against the odds she had a chance to get away, what could I possibly do? Step up, and I would identify myself as a troublemaker at the very least. Use my gift, and the rebellion would be in jeopardy. And I might endanger Flint. Too late now; the crowd was in and though the gates out to the encampment still stood open, they were guarded.

The Enforcers stationed themselves around the circle, blocks of black amid the color. I willed Stag Troop not to come close to me, and they did not, but placed themselves directly in front of the raised seating. And now, as the trumpets sounded again, along with a rattle of drums, the royal party came out from the fortress.

In my imagination, King Keldec had long been a kind of monster, a man eaten away by his fears and weighed down by years of cruel acts. I had not been able to see him as human. But the man who moved with leisurely pace to seat himself in the center front of the raised area was nothing remarkable to look at. He'd come to the throne at the age of twenty; that made him six-and-thirty. He looked younger. His hair was brown, his face thin; his features held an expression of surprising mildness. He wore a richer version of his warriors' black garb. It startled me that a man who wielded such power and authorized such evil acts could appear so . . . ordinary.

Queen Varda was beside her husband. She was small, about my own height: a pale woman in a red gown, with her dark hair swept up high. She reminded me of a bird of prey, perhaps a merlin. There was an unnerving intensity about her features, as if she were only waiting to spot her quarry and strike. The last empty places filled up with folk who must be the king's inner circle: councillors, advisers, courtiers. Perhaps Enthrallers and other canny folk.

A court official with a booming voice made a short speech of welcome; then the king rose to his feet. The crowd, hushed already, grew quieter still.

"Welcome, good people of Alban, to my fifteenth midsummer Gathering!" Keldec's voice was strong, ringing out across the open area. "This is a time of celebration, a time for our subjects to show their strength and skill, a time for all who live in our fair realm to demonstrate their loyalty. Our chieftains will renew their promises of service for the coming year. There will be displays of prowess and endurance, contests in which both men-at-arms and ordinary folk will participate.

"You know, my people, that the Gathering also provides an opportunity for reward and punishment. Not all of you have pleased your king since last we met in this arena. Not all have acted with perfect loyalty. At this Gathering, those who have offended me will receive their just deserts. And those who have pleased me well will be generously rewarded. Prepare for three days of matchless entertainment, three days of challenge, three days unparalleled in the year. You have traveled far to be at Summerfort. In recognition of that effort, when each day's events are over, my household will provide roast meat enough to feed you all, and a cup of ale apiece."

Applause from the crowd, along with some cautious shouts of acclaim.

"Let us proceed," Keldec said. "My people, show me the best of Alban!"

The day's events began with quite ordinary contests of strength—bouts of wrestling, a tug-of-war, a race in which men carried sacks of grain—and I began to wonder if Father had been wrong about the dark side of the Gathering. The court official announced each event in turn. It soon became plain that the onlookers were required to demonstrate their enthusiasm with shouts, whistles, and screams—encouragement or abuse seemed equally acceptable. Folk who were too quiet found themselves singled out by armed men, pulled from the crowd, and subjected to what looked like uncomfortably intense questioning. One or two were taken away and did not return. Very soon everyone around me was yelling.

And then things began to change. Feats of strength, such as an active young farmer or fisherman or a man-at-arms might be expected to excel in, became feats of impossible endurance. The tug-of-war was run again, this time with a different rope, crafted from something that made the competitors' hands bleed. Anyone who let go was dragged out of the way by two Enforcers and pelted with missiles by the crowd—someone had provided a supply of rotting vegetables, and when that ran out, folk threw stones. A hardy or desperate few saw out the contest to the end, their faces white with pain, their bloody hands slipping on the rope. Queen Varda laughed. At least, at the end of that display, both winners and losers were allowed to return to their places. I could not pretend enjoyment; I failed even to mime shouts of enthusiasm. I hoped the folk around me were making enough noise to cover my silence.

There was a contest in which men had to heft a log above their heads, the victory going to whoever held it there for the longest count. There were some twenty brawny fellows competing, and at first it was done with goodwill, the crowd applauding winners and commiserating with losers. Contestants were paired in a series of man-against-man challenges. One by one they dropped out of the competition, wheezing, red-faced, slick with sweat.

The king leaned forward to speak to his official; the official held up his hands for silence.

"The king wishes this man and this man to meet in the final challenge." He indicated a tall, dark-haired individual and a shorter, stockier fellow. The two of them looked pleased—there had been eight other men still left in the contest. The others made to return to the crowd, but there were Enforcers in the way now, and heavier logs were being wheeled in on a low cart. Much heavier logs; they looked far too big for one man to lift. "The king wishes the stakes to be raised," the official said as a pair of Enforcers man-handled each log in turn off the cart, standing them upright on the ground. "He is sure you, Morr of Glenbuie, are keen to make amends for certain remarks that were brought to his attention, remarks suggesting some concerns about the Cull in the east of Glenbuie territory. Your chieftain has nominated you to be his champion in this contest, in recognition that a grave error of judgment was made. If you prevail, your kin will remain safe at the next Cull."

Even across the distance, I saw that the dark-haired Morr's face had blanched. After one quick glance up at his chieftain in the stand, he squared his shoulders and set his jaw, ready for what might come. He had not known, it seemed, that being chosen for this contest was anything but a recognition of his strength.

"And you, Dubhal of Scourie." The official turned to the shorter, broader contestant. "You have a daughter who's a fine spinner, don't you? Living in Brightwater settlement? Known all across Scourie for her talents, or so the king has heard."

I hugged my shawl around myself, knowing where this was headed. The folk next to me were hushed with anticipation.

"I have a daughter, yes, my lord." Dubhal rubbed his hands on his tunic, stared down at his boots.

"Look at me!" The official nodded toward one of the Enforcers, who stepped forward and delivered a ringing blow to Dubhal's jaw. He reeled, then steadied.

"Answer the question!" barked the Enforcer.

"What you said . . . it is correct, my lord." A deep, shuddering breath. "But my daughter . . . Ana . . . yes, she's good with her hands. A good worker. Nothing more, my lord, I swear."

"Nothing more. That's not what the king heard. Folk are saying your daughter is smirched. They're saying no ordinary hand can spin so fine."

"That is a lie, my lord. Ana comes from a long line of spinners; she learned young. It's no more than that."

Dubhal's voice was shaking now. With an effort, he looked the official in the eye. "I'd stake my life on it, my lord."

The king's mouth curved in a slow smile, and a sigh went through the crowd. My gut was churning. I wanted to run, to get out, to be gone before I had to see what unfolded. But there could be no running, with folk all around me and guards on the gate. Besides, there was a part of me that held me still, a part that whispered, *Bear witness. In times when it's hard to put the cause first, the memory of this will make you strong.*

"You will pit your strength against each other," the official said. "Three times, added weight each time. Outlast your opponent twice and victory is yours." He turned toward the crowd, and people obliged with shouts of approval.

"Black Crow save us," muttered the young man standing behind me, "look at the size of those things. They won't last to the count of five."

"Shh!" hissed someone else.

"Morr," the official was saying, "you understand what is at stake for you here. Dubhal, win this contest and the queen will consider offering this daughter of yours a position at court, where her special skill can be put to appropriate use. Lose, and she will be culled."

Dubhal opened his mouth as if to protest, then closed it without saying a word.

The contest began. They lasted a long time—far longer than I would have thought possible for any man. It was desperation, maybe, that gave them the strength to go on.

Muscles straining, eyes bulging, feet planted square, the two of them stood facing each other with the huge logs up over their heads. The crowd was roaring encouragement: *Hold on, lad! That's the way! Keep it up, man, you can do it!* And abuse: *Your daughter's smirched! What does that make you, big lump?*

It could not go on forever. Morr's legs began to wobble; he shifted his feet, his face scarlet with effort. His whole body was trembling. A moment later the log came down, thudding to the ground and narrowly missing his opponent's feet. Dubhal had won the first round. He bent his knees, set his log carefully down. Pain was written all over his body.

"They'll do it different next time," said the young man behind me. "You're looking a bit pale. Here." He offered me a flask. "Honey mead; should do the trick."

"Thank you, but no. I'm all right."

"First time at the Gathering?"

The last thing I wanted was to get into a conversation, even with this apparently harmless person. I nodded. "I'll be fine."

"Takes a body that way sometimes. Change your mind, just ask."

"Thank you."

"They won't last so long this time. Arms will cramp up. Just watch."

He was right. Almost before the two contestants had time to draw breath, Enforcers came forward to push great iron rings onto the ends of the logs—two men to hold the wood, a third to add the extra weight. Surely neither Morr nor Dubhal, strong as they were, would be able to lift the burden at all, let alone hold it high. What would the king do if both failed—treat both as losers? Subject one man's kin to the Cull and destroy the other's daughter?

The king raised a hand: the signal to begin. The contenders gripped their impossible burdens, clenching their teeth, and lifted. Morr staggered. Dubhal was steadier. The weighted logs came up to chest height, then with a mighty heave were raised high. The crowd began to count.

But what now? Enforcers had come forward to sweep their staves about, at first only distracting the two burdened men, then, as Morr and Dubhal stood doggedly in place, tapping them on the ankles, the knees, the shins. Then hitting. Then striking so hard that Morr winced in pain and Dubhal let out an explosive breath, cursing. The counting became a chant, two chants from opposite sides of the crowd. *Scou-rie! Scou-rie!* And *Glen-duie! Glen-duie!* Even so might folk have cheered on their village teams at a game of ball, all in a spirit of fun, with the opposing sides sharing a few jugs of ale when the match was over.

But this was the Gathering, and such chants carried their own peril. The nearest guards turned their heads sharply toward the sound, and it soon died. In these games there was only one real player, and that was Keldec.

The staves were working in and out now, teasing the contestants who sweated under their loads, poking them between the legs, prodding them in the small of the back, rapping at their feet. And in an instant it was over, the two of them dropping their burdens at once, the logs crashing down, making the Enforcers jump back out of the way. Morr and Dubhal collapsed onto the ground, wheezing. If one had released his log before the other, I could not have said which it was. Indeed, I wondered if a moment had come when they'd looked each other in the eye and decided in silence, *Enough*.

There was a brief consultation: the official, the Enforcers, the king leaning over from his seat to speak with them.

"Second round goes to Morr," the official announced.

"Convenient," murmured someone in the crowd close to me, and was immediately hushed by others. It was indeed convenient; a drawn round would have required the men to lift twice more, most likely impossible, while this result made the third round the decider. The people around me were talking about chains, whips, dogs. It took all my will not to crouch down and cover my eyes. *Oh, Tali. What will it be when your turn comes?*

For the third round, they used magic. A more powerful magic than I had imagined existed within Keldec's household, for though we knew from Flint that he had canny folk there, I had assumed their gifts were similar to those I had encountered elsewhere in Alban: keen sight like Tali's, acute hearing, a gift for music or handcrafts, or a knack with animals. The most unusual gift I had seen a canny human use was Sula's: she was able to draw heat into water, which proved useful both for cooking in clay pots and for providing comfortable baths in winter.

What unfolded now told me there was at least one

gift among Keldec's folk that might be brought into play in a battle: a gift of fire. The third round began, the contenders crouching to lift their burdens, which now wore a second pair of iron rings. Morr and Dubhal gripped the logs, strained to rise, struggled up to standing. Facing each other once again, they lifted their burdens high.

"One thing I'll say," the man behind me murmured, "they've got bollocks, the two of them."

"Here comes the fellow with the flame," muttered a woman.

I saw no flame, only a member of the king's household, a dark-haired man of middle height dressed in the robe of a councillor, stepping down from the raised seating to walk forward and stand a few paces from the burdened men, both of whom, miraculously, were still fairly steady. The Enforcers stood back; it seemed the staves were not required for this round.

The robed man raised his arms. His left hand pointed toward Dubhal, his right toward Morr.

"Here it comes," murmured someone. There was no counting now, no shouts of abuse or encouragement. A profound hush lay on the crowd.

The robed man made a pass with his hands, very like the one I had seen Sula use to heat water at Shadowfell. For a few moments nothing happened. Then smoke began to rise from the two logs, threads at first, growing to small clouds. Morr staggered; Dubhal coughed. Then both shouted at once. Flames were licking the wood, catching at their hands. The logs were afire. It seemed a charm too powerful to be worked by humankind. But the Good Folk would not enter this place of iron, I was sure of it. That man out there was a canny human like me.

I could hear Dubhal's breathing even from so far away, a desperate, agonized gasping. Morr was silent, his teeth clenched in a death's-head grimace. *Call a halt,* I willed the official. *Make it stop.* Around me the crowd watched with appalled fascination.

I had thought Dubhal on the verge of collapse, but it was Morr who fell first, his burden rolling away to lie flaming on the ground. Dubhal did not drop his log straightaway, but held on long enough to be quite sure there was no mistake. Then, sobbing with pain, he let it go. Morr was curled up in agony. Tears ran down Dubhal's face. Nobody stepped forward to help them, but the robed man made a quick gesture this way, that way, and the fires went out as if doused in cold water.

The king rose to his feet. He was smiling. "Dubhal, your effort has pleased me well. I will send my physician to tend to your injuries. A fine, strong man like you might even find himself among our Enforcers one day, who knows?" A pause, then, as he bent to say something to Queen Varda and to listen to her response. "The queen wishes to meet this talented daughter of yours. Is she here today?"

"No, my lord." Dubhal's voice was a desperate gasp; his hands were shaking as if palsied. What he needed was cold water, quickly—where was this physician?

"Indeed." Suddenly Keldec was chilly. "Why not?"

"My lord, she is heavy with child and could not travel."

The king bent to consult his wife again. Straightened to look once more at Dubhal. "The queen does not want a spinner with a squalling babe. Make arrangements for it to go elsewhere; then bring your daughter to court. We are not unreasonable; in recognition of the strength you have shown today, we will wait until our return to Winterfort in the autumn. Be there within ten days of our arrival, or the queen may not be so favorably disposed toward you."

"Thank you, my lord king. You are most generous."

"Take him to my physician," Keldec said. As Dubhal was led away, the king's gaze found the hapless Morr, who had got up into a crouch, his injured hands held out before him.

"Morr of Glenbuie. Stand up before your king."

He forced himself up.

"As your chieftain's champion in this contest, you have failed. What have you to say for yourself?"

Morr spoke. His voice was faint, and I could hear nothing of it.

"Speak up!" the king snapped. "Let all those gathered know your shame."

"I did my best, my lord king." He turned his head to look at his chieftain in the stand. "I did my best, my lord Sconlan. I regret . . ." He sagged at the knees and fell to the ground, apparently in a dead faint.

Keldec made an impatient gesture. Two Enforcers— one was Flint—stepped forward to pick the man up and remove him from the open area. They did not carry him into the fortress, but across to an outbuilding set against the wall, so close to where I was standing that I pulled my shawl up over my mouth and looked down at my feet, willing Flint not to see me. My heart hammered so hard as he went by that it seemed he must surely hear it, but he passed without a sideways glance. Not long after, he and his comrade emerged from the building without Morr and went to resume their places near the king.

The games went on. What we had seen was only the start of it. It became plain to me that there were few bouts or contests here that were not devised as punishment for those who had offended the king. The events grew more and more brutal as the day progressed, a sequence of cruelly devised entertainments that saw folk hobbling from the field with terrible injuries, the kind of hurts that would blight the whole of their lives. Craftsmen with fingers gone. Archers blinded. Horsemen crippled. It came to me that Keldec was not only evil, he was deranged. When I could no longer bear to look at the games, I watched him, and I saw how often he bent to seek the queen's opinion, and only decided one way or another after she had whispered in his ear. I saw too that the man who had performed the trick with fire now sat on Queen Varda's other side, and spoke to her often as if he were a trusted confidant.

There were other kinds of hurt on show, other kinds of atrocity. Taunting, humiliation, mockery. The requirement to insult or damage a loved one publicly in order to avoid a worse punishment. The requirement to stay quiet and compliant as a friend or family member was assaulted.

Eventually came a break for everyone to take food

and drink. There were communal privies out in the camping area, and some folk were going out to use them. I was
sorely tempted to follow them and run for the forest. Every
instinct urged me to flee this charnel house. But there
would be no escape; the river mouth was in full view from
the sentry point in the Summerfort tower, and there was
no way I could cross without being spotted. One woman
heading in the wrong direction would be immediately noticed and brought back to account for herself.

The friendly young man offered me a share of his provisions, and I accepted some bread and cheese, but found
I could not eat. After the meal, the official announced
that the next event was a fight between two Enforcers. My
tight belly relaxed a little. This, surely, would be a straight-
forward display of strength and skill, a reminder to us all of
the power the king held in his fist.

I knew the king's men were ruthless. They were dedicated to the task. I had seen them as they swept down on
Darkwater, bringing death and destruction. I had not seen
them pitted one against another like this. Their movements had an economy of style, a fluid control that made
their bout a deadly dance. Short sword and knife flashed
in the sunlight; it was both beautiful and terrible to be-
hold. How had my brother, fourteen years old, untrained
in fighting and armed with a homemade spear, managed to
stand up to the king's men even for an instant?

Both combatants wore the emblem of Seal Troop; they
were comrades. Perhaps that was why the bout stretched
out so long, with the skill and strength of the fighters

making it near impossible for either to prevail. Caught up in the excitement, the people around me shouted, cheered, groaned when one or the other combatant was forced to give ground or release a punishing hold. But not the watching Enforcers. I'd have thought fighting men might lay wagers on such a contest; at the very least, I would have expected them to be yelling encouragement with the rest. But they were uniformly grim and silent.

It went on and on, and as it progressed, the crowd grew quieter too. Both fighters were flagging; soon, surely, one must make a small error of judgment and lose a weapon or fall to his knees in surrender. They'd already stayed on their feet and in possession of their weapons for far longer than I'd expected.

The king rose to his feet; the combatants stepped away from each other, breathing hard.

"Set aside your weapons," Keldec said.

A pair of guards came forward; the fighters handed over their swords and knives. It seemed common sense had prevailed, and the bout would be declared a draw.

"My people," the king said, and spread his arms out as if to embrace all of us, "I am sad to tell you that even within the ranks of my own most loyal fighters, acts of disloyalty sometimes occur. This is rare; my Enforcers are the best of the best, warriors unparalleled, a force truly to be feared. I expect of them what I expect of every man, woman, and child in Alban: complete and unswerving loyalty. These men you see before you have erred since last we gathered here. Erred in small ways, perhaps; but small mistakes can lead to more significant blunders. If not unchecked, disobedience will spread its creeping evil like a canker through the community. My people, I do not tolerate dissent in any form. That it can occur within the ranks of my own fighting force is deeply troubling.

"Hence this combat you have witnessed today, an even fight between two skilled warriors. Warriors I trust, or trusted." Keldec's tone was that of a disappointed father, sorrowful and benign. Perhaps, when an Enforcer displeased him, a public humiliation such as this was all the punishment meted out.

"It pains me to do this," the king said. "But justice must be served, and lessons learned. Men!"

The two fighters stood shoulder to shoulder, arms by their sides.

"You will fight to the death. Unarmed. Win this combat and your indiscretion will be overlooked. This time."

The men's self-discipline was exemplary. They might have been responding to a request to provide a demonstration bout for new recruits. They squared off, facing each other at two strides; four Enforcers moved from the ranks of Stag Troop to stand around them, marking the boundaries of the combat area. They fought. I imagined how it would be, knowing you must kill a comrade to save yourself, to prove your unswerving loyalty. Knowing, I supposed, how arbitrary, how unfair this penalty was, for both had shown themselves to be peerless fighters, and surely either could prevail. What if they'd refused to fight? Perhaps the king would have thought of something still crueler, something ingenious, something that might have ended up with both men dead.

It seemed as if this one contest might go on all afternoon, so evenly matched were the two. One would get the other down on the ground, only to have his opponent wriggle from his grasp or surge up in a display of sheer force. One would leap on the other's back and cling like a barnacle, seeking to choke his adversary, and would be dislodged when the first whirled around in circles until he shook the burden off. The sun moved across the sky; the shadows lengthened. By the fortress gates a fellow with a drum began to hammer out a steady beat, as if to signal change.

At last, at long last, one of the fighters began to flag and, sensing this, the other delivered a series of swift strikes, to the belly, to the lower back, to the face. When his opponent staggered, he moved fast as an attacking wolf, and in a flurry of movement brought the other to the ground, facedown with his arms pinned behind his back. The crowd's cheers were somewhat muted; it had been long, and folk were tired. Besides, Keldec was full of surprises.

"My lord king." The victor's voice was remarkably steady. "I am without weapons. Will you allow the use of a knife for a merciful ending?"

Please, I begged silently. *If this must happen, make a quick end to it. Or change your mind and spare them both. You said their errors were small.*

Keldec had watched the entire bout impassively. Now he consulted his wife again, and I saw her little shake of the head.

"Were you not listening, Buan? No weapons. Make an end of this."

Something odd happened then. When Buan released his hold on the fallen man's arms, the other made no effort to get up and fight until the last. Instead, he rolled onto his back, eyes on Buan, who knelt above him. I could not see what passed between them in that last moment, but perhaps it was a recognition that to be finished quickly by a man you trusted was not such a bad death. Buan put his thumbs on the man's neck and pressed down, dispatching him with an efficiency no doubt born of long practice. He stood and faced Keldec. "Hail the king!" he cried out, and a great shout arose from the Enforcers stationed around the area, "Hail the king!"

Enforcers from Seal Troop came with a stretcher and bore the dead man away. With a wave of the hand, Keldec dismissed Buan, who bowed low, retrieved his weapons, and disappeared into a group of his comrades. He would be spared to fight another day.

I wondered what the loser had done to deserve death at the hands of a friend. It was a brutal code to live by; a man might almost wish to be enthralled into obedience, since that would mean he was incapable of offending the king. I prayed that somehow Flint's unauthorized trip back to the isles had not been reported to the king. Let him not be dragged out there before my eyes to face the same harsh discipline. And what lay in store for Tali?

The day was not yet ended. Folk were hauled up and punished for saying one word out of place, for setting one foot over a border, for speaking up to defend the good name of a wife or child or elder. I felt sick, sad, furiously angry. If the gods still looked down on Alban, they must be hiding their faces now.

When the rebellion comes, I thought, *when our great battle is won, we will restore the Gathering to what it should be. But we will not forget what it was allowed to become; folk need to remember, so this can never happen again.* I tried to imagine Regan's final plan in action: a great force of men-at-arms and ordinary people, of Good Folk and rebels, surging forward over this flimsy barrier to take on the king's army in open combat. I tried to think of myself there in the middle of it, using my gift to make things happen. But my eyes were full of horrors, and I could not see it. Even if Regan won his battle and the king was deposed, how could the damage wrought in Alban be set right in one generation, or in two, or even in three? Every man and woman who stood here and watched this unfold without protest, every single person who failed to speak up against what they must surely know to be wrong, was as guilty as Keldec himself. The stain of it was on us all.

It was late afternoon; in the viewing area most folk were sitting down, weary from the long day, perhaps anticipating the roast meat and ale the king had promised. When the horn sounded again, nobody seemed especially excited. But when the king himself stood up to speak, all eyes turned to him.

"Owen Swift-Sword!" Keldec called. "Step forward."

A man walked out from the ranks of Stag Troop to

stand facing the king, and a jolt went through me. It was Flint, his face bare of the Enforcer mask. He dropped gracefully to one knee and bowed his head. Beside me, folk craned their necks to see.

The king waited. Four Enforcers advanced, one from each corner of the open area, to stand around Flint at a short distance. He remained kneeling, head down. What was this, a public execution? A battle of one against four? Cold fingers closed around my heart.

"Look at me!" The king spoke with crisp clarity. "You are called before this assembly to answer an accusation of disloyalty. You are a king's man, a troop leader, a trusted servant of your monarch. You have given years of fine service; you have acted with courage and discipline. You have lent your king the strength of your arm and the comfort of your wise words. In the face of doubt and distrust, I have spoken up for you; in the face of twisted words and whispers in the dark, I have believed in you." There was an intimacy in the king's voice, as if he saw Flint as a true friend, almost a brother; he sounded utterly sincere. And then, in the blink of an eye, the tone changed. "If you have betrayed the trust I placed in you, if you have thrown back in my face the precious gift of friendship, you will pay the heaviest of prices. What have you to say for yourself? Speak now!"

Flint lifted his head; he looked the king in the eye. His face was chalk-pale. "I am loyal to the kingdom of Alban," he said. His voice was soft, but the crowd was quiet too, captured by the intensity of this exchange. "I challenge any man to provide material evidence that this is not so. I repudiate the accusations made against me; there is no proof. My lord king, I throw myself on your mercy, knowing a king of Alban does not lightly make the choice to punish one who has been among his staunchest supporters. If you believe that I have done you wrong, if you give credence to the testimony of those who have accused me, then I accept that. You are the king. I accept whatever penalty it pleases you to impose on me."

For just a moment Keldec's self-control seemed to falter; he appeared moved by Flint's words, which had been delivered with powerful simplicity. Then Queen Varda got up and murmured in her husband's ear, and he nodded. When he turned back to face Flint, he was calm and assured once again.

"I am minded to be magnanimous," he said. "Nonetheless, a penalty must be paid, and be seen to be paid." He glanced to his left, toward the entry to the Summerfort tower. "Bring out the prisoner!"

No. No, let this not be. There must be many prisoners. There was no reason for it to be her, no reason for my heart to be pounding like a marching drum, no reason to panic, no—it was Tali. She came in with her head held high, her dark eyes blazing with defiance, and an Enforcer on either side. Her wrists were bound in front of her. She'd been hurt; I saw it in the way she walked. She had a black eye and a bruise on her cheek. They'd taken away the modest clothing she'd been wearing. Now she was in a kind of shift, long and coarse, with rents in it that seemed deliberately placed to reveal her body to the onlookers, for the pale curve of one breast showed through a tear in the bodice, and a rip in the skirt revealed a good part of her thigh. The tattooed ravens still flew, swift and straight, around her neck; the spirals and twists on her arms were fully revealed by the sleeveless garment. Her hair had lost its usual spring; it lay in sweat-soaked strands as if it had already given up.

Her guards brought her to stand not far from Flint, to one side of the square marked out by his four minders. She glared up at the king. Where another woman might have made pretense of compliance, apologized, groveled to save herself, Tali's furious defiance was written on every part of her. Whatever Keldec planned for her, she would go down fighting. Queen Varda said something to a woman sitting behind her—a sister, a friend, a confidante—and both of them laughed.

"I'm told this young woman is something of a fighter," the king said levelly. "Skilled to a remarkable level. Strong to what might be considered an uncanny degree. What have you to say for yourself, girl?"

She glowered at him, then spat on the ground in front of her. One of her guards stepped forward and delivered a heavy blow to her cheek; she staggered, then straightened her back and lifted her chin.

"Nothing to say? No explanation for your ability to account for several men without resorting to any kind of weaponry? No excuse for taking out your anger on a group of peaceable travelers in the middle of the night?"

"If you consider beating and attempted rape peaceable

activities, then there is little point in my offering you any explanation."

A horrified gasp from the crowd as she delivered this statement; she had committed the unthinkable offense of insulting the king to his face, in public. I was cold all through. *Oh, Tali, you have just ordered your own death. Couldn't you have pretended to be less than you are, just for long enough?*

The king had returned his attention to Flint. "Owen Swift-Sword! Three of your comrades took this woman into custody after hearing of her suspect behavior. If she were your captive, what penalty would you impose on her?"

Flint had not even glanced at Tali, nor she at him. Only, when she'd spoken, I had seen him start, then recover himself. Before he came into the open area, he had not known she was at Summerfort. I was sure of it. And it was clear from the king's words that Keldec knew nothing of what Tali truly was. That she and Flint found themselves out there together was no more than a cruel twist of fate. "It is not for me to recommend punishment, my lord king," Flint said. "That authority is yours."

"I asked you for an answer." Keldec's voice had an edge in it now. Members of the royal party sat up straighter. The four Enforcers around Flint set hands to their weapons.

"As you wish, my lord king. I would put the woman to the test; ascertain whether what has been said of her is true. She could not be recruited to the Enforcers, of course. But if she is indeed a fine fighter, there would be work she could do in your service. Specialized work. Combat skills can be put to many uses."

"Put her to the test. How?"

"I would not do so here at the Gathering, my lord king. The potential of a warrior takes some time to assess. There is a series of tests we use for men seeking to become Enforcers; they are carried out over a full season. Any new fighter coming into your service undergoes that training. There is no reason why a woman should not do the same, provided she is capable."

Another burst of laughter from the queen and her women. It was plain they considered the idea ludicrous. Many within the crowd laughed along with them.

"I see." I could not read the king's mood from his face; I had no idea where this was heading. "And what then?"

"If she failed, it would be up to you to decide her fate, my lord king. If she met our requirements, there would be many ways in which she could assist us. Helping train new recruits. Acting as a sparring partner for our men. Perhaps a position as a personal guard for my lady the queen, if I may make so bold as to suggest that."

"This is nonsense." Varda's voice was clear and high, like a blade cutting across Flint's measured words. "A female guard? Ludicrous. The girl's all spit and defiance, with no substance behind it. I declare Queen's Privilege."

I had no idea what she meant, but whatever Queen's Privilege was, her words silenced the crowd. No laughter now; every face was turned toward Keldec.

For a moment he hesitated. Plainly this was not part of his plan, but it seemed the rules of the Gathering meant he must agree. "Of course, my lady. Will you stand and speak to our people?"

Queen Varda stood. Although she was a little person, something in her drew every eye.

"Here we have a trusted servant who has betrayed his master," she said, casting her glance over Flint. "And here an upstart country girl with no common sense, a woman who has behaved as no woman should, a person whose abilities tell us she is surely smirched. The solution is obvious. He must demonstrate his loyalty. She must be rendered harmless. Owen Swift-Sword, you are expert in combat. You would not otherwise have risen to be leader of Stag Troop. But you have another skill, do you not? Explain to the king's subjects the nature of that skill."

My gut twisted; my heart lurched. *Oh no. Oh no, not this. Please, not this.*

"My lady, I have on occasion performed an enthrallment at the king's request." He sounded calm and courteous; his voice was under expert control.

"Oh, come, Owen, you can do better than that. Are you not foremost among the king's Enthrallers, the most skilled of all, the one they say never makes an error? I've seen you do it. Over the years of your service you must have provided my lord with—how many—ten, twelve of his most loyal retainers? No false modesty, now."

The playful note made me sick; she might have been teasing a suitor.

"Twelve, my lady."

Tali began to struggle between her captors, fighting to

free herself. At a nod from the king, one of Flint's minders went in to assist the two who held her; Tali got in a couple of well-placed kicks before he landed a blow to her lower back that saw her bent double, choking with pain. Her captors forced her upright. Her face was gray.

"Twelve." The queen might have used the same tone in speaking to a beloved pet as she stroked it. "Well, Owen Swift-Sword, let us make that thirteen. If you would have this young woman join the king's household, in whatever capacity, her attitude must change. We must be absolutely sure of her loyalty. A girl who spits at the king, who mocks his authority, can only be rendered compliant by enthrallment. On this occasion, that process must be entrusted to the most reliable of our Enthrallers: yourself. This will not only ensure the girl's loyalty; it will allow you to demonstrate yours." With a sweet smile, Varda resumed her seat.

"It shall be as the queen wishes," Keldec said, his eyes still on Flint. "You will perform this enthrallment now, here, before the eyes of my people. Do this well, provide us with good entertainment, and both your offense and this woman's will be set aside."

Flint had dropped his gaze; he was apparently examining the ground at his feet. "You are aware, my lord king," he said, "that an enthrallment is usually carried out overnight; it is necessary for the . . . subject . . . to be in a heavy sleep before the charm is worked. And better if he or she is left to wake from that sleep naturally."

"Come now, Owen." The king was affable; if he had

310

not been well pleased by his wife's intervention, he was not going to reveal that in public. "We have seen you do this before, and do it most effectively. We have the means to make a person sleep and wake as required." He glanced up at the sky. "Time is passing. Tell your comrades what you need and let us get on with this."

Sick to the core, I watched as they prepared the area. My mind sought frantically for solutions—perhaps both Tali and Flint could fake the enthrallment, perhaps she could pretend to be changed, pretend to be loyal and become a second spy at court, perhaps I could provide a distraction, allow them to run for it. No. We were surrounded by guards, right under the eyes of the king. I must not expose myself to view; to rush out there was to become another victim of this sorry day and lose Regan his most powerful weapon. And how could Flint fake this? The charm must be sung aloud. Once he had done that, with his hands on Tali's head, there would be no reversing it. There must be other Enthrallers here, folk who would know if he erred, folk who would not need to block their ears while the magic was worked. There was no way out. I must stand here as the man I loved destroyed my friend before my eyes. Flint's strength of purpose would see him go through with this foul act rather than reveal his true allegiance. Tali's iron will would keep her from showing by so much as a single glance that she knew him; it would keep her from offering a bargain, her knowledge of his double life in exchange for her release. Likely there was no bargaining with Keldec anyway; if Flint refused to do this, his life would be

311

forfeit, and the task of enthralling the rebellious girl would be given to one of the others, who might botch the job.

I was not as strong as they were. I was not even strong enough to keep the tears from falling as I watched them. She was so full of life, so brave, so much herself. She was doing her best to stand straight, though it must be costing her dear after that last blow; she was trying to hold her head high. *Don't turn around,* I willed her. *Don't see me,* though the fading light made it near impossible that she would distinguish my face in the crowd even if she did turn my way. And at the same time I thought, *Look at me one last time, Tali. Let me see the courage in your face and the light in your eyes. Show me the fighting spirit of Ravensburn.*

They brought out a pallet, which they raised up on benches so the crowd could see. They fetched a pair of flaming torches, which they set in iron holders. These were not yet necessary for light, but perhaps they enhanced the spectacle. Here was a black robe, which Flint put on over his plain attire. Here was a warm blanket, which he placed, folded, on the pallet. Now a pillow. Last, a flask and a small goblet. The Enforcer who held these items was the man I had seen in a dream, talking to Flint atop the guard tower. Perhaps a friend; perhaps a betrayer. What was happening here made a mockery of right and wrong; it set everything in confusion.

Cry out! my heart told me as they tipped back Tali's head and forced a draft down her throat. *Cry out shame!* There he was, grave and still, waiting at the head of the pallet until she collapsed in her captors' arms and was lifted up to lie there, as still as an enchanted princess in an old tale. Her dark head on the pillow, the brave necklace of raven flight, her arms ringed with the patterns of her ancient clan. They took off her boots. The guards stepped back, and Flint moved to lay the blanket over her, as gently as if he were tucking a beloved child in bed. Now Tali was covered to the neck, her modesty restored. Her prone form looked surprisingly small.

Flint spoke to the other Enforcers and they moved back a little, leaving Enthraller and victim alone in the circle of torchlight. Perhaps the preparations had taken longer than I imagined, for now the sky had a reddish tinge. The air was perceptibly cooler. I shivered, lifting my hand to wipe away the treacherous tears. *Bear witness. You must bear witness as you did once before.* I was back in the cottage at Corbie's Wood, the cottage that had long been home and refuge, place of wisdom and peace. Standing hidden, watching through a chink in the wall as they forced the draft down my grandmother's throat. Watching as they changed her forever.

"Cold, are you? Here, wrap this around your neck." The young man offered me a woolen scarf, and I took it rather than risk words. "What's this, tears? Have you never seen an enthrallment before?"

I shook my head. Out there, Flint had laid his hands along the sides of Tali's head.

"It's not so frightening," the man said quietly. "The fellow will sing a bit, and the woman will sleep. Then they'll wake her up again and she'll have lost her argumentative

313

ways. A remarkable thing. No need to be upset about it." And, as an afterthought, "They say this fellow, Owen Swift-Sword, is the best of them all. In a way he's doing the lass a favor."

I nodded. He passed me a handkerchief; I took it and mopped my cheeks. Grandmother before enthrallment had been a strong, wise old woman. The charm had done her no favors; it had been botched. She had survived only to endure a life-in-death.

"He won't make any mistakes," the farmer said, his eyes on Flint, who stood still as stone, eyes closed, hands gentle against Tali's face. He had not yet started to sing the charm.

I realized, suddenly, the implication of the man's words. Of course Flint wouldn't get this wrong; he never did. Tali would not wake as a witless, shambling mockery of herself. She would not be like Grandmother or that poor man-child Garret whom I'd encountered last autumn. No, the enthrallment would work the way the king wanted it to, and Tali would become as faultlessly loyal to Keldec as she had been to the cause of freedom. The first thing she would do when she woke was expose Flint as a spy. The second thing she would do was identify me as a rebel and as a Caller. The third thing would be to tell what she knew about Shadowfell. The cause was doomed.

I had to get out. I had to get away. If I could make it up into the woods and find Sage, if I could run as far as Brollachan Bridge before they tracked me down, perhaps I could use the Good Folk to get a warning to Regan.

One of Sage's clan, in bird form, could fly to Shadowfell in the morning, tell the rebels it was all up, bid them scatter across Alban and go to ground. I must get out now, quickly, before the enthrallment was completed. Before the new Tali woke. But the crowd had moved in close, blocking any way out. To push through would be to attract immediate attention. I was trapped.

Flint was singing the charm. It might have been a lullaby, so quiet and gentle was it, falling on the ears like soothing balm. Insidious. Evil. An ancient art, devised for healing the wounded mind and spirit, turned to a tool of power, a blade that would reach into a person's mind and twist their very being to the king's will. Wrong. Oh, so wrong. And yet so beautiful to hear. Many people in the crowd had stopped their ears or covered those of their children. There was an Enforcer stationed not far away, but his gaze was not on us. Caught by Flint's voice, he stared at the blanketed form of Tali and the somber one of the Enthraller. Willing away her very self. Willing away all that had made her so magnificent. *Farewell, Tali. Farewell, bright spirit.*

Perhaps it was over quite soon. It felt long. I became dizzy and had to lean on the wattle fence to stay upright. My tears had dried up. I was numb; my mind was refusing to accept what was coming. Maybe she wouldn't see me. She couldn't know I was here, would have assumed, surely, that I'd have fled to the woods as soon as I could once she was taken. She would accuse Flint first anyway. That would grab everyone's attention. I must seize that moment to slip

315

through the crowd and out the gates, then head up to the forest before it was too dark to find a way. Perhaps, by some miracle, I could get across the river without being spotted. None of it seemed real. Perhaps I would wake soon to find myself in the mountains with Tali sleeping beside me, and this would be only another dream.

The charm was finished. Flint stood silent for some time, still cradling Tali's head. Then he removed his hands and took a step back. I felt, rather than heard, the crowd's indrawn breath.

Flint glanced over at the Enforcer who had been helping him and gave a nod. This man advanced toward the pallet; another Enforcer came in on the other side. One lifted Tali to a sitting position, tipped back her head, stuck his fingers in her mouth to hold it open. The other produced a tiny bottle, from which he dripped what seemed a very small amount of something onto Tali's tongue. She was lowered gently to the pillow; the blanket was drawn up again. As a loyal warrior of Keldec, she would no longer be beaten and reviled, but treated with respect.

Again we waited. The torches flared in the breeze, sending sparks high into a sky in which the rose of sunset mingled with the gray-blue of a summer dusk. I had to reach the cover of the forest before it was too dark to find my way. There'd be no returning to Shadowfell now; the best I could hope for was to get a message to the rebels before the king's men got there. It would be life on the road again, fleeing from one small settlement to the next, half a step ahead of the Enforcers. Oh, gods, let Sage or some of her clan be up there in the woods tonight. Let me not be entirely alone.

Tali stirred. A ripple of excitement ran through the crowd. She moaned, lifting her head, rubbing her eyes. She sat up.

There was a moment, no longer than a single indrawn breath, when I thought she would leap to her feet, herself once more, defiant and strong. Then she tried to stand, and her legs gave way, and she collapsed to the ground beside the pallet. A sound came from her, a terrible, wrenching wail that had no words in it, only blind animal terror. One of the Enforcers came up to her, an imposing figure in his high boots and black clothing. He reached down to help her to her feet, but she shrank away, curling in on herself, pressing close to the bench that supported the pallet. A babbling spilled from her, mindless, meaningless, its only message utter panic.

I fought back a wave of nausea. Gone. She was gone. The peerless Enthraller, the man whose skill had never before let him down, had made a mistake. The charm had gone wrong, and Tali would never be herself again. Nor would she ever be a servant of Keldec; that wreck of a woman would not be training new recruits or standing guard at court. Flint had destroyed her. Didn't they say it was the strongest, the most defiant, the most courageous who were hardest to turn? A vile thought came to me. Could this have been deliberate? Had Flint taken this path so Tali would not become subject to Keldec's will? Would he ruin a friend's mind if the alternative was her betraying the cause?

"Black Crow save us," muttered the young farmer. "I thought they said this fellow had never lost one."

"First time for everything," put in someone else. "Look at her! Like a helpless infant. See, she's wet herself."

Two Enforcers had hauled Tali upright; there was a dark patch on her shift and a puddle at her feet. She fought them, not with the harnessed force of earlier, but wildly, like a frustrated child. Neither of them hit back now; they only held her.

Flint had neither moved nor spoken. The torchlight played on his grave features as he looked up at the king. The crowd was alive with murmuring, whispering, conjecture; above that came the sounds of Tali's terror.

I was twelve years old again, back in my grandmother's house, watching from my hiding place as she woke from a long sleep, after the Enthraller charmed her. The confusion in her eyes—why were these men here, leaning over her bed? The pathetic cries—her words were all fled, she could remember nothing. The smell as she lost control of her bowels. Knowing I could not come out to help, could not comfort her until the king's men had left the house. Knowing the wise woman I had so loved was gone, gone forever. And later, knowing that the pitiful remnant there before me, shuddering, weeping, unable to help herself, had no one to turn to except me.

King Keldec rose to his feet. The crowd quieted. Flint had failed; perhaps he would die regardless. Perhaps I would lose both of them before this dark day ended.

"Twelve out of thirteen is, I suppose, still a fair record,"

318

Keldec said with a little smile. He spoke above Tali's wailing. "And there is no doubt you have provided us with entertainment, if not exactly the kind we anticipated. You must sharpen your skills before next time, Owen. Had this been a man, a potential recruit to our Enforcers, I would view your error with less leniency."

"Yes, my lord king." As calm as if this were an ordinary day; as if Tali were not crouched there at his feet, sniveling like a beaten child.

"Since this was done under Queen's Privilege, it is for my lady to have the final word," said the king. "It is late; my people are weary and in need of some supper and sleep. Tomorrow is a new day, full of fresh diversions for all. My lady, will you speak?"

She stood, regal in her crimson gown. "Thank you, my lord king. People of Alban: we know the power of enthrallment, how it can turn a wandering mind back to the path of patriotism and loyalty. Sometimes, as with this woman you see before you, an individual is too warped, too blind, too set in her ways to be healed by the charm, even when fortunate enough to be in the hands of an expert such as Owen Swift-Sword. Disobedience brought this woman here; disobedience, defiance, a blatant disregard for the king's law. It is entirely appropriate that our attempt to help her has resulted in the pathetic spectacle you see before you."

A wordless roar burst from Tali, who was thrashing around in her captors' grasp. One of the guards put a hand over her mouth, then cursed as she bit him.

"Take her away!" Varda commanded. "The girl is not fit for this company, or indeed for any company at all. The sight of her offends me. Dispose of her. Take her right away. Now!"

A brief consultation between the Enforcers. Then Flint and the man I'd seen in the dream hauled Tali up, each taking one arm, and dragged her away, heading for the same place where they had taken the unfortunate loser of the log-lifting contest. Close to where I stood; too close. I hunched myself down. *Dispose of her.* What did that mean?

On the far side of the open area, the official was calling for quiet. Enforcers were already taking away the pallet and the benches on which it had stood. The trumpets sounded a new fanfare, and a pair of oxen came out through the fortress gates, pulling a cart laden with joints of roast meat and barrels that likely contained ale. As the eyes of the folk around me moved to this new diversion, Flint glanced over and saw me. He started in shock, then rearranged his expression to that of the king's man, remote, impassive. A practiced dissembler. He gave the very slightest jerk of his head toward the open gates to the encampment. Then they moved on, the two men heading out with Tali between them. This was the opportunity, the one chance. Too late for her, but not for Shadowfell.

"Sorry, need to be sick, excuse me—" Quickly, while everyone was looking at tonight's promised supper and exclaiming over Keldec's generosity. Quickly, before the king began another address to his loyal people. I pushed my way

320

through, bag over my shoulder, staff in hand, heedless of whose feet I stepped on. "Sorry—going to be sick—"

"My loyal people!"

I was out, beyond easy view of crowd or guards, an instant before Keldec's voice rang out again in what must surely be the final speech of the day. There they were, not far beyond the open gates and apparently heading across the encampment toward the river. They'd gone right past that outbuilding where several of today's losers had been taken. I ran after them, not sure what I could safely say with that other Enforcer present. What did the queen expect them to do, take Tali up into the woods and make an end of her? Abandon her when quite clearly she could not look after herself? They turned, saw me, and halted.

"Caaah . . ." Tali struggled in the men's grip, trying to say something. Her tone was loud and flat. A half-wit. That was what people would call her from now on. If she lived among ordinary folk, she would be shunned, ridiculed, ostracized. "Gaaah . . ."

"It's all right, Luda," I said, fighting to keep my voice calm as I walked over to the three of them. I took off my shawl and reached to wrap it around her shoulders, over the inadequate shift. My hands were shaking; my heart was drumming. "I'll look after you." Then, to Flint, "I am this woman's friend. I was her traveling companion until she was seized. My name is Calla, and I will take her home."

"And where is home?" asked the second Enforcer.

"West, then south by Hiddenwater," I said. That way

lay Tali's ancestral territory of Ravensburn, so it was not quite a lie.

"Out of sight first, Rohan," Flint murmured, drawing Tali toward the river again. "That's what the queen ordered. We want to be up there, under the trees, before folk start streaming out here again." And to me, "Give me that, it'll be quicker if you're not carrying anything." He took my bag and slung it over his shoulder.

Crossing the river was awkward. Here, where the Rush spilled into Deepwater, there were three separate channels. Tali was frightened; it took both men to guide her over, while I made my own way, using my staff for support. The river bottom was all sliding stones, and although the water came only to my knees, the flow was swift. I saw Flint looking at me, a little frown on his face. Trying to convey something with his eyes, perhaps an apology. *There should have been some other way,* I thought grimly, though I knew this was unfair. For him, for Tali, there was no way but the cause. Flint had put his position at court, so critical to Regan's strategy, ahead of Tali's survival. I knew that if he had consulted her on the matter, she would have expected no less. Andra had stayed silent in the woods while her brother died. It was a rebel's choice. You valued your comrades, you respected them, you fought alongside them. And sometimes you sacrificed them for the greater good. Right now, it was hard to accept that. It was hard to walk with Flint and not to judge him.

On the far side of the river, forested hills rose up from the loch shore. The two men took a path that meandered up the hillside through a stand of beech and birch; we climbed up and up in the long summer twilight. By the time Flint called a halt in a small clearing, evening shadows had robbed the forest of its color. Somewhere in the trees a bird sang a melodious, plaintive farewell to the day. Tali sank to the ground, hugging the cloak tightly around her. Her noisy protests had long since subsided to a weary whimpering.

"You'll camp here." Flint examined us in the fading light, his face giving nothing away. "Make no fire tonight. Head off west in the morning and make sure you keep her quiet. The smirched aren't welcome on the main roads. Don't make trouble again. Believe me, we'll be far less helpful next time."

"You have supplies?" Rohan asked. "Enough for your journey home?"

"We'll get by." Since neither man had brought supplies to offer us, his question seemed pointless. "Thank you for your help," I made myself add. I didn't seem to be able to stop shivering.

They looked at us for a moment, and in their eyes I saw what they saw: myself, small, slight, and visibly distressed; Tali with her tall, strong body and the mind of a terrified infant. A heavy pack. A long walk through rough terrain. Folk on the road and in the settlements who would either shun us or subject us to open ridicule because of what Tali had become. "We can manage," I said.

They looked at each other. Rohan lifted his brows, then turned and headed off down the hill.

"Travel safe," murmured Flint. For just a moment his gray eyes met mine, but what he read in them I could not guess. Love, disgust, gratitude, reproach—they all tangled in my mind, along with a bone-deep exhaustion at the thought of what lay ahead. He turned away, strode off down the path, and was lost in the shadows.

Chapter Twelve

Tali sat with her arms around her knees, quiet now. Around us the forest was hushed. The sound of the men's footsteps faded away. I knelt to unfasten the pack; my hands needed something to do. I would not remember that last sad season with my grandmother, when I had fed her, cleaned her, held her when she panicked, kept steady vigil day and night as she shrank and faded and crumbled away. I would not think of how it might be with Tali. And yet, as I rummaged for the last scraps of our food, as I made sure the iron weapons were still well wrapped so I could call to Sage once I was certain the Enforcers were gone, that was the only image in my mind.

"Should be safe to talk now."

My skin prickled. I did not dare turn around.

"Neryn. They're gone." And after a moment, "Neryn?"

I turned. She was still in the same position, on the ground, hugging her knees, watching me. Her face was a pale oval in the dimness of the forest shadows; her dark eyes were sharply aware. Around her neck the ravens flew their steady course, strong and true.

"Tali?" It came out as a shuddering sob.

Her eyes widened in shocked realization. "You didn't—you can't have—oh, Neryn!"

I put my hands over my face. A moment later, I felt her strong arms around me, and the warmth of her against me.

"Black Crow save us," she muttered. "You thought it was real. All this time, you— By all that's holy, Neryn! How could you believe for a moment that Flint would do that?"

I couldn't speak. She held me as I wept; as I tried to reshape everything that had happened since they first brought their captive out before that crowd. After a while she released me and stepped away. She cleared her throat.

"I hope you brought my spare clothes," she said, kneeling to look in the bag. "The sooner I get this wretched thing off the better. Oh, good." She drew out her neatly folded trousers, her tunic, her shirt. "Take a few deep breaths, Neryn. Sit down and drink some water. We must move on quickly. That other fellow seemed mild enough, but he's an Enforcer, and no Enforcer can be trusted. Who's to say someone may not have a change of heart and come after us, thinking it might be tidier to finish us off and get rid of the evidence?"

"How did you—" I choked on the words, then tried again. "That was so real. It was just like—I never for a moment— Flint didn't know you were there until they brought you out, did he? How could you know what to do? And how could he fake it with the other Enthrallers there?"

She had stripped off the torn shift and was getting into her own clothing. Even in the near darkness I could see the bruises on her pale skin, the marks of a savage beating. "I guessed what he'd do. I knew he wouldn't enthrall me. I told you once he'd never do that to a friend, did you forget? So there were only two choices—pretend it had worked or pretend it hadn't. Do the first, and I'd be stuck at Summerfort playing the same sort of part Flint does, and you'd be on your own with nobody to look after you. Do the second convincingly and I had some chance of getting away. As for the other Enthrallers, I don't know the answer to that, but Flint did tell me once that the singing is mostly for show. The real magic is in the part you can't see, when they lay their hands on a person. The risk was that folk might not believe Flint could bungle an enthrallment. My acting must have been good enough." She winced as she pulled the shirt over her head. "It must have been extremely good. I hadn't imagined for a moment that you thought it was real. You were so self-controlled." She put on the tunic and fastened the belt. "I'm sorry you were upset. I had to keep up the pretense while that other fellow was here, amiable as he was." After a moment she added, "My guess is they were expected to bring me up here out of sight, then dispose of me permanently. That's more in line with Keldec's usual approach. Seems there's at least one kindhearted man among Flint's fellow warriors."

I said nothing. I had misjudged Flint yet again. I had sent him away without so much as a smile when he had risked everything to save Tali and to bring us to safety.

"Neryn."

"I know, we have to move on. Here, I'll take the bag."

"I'll carry it. Thank you for bringing my weapons." She waited while I picked up my staff and put on the cloak she had passed back to me. "I won't lie to you; we may find ourselves in real trouble soon. Whichever path we take from here, we'll be near the Rush valley when people are heading home from the Gathering. If anyone who was down there just now spots me walking up the valley and obviously in my right mind, we'll be reported straightaway. I don't need to spell out what the consequences of that would be. Even if nobody sees us, even if we have perfect weather and move as fast as we possibly can, we'll reach Shadowfell much later than we originally planned. We could go to ground somewhere until the crowds have dispersed. But then we'd have no hope of getting you to the Lord of the North and back again before winter."

"I have a plan. At least, I had a plan I was going to use when I thought—"

"When you thought you'd have to convey a half-wit all the way to Shadowfell?" I heard a smile in her voice. "Tell me."

"I thought Sage or some of her clan might be close by; they were camped here once before. There were no Good Folk down at Summerfort, not a trace of them. Up here, farther from the iron weaponry, I thought some of them might be prepared to come out if I called them. I would have asked them for help to get you safely to Shadowfell."

"Still will, I hope, especially if they can do so quickly.

I've a good chance of getting you to Shadowfell alive. I can take you on to the north. But I can't achieve the impossible. You might still reach the Lord of the North before the autumn storms set in. But you wouldn't get back; you'd be there for the winter."

"And so would you," I said, realizing what that would mean for the rebels. Her role was vital, not only for keeping bodies strong and morale high over the long shut-in winter, but for helping Regan plan ahead. They would struggle without her. "Of course, someone else could go with me."

"Someone could. There's no predicting what Regan will want. If he's there to make the decision." A silence. "But after what's just happened, you may prefer it to be one of the others."

"You'd always be my first choice," I said. "But only if you wanted the job."

"Will you call the Good Folk, then? Or are they not here?"

"Oh, they're here," I told her. "I can feel them all around. But I may not need to call."

"Why no—"

Lights appeared in the forest around us, closing in from the shadows under the trees. We stood silent as small beings came into view, eight of them in all, each carrying a tiny glowing lantern. They made a circle around us at a distance of a few paces, then sat down, placing their lights carefully on the ground. Rather than tower over them, Tali and I sat down beside them.

No Sage. No Red Cap. But these were familiar faces:

the doubting Silver was here, delicate and fey in her shimmering gown, and beside her were others of her clan—Daw, Gentle, Blackthorn, and more. Despite Silver's misgivings, they had helped me before. They would help me again. "Thank you," I murmured. "Oh, thank you for coming here."

"A wee birdie told us you were in strife," said the little herbalist, Gentle, speaking as if it were only a day or two since she had last seen me. "Thanks to your courage and your friend's quick wits," she glanced at Tali, "you're out o' trouble for now. But you'll be needin' to get awa' soon."

Silver spoke. Her voice was like the ringing of a lovely bell; her face wore a familiar frown. But her words surprised me. "We believe that if you attempt to return to Shadowfell on foot, even on side paths, the Enforcers will catch up with you. You escaped tonight only by luck and quick thinking. We could not help you; not in that place of iron."

"How do you know what happened if you cannot go there?" Tali asked.

"A crow flew over," said the bird-man Daw. "We have followed your journey, all of it, in one way or another. Our people are out and about, crossing Alban as never before, since Sage brought the word. Much change. Much disturbance."

"You cannot reach the Lord of the North by human pathways," Silver said in a tone that brooked no argument. "Not before the autumn. But . . . there is another way. A way that may be confronting to humankind, but a quick one."

"A very quick one," said Blackthorn, the clan's wizened elder. "You can be on the Lord's doorstep tomorrow."

"Tomorrow?" Tali sounded incredulous.

"That would be . . . a gift," I said. No more long days of walking; no need to hunt, fish, and forage on the journey; no constant looking over our shoulders. No need to find our own way through the wild and perilous north. The relief was such that I felt faint.

"The Northies have sent you a guide," said Blackthorn. "Something of a surprise."

"What guide?"

Gentle said nothing, only looked up into the trees; the others too turned their gaze upward. There, perched on a branch above us, was a pure white owl, his feet neatly clad in small felt boots. The boots were a warm blue and had some kind of embroidery on them. I had encountered this creature before. When I had been struggling to survive on my own, after Flint first told me he was an Enthraller and I fled from him in revulsion, on a night when I might have died of cold, this being had come to help me. He was powerful, and he was from the Watch of the North.

I rose to my feet and bowed, then looked up to meet the being's gaze. His face was not quite that of an owl; there was a suggestion of a young man about it too. "We have met once before," I said, "and I am deeply in your debt. May I know your name?"

The owl being blinked his great eyes. "Whisper," he said. "Word came that you're seeking the Lord o' the North. The Big One's sleeping and canna be woken. Maybe your call can stir him. We've waited long for that. I'll be taking you tae his hall. Now, straightaway. Ready?"

I longed to say a simple yes. This was just what we needed. But I must explain, for the offer was based on false hope. "My gift—it's not—"

"Wait," Tali said, and all eyes went to her. "Straight-away? You're saying we can't go back to Shadowfell first?"

If I had not known before how much it meant to her, getting back there and seeing Regan before he headed out on another mission, I heard it now in her voice.

"As I see it, you have a choice," Whisper said. "And you wouldna be wanting tae dawdle over the choosing. The two of you come wi' me and reach the Big One by morning. Or the Caller comes wi' me, and the fighting lassie returns tae Shadowfell on her own."

I could not let this go on. "Whisper . . . I can't use my gift to wake the Lord of the North. I understand that his people need him back. I need him too, so I can learn about the magic of earth. But . . . a person like me doesn't sum-mon a Guardian."

Whisper regarded me gravely. "Then you'll be needing tae wake him some other way, lassie. Come on now, make up your minds. Is it the two of you or only the one coming north?"

Silence. Tali's jaw was clenched tight. I wanted to tell her she could go back to Shadowfell, I would be fine, some of the Good Folk could bring me safely home when my training was completed. But I couldn't give her anything but the truth.

"You won't be safe on your own," I said quietly. "You said it yourself; the moment someone spots you, they'll report you to the Enforcers. Now that the king and queen have seen you, along with their court and their guards, you won't be able to go about openly at all. Not in this region anyway." After a moment I added, "You're not the easiest person to disguise."

Tali's mouth twisted. "Now, that's new, you telling me *I* won't be safe. Neryn, forget strategy for a moment. What do you want me to do?"

We'd started this journey in wary cooperation, at best. This question told me how much that had changed. If I had not been quite sure before that Tali trusted me as a comrade and as a friend, I was sure now. I spoke as if the Good Folk were not present, as if the two of us were alone together by our campfire.

"I'd like you to come with me. I know you want to go back; I know how worried you are. But I would feel much safer if you were with me, and . . . when we were in the isles, it was much easier to learn, much easier to get through the long days, because I knew you would be there waiting for me. I'm not used to having friends to support me. It makes it much easier to be strong."

One of the Good Folk gave an audible sigh, as a listener might at a poignant moment in an old tale. Silver glared at the little creature and it fell silent, looking down at its three-toed feet.

"Very well, then, if that's what you want." Tali's tone was gruff. She seemed to be avoiding my gaze. "Can't say

I'm overkeen on heading up the valley alone. Regan and the others would probably be gone by the time I reached Shadowfell anyway. One thing, though."

"Oh, aye?" Whisper was sounding somewhat cool now.

"I'm not leaving my weapons behind. They've come all this way and I'm keeping them. They can stay wrapped up; I'm getting used to that. But if I go, they go."

"You ask much."

"So do you." She met Whisper's owl-eyes with a steady gaze.

"Aye, well." This seemed to be a yes. Whisper lifted his wings and flew down to land beside us. "We'd best be on our way. Gather your bits and pieces and follow me."

Our passage to the north was indeed quick. Quick, dark, and confronting enough to turn a person's hair pure white. I should have remembered that the magic of earth included the magic of stone. I should have remembered how it was last autumn, when the king's men almost caught me in a narrow defile. I had pressed myself up against the sheer cliff face and asked a stanie mon to hide me. For a little, that day, I had believed I would be entombed, immobile, within the rocks until I died, perhaps of sheer terror. Only when I'd remembered the need to address the stanie mon in a particular kind of verse, the kind used in a children's game, had he released me.

Whisper led the two of us up the hillside, with the Westies coming beside and behind, lighting the way with their small lanterns. Tali carried the pack; I brought my staff. We climbed steadily for some time, until we were high above Summerfort. By daylight there would be a fine view of Deepwater and the forested hills all around.

"Ready?" Whisper said, halting abruptly and turning to face us.

Tali spoke for the two of us; I was still catching my breath. "We're ready."

"Sure?"

"Yes, we're sure!" I caught Tali's unspoken words: *Get on with it, will you?* Perhaps she was remembering being caught up and whirled around in the descent from that cliff top on Ronan's Isle to the Hag's boat.

"Very well. Wee folk!" Whisper was addressing the Westies, his tone somewhat patronizing, though he stood no higher than Silver, who was the tallest of the group. "Step back. When we're gone, douse those lanterns and make your way home, quick as you can. You can tell the messengers the Caller's safe, and on her way north."

"There is no need to spell it out for us," said Silver testily. "Farewell, Neryn. Go safely."

"When you reach that place, Neryn," put in Gentle, "see to it that the lassie there gets some salve for her cuts and bruises. I'd have done it myself if we'd had more time." She looked up at Tali. "You're a braw fighter, lassie. Strong to the core."

"I wondered . . ." Tali was unusually hesitant; she glanced at Daw. "I know there are birds carrying news. Have you any news of Regan, our leader? When we left, he was heading for Corriedale. But he might be back at Shadowfell by now—"

"Nae time for chatter," Whisper said. "We must go *now.*"

But Daw, ignoring this, said, "He went to Corriedale. He returned to Shadowfell. More, I do not know."

Did I imagine the sudden glint of tears in Tali's eyes, bright in the soft lantern light? "Thank you," she said, her voice a murmur.

"Now," said Whisper, and this time everyone obeyed. The Westies retreated. Tali and I stood still, waiting for whatever might come, another whirlwind, a magical charm to make us fly, a vehicle of some kind, though what could cover the miles from here to the north in a single night, I could not imagine.

"Grasp hands," Whisper said. "Keep hold and dinna let go. This will be long; hold still and quiet until I give you the word. Got that?"

We nodded; I was not sure if the period of silence had already started.

"Now, then," said Whisper, and everything went dark. Pitch-dark. Utterly dark, as it had been the other time, when the stanie mon had hidden me within a wall of stone. And it was silent; the small creaks and rustles of the forest creatures, the movement of trees in the breeze, the soft tread of our feet, all were gone. There was nothing; only Tali's hand in mine, and the thunderous beating of my heart.

Tali's fingers tightened on mine momentarily, then relaxed as she imposed her customary self-control. After the first jolt of panic, I drew on the Hag's training to keep my body still, breathing in a pattern. If there was anything I had learned in the isles, it was to maintain my balance when I could not see; I had spent long periods standing in that cave with my eyes shut, simply breathing. But this was harder. In the cave, even when the Hag was not guiding me with her voice, there had always been the sound of the sea.

I felt no sense of movement. As far as I knew, we remained standing on the hilltop above Summerfort, under the trees, and the forest creatures were carrying on their nightly business around us as always. Only, we had been rendered blind and deaf.

Time passed—a great deal of time, or so it seemed. I maintained my steady breathing; I tried to keep my thoughts from wandering to treacherous areas, such as whether what Flint had done for us would put him in still more peril. Or whether, when the shocks of today had subsided, Tali would be furious with me for coming to Summerfort instead of escaping up the valley and leaving her to fend for herself as the rebel code required. I tried to banish the vile sights and sounds of the Gathering from my mind, but they would not go away.

Gods, it was dark! I tried to shift my weight onto one leg, then the other, without actually moving. My knees were starting to feel odd, shaky, even though all I had done was stand still. My throat was dry; I wanted to cough. And I needed to relieve myself. Whisper had said we would be there by morning. We didn't seem to be going anywhere. But perhaps, in some strange way, we were already traveling. Perhaps this *was* the journey north. Perhaps, to get there, we must maintain this pose all night. What would happen if one of us moved? If one of us, in a moment of in-attention, asked the other how she was feeling? Would that leave us where we'd started, on the hillside above Summer-fort with enemies all around? We might never reach the Lord of the North. I fought back a yawn. *Weapons sharp. Backs straight. Hearts high.*

By the time our long vigil came to an end, I was almost beyond noticing. Half-asleep on my feet, I heard a scraping sound, as of a stick drawn across a rough stone surface, and I felt Tali's grip tighten on my hand.

"Close your eyes," said Whisper from right beside me. "Count to five. Now open them."

When I did so, there was light: not the first rays of the dawning sun, nor yet the welcoming glow of the Good Folk's lanterns, but a cool blue light like ice under a full moon. It was so bitterly cold that my breath caught in my chest.

After the time of utter darkness, even this low light was an assault on my eyes, and for a little I struggled to see clearly. One thing was certain: we were no longer in the forest. As my vision accustomed itself to the change, I saw before me a landscape of stone and shadow, remote and still, lovely in its chill perfection. We stood on a hillside, facing north. And now, to the east, the sun rose over snow-capped mountains, touching their higher slopes with rose and gold. To the north were more great peaks. What was it Tali had said once, that people hadn't seen real mountains until they came north of the river Race? Above us arched a pale and cloudless sky, and as we rubbed our eyes and stretched our aching bodies, an eagle flew over, its power-ful wings bearing it westward.

"Aye, well," said Whisper, who was on my left and ap-parently none the worse for wear after the long night's vigil. "You might be wanting tae splash your faces and stretch your legs before we move on. Down that way there's a wee stream. You might be needing tae crack the ice first. I'll wait for you here."

There was indeed a stream, and a hollow where a few straggly bushes grew, providing some cover while we per-formed our ablutions. Tali broke the ice with the heel of her boot. The bracing chill of the water was welcome, ren-dering us sharply awake. Together, we went through a se-quence of exercises familiar from our time on the skerry, limbering up our cramped bodies.

"*Move on,*" Tali murmured. "How far, I wonder? I have to say, you've looked better in your time, Neryn."

"You look surprisingly good, all things considered." In fact, she looked pale and tired, and she was not moving with her usual confidence. She was surely in pain; it wasn't long since she'd been beaten by the king's men. "But you need that salve."

"What I crave right now is sleep. But after last time, I'm not fool enough to hope for anything. We were probably lucky to get a wash and time enough to relieve ourselves."

We did not need to walk far. Whisper led us to a hall whose entry was in a fold of the mountain. It reminded me of the passages and chambers, the stairs and doorways of Shadowfell, and I wondered whether once, long ago, a powerful entity such as the Hag or the Lord had made a home there.

Inside, the Lord's hall was far grander and more spacious than Shadowfell. Even indoors it was bitterly cold. The arching walls were the stone of the mountain, but here and there paler patches glinted and glowed in the light of suspended lanterns, suggesting ice. Great skins softened the rock floor, skins of creatures whose kind I could only guess at. Wolves three times bigger than any known to man; jet-black cattle with hair as soft as a cat's.

Whisper led us deeper in. Chambers opened to one side or the other, and there were many folk about, not men and women but Good Folk, though they were generally taller than the Westies, some of them of a height with humankind. Most were clad in gray, and some bore weapons. None of them were talking.

We came to a halt outside a doorway covered by a curtain of sturdy weave, patterned in various shades of gray. Whisper did not announce our presence, but suddenly the curtain was drawn aside and there was a wee woman in a gown and apron, her startling red hair as curly and wild as Sage's, her eyes bright as glass beads, and a welcoming smile on her face. A wave of warmth came from the chamber behind her.

"Ye'll be wantin' a bath and a bittie breakfast," she said. "Come on, then, dinna stand aboot lettin' in the chill." This small personage addressed Whisper. "Ye can leave the lassies tae me," she said. "They'll no' be fit for anything until they've had a cleanup and a guid sleep."

Whisper went off without a sound. Perhaps he too was tired.

"Bath first," the wee woman said. "Ye'll be the Caller, nae doot. And ye the keeper."

"I'm Neryn." I was not quite tired enough to forget the importance of courtesy. "And this is Tali. A bath . . . Thank you, this is more than we hoped for." There were indeed two bathtubs in the chamber, ready and waiting for us. They must have known we were coming before we reached this hall. And there was a hearth with a fire; it was blissful to feel the warmth of it.

"Aye, weel, ye'll be cold. 'Tis no' the easiest way tae mak' a journey, Whisper's way. Quick, aye. But chilly. And hard on the knees. Strip off your things. Here, let me help ye."

At the sight of Tali's bruises, she sucked in her breath. "Ach! I'll be findin' a salve for those. Ye puir lassie. Into the tub wi' ye, go on now. Ye can ca' me Flow." After a pause, she spoke again, and her voice was shaking. "Is it true, what the messengers hae been tellin' us? Can ye really wake the Lord?"

In the face of her naked hope, I found myself incapable of telling her how unlikely that seemed. "I can't be certain of anything, Flow. I will do my best, I promise."

When we were washed, fed, and clad in new clothing that fit us perfectly, Flow led us to a little round sleeping chamber with a pair of shelf beds that appeared to have been hewn out of the rock. Each was furnished with pillows and soft bedding, atop which was spread a fur cloak, luxuriously warm.

I had never seen Tali so exhausted. Flow had salved her

bruises, using a mudlike mixture, and covered one or two with dressings of moss and linen held on by neat bandages. Perhaps that had reminded Tali of the beating and of what had come before and after. I would not ask her about it. If she wanted to tell me, she would do so in her own time. Not now; both of us were dropping with weariness.

I sat on the edge of my bed, watching Tali as she checked every corner of the chamber, then came back to lean my staff against the wall close by her own sleeping place. Her staff had been lost when she was taken prisoner.

"What are you doing? Lie down and rest."

"It feels wrong to have nobody on watch. But the fact is, I'm too tired to do anything about it."

"We're safe here. I'm sure these people have their own guards."

There was a silence, during which she folded her arms and looked down at the floor. Then she added, "I've failed you once, maybe twice. I wouldn't want to do it again."

"Failed me? How?" What was she talking about?

"In the isles, I let them take me from the skerry and leave you alone out there. By Deepwater, I had to leave you on your own again. I should have known you'd come after me. I should have known you wouldn't put your own safety first. And now look where we are."

I blinked at her. "Safe, warm, bathed and fed, and exactly where we intended to be."

"But—"

"Lie down, shut your eyes, and stop thinking so hard. If you weren't so tired, you'd know you're talking nonsense."

"But, Neryn—"

"If we don't sleep now, we won't be at our best to face whatever comes next. Do as you're told—lie down, and not another word out of you."

She managed a smile, then winced in pain as she lowered herself onto the bed.

"I know you're worried about Regan," I told her. "But they said he went back to Shadowfell, and he has good advisers."

"Mm." She pulled the covers over herself and lay down.

"Sleep well, Tali," I said. But there was no reply.

We woke and found ourselves feeling better; Flow brought us a meal, which we ate hungrily. It could have been morning or evening when Whisper came to fetch us.

"I'll show you where the Lord lies," he said, and led us through a maze of passageways to a grand chamber, its roof so high above us that it seemed lost in shadows. Silent attendants stood in ranks to either side of the hall, which was illuminated by a double row of flaming torches. At the other end of the room, on a pallet set high on a dais, a man lay sleeping. One guard stood at the head of his bed, another at the foot. They were tall, broad beings, manlike, but each would have dwarfed even Big Don. Their caplike helms and breast-pieces were of a glittering substance I could not identify, and they held spears of pale bone. Brothers, I guessed, for their faces were nearly identical, strong-boned and impassive. Their eyes were as gray as their garments. I was reminded of Flint.

As Whisper led us forward, the vast cavern seemed full of an expectant hush. These people thought, perhaps, that I could work a miracle. Or their long-held hope had made them clutch at straws. Hadn't someone said the Lord of the North had been sleeping for hundreds of years?

We came before the dais. The guards did not move.

"You can go up," Whisper said.

I climbed the steps to the pallet; Tali stayed at the bottom, my staff in her hand. I looked down at the Lord of the North.

He was tall and appeared to be in his prime. His clothing too was gray, and over it was a coverlet of pure white fur. His face was snow-pale, his hair was dark, and his wide-open eyes were the color of a chill dawn sky. I waited until I had seen his chest rise and fall seven times before I accepted that he was not dead.

I cleared my throat, but found no words. This was not sleep, surely, but something deeper, a kind of living death that lay far beyond the limits of my understanding.

"Can you help him, lassie?"

I started in shock. The deep voice belonged to one of the formidable guards. He'd turned to look at me, and I saw the same hope on his face as I had seen on Flow's. These folk loved their lord. Above all things, they wanted him back. "I don't know," I said. "Whisper, how long has he been like this?"

"Long years," Whisper said. "Long, long years. We've done our best tae tend tae him. We've kept things going in his ha'. We've waited. But we canna bring him back. Before he lay down here, he ordered us not tae wake him."

344

"Doesn't that mean—?"

"He didna give *you* any orders."

There was no arguing with that. "You say he lay down. He put himself into this trance? Why?"

"You'd best talk tae Flow. She'll give you the story. We'll leave him in peace now. We dinna expect you tae bring him back in an instant. Stane moves awfu' slow."

As we made our way out between the rows of silent attendants, Tali asked him, "May we move about here? Talk freely to folk?"

"Aye, wander as you please. Anyplace we dinna want you prying, there'll be a guard on the door."

"I've seen some unusual weaponry here," Tali said. "Is there perhaps an armory? A master-at-arms, a person who is in charge of such things?"

"Oh, aye. There might be both. I'll have a wee word."

Later in the day—or possibly night, for in this underground hall there was no way of telling if it was light or dark outside—we had settled in a small chamber where there was a hearth with a fire. Flow had suggested we would be more comfortable there, and had offered a choice of mending or cutting up root vegetables for our supper to keep us occupied. She had promised to tell me the tale later.

I was working my way through the mending; Tali had already accounted for the parsnips and carrots, wielding Flow's bone knife with precision. When someone marched in without knocking, she was on her feet in an instant. The implement, rock-steady in her hands, was aimed straight at the being's heart.

"Friend," the visitor said, holding up open hands to show he meant no harm. Tali lowered the knife but stood her ground. I set down my sewing.

Five of them came in, and the chamber was suddenly full. They were uniformly clad in short hooded cloaks over plain gray clothing and sturdy boots. Most striking were the leather protective garments they had on, arm braces and breast-pieces not unlike those worn by the warriors of Shadowfell. Three resembled shortish human folk, one was more wolf than man, and the fifth seemed to change its shape each time I looked. Two bore staves; all had sheathed weapons at their belts. Fighters.

"Next time, knock," Tali said, putting the knife down on the table.

"Then we wouldna hae seen how quick ye were."

"You want a demonstration of my fighting skills, just ask." Tali folded her arms. Her stance, feet apart, chin up, was all challenge.

"Er . . . this might not be the place for that," I put in.

The spokesman for our visitors folded his own arms. He had to tilt his head back to look Tali in the eye, but there was something in both his stance and his expression that suggested he'd be happy to give her a good fight if she wanted one. "As tae skills, we've heard ye might have a thing or two tae teach us."

"You know nothing about me!" she snapped. "How could you?"

"A bird," I suggested. "Yes?"

"Your tale came before ye. A wee skirmish wi' the king's

346

men, aye? One agin four or five, that's what we heard. Not to speak o' the way ye train those fighters o' yours, back hame."

Tali scowled. "That doesn't explain your storming in here and almost getting this knife through your chest."

"Stormin'? Lads, were we doin' any stormin'?"

The other four shook their heads.

"Ye want tae see stormin', just say the word," the spokesman said.

It was time to intervene. "My name is Neryn," I said, "and this is Tali. You have a fighting force here? I thought the Good Folk shunned conflict. I thought you would sooner go to ground than become involved in such things."

The five of them took this as an invitation, strolling over to seat themselves on the benches beside us. One reached out to help himself to a piece of carrot; Tali's glare stopped him before he set a finger on it.

"Ye got it wrong, lassie," said one of the others, a red-bearded fellow almost as broad as he was tall. "The disputes o' human folk, aye, we steer clear o' those, unless one o' your kind comes along—a Caller, that is. Even then we dinna much care tae get caught up in them. Oor ain fights, they're a different matter."

"Your own fights?" asked Tali. "Against whom?"

"A' sorts. Brollachans; trows; wolf-men. There's some grumly old creatures in the north."

"Then there's clan disputes," put in one of the others. "Over land, over law, over trifles. The winters here are lang; folk need somethin' tae keep theirselves occupied."

Tali and I exchanged a glance.

"How many fighters do you have here?" Tali asked.

"Ach, that's no' information tae be given oot lightly. Ye dinna hae oor names yet, and already ye want oor strategic secrets. We're no' fools."

"Understood." Tali was smiling now. "If the situation were reversed, I surely wouldn't give you that information. As for names, you have ours; if you choose to introduce yourselves, I have a suggestion you might perhaps want to consider."

They looked at one another.

"It's to do with the long winters, and not getting restless, and honing your combat skills."

"Oh, aye?" The red-bearded one sounded unimpressed, but there was no concealing the glint of interest in his eye.

"Piece of carrot, anyone?" Tali asked.

Grins broke out on every weathered face. "Scar," said the spokesman.

"Stack."

"Grim."

"Steep."

"Fleabane."

"His mither was a herb-wife," said Scar in explanation.

"A suggestion, ye say." Stack stroked his beard thoughtfully. "What suggestion might that be?"

"Seems we have the same problem: an army that needs to keep busy over the winter months, so it's ready for action once the thaw comes. And by busy, I don't mean folk getting into foolish disputes among themselves. I have ideas that I may be prepared to share once I know you better. If you want my help, I'm offering it."

"At what price?" The wolflike being, Grim, was staring at Tali through narrowed eyes. He looked as if he might leap to the attack if she said a wrong word.

"I'd like to see your armory and talk to you about your weapons," she said with perfect calm. "In time, I'll tell you more about our future plans, though you may know something of that already. It seems messengers have been carrying the word about our cause to the Good Folk all over Alban." She hesitated, glancing at me. "Our leader would be interested to know you have a fighting force here." I saw her deciding not to ask them if they were immune to the fell effects of iron. "You've done a remarkable job to keep that going all this time without your Lord."

"Aye, 'tis a lang while," said Steep. "The best we can dae, while we're waitin', is keep fightin'. Keep oor heads up."

"Weapons sharp, backs straight, hearts high," I murmured.

They stared at me with new respect. "Aye," said Scar after a moment. "Aye, ye got it exactly."

"Like you, I don't much care for being idle," Tali said. "Neryn has a job to do here. While she's working on it, I think I can help you; I think you can help me. But, of course, it's your decision. The only thing is, there's a limit to how much of the day I can occupy in chopping vegetables."

The fighters roared with laughter. Then, without another word spoken, they were all on their feet. "Come on, then," said Scar. "Lang way doon tae the armory. Best be movin'."

Trust had come with surprising speed. Tali glanced at me, brows raised.

"Go on," I said. "I'll be fine. Flow's not far away, and the place is full of guards."

"Guards?" Steep spoke with derision. "Ye mean them in the ha'? Just for show, they are, save for the Twa. The real fighters, we're a' doon below. We're the strong backbone o' this place; wi'oot the likes o' us, wha'd keep the Southies in check?"

They left the chamber with Tali in their midst. I picked up my mending, but my mind was on the Lord of the North with his open, empty eyes and his noble features clean of expression. I felt the weight of expectation from this household of loyal folk, all of them hoping I would be the one to do what their lord had forbidden them: wake him from his deathlike sleep. A sleep he had imposed upon himself. What could drive a Guardian to do such a thing?

"'Twas long ago," Flow said. The two of us sat with the mending basket between us. Tali had not returned; I decided to take that as a good sign. "A sad tale, simple enough. In the old days there was a Lady here, his wife. They had a wee daughter, just the one. Our folk, ye understand, live lang, but dinna often bear children, so this lassie was rare and precious. Everybody loved Gem; she danced around this gloomy old ha' like a bright butterfly. She was full o' questions, wanted to know the makin' and workin' o' everythin'. Hardly stopped movin' frae dawn tae dusk. When she grew up a bit, her father began tae teach her the magic o' stone, the spells and charms, the deep knowin'. Folk would come on the twa o' them, the tall man and the half-grown lassie, heads together over some old scroll or conjurin' up creatures out o' the bare rock." She folded up the garment she had been mending and reached into the basket for another.

"What happened?" I asked, knowing it could be nothing good.

"Many enchantments she learned from her father; she was skilled in that work. But she was always wantin' more. The Lord, ye understand, would hae kept her safe at home, nae wanderin' beyond the ha' unless she took him along wi' her. He didna ken that a' lassies want tae run free when they start tae grow older; a' lassies want tae be let off the leash and mak' their ain errors.

"Gem took tae slippin' oot. She was clever, she had spellcraft, she learned tae get by her father's guards unseen. The Lord had given her the kennin' o' deep magic. Mebbe he forgot tae teach her common sense. One day in summer, Gem went missin'. Naebody saw her leave, but she wasna tae be found anywhere in the ha'. Ye ken how steep the paths are in these parts, sheer up and doon on either side. The Lord used a spell tae find his daughter, but it was too late; she'd lost her footin', or somethin' had startled her, and she'd fallen tae the rocks far below. Broken. Dead. The cruel part o' the tale is, the lassie was skilled in magic. She could hae changed her form and flown oot o' trouble. But she was still young, and she wasna quick enough." She fell silent for a little, her sewing forgotten in her hands. "They'd been arguin' that same mornin', before Gem left. He wasna happy wi' her work on some charm or other, and she lost her temper and shouted at her papa. *Why canna ye leave me be? Why canna I be free like the creatures on the mountain?* 'Twas only a small quarrel; she loved her father weel. But that lay heavy on him once she was gone."

"What about Gem's mother?"

"She faded." Flow resumed darning the stocking she was holding. "Grief shrank her down tae a shadow. In the end she went awa'. Couldna bear tae be in the place where her only child had perished. And he was left on his ain-some. One day he lay doon and didna get up again. Told us, before he crept awa' inside himself, that we werena tae wake him. We've watched ower him ever since, hopin' things would change, but they havena. Until the twa o' ye came along." She cast me a sideways glance. "We never had a Caller before. We're thinkin' mebbe ye can do what we're forbidden tae try." Hope shone in her eyes.

"It must have been very hard for everyone here," I said eventually. "Losing Gem, and then the Lady, and him as well."

"Gem was oor wee one, the only bairn ever born in this ha', and we a' grieved for her. The Lady, aye, 'twas indeed sad. As for him, we tried tae coax him oot o' his sorrow, but he was deaf tae us."

"But you've kept the household going, kept it all ready for him." Hundreds of years; such hope.

Flow sighed. "It's been hard, sometimes, tae gae on believin' that someday he'll wake. The lads, the Twa, they've been staunch; they havena slept more than a snatch since he lay doon there."

"The Twa—you mean his two guards?"

"Aye, lassie. 'Tis special hard for them, since they were always by his side before. We're thinkin' ye might be the last chance. If a Caller canna reach him, wha can?"

I hesitated. "I think . . . I must speak honestly, Flow. I don't believe I should call a Guardian as I might a less powerful being; it feels wrong. I need time to think about it, work out another way. . . . But Whisper said stone moves slowly. We had some hopes of returning to Shadowfell before the winter."

"We've waited lang. We can wait a bit more. Could be you'll know when it's time."

In the isles Tali had been counting the days until we might move on with our journey. Here she was busy from dawn till dusk with the northern warriors, somewhere down below. She fell into bed each night content but exhausted and slept soundly until morning.

My days were spent with the Lord of the North, in the great silent cavern where he lay with his eyes on nothing. The ranks of attendants who had been present when I first entered this chamber were gone now, but the Twa kept me company. They stood alert, spears in hand, while I sat by the Lord's pallet and tried to find answers.

This was surely a charmed sleep, a spell turned inward

that could only be undone by magic. As a Caller, I had no magic of my own; I was neither fey nor a mage. My time with the Hag had made it clear to me that my power lay in opening myself to natural magic, becoming a conduit through which it could flow. But I would not call a Guardian. To attempt that seemed not only presumptuous and foolish but, under the current circumstances, perilous. If the Lord had put himself into an enchanted sleep, then ordered his household not to wake him, he wasn't going to be well pleased by a human woman breaking the spell, then asking him to teach her. It seemed to me I must find a way into his slumbering thoughts and seek there the answer to bringing him back. How I might go about this, I had yet to work out.

Meanwhile, I imagined him as a friend who had been grievously hurt, someone I could not cure, and I did what I might have done if he were human. Sang songs. Told stories, including my own with its losses and its learning. Talked to him of other things: the turning of the seasons, the harvest, the weather, my hopes for Alban's future. At my request, Flow prepared for me the meals the Lord had most enjoyed and brought them on a tray so I could eat by his side. I always asked him if he wanted a share. I encouraged the Twa to talk to me about the past, not the sad past of Gem and her mother, but the time before, when this household was full of laughter and life. The Lord lay quiet as our talk flowed over him; under our smiles and tears he remained impassive. The days went by.

Tali was making better progress. She was helping train

the Lord's fighting forces, or rather, training Scar and his fellow leaders to do the kind of work she did at Shadowfell. At the same time, she was making these folk into comrades, talking through our strategy, explaining why it was so important that we all work together. She was listening to their contributions, some of which, she told me, were immensely valuable.

I was glad she was so busy. It stopped her from worrying about Regan and the others, from trying to guess where they'd gone after midsummer and what risks they might be taking. Tali either absent or fast asleep was a great deal easier than Tali bored, restless, and anxious.

Early on I had asked the Twa for their names, so I could address them individually. They did leave the Lord's side occasionally, but not for long, and never at the same time.

"Names?" one of them echoed. "We're the Twa. The ane, and the other."

"But didn't your mother and father name you when you were babies? They cannot have given you only one name between you." Then again, perhaps that was quite common among Good Folk.

The other guard took off his shining helm and scratched his head. Both of them had long, thick fair hair, worn neatly plaited. "Lang time ago," he commented. "Mebbe. But I canna recall any names." He looked at his brother. "The ane, and the other. That's us."

I asked Flow about it later, and she said nobody could remember. "The ane, and the other," she said. "All this time, only those."

I had sown a seed in the minds of the Twa with my question. One morning, as I approached the dais where the Lord lay, ready for another long day's vigil, they were not standing silent as usual, but were engaged in a lively conversation.

". . . but dinna ye think, if we had our ain names, we wouldna be the Twa anymore? That would be awfu' hard."

The other guard shook his head. "The Twa are strong as granite, laddie. A wee thing like a name canna split us apart. Tae my thinkin' there's pride in a name. A man can be part o' the Twa, and be hissel' at one and the same time. Dinna ye think so?"

"Isna it a bittie late for namin', wi' the Lord gone awa' inside himsel', and nae work for the Twa but keepin' watch ower his sleep?"

I came up the steps to stand beside them. "It's never too late for naming," I said. "But only if you both wanted it, of course."

The Twa exchanged a look, then spoke at the same time.

"What ye sayin'?"

"Ye got names for us?"

Already, in my mind, I thought of them by the names I had given them. Not mountain names like those of the fighters; perhaps not names for Good Folk at all. "I have suggestions."

"Let's hear them, then."

I looked first at the brother who was just a trace taller, his eyes perhaps a little lighter, his hair slightly paler. "For you, Constant." I turned toward the other. "And for you, Trusty."

Neither said a word.

"Chosen in recognition of your long and faithful service to a lord who cannot honor you himself," I said. "But if you don't like those, we could think of some others. And, of course, you will always be the Twa."

It was only after I had settled myself on my stool at the Lord's bedside, and one of Flow's helpers had come in with breakfast for the three of us, and gone out again, a small figure hurrying away across the huge, empty chamber, that the Twa made comment.

"Constant," said the one. "There's a guid ring tae that. I like it weel enow."

"Aye, and Trusty, that's a name like a strong helm or a thick winter cloak," said the other. "A fellow can wear it wi' pride. Ye give us a guid gift, Neryn."

"Then I'm happy."

"No ye're no'," Trusty said, setting down his spear and lowering himself to sit on the step beside me. Constant sat down on my other side. I passed them their bowls of porridge from the breakfast tray.

"No' happy at a'," said Constant. "No' in yersel', I mean."

"I don't know how to reach him," I said. "Compelling him to come out of the enchantment is wrong, I feel it in my bones. I need to . . . coax him out. He needs a reason for coming back."

"Ye give us a gift," Trusty said. "Canna ye offer him the same?"

357

I recalled that campfire on the cliffs of Ronan's Isle, and sharing our soup with the Hag and Himself. It seemed a long time ago. "How can I? Where he's gone, I can't reach him. And I don't know what he would want."

This was greeted with a weighty silence, during which I realized that of course I knew; there was only one thing the Lord wanted, and nobody could give it to him. "I can't bring Gem back from the dead," I said. My mind was still on the Hag, and the teaching she had given me, teaching that had allowed me to single out one mind from many and direct my call there. The test she had set me, in which I had chosen not to call away the gull, which would have snatched up the wee fish, but to summon a far more powerful being: Himself. My mind raced ahead into the realm of the impossible. The near impossible.

"I have a question for you."

"Aye?"

"The Lady, Gem's mother . . . Flow said she faded and went away. Where did she go?"

Their spoons stilled in their hands.

"Awa'," said Constant.

"Whaur, we canna tell ye," said Trusty.

"If I could bring her back, would he wake?"

"If that didna wake him," said Constant, "naethin' would."

"Can ye dae it?" asked Trusty, his voice vibrant with sudden hope.

"When I was in the isles, I did call a being of some power. He was dear to the Hag, like a husband. But when

I did it, he was quite close by, under the sea. In my mind, I could feel my way through the water and find him."

"Neryn," said Constant, "I dinna want tae tell ye this, but the Lord, he's the only one will know whaur the Lady went. And he canna tell ye until he wakes. The truth, it's hidden inside him; tucked awa' deep like a shining jewel in the heart o' stane."

The image was powerful. As I considered it, an answer came with such force that I sprang to my feet, almost upsetting my porridge bowl. "The magic of stone! That's what he's done, anchored himself in stone, made himself part of it, and hidden the sorrow away inside. . . ." *Stane moves awfu' slow,* Whisper had said. Never mind that; I must work as I had never worked before. "I'm going to need your help," I told them.

Chapter Thirteen

Perhaps I showed a confidence I did not truly feel, for once I had explained what I intended, it was not only the Twa who helped me but the entire household. I had them move the Lord out of the vast hall and into the chamber he had shared with his Lady, a spacious room but far smaller than the other, with hangings to soften the walls. At my request a fire was kindled on the hearth and oil lamps were brought in to banish the shadows. The Lord of the North lay on his bed, as still and remote as ever.

I asked that we be left alone—the Lord, the Twa, and me. There were to be no interruptions. We entered the chamber and shut the heavy door behind us.

Constant and Trusty took up their usual positions, spears in hand. I stood by the Lord's bed, took his cold hand in mine, and shut my eyes. Somewhere within the stony chill of the sleeping man, there was life. Somewhere within the fearsome spell that locked him away, there was a person who had loved, and loved well. A fine person, one who had earned the devotion of his household, a devotion that had endured through three hundred years of waiting. I would not call him; every instinct told me that was wrong. But if I could find his Lady in his thoughts, if I could find something that convinced me her return would wake him, I could call her.

I went through the long preparation the Hag had taught me: breathing, concentration, awareness. But I changed the manner of it. I did not seek the fluid, ever-shifting movement of water now, but the heavy, monumental existence of stone. Not dancing, spraying, flowing, crashing, but waiting, holding, staying, being. I stood immobile, my breathing slow and slower, searching. Within the stillness that wrapped the Lord of the North, I sought the little signs of movement and change. For the wisdom of the north was not only that of stone, but also of earth, and from earth springs life. If he was a rock, monumental and still, I would be a growing tree, and as a tree sends its roots deep into the earth, I would find a way to the secrets at his heart. When I was ready, I made my mind a seed, lying in the winter ground as snowstorm and windstorm harried the mountains above. I felt the little death that was the cold season. I felt the spring thaw; I felt the ground soften and warm around me, and I stretched out tiny roots into the soil and pushed a single green shoot into the air. *I am alive. I rise from earth. I am the awakening of Alban's deep heart.*

Rain fell on me; breezes stirred me; wandering goats nibbled at my leaves. Seasons passed and passed, and I thrust my roots deep into the ground, finding ways between the stones, gripping tight, winding and binding and fastening myself there. In my crown, generation on generation of birds nested. Martens climbed my trunk and raised their young in my hollows. Autumn by autumn, my leaves changed color and dried up and fell to form heavy drifts around my feet. My seeds were carried by wind and bird and insect; my children flew far and wide, settling in their own soil. Spring after spring saw my new leaves sprout, the fresh green of hope. Kings and chieftains rode by me on their proud horses; sheep grazed around me; farmers and herdsmen rested in my shade. Fey folk too visited me, joining hands to dance around my trunk, making crowns from my leaves, living in my canopy. Good Folk, respectful of my gifts, wise in ancient ways.

I grew old, old beyond human measure. My strength waned; insects ate at my core, and my branches grew brittle, snapping in autumn gales. A storm toppled me; I fell to lean against a younger tree, grown from my seed. Mosses crept over me. Small creatures found a refuge in my decaying wood. Beetles dwelt in the shadowy recesses beneath my great body. In death, I was wrapped in life. And underground, in the caverns of Alban's heart, my roots still held fast.

"Dinna ye think," whispered someone, "that there's a bittie mair warmth in his cheeks?"

"Aye," murmured someone else, "and a touch o' light in his e'en, would ye no' say?"

I sucked in a breath, opened my eyes, felt my knees give way. Before I could fall, Constant was on one side and

Trusty on the other, holding me up. They helped me to a bench by the fire. The chamber was moving around me, even when I was sitting still. It might have been morning or night; I might have been standing there for days.

"Not finished," I managed. "Can't . . . rest . . ."

"Ye'd best tak' a bite tae eat and a wee sip o' mead," Constant said. "Ye been standin' there lang. For a human lassie, verra lang."

The household knew I wanted no distractions. Trusty went off to fetch food and drink. When he came back in, Tali was waiting at the door to escort me to the privy.

"All right?" She frowned as she scrutinized my face.

"Mm." I was too tired to think, let alone have a conversation. Besides, if I started to talk about this, I might lose any belief that what I was attempting would actually work.

"You don't look it. Make sure you call if you need me. I'll be right outside the door."

"What about . . . ?"

"Scar and the others can manage without me."

"You need not—"

"Yes, I do."

I took to sleeping as Constant and Trusty did, in short snatches when I could no longer keep my eyes open. There was a shelf bed by the wall, probably intended for the Lady's maidservant, and that was where I lay, under the fur cloak I had been given when I first came here. The Twa were too tall to use this bed, but took turns to stretch out on the floor.

I lost track of the passing days and nights. From that first delving, when I sought a pathway into the Lord's enchanted sleep as a tree would search for a crevice through which to slip its root, I moved deeper and deeper, searching for traces of the Lady. For all my weariness, I found it easier each day to sink into the state of trance; I felt the weight of earth in my body, its slow rhythms in the beating of my heart, and in my bones the endurance and strength of stone. I was no longer hungry, though the Twa made me eat. I became patient. Day by day, as Tali took me to use the privy, to wash, to change my clothing, I saw that the lines on her face were deeper and her eyes more troubled, but I did not think of the passage of time or of what it might mean for us. I was not aware of thinking much at all.

Step by slow step I moved down the pathways of the Lord's mind. Day by day, night by night, I walked there, and saw revealed, as bright spots in the darkness, the things he had loved, the things he had lost, the good things he had chosen to set aside. Gem was everywhere: a tiny babe, her cheek peach-soft under her father's astonished touch; a dark-haired child, tossed high in the air, laughing in delight; a quicksilver girl, full of curiosity; a frowning student, bending over a great scroll with questions in her eyes. Gem running. Gem climbing. Gem playing a little harp. Gem casting a spell and turning a cat to stone. Gem shouting at her father. Always that: the furious words, the swirl of her long hair as she stormed out of their workroom. *She left me. My Gem left me. The last thing I ever said to my daughter was, Disobedient wretch! If you cannot master yourself, how will you ever master your craft?*

The Lady was more elusive. From the Twa, I learned that her name was Siona, and that she came from the far north, land of eternal ice. But I did not see her anywhere in the Lord's thoughts; it was as if the loss of Gem had erased his wife from his memory.

"Did they have a falling-out?" I asked the Twa on a day when frustration had made me give up my quest early enough to take supper by the fire with them, all of us weary and despondent. "A quarrel? Did they part on bad terms?" It was hard for me to accept, still, that the Lady had chosen to walk away when her man was sunk in his grief.

"He loved her weel," Trusty said. "And she was right fond o' him. But after Gem died, they had words. Words that would hae been best left unsaid."

"Tell me, if you will."

"He blamed himself. If he'd heeded Gem, if he hadna shouted at her, if he'd done this or that different . . . He couldna see past that. A' tangled up in it, he was."

"The Lady reminded him she was grievin' too," Constant said. "But he was deaf tae her; he was fu' up wi' his ain hurt. She waited awhile, and he didna seem tae change. So she told him that while she was by him, she couldna heal."

"He didna listen. The next day he woke up and couldna find her. Asked us where she was; didna believe us when we told him. Nine-and-ninety days he waited for her to come tappin' on the door, fu' o' contrition. But she didna. So he lay doon, and ye know the rest."

"Why is it ye need the story?" The Twa had been keenly interested in what I was doing, and so were the folk beyond the closed door. I'd been giving Tali brief reports on my progress, which she shared with the rest of them; apparently they hung avidly on every word.

"His mind is full of Gem; in particular, his argument with her before she ran out and fell to her death. Sometimes I see his life before, but nearly always with her. Lady Siona simply isn't there. This will be the first time I've tried to call someone when I have no idea where she is. And the first time I've done it when the person is probably far away. Without an image of her in my mind, I don't know how I will go about it." They had described her to me, of course. *Like moonlight,* Constant had said. *Like a willow,* Trusty had added. That was not much help.

"Ye might speak tae Flow," Constant said now.

Tali, true to her word, had been keeping guard outside the door. She came with me to find Flow in her small, warm chamber, and I explained my difficulty.

"He doesna think o' her at a'?" The little woman was working on a pair of shoes, tiny needle flashing as she embroidered a delicate pattern of leaves and tendrils. "Aye, weel, mebbe that isna sae surprisin'. He's set her awa' deep as deep, hopin' he willna need tae look at what he's done. If he hadna been sae wrapped up in his ain grief, he'd hae seen the twa o' them needed each other. He didna understand until it was too late. And then he couldna face the truth: that *he* had driven her awa'."

"You think that's what holds him so long in this spell? But what if I summon her and she doesn't want to be here? Surely, if she really wanted to come back, she'd have done so long ago. And what if she comes and he still doesn't wake up?"

Flow lifted her gaze from her handiwork. "I canna answer that, lassie. Ane thing, I can help ye wi'." There was a big basket in the corner; she moved to sort through the contents, then returned to the fireside with a folded cloth in her hands. "Ye wanted the image o' Lady Siona. I crafted this soon after she came here as his bride; it hung on the wa' by their bed, but when he fell intae his lang sleep, I set it awa' for safekeepin'. A guid likeness."

Unfolded, the cloth revealed an embroidered picture of a slender fey woman in a white gown, standing by a window through which pale light streamed. The stitches were small and fine. Lady Siona might have been standing there in miniature, so real did she seem. Her hair was wheaten fair and rippled over her shoulders in waves; her eyes were palest green, her face heart-shaped, with a sweet mouth and a small, straight nose. She was somewhat like Gem, but at the same time very much herself.

"O' course, she'll be aulder now," Flow said, running a hand over the embroidery. "Oor folk are lang-lived; but time and sorrow will hae made their mark."

Tali gasped. I felt my eyes widen. The image had changed under Flow's fingers, the Lady's hair now touched with silver, her face still beautiful but older, wiser, her eyes shadowed with sadness. I was reminded sharply that this place was not Shadowfell, and its folk were not of humankind. I gazed at Siona's embroidered features, trying to fix them in my mind.

"Ye can tak' this wi' ye, Neryn. Get the Twa tae put it back on the wa'. Then she's wi' him, even if he thinks he doesna want her." After a moment Flow added, "Ye might try a different approach. Feel the way, no' wi' your mind, but wi' your heart. Havena ye ever had a fallin' oot wi' someone ye loved weel? A quarrel that made a gulf between the twa o' ye, and caused ye tae wish ye could wipe your mind clean o' him, and yet deep down, despite all, he was still as dear tae ye as ever?"

She and Tali were both looking at me. I felt my cheeks flush.

"Aye, ye ken weel what I mean," Flow said, saving me from the need to answer. "Could be true love is the key ye need tae unlock the Lord's last secret. Tae find your pathway in. I'll be biddin' ye guid night now."

It was late; on the threshold of the Lord's chamber Tali stopped me, putting a hand on my arm. "You look terrible, Neryn. Pasty, thin, worried, a shadow of yourself. Don't tell me you're going to try this tonight, without resting first."

It was a fair comment. I was so tired I could hardly think straight. "Tali, how long have I been doing this? How many days have passed?"

Her hesitation was an answer in itself. "Quite a few," she said eventually. Unspoken was the fact that while the Lord slept, I could not learn from him; that we needed to get home to Shadowfell before the season made it impossible.

"You've finished your work here already, haven't you? Teaching those warriors how to use their long winters profitably. Learning all about their weaponry."

368

"Don't add me to your concerns." She attempted a re-assuring smile. "I thought it might do you good to go out-side for a bit, that was all. Fresh air and exercise. Sitting in that chamber all day and all night isn't doing your fitness any favors."

I managed a smile of my own. "There's no choice," I said. "When we get home to Shadowfell, I'll practice hard to make up for it."

"Here's a suggestion. For this one night at least, have a proper sleep and tell those two fellows to do the same. I can stand guard in their place, if they want that. I'll have an army of volunteers to keep me company. Tomorrow, come out for a walk with me before breakfast. It need not be long. I want you to see the sunlight, even if it's only for a short time."

"If you insist."

"I do. I don't want to have to spend another winter run-ning up and down the Ladder with you. Besides, Flint told me in no uncertain terms to look after you. He'd hardly be impressed if he could see you now." A speaking pause. "True love, hmm?"

"She wasn't talking about me."

"Ah, well," said Tali lightly, "what would I know?"

Next morning she led me out of the Lord's subterranean hall, with Scar as a guard, and up a winding pathway be-tween the rocks to a level vantage point. We watched the sun rise over the mountains, brightening the wide bowl of the sky and touching the clouds with rose and gold. For a while we sat in silence; Scar leaned on his spear at a little distance. Although I had done as Tali suggested and lain on my bed all night, my sleep had been fitful, full of tangled thoughts of failure and disappointment. And I had dreamed of Flint, a disturbing dream in which he stood before the king and underwent an interrogation that turned his face white and made him bunch his hands into fists.

"About Flint," Tali said now, as if she had read my thoughts.

"What about him?"

"Did he explain his mission in the isles to you?" That she trusted Scar was obvious; she made no attempt to lower her voice.

I thought of that brief, precious time on Far Isle, when I had spent a night in Flint's arms. "No," I said. "Did he tell you?" When had that been possible?

"He was under orders to kill a man. He told me while you were sleeping. He didn't do it. Instead, he made the fellow disappear. Arranged for the local folk to spirit him away. The target was his old mentor."

"The mind-mender? I thought he was dead."

"Old and frail, but still living. And still a powerful influence on the folk of the isles, who, as you noticed, are of a different breed from the folk of the mainland."

I could hardly think what to say.

"The king couldn't have known before the Gathering," Tali went on, "or Flint would have faced a much harsher penalty than having to perform a public enthrallment, even of a difficult individual like me. But there are folk at court who don't trust him, and who've made that fairly clear to him. A perilous path."

"He shouldn't have rushed back to see if I was safe. That must have aroused suspicion, however plausible an excuse he thought of."

"If he's not more careful, one day he'll take a step too far," Tali said. "He could be his own destruction, and maybe yours as well. In my mind, true love is overrated as a solution to practical problems."

We sat on awhile, not talking, then made our way back down to the Lord's hall. The position of the sun made it sharply clear that autumn was advancing—I had been many long days closeted with the Twa, sending my creeping tendrils through the hard stone of the Lord's mind. *Today,* I prayed. *Let it be today that I find the key.*

In the Lord's chamber the fire was burning on the hearth, the floor was swept clean, and the embroidered image of Siona looked down at us from the wall. The Twa were waiting for me.

"Today, ye think?" asked Constant.

"Dinna push the lassie; she canna tell ye if it's today or tomorrow or some other day," said Trusty.

"Just sayin'."

"If I find her today, I call her," I told them. "Whether she will come, and whether he will wake, there's no telling."

To begin with, it was like so many other days. The long preparation, the breathing, the sinking deep. The slow reaching out, searching within the forbidding stone of the Lord's mind for the wee pathways in, the cracks and chinks still open to the passage of thoughts and feelings, memories and dreams. The images I had seen so often before, his daughter in all her moods, his beloved Gem; the day he lost her, and the guilt that would not go away.

Love, I thought. *Love heals all.* And I made an image of Flint, whom I loved above all others: Flint tending to me in a little hut halfway up the Rush valley, Flint keeping one eye on me as he stirred a pot of porridge, Flint risking everything to shield me from harm. Flint on the jetty when the Hag brought me back from the skerry, with his heart in his eyes. Flint's body against mine. Flint calling me *my heart.*

I searched again for Siona, a trace of shining hair, a soft pale gleam, a pair of green eyes, a wistful smile on lips surely made for laughing. And there she was, playing a game with her little daughter: Siona hiding behind a tree trunk, her white gown clearly visible while Gem hunted here and there, calling. Siona jumping out to catch up her daughter and whirl her around. The image faded, and here was another: Siona by her window, as in the embroidery; Siona turning to greet her husband, rising on tiptoes to kiss his cheek, her hands light on his shoulders. Siona smiling, with an invitation in her green eyes. *I need you.* The thought was so powerful I staggered, almost letting go of the Lord's hand. *I need you! Come back to me!*

It was time. His longing flowed through me, as strong as living stone, as urgent as true love itself. I opened myself wholly to it, let it take me, sent it out to the woman who walked through my mind and his, wherever she might be. *Come home, Lady Siona! Your Lord needs you! Come now!*

The Twa told me later that my call was silent; at the time I did not know if I was shouting or singing or only calling to her in my mind. Afterward I fainted. I came to on my little bed to find Constant wiping my face with a damp cloth while Trusty hovered behind him with a mead cup in his hand. The chamber was as before, the fire burning on the hearth, the picture of Siona looking down on her sleeping husband. I sat up gingerly; my head was throbbing and my limbs felt as if they belonged to someone else, perhaps a rag doll.

"Dinna try tae talk," Constant said. "Ye're lookin' peaky."

"Ye did it, aye?" asked Trusty.

I took the proffered mead, drank, felt somewhat restored. "I tried, at least." But had it worked? Might we wait days and days, as the Lord had, only to discover that she was not coming back?

Trusty moved to set the mead flask down, and halted in his tracks. "His e'en," he whispered. "His e'en—they're shut."

It was true; the Lord's eyes no longer stared blankly upward, but were shielded by their heavy lids.

"Breathin' still," Trusty said, laying his hand on the Lord's chest, "but sleepin' noo. Guid sleep, ye ken?" A tear ran down his broad cheek. "Aye, sleepin' like a babe." He knelt down by the bed, laying his big hand over the Lord's cold fingers.

"She's comin'," Constant said in a tone of awe. "Ye've done it."

I opened my mouth to tell them they should not get their hopes up, that this might be only coincidence, but before I could speak, someone knocked on the door. We had laid down the rules so clearly—no interruptions at all while I was working—that all three of us turned our heads at once, and now even I was tight with anticipation.

"Open it, Constant."

He slid the bolt back and swung the heavy door open, and there she was, with what looked like the entire household behind her: a tall, slender fey woman in a white gown, her hair a blend of gold and silver, her face as sweet as in Flow's embroidery, but shadowed with the passing of time and the bearing of a great sorrow. Around her brow was a circlet of pale flowers. Siona did not ask to be let in; she did not say a word. Constant gave a little bow, scrubbed his hand over his cheeks, and stepped back so she could walk past. Trusty rose to his feet and came to stand beside me; I had tried to rise, but my legs would not hold me.

Siona ignored us all. She stepped over to her husband's bed, sat down on the edge of it, and reached out a graceful hand to touch his forehead, his cheeks, his strong mouth, as if relearning him. There was tenderness in her fingers as she brushed them across his closed eyes, then stroked his dark hair where it fell back from the strong forehead. There was love in her eyes, a love that acknowledged the errors of the past and forgave them. I held my breath as she bent forward and kissed him on the lips.

He stirred; he opened his eyes, and they were no longer blank, but full of all he had held trapped inside, full of all that had not been said, all that had played on him during the long years of silence. He opened his mouth to speak, and Siona laid her fingers across his lips.

"We'll be awa', my lady," Constant said quietly. "Come on, Trusty. Neryn, can ye walk?"

When it was obvious I could not, he picked me up bodily—not difficult for such a giant—and bore me out of the chamber, with Trusty coming behind. It was the first time the Twa had been away from their Lord, both at once, since the day I had met them. As Constant carried me toward my bedchamber, as careful as if I were a basket of eggs, I fell asleep in his arms.

I woke to find myself tucked up in bed. For a while, I lay there watching the oil lamp throw patterns on the stone walls, not ready to get up and face the immensity of what it seemed I had managed to do. Lady Siona had come home; the Lord of the North had woken from his long sleep. If I felt anything, it was an awareness of my own temerity for daring to meddle in the lives of such powerful and ancient beings. All very well for the Hag to say I need not worry about overreaching myself. When I'd called Himself, I had already got to know both him and her; I had been fairly sure neither would take offense. This was quite different.

After a while Tali came in with Flow behind her.

"You're awake," Tali said. "Good. He's asked to see you."

It was an effort to get up and change my clothes; an effort to brush and replait my hair. Flow set food and drink before me, then stood with hands on hips watching me eat.

"Is it all right?" I asked. "Is he angry? Is Lady Siona happy to be back?"

"I don't think you need worry about that," Tali said with a crooked smile. "Nor will you have to give lengthy explanations, since everyone including the Lord and Lady seems to know all about Regan and the rebellion, as well as your own history, even some bits that are new to me." She lifted her brows in query.

"Oh. I did talk to him quite a bit, told stories and so on. In the first days I couldn't think what else to do. I didn't realize he could hear me; he was sunk so deep in his sleep."

"Saves explaining anyway," she said. "When you're ready, we'll go."

Beyond the door of our chamber, the household was transformed. There were lights everywhere and folk bustling about; the uniform gray cloaks had been discarded to reveal garments decorated with feathers and fur, and as they met in the hallways, members of the household were stopping to greet each other with smiles. As Tali and I passed, folk reached out to touch me, to thank me, to offer shy nods or extravagant bows. There was no doubt that in their minds I had achieved the required miracle.

The Lord of the North received us in a council chamber, where he sat at a table fashioned from a huge stone slab set across two slightly less monumental blocks. He was alone save for the Twa, who stood guard on either side of him. They made no move as I came in, but Constant smiled and Trusty winked.

I advanced to the table. "I am Neryn, my lord, the Caller. You asked to see me."

He rested his chin on steepled hands and regarded me across the table. It felt odd to see his features released from the sleeplike spell; they were full of bright intelligence and alive with question. He continued his scrutiny for some time without saying a word.

"My lord," I said eventually, "I hope the action I've taken has not offended you. It was hard to know what to do. Your people needed you. The Twa, Flow, Whisper, your warriors—all your folk were desperate to see you restored to yourself. But I also had a purpose of my own for seeking you out. I need your guidance. I'm told you already know about King Keldec and the way he has changed Alban for the worse; about the planned rebellion. I have an important part to play in that, but without your assistance, I cannot do it."

"I understand this," he said, his voice deep and sure. "While I lay silent, I was not deaf to the tales you told me. You spoke with sincerity and passion. As for offense, none was taken. You brought my lady home. You brought love back to my lonely hall. You helped me, and now I will help you. They tell me you want to learn, and they say time is short. What is it you seek from me?"

"To learn the magic of earth and stone," I said, "so I can use it to strengthen my gift."

A smile curved his thin lips. "What was it you used to bring Lady Siona back to me, if not the very magic of which you speak? I felt your tendrils in my mind; I felt you seeking out the secrets I had hidden deep. You understood the heart of an oak; you became one with earth; you trod the slow pathways of stone. Besides, did you not call one of my beings out to help you, long before you knew you would be traveling here? Did not you bring forth one of my own to crush your enemy? In the magic of stone you have a natural ability, and you are already proficient."

"My lord, I am happy that I could be of service to you and to your household. Yes, I have done those things you mention. But I still have much to learn before I can use my gift for the good of Alban. You know, I think, that our leader—the leader of the rebels, Regan—plans a confrontation next midsummer, at Summerfort, while the king and his forces are all gathered there."

"And the plan is that you call my kind to the assistance of your human rebels. Yes, if I had not learned that from the tales you told by my bedside, my guards would no doubt have recounted it." He glanced in turn at the Twa. "You have made some fast friends during your time here, Neryn."

"I know, my lord, and I am glad of it. My lord, the Hag of the Isles taught me to be fluid as water; to move as the sea does, to learn the shapes of things, to single out one being among many and call to it. And in this hall . . . calling the Lady Siona was something new for me. I have never before tried to call a being who was far away and in a place unknown to me. Since I managed to do it, and do it successfully, perhaps I do have more ability than I thought. But . . . I cannot imagine that the forces we'd need at Summerfort, the uncanny forces, could be there in some kind of disguise, ready to reveal themselves on command when they were required. Regan's plan depends very much on the element of surprise. The loyal chieftains will have their men-at-arms ready, of course, and the rebels can be in the crowd. Your folk . . . they would be far harder to hide. I believe I would have to call them from afar. I would need to send a call strong enough to summon many, but precise enough to fetch only those able to fight alongside us." I hesitated. "There's the question of cold iron. Is it true what your folk have said, that there is no charm or spell that renders immunity against its destructive power?"

"Ah," said the Lord of the North, sitting back and folding his arms. "The heart of the matter. Not only will you need to call with strength and precision, you will need to do it quickly, if I understand the plan. You'll have a few moments, no more, before this king senses trouble and orders his forces to attack. And your rebel army, I imagine, is somewhat more makeshift than Keldec's."

"Makeshift but well drilled," I said.

He smiled again. "That does not surprise me; I understand your friend has transformed my own army during her time here. You can expect their support when the time comes."

This was a remarkable offer. "Thank you, my lord. Regan will be well pleased with that news."

"So. I will help you to refine your call in the manner you require. I will give you the rudiments; you must practice after you leave my hall. They tell me time is running short for you."

"I do not know how long we have been here already, my lord. But we do need to return to Shadowfell before the end of autumn."

"Then time is indeed short, and we have work to do. As

379

for the matter of cold iron, my answer will not please you. I have no charm by which its influence may be kept at bay. My own fighters have a natural resistance to it, but that is not so for many of the Good Folk. You'll have seen its effects. You'll understand why our people keep away when it is present. The Westies in particular. Call them into a place full of iron weaponry, and you'll earn lasting enmity toward yourself and your kind. That is not the way to begin a new age."

The weight of this was heavy in my heart. "So there is no shield against iron," I said.

"That is not what I said."

I waited, not daring to breathe.

"Fire masters iron," the Lord said quietly. "You've seen a smith at work, yes? I think the answer you want may lie in the south. You should seek out the Master of Shadows."

Torn between dismay and hope, I protested, "I only have from spring to midsummer, and I must travel east to visit the White Lady! I saw the Master of Shadows. He told me I needed to learn something from each of you, from each Guardian, before I could use my gift fully. He did not . . . He implied that meeting him that day and undergoing his test was sufficient for his part of my training. I don't think there can possibly be time. . . ." Tali would be horrified.

"Perhaps not. And perhaps I am wrong. All of us would like a charm of defense against iron. I have not heard of its ever being used; it does not appear in the lore. Possibly it does not exist. I suggest only that if it did, that is where it would be found."

"I see. Thank you, my lord."

"No need for thanks." He waved a hand dismissively. "Tonight there will be feasting and celebration. Tomorrow we start work. My gift to you will be to ensure you leave this place with some, at least, of the answers you need. Go now, Neryn."

Over the days that followed, while the household grew bright and joyful under the benign eye of Lady Siona, the Lord of the North took me down to the caverns where his warriors honed their skills to work on my call. He taught me to concentrate my energy tightly, to encompass a whole group of folk with my mind, to see the one-in-many that would allow me to bring five, ten, twenty beings to me in a matter of moments.

He used his own folk as the material of my practice: not only Scar and his fellow fighters, but Flow, Whisper, the Twa. He made me call others, folk from beyond the confines of his dwelling, folk of whom I had only a faint notion. He made me place his people at risk; he made me put them to the test. It was not comfortable learning, but I did it without protest, though it troubled my dreams at night.

It became clear to me that the Lord loved to teach. He worked me rigorously. He spent long days with me, and set high standards. When I struggled or made errors, he did not grow angry, merely analyzed the difficulty and made me try again. He was good at explaining, always providing reasons for what he told me, spelling things out in logical sequence. I often remembered those images of him with

Gem, the two of them engrossed in their discoveries, the same delight on their faces, the same shining enthusiasm in their eyes. As a fey girl, she had doubtless been more apt than I. As his daughter, she had probably challenged him far more. I knew I could not measure up to her, and I did not try to, only felt glad that he took some pleasure in working with me.

As for Scar and the others, it helped that they were willing participants. I had given them back not only the Lord for whom they had waited so long and so faithfully but their Lady as well. They were all too ready to subject themselves to whatever the Lord required of me: calls out to the mountainside at odd times of day, calls to leap into a mock battle, a call that brought a huge creature suddenly into their midst, a being of mud and shale and old tree roots that sat there scratching itself and whimpering, until the Lord called Whisper to make it small and carry it out-side to be released among the rocks.

And, after a while, calls that encompassed not only the folk of the north, but Westies as well. Calls that traveled over countless miles of mountain and loch and forest, all the way to the wooded hills by Silverwater. Not Sage; not Red Cap. But I called Daw, the bird-man, and others of that clan, at first on their own, and then at the same time as folk from the mountains. They were not best pleased to find themselves here in a northern hall, but the Lord's household greeted them courteously, and provided re-freshments before he used his own magic to convey them home again.

"We lack the time for you to learn dismissal as well as summoning," he told me. "When you called a stanie mon, you were able to reverse the call with the same kind of rhyme. A creature like that thinks very simply; the childhood rhyme you used was ideal for his understanding. For others it is more difficult. If you were able to stay with us over the winter, I could teach you. But your friend is eager to depart, and I think she will not leave you behind."

"She's concerned about our comrades. And she needs to be there for winter, to keep them strong and to help Regan with strategy. I need to report to him as well. But I thank you for the offer; perhaps, at some time in the future, I might return here and study further with you, my lord."

"My door is open to you, Neryn. For a human woman, you learn well. As for the matter of reversing a call, should you win your battle, those of our folk who survive will make their own ways home."

Those who survive. Despite all I had learned, midsummer remained a grim prospect.

Only once did the Lord of the North speak to me about the choice I had made, when faced with the need to wake him. It was after a long day's training, when Tali and the warriors had left the cavern where we worked to go upstairs to supper, and only he and I were left, with the ever-present Twa close by.

"You chose not to call me out of my slumber," he said. "You chose instead to call my wife. A very wise choice, when it came to it. I heard that Flow advised you."

"Yes, my lord." I was somewhat reluctant to talk to him

of true love, and the presence of Flint in my thoughts when I had called Lady Siona to her husband's side.

"If you would raise a mighty army to do battle against this king, your command of your gift must be total. You must be prepared to summon anyone. Is not your cause served best by the most powerful beings in your realm?"

"I believe, my lord, that it is served best by the wisest. Indeed, perhaps the wisest *are* the most powerful."

The Lord gave a slow smile. "I wish you were staying," he said, almost as if he were an ordinary man.

I had expected a test, like the one to which the Hag had subjected me before I left the isles; something that would require me to demonstrate mastery of all he had taught me. But the only thing he made me do was send Whisper away without using words. My call was to be quite specific: Whisper was to fly over the Rush valley, from Shadowfell to Summerfort, and return with a report as soon as possible. I knew there were other winged beings, lesser ones, that regularly carried out this kind of task. But I did as I was bid, and one morning Whisper flew off across mountains whose peaks sparkled under the rising sun; already, in the highest places, there was snow. How long such a journey would take, I did not know. The instruction had been to fly, not to travel the quick way, in darkness and silence, by magic.

Once Whisper was gone, it seemed the formal part of my training was over. The next morning the Lord took me walking on the mountain, just the two of us, without even

Constant or Trusty. I wore my fur-lined cloak and carried my staff. We climbed a steep and perilous path. He made me walk on the inside and hold on to his arm.

The sky was gray; ominous clouds massed in the north. Shadows lay over the peaks and the land was eerily still. Our path led to a broad shelf, behind which rose a sheer cliff face, dauntingly high. At its foot a little cairn had been erected, white stones placed with precision, and over the cairn crept a mountain plant dotted with five-petaled yellow flowers. We halted beside it.

"This is where she fell," said the Lord of the North. "Here she lies, under the stones. Some lessons, a person can grasp quickly, if he has a mind to it. Some are harder, learned over long years of struggle and confusion. The lessons of loss are hardest of all. Take to heart what you taught me, Neryn; cherish what you have, for in an instant it can be gone. And when it's gone, let the memory not be a weight that drags you down, but a bright light leading you forward. She was like that. Gem. A light. Quick and shining and full of life."

His words conjured an image of Flint, white-faced, white-knuckled, standing tall before Keldec's hard questions. I remembered our night on the island, a precious gift in a world of doubt and hard choices. Tears brimmed in my eyes.

And there beside us was Lady Siona, come from nowhere. She wore a white fur cloak and carried a little lantern shaped like a cat. I had hardly spoken with her, immersed as I had been in the long days of learning. Now she smiled at me, and reached out a hand to wipe away my tears.

"You have brought such happiness, my dear," she said. "I think you have touched the heart of every man and woman in our dark old hall. As she did, our lovely daughter." She bent to place the lantern by the cairn. "You do not weep for her, I believe, but for a dear friend of your own. Perhaps Whisper will bring news of him."

But Whisper, when he returned, brought news of a different kind entirely.

"Neryn! You need to get up, now, quickly!"

"Whaa . . . ?" It could not be morning yet, surely. I closed my eyes again, burying my face in the pillow.

"Wake up, Neryn! We have to go, now, straightaway!"

I forced myself to sit up, rubbing my eyes. The lantern was lit, and I saw that Tali was fully dressed. Our staves were propped together against the wall, my old one and her fine new weapon crafted of old oak, a gift from the northern warriors. Beside them were two bags, one full and strapped up, the other—mine—apparently packed, but open.

"It's the middle of the night," I protested. "What is this?"

"Get up. I'll tell you while you get dressed. Here." She even had my clothes ready—gown, tunic, cloak, walking boots. Something had happened. Something bad. I heard it in her voice.

"What?" I said, shivering as I took off my warm nightrobe, a gift from Flow.

"Whisper. He's back, and he's brought ill news. He saw . . ." She was struggling to get the words out.

"*Say it,* Tali."

Tali shook her head. I saw her take a deep breath and gather herself. "Some of our people, making their way back to Shadowfell. They were in trouble. Bad trouble. Hurry up, Neryn, get your boots on."

"Why didn't you wake me earlier?" I wrenched my hair into a rough twist and knotted it at the nape. I thrust my feet into my boots, then gathered my small items and shoved them into the pack.

"You needed sleep. It made more sense to get everything ready before we woke you." She gathered her pack and staff. Flow was in the doorway now, picking up my pack, motioning to us that we should follow her. The place seemed full of flickering shadows as we walked along the passageways to the Lord's council chamber. The door stood open; within were the Lord of the North and Whisper, the Twa, and the warrior Scar.

It was all happening so quickly; too quickly. The Lord bade me a grave farewell and kissed me on the forehead. He reminded me that I was welcome to return whenever I wished. Scar and Tali thumped each other on the shoulder without saying anything. Flow embraced me. Constant and Trusty bent to hug me in turn. I was crying and so were they. And still nobody had explained, not properly.

"Tell me what you saw," I said to Whisper. "Please."

"Three fighters. Twa men, one woman, bearing a wounded warrior on a stretcher fashioned o' bits and pieces. Ane verra tall fellow; ane wi' the same raven markings as the lassie here. Frae that, I knew them as some o' your band. The woman was big and strong-looking, wi' red hair. I didna get a guid look at the fellow on the stretcher. Going quick, they were, even wi' that burden."

"Big Don," I said, with a heavy feeling in the pit of my stomach. "Fingal. Andra." On a new mission, begun after midsummer. Fingal would have been traveling with Regan. "Where?"

"Coming ower frae Wedderburn, that's my guess."

"We have to go." Tali's voice was uneven. "Now."

The Lord nodded at Whisper, and said quietly, "Fare-well, Neryn. Farewell, warrior. You have done good work here. Whisper will convey you to Shadowfell. May you find better news there than these tidings suggest. Know that when the time comes to put your plans into action, the North stands ready to support you."

"Thank you, my lord. For everything," I managed. But Tali, caught in the nightmares of her imagination, did not say a word.

Chapter Fourteen

Whisper's magic got us to Shadowfell by morning. Standing in darkness, silent, while he worked his long charm, I felt my mind filling with unwelcome possibilities. That had been Regan on the stretcher, surely. Had they been attacked by the wayside? Fallen foul of the Enforcers? Regan's Rebels were skilled in crossing country unseen, in avoiding danger, in staying out of trouble even when the risks were high.

In the enforced silence of traveling Whisper's way, I could not ask Tali the hundred questions that were in my mind. But I had seen the horror on her face when Whisper spoke the name. Wedderburn. Wedderburn, whose chieftain, Keenan, was the son of the man who had massacred Regan's family. Had he gone there, ignoring her wise caution, and precipitated a disaster?

He was alive, at least, and perhaps not too badly hurt. If his injuries were serious, they surely would have stopped somewhere, not attempted to carry him all the way home.

But maybe I'd got it all wrong. In the back of my mind was Flint, and the risk he had taken to get Tali away from Summerfort. Perhaps the rebels had not gone to Wedderburn at all; perhaps Fingal had persuaded Regan against such rash action. This could have been a rescue mission. The injured man could have been Flint: Flint uncovered as a spy, Flint pursued by his own.

Light came, and awareness of time and place, and we were on a different mountain, on the threshold of Shadowfell. It was day, and winter-cold. Blue shadows lay across the fells. All was quiet. Before my eyes had time to adjust to the sudden brightness, Tali strode ahead, not prepared to wait even an instant. Whisper and I followed more slowly.

As we walked up to the door guards, it was plain that something had gone terribly wrong. Gort and Dervla were on duty, with wooden staves in hands, suggesting some of the Good Folk were close by. As she saw us approaching, Dervla rested her staff against the wall and walked forward with hands out, almost as if to fend us off. Gort went inside; I heard him calling for Fingal. So they were home already.

Dervla had taken hold of Tali's arm. As Whisper and I came up behind, she said, "There's bad news. You'd best come inside and sit down."

Tali shook her off. "Tell me! Say it straight out!"

"Tali," I said, trying to stay calm though my heart was thudding, "we should do as Dervla says, go in, hear the whole story."

"Say it!" shouted Tali, and raised her hand as if to strike Dervla across the face. Dervla lifted her staff.

"Tali."

Fingal was in the entranceway. Behind him was the taller Brasal, and beside him Bearberry, the badgerlike warrior of Shadowfell's Good Folk. Their faces told of a loss greater than those I had dared to imagine.

At the sight of her brother, Tali lowered her hand. "Tell me what's happened," she said in a tone like a barbed blade. "Now, straightaway."

"Regan's dead," Fingal said, and for a moment I closed my eyes, willing this to be a nightmare from which I would soon wake. "Killed. Cian and Andra were both wounded in the same action, Cian seriously. We got him home; he'll live. But Regan is gone." He delivered the news flatly, as if he were too tired and sad to care much about anything.

"He can't be dead," Tali said. "You were carrying him on a stretcher, Whisper flew over and saw you, why would you carry him all the way home if he—"

"He's dead, Tali. It was Cian we carried back; his ankle is broken. We had to leave the others behind."

She stood frozen, staring at him as if he were speaking a language she did not understand. As tears pricked my eyes, I asked a question whose answer I did not want to hear. "Others?"

"Little Don. Killen. Young Ban. They're all gone. Tali, Neryn, come inside." Fingal cast a glance at Whisper. "And your companion. The place is clear of iron."

"Where did this happen?" Tali's tone was sharp and cold now. "Who killed them?"

"It was simple enough. Regan was sent information from within Keenan's household. Strategic information of some

391

value, with a promise of more. It seemed reliable, though we had our doubts. Regan was confident that we could get in, speak to the informant, and get out again without arousing suspicion. He insisted on going himself, despite all our arguments. He wanted to do it as a two-man mission; we convinced him to take a bigger team. Three went into the household: Regan, Andra, and me. The rest waited in concealment beyond the walls of Keenan's stronghold. Bearberry acted as messenger, using his special abilities to go unseen."

"And?" It was like an interrogation; had Tali forgotten that the rest of us were shocked and grieving too?

"We went in openly, as folk seeking a few days' work. It's a big establishment; there was plenty for us to turn our hands to. We shoveled dung and hauled bags of oats, and Regan spoke to his informant, who happened to be working in the stables alongside us. Regan was confident of maintaining his cover. He never thought someone would recognize him as the island heir everyone believed had been killed alongside his father, years ago."

"You let him die," Tali said, staring straight at her brother. "You were his guard, and you let him be killed. You failed him."

Fingal was chalk-pale, the raven tattoos standing out sharply against his skin. "He found out he'd been recognized, not by Keenan but by one of his councillors, an older man. He sent me off to find Andra; our escape plan had us crawling out through a drain that ran under the wall, down from the stables. We waited for him under cover, as planned, and he didn't come. While we were down there, thinking he was just waiting for his moment to get away, they'd apprehended him and dragged him off to account for himself to Keenan. He . . ." Fingal's gaze faltered; he looked down briefly, then with a visible effort of will, met his sister's eyes again. "He was decapitated, Tali. Our comrades out in the woods saw his head displayed above the gates of Keenan's fortress. Bearberry came to get us out. There was no choice but to leave Regan behind."

Tali might have been made of stone.

"The others," I managed. "What happened?"

"Keenan's sentries spotted us slipping across his border and gave chase. There was a skirmish. We accounted for Keenan's men, but we lost three more of our own. Andra's shoulder wound was superficial, but Cian couldn't walk. Bearberry sought out the Westies; they made us a stretcher, brought food and water, helped us to get away safely. And they gave us a solemn promise that they would bury the bodies of our slain, to keep them safe from wolves and from human predators. For Regan, there could be no such promise." Fingal drew a ragged breath. "Once we were well clear of Wedderburn, Bearberry enlisted the aid of some strong, fleet-footed beings of his acquaintance, and we were conveyed home with speed. Andra's recovering well. Cian's ankle will mend, thanks in part to the Folk Below, who sent their healer up to assist me. That is the story. We lost four fine men, among them our leader. Regan made an error of judgment, and now he's gone. Yes, I failed him."

At this point Brasal stepped past both Fingal and Tali, put his arm around my shoulders, and ushered me in through the doorway. I was aware of Bearberry moving out to speak long-overdue words of welcome to Whisper and to draw him inside.

"Tali—" I said, glancing over my shoulder. She looked as if she might never find the will to move again.

"Come," Brasal said in my ear. "You, at least, I can look after. We're working on small things; that's the best we can do right now."

They had hoped that with our return, Shadowfell might begin to come back to itself. They had expected that Tali would take charge, make sure everything continued as usual, rally the shattered household, and make plans for the future. She was so strong, so certain, that she could be relied on even in a catastrophe like this.

Instead, she went to ground like a wounded animal. There was, first, a hideous shouting argument between her and her brother, in the infirmary, which could be heard throughout the network of caverns and passages that made up the rebel headquarters. I sat in the dining chamber with the much-reduced household—apart from the recent losses, many were still out across Alban on their autumn missions—holding a cup of ale between my palms and willing the nightmare to be over. Around me sat Milla, Eva, Brasal, and Big Don, all of us silent as Tali's excoriating words to her brother rang in our ears, bitter, accusatory, furious, cruel. That they were not in any way justified only made it worse. It had been plain from Fingal's story that

Regan had instigated the mission to Wedderburn, and that Regan's own lapse in judgment had taken the team into deadly peril. But she kept on shouting: *You should have been there, you should have saved him.* And worse: *If I had been there, he would have lived.* Fingal was not saying much, but when he did speak, his voice was harsh with grief.

"This isn't Tali," I murmured. "Has losing him sent her completely mad?"

"Give her time," said Milla, who, like all of them, was looking wan and exhausted. "She hasn't accepted that he's gone yet. She needs to weep, and rest, and think about it on her own. By morning she'll be back to herself and giving orders, see if she isn't."

Milla was wrong. Tali took her weapons, a waterskin, and a blanket, and climbed to the ledge at the top of the Ladder. We left her undisturbed awhile, thinking that if she planned to throw herself down, she would not have taken anything at all. When the day was beginning to darken toward dusk, we discussed who should go up to talk to her, and I was chosen.

As I climbed, the memory of midwinter morning and Regan's stirring prayer was strong in me. His shining blue eyes; his face, bright with dedication, courage, and hope. *Farewell to the dark. Hail to the light. Lead us into a new day.*

Tali was huddled at the very back of the ledge, her arms around her knees, her head down. The blanket was wrapped around her. I suspected she had not moved in a long time.

"Go away!" she snarled as I approached.

I sat down on the rocks a few paces from her. "It'll be dark soon," I said. "Could be sensible to come down before then."

"Go away, Neryn!"

I waited awhile before speaking again. "Regan wouldn't want this," I said quietly. "He would expect us to grieve, of course. But he wouldn't want anger. He wouldn't want us to turn on each other."

She lifted her head, revealing in the fading light a ghost-like caricature of her true face. "What would you know?" she snapped. "If it hadn't been for you, I'd have been with him, and he wouldn't be dead! Get back down those steps before I throw you down!"

I retreated. I knew how strong she was, and I thought I saw madness in those haunted eyes.

She was not down by morning. We kept a vigil at the foot of the Ladder, taking shifts, so there would be a friend close at hand to help her when she moved. The longer this went on, the weaker she would be when she finally gave it up, and the Ladder was dangerous. Ordinary work, already neglected since the news of Regan's death came in, was now almost abandoned, though Milla and Eva kept us fed, and a pale, silent Fingal continued tending to the injured Cian. Bearberry and Whisper had gone down the spiral stair into the domain of the Folk Below. We sat around the table and spoke in low voices about the future, and I heard one or two of the rebels saying maybe it was all over; that they might head south before winter, in search of work or the scattered remnants of family. When Milla turned on them for so quickly losing hope, one man pointed out that without a leader, the rebellion could not go ahead; without a vision for the future, folk soon lost the will to fight. How could we maintain the push toward midsummer, how could we retain the support of the loyal chieftains without Regan? There was nobody like him.

We did talk about it. We thought of folk who might lead: Milla, who had been with Regan almost from the first; Big Don; Fingal. But Milla, for all her strength of character, was no warrior; Big Don had the presence to lead, but lacked a gift for strategy; Fingal could not do the job with the weight of his sister's scorn on his shoulders. Others we considered, trying to see a way out of the darkness, but we knew in our hearts that there was only one choice.

When a third day dawned and Tali still had not come down, I climbed the Ladder again. This time, before I went up, I talked to the others and had them make some preparations; if I did not hold on to hope, then I could hardly tell Tali to do the same.

I took another waterskin with me; hers would surely be empty by now. I took a bannock wrapped in a cloth. In my pouch I took something else.

Tali appeared to be asleep. She lay against the rock wall, long lashes soft on her pallid cheeks, blanket over her. Her face was gaunt and gray; she looked ten years older. As I came out onto the ledge, her eyes sprang open. "Are you deaf?" No angry snarl this time, but a harsh whisper. "I told you to leave me alone."

"If you wanted to die," I said, my heart thumping,

"you'd be dead by now. If you plan to live, it might be a good idea to eat and drink. I've brought you something. And I'm not going away, so there's no point in snarling at me." I set the food and drink beside her, then settled cross-legged not far away. "You could do with a wash," I added.

"I don't want this, Neryn." Her voice was a thread.

"Yes, you do. Sit up. Here, let me help you. I'm the leader today, and the leader says eat. Slowly, or you'll make yourself sick."

She sat; I could see she was dizzy from hunger. When I put the waterskin in her hands, she almost dropped it. She drank.

"Good. Pass it to me. Now, one mouthful of bannock."

"You don't have to feed me," she muttered, taking the morsel I had broken off and putting it in her mouth.

I waited until she had eaten half the bannock and taken more water. "Good," I said. "Without this you won't be able to get down the Ladder, and I imagine you don't want the entire household watching as Big Don carries you down over his shoulder."

She narrowed her eyes at me. "I'm not coming down," she said. "I can't. I can't do it without him. I can't do any of it."

"You know what everyone wants," I said. "There's nobody else who can lead us. Not the way Regan did."

She closed her eyes as if my words hurt her. "They'll manage. Someone will step up. Big Don. Andra. Someone. You could do it."

"You're not thinking straight. I'm part of it, certainly,

an important part. But my role is quite different. Tali, we've talked about this, the rest of us. Nobody else can lead us. Only you. We need you." I did not add what was in my mind: that Regan would not have wanted her to give up, that what he would have expected was that she step in and take his place. He'd have wanted her to see his vision through to the end. Surely there was no need to tell her that, for she had known him better than anyone.

"I have something for you," I said. "I forgot that I'd put this away for safety, or I'd have given it back to you long ago." From my pouch I took the little wooden raven that I'd retrieved from her belongings after she was taken by the Enforcers. She reached out her hand and I laid the token on her palm. "Remember those ghost-warriors at Hidden-water? *Weapons sharp; backs straight; hearts high.* They believed in you. Ultan's heir, they called you. You come from an ancient family; to those warriors, and to everyone here at Shadowfell, you are a true embodiment of fighting spirit. You think the cause is lost with Regan's passing. But if you find the strength to stand up again, if you can survive this and march on, the cause stays alive. We have less than a year to achieve this, Tali. You're the only person who can make it happen."

Her fingers closed around the little raven. "Neryn," she said, her voice shaking like that of a hurt child, "I never told him. I was so strong, so determined to keep to the rule we'd agreed on, I never told him how I felt. Never breathed a word. Not once." Her lower lip trembled; tears spilled from her eyes. "Oh gods," she said, scrubbing a hand across her cheeks, "what am I, some foolish girl of twelve summers?" She put her head down on her knees.

"You loved him," I said. I had not suspected this, not for a moment. They'd been close; many times I had seen the red head and the dark bent over a map or document, or heard their voices in intense, private discussion. I had known they were old and true friends. But this . . . This explained much.

"He died not knowing," she whispered through the flood of tears. "Alone. Without anyone. And then they butchered him. When he most needed me, I wasn't there. . . ."

I put an arm around her and let her weep. When she had no more tears left to shed, I took out my kerchief and wiped her face. I offered her the waterskin again. "Come down, at least, and have a proper rest," I said.

"Neryn."

"Mm?"

"You're not to speak of this. Not to anyone. You understand?"

"Of course not. Tali, he knows. Wherever he is now, he knows how you feel and he honors you for it."

"Honor," she echoed. "Look at me. Hardly an image worthy of honor, is it? All right, let's get down that wretched Ladder. This time, you'd better go first and hope I don't fall."

Big Don was at the foot of the steps; he stayed there until we were safely down, then went away as we had arranged earlier. Tali and I went first to the privy, then to the women's quarters, where the only occupant was Andra, resting on her pallet with a bandage around her shoulder.

"How is it?" Tali asked, making a brave effort to stroll across and sit on the edge of Andra's bed with her old assurance. "Much pain?"

"It's mending." Andra too had been prepared in advance. "Aches at night, but the healer from Below put some kind of poultice on it, and it's bearable. Be a while before I can use a sword again."

"Not too long, I hope," Tali said in a wraith of her old voice. "I have work for you."

"I'll do my best," said Andra with a smile. "You all right?"

"I've been better."

"To be brutally honest, you stink."

At that point Eva and Milla came in with the bathtub and two buckets of water.

"It's a conspiracy," muttered Tali.

"Guilty," I said. "We have to share this bedchamber with you, don't forget."

She submitted to a bath; Milla washed her hair for her, Eva helped her in and out, I held the towel ready for her to dry herself. She drank half a cup of mead and ate a bowl of porridge. She lay down on her bed and slept for the rest of the day. Beyond the bedchamber door, the household of Shadowfell crept about on soft feet, hardly daring to hope. She was still asleep at suppertime, so we left Andra watching over her and gathered in the dining chamber, none of us saying much. If anyone had noticed Tali's swollen, reddened eyes when she came down the Ladder, nobody mentioned it. Nobody asked me what I had said to her. Instead, we spoke of other matters: the best way to prepare cheesy bannocks, which loch harbored the biggest trout, how soon the autumn storms would set in.

We were sitting over our mead when she came in. She was wearing clothes borrowed from someone bigger; they emphasized how gaunt and pale she was, shrunken by grief. But she held herself tall, her shoulders square, her dark eyes daring any of us to pity her. Behind her came Andra.

"I have something to say," Tali began. "First, I regret my unfortunate loss of self-control when we first arrived here. It won't happen again. I offer my brother a public apology." She glanced at Fingal, who had said barely a word throughout the meal. "There's no blame to be laid for what happened. We are warriors; we take risks; sometimes we misjudge the way things will fall out." She cleared her throat and straightened her back. If anyone thought this was not costing her, they did not know her as I did. Andra moved in closer, ready to support her if she faltered.

"I won't waste words," Tali went on. "Regan's gone. Someone has to step up and take on the duties of leader. I'm offering myself as a replacement. Not that anyone can really take his place; he was himself, a beacon of hope, a shining light in the darkness." Her voice was shaking. "But he'd want us to go on; he'd want us to see this through to the end, no matter how heavy our losses. I don't forget the sacrifice of Killen, young Ban, and Little Don, who also fell at Wedderburn. Three fine men. Nor of all those we've lost over the years since Regan's passion and vision brought us together and gave us the hope of a better future." She swayed; Andra took her arm, steadying her.

"Andra has agreed to take on my old job, training you and keeping you all in order," Tali said. "And I'll be leader for now, if you want me. When all the others get back, when winter sets in, we should give everyone the opportunity to volunteer, then put it to the vote. But Neryn says you need someone to take charge now, so I'll do it. If you'll have me."

A roar of approval gave her the answer.

"Good," she said, sounding surprised. "Good. I'll hold a council the day after tomorrow, all of us and any of the Folk Below who want to be present. I'll hear everyone's report on their activities since Neryn and I went away. Neryn will provide ours. We need to start planning, and planning fast. We only have until midsummer to achieve this. We must work as we've never worked before." She brushed a hand across her cheek. "We're doing this for you, Regan," she said. "We're doing it for all our fallen. Maybe you're gone from this world. But you're always with us, here at Shadowfell."

"My lord king."

"Close the door, Owen. Come close, sit down. We are alone; no need for formality."

He sat. Accepted a goblet of mead poured by Keldec's own hand. Waited.

"I have news. Momentous news. Or so it seems."

"My lord?" It was a long time since he had seen such a look in Keldec's eye, or such animation on his features. What was coming?

The king leaned forward across the table. His voice fell

403

to a conspiratorial murmur. "Word has it that a Caller has been found."

His heart went cold. "A Caller? I had thought such a phenomenon did not exist in today's Alban, my lord." He managed to keep his tone cool, his manner calm. "After our lengthy search throughout your lands, our exhaustive questioning of your people, if a Caller were there to be found, I believe we would already have found her."

"Him," said Keldec.

He drew in a slow breath, then released it. "My lord?"

"A young man. In the south. The queen received a message to that effect earlier today; this fellow was discovered by some of her people. He's on his way here for questioning." Keldec's eyes were bright. "If it's true, what the old tales tell us about the powers of such a person, this may prove a weapon of inestimable power, Owen. Think what we could achieve with the Good Folk at our disposal. We could create a powerful army indeed. We could spread our authority far beyond the borders of Alban. Our line might become foremost in the known world." He paused. "Provided the Caller is loyal, of course. Such power, wielded by a person of rebellious nature, would be deadly to us and to all we hold dear. Once this man is brought to Summerfort, I may have a particular need for your services."

"I understand, my lord king."

"You seem very calm in the face of such news," Keldec observed.

"My lord, I am . . . I am taken aback, I confess. I hardly know what to say. A Caller . . . I had begun to think the

404

notion nothing but an old wives' tale. How soon will this young man be here?"

"That I cannot tell you. Six days, maybe seven. Be ready when the time comes."

His mind raced. How could he get this news to Shadowfell, how could he warn Regan, warn Neryn, that the whole balance was about to change? "I'd planned to ride to Wedderburn in the morning, my lord," he said. "There's been word of a problem there, incursions across the border by parties unknown. Keenan requested our advice."

"Send Rohan."

"I had intended that we both go, my lord, with a party of four or five men. I believe a troop leader's presence is called for in this situation. We must ensure all of your chieftains remain steadfast in their loyalty. Offering assistance on such occasions helps to strengthen that loyalty. I can be back by the time you require me."

"Go, then, if you wish. Six days. No more."

"Yes, my lord king."

By night, while Keenan's household slept, he climbed the wall above the gates to Wedderburn's stronghold and cut down the rotting, crow-pecked remnant Keenan had nailed up as a warning. The russet hair, the ring in the left ear, confirmed what his instincts had already told him. With the head in a bag over his shoulder, he slipped away to the place in the woods where he'd left a horse hobbled, waiting. The creature jittered and trembled when he tied the bag behind the saddle. With quiet words he settled the animal, though his heart was beating hard, like a drum sounding a call to battle. In his dark clothing, under a waning moon, he could stay unseen until he was well across the border. There was nothing on his person to identify him: no heavy Enforcer cloak, no stag brooch, no silver to the harness, no rich garments or wax-sealed dispatches. No longer a king's man. Only a man.

He mounted and rode steadily away from Wedderburn, across the hills, carrying Regan home to Shadowfell.

ACKNOWLEDGMENTS

My thanks go to Gaye Godfrey-Nicholls and Tamara Lampard for their wise advice on elemental magic and ritual. Gaye also crafted another great map from my sketchy instructions. Michelle Frey at Knopf USA and Brianne Tunnicliffe at Pan Macmillan Australia exercised tact and professionalism throughout the process of polishing the rather raw initial manuscript into its final form. I thank Claire Craig, Jo Lyons, and all at both publishing houses who played a role in the development of the book. To my family, thanks for being prepared to brainstorm at short notice. And to my agent, Russell Galen, the usual appreciation for his support along the way.